Fires, Feuds and Fun
A Dodecanese Summer

Fires, Feuds and Fun: A Dodecanese Summer

Published in Great Britain by

Travel Pastime Books
Hall Farm
High Catton
York YO41 1EH
UK

ISBN: 979-83-73259-39-2

Fires, Feuds and Fun
A Dodecanese Summer

Rosemary Vulliamy

TRAVEL PASTIME BOOKS

Note

My novel was born out of missing the opportunity to travel, especially to Greece, during Covid lockdowns and restrictions. Writing it enabled me to relive the enjoyment, fun and specific characteristics of the Dodecanese islands which I hope readers will also vicariously experience and enjoy.

The chapters describe aspects of life in the village of Kefalos, including some that may soon be lost, such as bread making in traditional outdoor ovens and the annual fish festival. The explorations of actual villages, ruins, castles and monasteries in the Dodecanese on foot along ancient footpaths and by bicycle and bus draw on extensive diary notes and could be repeated by interested readers. The interactions with the local Greeks and the British, who have built their livelihoods on the islands particularly in Kefalos, are based around actual events and experiences. However, the characters are developed through imagination and conjecture and do not portray real individuals.

Acknowledgements

A huge debt of thanks is due to my husband, with whom I shared my Dodecanese adventures, for his encouragement and support in writing this novel and for taking the photographs on the front and back covers. I am also very grateful to my friend Christine Kyriacou who made valuable content suggestions and checked Greek spellings and to my relative Jo Patterson for the book cover design. Thanks also to the community of Kefalos who made our many visits so enjoyable.

Contents

1

A Home for the Summer

I struggled to push up the bolts locking the internal sliding doors and awkwardly shoved each one back as the bottom runners squeaked in protest. Then I unbolted the external sliding louvre doors. These slid back easily to reveal, like a theatre set, the wonderful panorama of Kamari bay. I stood there squinting into the early morning sun as my eyes adjusted from the darkened interior to the brightness.

I sighed appreciatively as the familiar view came into sharper focus. Mount Dikeos, the top of which was hidden in soft white early morning cloud, rose above Kos island's small central mountain range and formed a backdrop to the west. To the east the silhouette of the volcanic island of Nisyros and its islets rose mistily out of the sea. Brown sun-baked cliffs encircled the bay and, below, the square white flat-topped buildings of the houses, studios and restaurants clustered closely together between the cliffs and the sea.

This morning the sea was totally still, shading from navy on the far side of the bay to brilliant azure where it lapped the beach below. Unusually there was no activity in the little harbour. It was home to an assortment of small brightly coloured fishing boats, moored side by side, sterns secured to the jetty. Some were amazingly tiny given the strength of the winds and the suddenness with which squalls can arrive.

Three much larger tourist vessels, made top-heavy by their wide upper decks crammed with seats, were tied up at the end of the harbour wall. Later in the day these would be carrying holidaymakers to and from nearby popular beaches and for day trips to Nisyros. Outside the harbour in the shelter of the steep hill rising behind our house, a small flotilla of five tourist yachts were moored with their occupants seemingly still asleep.

Behind the harbour and at the bottom of the hill on the side of which our home for the next six months was perched, the owner of Scorpios was vigorously brushing the encroaching sands from the restaurant patio and straightening the tables and chairs in readiness for the first customers. Moving away from the restaurant, my eyes followed the line of motionless umbrellas and their equidistant positioned sunbeds along the water's edge to where two men had beached their fishing boat under the cliffs and were carrying out repairs. A great feeling of well-being surged through me. This was the first morning of many such mornings that I was going to spend here.

For the past seven years I'd come with John, my husband, for a fortnight's holiday in the Greek town of Kefalos. On at least the last three occasions, when it was time to go home, which we were always very reluctant to do, we had threatened to come and live here for the entire summer. We wanted the opportunity to enjoy the sun, sea, holiday atmosphere and activities of the island for longer and have more time with the friends that we had made during our visits. Also, we were keen to have the opportunity to visit some of the other nearby Dodecanese islands.

During the grey cloudy days of the previous November we had decided to make these holiday conjectures an actuality. At the end of April, when the fixed-term contract for the university research project that we had been working on came to an end, we took a break from work. We rented our house out for six months to some visiting academics and so here we were on day one.

Finding an appropriate place in Kamari, the seafront of Kefalos, to be home for six months from the beginning of

May until the end of October had seemed likely to prove difficult. The rentable accommodation there was almost entirely holiday studios of the one room for living, sleeping, cooking on a two-ring hotplate and showering in a cupboard variety. While we had always been content with this for our two-week break of holiday activities, something more homely, spacious and interesting was required for a longer stay.

Initially, as anticipated, the possibilities seemed very limited but, in the event, finding our house had proved remarkably easy. We spent three days tromping around the roads and dirt tracks of Kamari following up notices in shop windows and leads suggested by shopkeepers to rooms and apartments to rent. Each advert promised attractive, larger and different accommodation but then turned out to be the usual studio, only thinly disguised by the addition of a full size cooker or a sofa and TV.

Although it was only early days in our quest for a home, we had felt a bit dispirited because we had set our hearts upon living in Kamari and it looked as if we might not find anywhere suitable. To get in a more positive mood, we decided to treat ourselves to grilled snapper in one of our favourite restaurants down on the beach just outside Kefalos. Occasionally back in England I managed to buy snapper and I grilled it with olive oil and dried herbs purchased the previous summer but I could never achieve the same wonderful taste as when it was cooked over charcoal in Kos. However, maybe this was also due in part to the contrast between sitting in our kitchen eating snapper and eating it outside on a balmy Mediterranean evening looking through the tiny twinkling coloured lights of the verandah at the sea and brightly moonlit sky.

We were pleased to find Spiros the owner of the restaurant, who occasionally took a turn as chef or waiter, was there because we hoped from past experience he might be able to help. A tall rotund figure with a head of thick wavy dark grey hair and a bushy moustache he was a man of many parts, who knew everyone and everyone knew him. After enjoying our excellent snappers, which were served, as customary, with rice, chips and tomatoes, in order to celebrate our return to Kos he brought each of us a large complimentary baklava.

As we munched our way through the rich sticky honey soaked pastry, we described to him our fruitless attempts to find somewhere appealing to live. He listened and questioned us to ascertain exactly whose accommodation we had looked at and delivered pejorative evaluative comments for each.

'I could have told you Dolphin apartments wouldn't do, dreadfully small and cramped, you couldn't survive there for more than a week.'

'Oh not Sunlit studios, they are so dreary, Savas hasn't redecorated them in years.'

'Don't even consider Cliff View studios, they have had terrible subsidence problems.'

Finally adopting a hurt expression he admonished us for not consulting him about our requirements. Of course he definitely knew just the place, and if we had come to him straightaway we could have saved ourselves a lot of unnecessary effort. By then it was past ten o'clock and most of the customers, rendered content and immobile by large platters of fish, moussaka, lamb kleftico or pastitsio, were at the coffee or free coffee liqueur and chatting stage.

Shouting to his wife in the kitchen, presumably to tell her where he was going – our knowledge of Greek, like most of the English visitors to Kos, being reprehensibly non-existent – he beckoned to us to follow him. Ten minutes later, after a ride in the back of his old, extremely fishy-smelling truck along the bay and bumping up the hill behind the harbour, we had arrived at what I immediately knew was indeed just the place.

A small traditional Greek house, it was enlarged by an

almost-the-same-size concrete bunker-style extension, the sliding doors of which opened out to reveal a magnificent view of the bay. However, I knew not to show any enthusiasm as this would incur wrath from John later. He would know that this was just right for us but would want to go through ritual bargaining to make sure it was secured at the best possible price and one that we could afford. The challenge of trying to secure a bargain was one he thoroughly enjoyed. Sure enough John was quick to point out that the kitchen was impractically tiny.

'Ah but,' countered Spiros looking at me, 'it has a cooker and an outside bake oven for making bread.'

'The shower room has a sloping roof,' John responded, 'and only a midget could shower standing upright.'

'Ah but,' said Spiros, 'considering the house is halfway up the hill the flow of water to the taps is remarkable.'

'Maybe,' said John, 'but the two bedrooms are exceedingly small and, apart from stone shelves in the larger of the two, there is nowhere within them to store anything.'

'Ah,' replied Spiros, 'but the extension is unusually big and it has a cupboard for cleaning things and garden tools.'

'Still,' said John, 'there ought to be a shed for garden tools.'

Thus the debate over the benefits and limitations of the property went backwards and forwards for what seemed to me, waiting in anxious anticipation, an interminable time. At one point, Spiros was extolling the virtues of the potential garden area outside the house. With two olive trees and a network of metal poles and wooden beams covered in an ancient vine and a bougainvillaea, it provided a shaded seating area outside the backdoor. John was countering with complaints of time-consuming watering and the fact that the suggested patio had no table or chairs. I tried to interject as I loved the idea of having a garden. However, my comment deteriorated into a cough at a glare from John.

Eventually, all pros and cons exhausted, rent was suggested, received with unbelieving indignation and rejected. Ultimately a price was reached acceptable to both as victory. Smiles, handshakes and embraces were exchanged. We had a home.

After three days of settling in and deciding where things should be put and how things should be done, we got into what was to become our early morning routine. John would drive down to Sophia's supermarket by the harbour to buy fresh rolls for breakfast. While he was gone, I brewed some coffee and laid the unturned oil drum we were using as a patio table. We had moved the two plastic chairs in the living room out onto the patio. Having breakfast outside was a real treat and a lovely relaxed way to start the day.

Three coughs of the starter motor and our hire car spluttered into life ready for the breakfast run. The car, which we hired for the duration of our stay, was an old black Marbella. We very soon realised that it had various idiosyncrasies, of which the requirement for three presses of the starter button to get it going was a crucial one. The Marbella had once been part of the Explore hire fleet owned by the local family company from which we had always hired a car for our holidays. When the Marbella was withdrawn, it was then used by a cousin of theirs until she returned to live in Athens. Referred to by us as Mabel, which seemed to suit the old car's personality, we had negotiated to have it on loan for six months at a very cheap rate.

The sound of Mabel's engine gradually disappeared as the car, avoiding potholes, bumped down the sandy track that at the bottom of the hill met the road. To the left the road wound its way up to the back of Kefalos old town. The town towered atop the cliffs, with traditional houses and narrow streets at its centre. On its ever-expanding outskirts, modern homes fanned out into the countryside behind.

Turning off the track to the right a few metres further on and past the little blue and white chapel clothed in bright pink bougainvillea, the road arrived at the harbour from where it swung left through 90 degrees to run alongside the bay. On the corner were two small supermarkets facing each other across the road. Both sold identical postcards, suntan oil, sun hats, shorts and T-shirts for tourists, a few basic groceries but, and most importantly, freshly baked rolls.

On our first morning John happened to choose Sophia's for his breakfast purchases because he could park in the road directly outside the door. This established our allegiance and from then on it was inconceivable to switch patronage. Local practice dictated that you shopped solely in one or the other, not that, as they stocked exactly the same things, you would alternate between them for reasons other than sharing out your custom on the grounds of fairness.

When John returned we sat on the patio enjoying the early morning sun, which had arisen from behind Nisyros. We tucked into our Greek yoghurt, honey and bananas followed by Sophia's rolls and cheese and planned the day. I would drop John off at Meltemi, the windsurfer hire business named after the supposedly reliably strong wind that blew throughout the summer months. This rendered the sheltered waters of the bay ideal both for beginners and those experienced windsurfers that liked to speed across the bay or head out to sea on flat water.

John was keen to go there to meet up with Seb the Greek owner in his thirties to find out how the business was doing. Hopefully it was doing well, as it had been arranged that he could do some part-time work helping out. We had saved hard to fund our self-elected sabbatical from work and we intended to live frugally. However, some earnings would be very helpful to pay for meals out and trips to the other islands.

While John was catching up on windsurfing news, I was going to drive into the old town and stock up on provisions. Then I intended to visit Betty and Mike, an English couple we had got to know at a barbecue several holidays ago and who had lived on Kos for six or so years. Betty had emailed me just before we left England to tell me that she was thrilled that her daughter Anna was getting married, although she was anxious about the wedding plans and would fill me in about everything when we met.

The plans for the day having been made, we lingered lazily over another pot of freshly brewed coffee. We watched as the first sunbathers ambled across the beach below us, consulted each other at length and selected the sunbeds and umbrellas that would provide their resting place for the day. Unpacking their brightly coloured beach bags, adjusting the sunbeds to achieve the desired angle for feet and shoulders and angling the umbrellas in order to blot out or to reveal the sun's rays, they settled down.

Tourism is the lifeblood of Kos and provides work and income for many of its inhabitants. Throughout the day and night from late May until early October, planes land and take off from the small airport in the centre of the island. They deliver holidaymakers in search of the reliable hot sun, warm seas and beach possibilities that Kos has to offer and return them at the end of their stay to less appealing climates and routines.

After taking the back road, which wound its way up the hill to Kefalos old town at the top, I parked outside the bank as I needed to withdraw some money. There I was pleasantly surprised to discover a shiny new ATM had replaced the old one which had such a scratched and faint screen that in the bright sunlight it was impossible to read any of the displayed information. You just had to guess where and what to press and hope for the best.

After making the withdrawal with unanticipated ease, my grocery shopping was quickly accomplished. Following a brief spot of queuing, from the butchers in the main street I bought a chicken, steak for John and some chopped lamb to make lamb kleftico. Next I went to the bakers to get some of their speciality fruit tarts and chocolate baklavas and hoped to see Angela who works there. Our liking for the fruit tarts had resulted in my getting to know her.

Angela had lived in Kefalos for nearly four years. She met her partner, who now worked in the pharmacy, when she was on holiday. At that time he had been a waiter in her favourite restaurant. They had kept in touch when she returned home to Wales and on her return for a holiday the following year she had decided to stay. As I hoped, Angela was there. The shop was busy and so while she served me we quickly exchanged news and arranged to meet for a coffee to catch up properly.

Then I went to Panayioti's supermarket in the back street parallel to main street for everything else that I needed. Shopping in Panayioti's is a pleasurable and artistic experience as every carefully dusted tin, bottle and packet is symmetrically and precisely placed on the shelves according to size and colour. Not only does this arrangement give fast easy access to the products required but also provides an all-round sparkling, colourful spectacle worthy of the Tate Modern.

I had first discovered the shop on the recommendation of Angela. Being in the backstreets it was off the tourist trail. I thought the shelves were so amazing I asked if I could photograph them. Very proud of his shop he was happy to agree, if somewhat surprised at my request. Today as I arrived outside the shop he was busily piling green and red peppers into a striped pyramid and mildly apprehending those that chose to roll down the pyramid rather than stay in position.

'Don't try to put them back I'll have those,' I offered obligingly as I needed some peppers.

When I left Panayioti's, I retraced my steps to the main street and crossed over to Zephina's, where I sat in a comfy wicker chair under an ample sunshade and ordered a cappuccino. Cappuccinos in Kefalos bear no resemblance to cappuccinos elsewhere in the world and certainly would not be recognised as such by an Italian. Kefalos cappuccinos are large cups of medium-strength black coffee with a large, or very large in the best ones, spiral of thick cream squirted on the top. I have become addicted to them.

Zephina's is one of four cafes situated on the corner of the crossroads on the edge of town and unusually is frequented by tourists and locals alike. The cafe next door to her has become the place of choice for the better-healed tourists. The drinks are twice the price but the sunshades are newer and thicker, the seats are armchairs and the occupants can hide from the road behind luxuriant pot plants.

Directly opposite, across the road is Hilltop cafe which although one building, as denoted by its variously coloured brick façade, caters for its different clientele by being divided into two distinct halves. One half has large glass doors in aluminium frames opening onto the pavement where there are wooden tables painted Grecian blue and kitchen chairs shielded from the sun by a faded awning. This is one of the favourite meeting places of the town's elderly men who swop gossip and banter over tiny cups of strong black coffee and glasses of water.

Over the dividing trellis, which is anchored to the pavement by pots, is the tourist half of the cafe with its huge overarching rectangular sun umbrella, smart patio chairs and tables with gaily coloured tablecloths. Four English women tourists whose skimpy T-shirts revealed deep red brown tans were loudly complaining about the taxi that they had ordered, which never turned up, thus requiring them to walk into town up the hill. By indulging in ice creams and baklavas they were compensating for their efforts.

As I alternately sipped my cappuccino and the accompanying glass of water Zephina's also provides, I indulged in the enjoyable pastime of watching the world go by, as indeed it certainly does on that corner. Vespas and quad bikes circled, crisscrossed, interweaved and narrowly avoided collision as riders hailed each other and the occupants of the corner cafes.

A teenage lad in trendy gear on a vespa screeched to a halt in front of me as his similarly clad friend walked into view. The two shook hands warmly, kissed each other on both cheeks, exchanged pleasantries and went their separate ways – a reminder that despite being surrounded by English people I was in Greece and young as well as old adhered to traditional greetings.

More elderly men wandered up to be warmly greeted by their compatriots who went into the cafe to bring out more chairs which, owing to lack of space on the pavement, they lined up in the road, backs to the traffic. The newcomers sat down gratefully quite unbothered by, or simply oblivious to, the screaming vespas, stuttering quad bikes and larger vehicles squeezing by, missing the chair legs by centimetres.

Four small elderly women, one very bent with a stick, walked in a line arm in arm along the road holding up the traffic. They were all dressed in black with black scarves on their heads. One sported hers tied around her head like a tourniquet. Could she have toothache? I wondered. However, as she was also wearing thick black woolly stockings, I concluded that despite the heat she liked to be well wrapped up. The women were saluted by the men and they waved back in return. On recognising one old fellow the sprightliest of the four disengaged herself from the line and went to sit with him. For the time I sat in the cafe, and probably beyond, they were engaged in earnest conversation.

Interrupting my reflections on whether romance was likely was the arrival of a shiny new police car, out of which jumped Kefalos's answer to the American police drama's Starsky and Hutch. They were bronzed young men in uniform with dark wrap-around shades, one with slicked back hair and the other with streaks and spikes.

After stopping and reprimanding a middle-aged Greek on a large roaring motorbike for some minor misdemeanour or other they swaggered over to the corner where two attractive young blonde tourists were about to remount their quad bike. After preventing the remount and carefully inspecting the tyres and brakes of the quad bike, an out-of-earshot interrogation ensued resulting in notes being made, of phone numbers and studios I concluded, as the young men returned to their car thumping each other on the arm and drove off grinning.

As a very hot looking German couple similarly clad in stiff canvas shorts and hiking boots, with walking poles at the ready, arrived in front of the cafe looking for somewhere to sit, I decided it was time I went. I indicated my intention to them before going inside to pay Zephina for my coffee. The German woman sat down thankfully once she had removed her large cumbersome rucksack. Why is it, when Germans go walking, the woman always has the back pack? I've often wondered this when John and I have encountered German couples when we have been walking abroad, and I've always been thankful that this isn't the way the English go hiking.

I took the main road down the steep hill from the old town. The main road follows the bay before climbing another hill and going north east along the middle of the island to the airport and Kos town. Betty and her husband Mike lived above their cafe at the bottom of this hill. They had sold their house in York and moved to Kefalos following a decade of going there each August for a holiday.

Over these holidays Betty, who worked as a primary

school teaching assistant, indulged in a dream of moving to Kos and opening a thoroughly English cafe serving tea with scones, tarts and cakes to appeal primarily to the English tourists and the growing number of English expats living in the area. Betty became increasingly disillusioned with her job as it continued to change substantially, requiring her to focus more and more on trying to increase children's literacy scores on national tests. Meanwhile Mike, who worked on his own as a hard landscape gardener, was going through a period of little work and customers failing to settle their bills. On return from their final Kefalos holiday, as Betty put it, 'We looked at each other and said OK let's go for it, let's do it.'

A great fan of the York Betty's cafe, which she regularly frequented for an after-school treat on Fridays and being called Betty, she decided her Kefalos cafe would have to be called Betty's 2. Purchasing the old run-down shop, which subsequently Mike renovated and extended to form their home and the cafe, had been beset with problems.

These peaked at an impasse when the building work had to stop because there was reported to be a site of archaeological importance in the garden, which would be disturbed by their proposed extension. However, after a long delay fraught with anxiety as to what they would do if the project had to be abandoned, a Greek neighbour suggested that he could arrange, via a friend of a friend, a payment to a particular official in the planning department which would most likely resolve the issue. The payment was made and not long after that, they were told that on considerable further investigation the conclusion had been reached that there were no remains of value under the garden. Work resumed and now several years after opening, Betty's 2 is well established on the tourist circuit including two tour buses a week from Kos town stopping off for afternoon tea as part of their excursion around the island.

Betty and I collected tea and slices of chocolate cake from the kitchen and settled under one of the striped umbrellas in the cafe garden.

'Now tell me about the wedding,' I prompted.

'Well Anna and Alistair have been living together for three years so I did wonder whether they would get married. Plenty of couples don't these days so when Anna last phoned and said they had set a date for the wedding I was really surprised but very pleased.'

'Will it be soon?'

'They've agreed the last weekend in August would be a good time.'

'It'll be in Scotland, I suppose.'

'Yes, well that's OK, it's what I expected because Alistair's family all live there but then she told me she wanted to get married on this island in Loch Lomond which is near where they live and apparently where he proposed to her.'

'Sounds really romantic,' I commented but added, 'as long as the weather cooperates. My experience of Scotland though is that it usually doesn't.'

'Exactly my reaction,' she agreed. 'I said to Anna that I hoped there was a nice building on the island they could hire because in the west of Scotland it's always raining. She said no there wasn't and that the ceremony would be out in the open on a little beach. Well I was horrified, but she was so excited by the idea and thought it would be so lovely and original. I just didn't really know what else to say.'

'Presumably they will go inside somewhere for a reception?'

'Oh yes, but first she said that after the service she thought it would be fun to have champagne and nibbles on the island. Just imagine if the weather is horrendous or even if it's OK but we're plagued by midges. However, then they do plan to go back to a local hotel in a castle, which is apparently quite luxurious, for an evening reception.'

'That sounds really good,' I said, glad to be able to be

genuinely positive.

Betty and I continued discussing the pros and cons of such a wedding ceremony of which there seemed to Betty to be rather more of the latter, until she went back into the cafe to work. She needed to help Maria, who assisted her in running the cafe, as they were expecting a Greek family and friends to come in for an English-style birthday party for their ten-year-old daughter.

On the way back, I caught up with John returning from Meltemi, just as he reached the harbour.

'Well what's the news? How are they all?' I asked as he got into Mabel.

'Oh where do I start, there's a lot. First I got a real surprise when I was walking there. I took the beach path and about three hundred metres before I got there, this building which I think was a shop originally but has just been empty for three or four years, is now another windsurfing centre. It looked really smart with plastic grass outside leading down to the beach but, as there's no wind today, apart from a few beginners trying to uphaul near the shore there didn't seem to be anyone about.'

'Is it an Italian company?'

'That's what I thought as there are an increasing number of Italians holidaying here now, but no, it's Russian.'

'Has it just opened then?'

'Yes it's only been open a couple of weeks.'

'Will it take some of Meltemi's customers?'

'They don't think so because Meltemi's mainstay are English, French and Germans who have pre-booked and the Russian company will probably only advertise in Russia.'

'What about people who just decide to have a go on holiday, or like you have always done in the past, wait and see what the wind is like and what else there is to do, then negotiate a price for as much windsurfing as they want?'

'Well Seb says that Meltemi is more friendly and they have better instructors and so, while I'm sure they'd rather not have competition, they don't seem too bothered.'

'So how is Seb?'

'He's fine. He has been really busy over the winter, putting down decking for the seating area in front of the hut, repairing the roof over it with new reeds, and Spiros got him some comfy armchairs from a hotel he works for that didn't want them.'

'Who else was there?'

'Yiannis. He was looking after a large group of windsurfers from Brighton but I managed a quick chat. Otto arrived from the Netherlands a couple of days ago but had gone to Kos town. Apparently Joel is working at a windsurfing camp on Fuerteventura at the moment but should arrive next week and Alain is finishing his MA in Paris but should be here in a couple of weeks time.'

'All sounds good.'

'Yes, but they are worried about my other bit of news.'

'Oh. What's that?'

'Last Friday, after midnight, someone set fire to Georgio's windsurfing hut on Paradise beach. By the time someone in the hotel up on the cliffs spotted the flames, the fire had totally taken hold and the hut and all his equipment was destroyed. Nothing like this has happened before.'

'Do they know who did it?'

'No. No one has any real idea who might have done it. It could be someone with a personal grudge against Georgio, or who was antagonistic towards him. His was a fairly new business and there was a lot of local opposition to it when he started, both from the other three watersports centres at Paradise, even though they don't have windsurfing gear, and from locals who didn't want to see any more developments on the beach. Alternatively, and this is what worries Seb, it could have been an unprovoked arsonist who might strike again.'

2

Bayfront Tourism and Creative Escapes

A couple of weeks after our arrival the days assumed a similar pattern. After our patio breakfast from Monday to Thursday John would usually drive around to Meltemi's hut to assist with windsurfer hire. The organised groups that were booked in for a week's equipment hire arrived early wanting to pack in as much time on the water as possible, even though first thing in the morning there generally wasn't much wind. However, the holidaying casual windsurfers, as John had once been, preferred a lie in and the more expert of them would wait for the wind to get up after lunch.

After breakfast I would spend a short time tackling those household chores that are the same wherever you are, like making the bed and washing up the breakfast things. Added to these was the particular chore of paddling in and mopping out the little bathroom while avoiding banging my head on the sloping ceiling. The shower tray was flush with the floor and so the water that collected on the small white tiles flowed around rather than down the central grating. Once these tasks were over, I would turn my attention to writing my diary entry for the previous day. This was a new activity for me but I thought that it would be good to have a detailed record of our sabbatical to look back on when we returned home.

A few years ago I had taken up watercolour painting but when working I had little time to give to it. However, this summer I envisaged producing paintings of some of the local farmsteads and fishing boats to portray those aspects of traditional life remaining on Kos. I hadn't the confidence to go out and paint *en plein air* as those that do so put it, as I didn't want my efforts to be scrutinised by passers by. I had lots of photos for inspiration from previous holidays and now I could observe first-hand the colours of the sky, sea and landscape and revisit local potential subjects. Currently I was working on a painting of a large fishing boat moored against the harbour wall. I was pleased with the way the boat had turned out but I was struggling to make its reflection look wet. Such activities kept me totally absorbed so that I was always amazed at how quickly the time passed.

My watercolour painting hobby like John's enthusiasm

for windsurfing also promised to provide me with enjoyable occasional work and some additional income. This morning I was going to drive some participants on an art holiday to Limonias where they could choose aspects of its tiny picturesque harbour and beach to sketch and paint.

Three years ago at a week's art course in the Peak District I had met Joan, a fellow participant, who at that time was a cookery and home technology teacher. She and her husband Terry were about to sell their home in England with the intention of buying a property on Kos to run as a centre for art courses and holidays.

Given our annual trips to Kos, I kept in touch with her to see how their plans were working out. After several visits to Kos scouting for somewhere suitable to realise their ideas, they bought a plot in the valley behind the buildings around the bay and below Kefalos old town. On the plot was an unfinished block of sixteen studios, eight on the ground floor and eight above. These had languished untouched for several years following the death of the would-be Greek developer. As Terry was a builder, he was able to use his skills and contacts to complete the block in such a way that it met all their requirements. The ground floor provided an apartment for him and Joan and a lounge, dining area and spacious art studio for course participants.

On the second floor were various rooms for them and any accompanying partners.

I left the house for the Art Centre and set off down the hill carefully observing the placement of my sandalled feet on the sand and gravel track. On one of my first walks down the hill, in high spirits with eyes focused on Kefalos town perched impressively high on the steep rocky hillside, I'd slipped. I skidded backwards, almost regained my balance again but unable to remain in the upright position fell heavily forwards and slid down the hill on my knees. The skin on my knees survived unscathed but only because the knees of my new pink jeans were shredded. Not being keen on the current fashion of jeans with rips in the knees, they were fit only to be cut down as shorts. Consequently, not wishing to reprise this detrimental performance, the track had my undivided attention.

As I joined the road to the harbour and passed the pristine little blue and white chapel decorated by the red bougainvillea which climbed through the surrounding wrought iron fence, the door opened. I smiled and greeted the very bent and misleadingly frail looking elderly woman in black who was coming out.

Athina visited the chapel every day to fill the oil lamps and replace the candles, brush the steps and water the flowers in their earthenware pots either side of the gate. She waved at me unsmiling. Apparently she hadn't smiled since her husband, a fisherman, had disappeared one night some 60 years ago. Her relatives, and she had many for she was a great-great grandmother to 22 children, believed her husband to have drowned that night. However, it had been a still night with a clear starry sky and neither his body nor his boat were ever found. The alternative explanation, fuelled by supposed sightings in the early years after his disappearance, was that he had followed his paramour to Rhodes. Reputed to be 107 years of age, Athina was probably the oldest person in a town characterised by the longevity of its inhabitants.

A hundred metres or so further on I called out 'kalimera' to Sophia and her daughter Iona who sat chatting in the doorway of their supermarket in readiness for their occasional customers. On the opposite side of the road Vasilis was similarly positioned in his shop doorway. I always liked walking along the Kamari bayfront taking in the sea air and enjoying the view and the activity.

In the harbour an array of tiny colourful fishing boats painted aqua blue, white and red with rectangular box-like cabins were jostling up and down tugging at the stern ropes that fastened them to the concrete jetty. The wind was getting up which meant the windsurfers would be pleased. The jetty with its little skeleton lighthouse reached out into the bay. This, together with a right angle of concrete and rocks providing additional mooring, protected the boats from the storms bringing violent and potentially destructive onshore winds.

Today the main activity was provided by two men who, shouting instructions to each other in increasingly loud voices, were paddling in and out of the water as they struggled to line up a seemingly extremely uncooperative speedboat with its trailer waiting on the stony beach. A few sunburned tourists intending to further darken their tans were embarking on a small boat to go for a day's sunbathing and swimming at Paradise beach.

This beach was aptly named owing to its deep sand and warm safe waters. Also, unlike the other best island beaches, it was unspoilt by tourist development apart from the longstanding hotel on the cliff top and the beach huts offering water sports and activities like the unfortunate Georgio's. Apparently a few days after the hut's incendiary demise, the police had carried out a few half-hearted enquiries which, as anticipated, provided no pointers to the identity of the arsonists.

I mounted the pavement separating the road from the

narrow beach of Kefalos bay, dodging around the large, inconveniently placed signboard recently erected by the municipal authority. It contained a supremely unhelpful plan of Kefalos shown as an artistic collection of orange shapes, of which only those indicating the position of the high school, the cemetery and 'the ground' – for football I presumed, given the Greeks' love of football shared with the English – warranted a label. Similar signs subsequently sprung up in all the nearby villages but these were festooned with labels recommending sites of archaeological, mythological and/or cultural interest.

The lack of such labels on the Kefalos plan suggested that there was nothing to see and nowhere of note in Kefalos. However, at the far end of the bay beyond Meltemi, on a rocky promontory opposite the picturesque islet of Kastri, are the ruins of the early Christian basilica of Saint Stephen. Any such ruins situated in England given its stunning location and bountiful remains of stone walls, mosaic floors and ornate pillars, would have lead to it being fenced off and charges made to enter. Instead, tourists laze on the basilica walls taking in the magnificent view of the bay and children chase over its neglected stonework and play hide and seek behind the pillars.

What the harbour signboard lacked in suggesting places

of interest it made up for in adverts. For a payment to the municipality Kefalos businesses could secure yet another opportunity to make their presence known. The Anchor Bar 'where the party never stops' instructed partying tourists 'to head for the harbour and listen out for us.' Unfortunately, there was no need to listen out on their karaoke night as the shrieking and caterwauling assaulted the ears of Kamari residents.

Although more muted where we were at the top of the hill, when the wind blew the sound of the would-be Buddy Hollys and Elvis Presleys in our direction, we were forced to sleep with the windows closed and shuttered no matter what the temperature. However, to be fair, apart from the karaoke Kefalos was very peaceful in the evening with tourists and locals alike mainly strolling around the bay or chatting over drinks or coffees in the many restaurants.

Reflecting the growing numbers of English tourists wanting properties for holiday homes or for their retirement, the Yorgos real estate business had a particularly large advert. It very optimistically promised potential clients a newly built white concrete bunker with shutters resembling three up and over garage doors to be available within six months.

Behind the beach, and further back along the tops of the

hills, numerous hollow concrete edifices had sprung up over the last decade. These partially finished homes, if they made any progress at all towards completion, and often it seemed that they did not, only did so outside the tourist season. Then numerous waiters and others engaged in tourism sought alternative employment.

There were a multiplicity of reasons these buildings, like the studio block bought by Joan and Terry, so frequently ground to a halt – the site would have encroached on an ancient olive grove or was considered to contain relics of the past as experienced by Betty and Mike. Alternatively, or in addition, the promised electricity or water failed to materialise, funds proved insufficient as innumerable complications arose and costs escalated. Also, in recent years the ongoing crisis in the Greek economy caused additional problems making builders and materials increasingly scarce.

By the harbour the wide pavement between the beach and the road around the bay consisted of smart evenly spaced yellow flag stones infilled with matching yellow cement. However, after two hundred metres, flagstones without the benefit of the securing properties of the yellow cement had disintegrated becoming irregularly spaced and wobbly. After a further two hundred metres the pavement reverted to what was the original narrow band of concrete along which, in order to avoid hire cars, trucks and vespas, tourists plodded in single file.

When I first witnessed the yellow flagstone improvements on holiday some years ago I was enthusiastic about them. However, my enthusiasm was regarded with extreme scepticism by the locals on the grounds that the project would never be finished. They assured me that it had only been started prior to the local elections by members of the party in power in order to provide an achievement to show for their term in office. If they won the election then there would be no need to finish the pavement. If they didn't, well there was no chance that the new party would be willing to complete the opposition's project.

In the event the elections did bring about a change in the ruling party and, as predicted, progress on the pavement ceased. Not only that but parts of the attractive blue metal railings strung between stone pillars, which prevented the less sure of foot, inebriated tourists or those prone to vertigo from falling in the bay or on the rocks, were taken down for painting and never reappeared.

Along the length of the new pavement palm trees and mauve and white hibiscus had been planted. These at least were a success, as despite their lack of water the trees grew surprisingly rapidly and were now quite tall and the hibiscus luxuriant and bushy. It seemed a shame there had to be a gap in this attractive greenery in front of Seagull studios where we had stayed for our first holiday on Kos.

The view of the bay and its narrow beach from the pool area would have been obstructed if the row of palms had continued without such a gap – something the wealthy studio owner was not prepared to allow to happen. The locals always referred to Seagull studios in revered tones for being the best studios in the area and this year to keep their status the balcony tables were graced with new striped umbrellas.

When at Seagull studios, each day John went off to windsurf. On his return he always used the tap in the courtyard at the back to wash his wetsuit and harness vigorously to try to avoid bringing sand into the studio. Alas one day a few grains eluded him. This led the next morning to the cleaner complaining long and loud to Mitsos, who ran the bar and managed the studios, about the activities of the occupants of number nine and the impact on the floor. Horrified he came immediately to inspect the unacceptable floor and on seeing the grains of sand he grew very excited jumping up and down arms akimbo. His normally fluent English deserted him as he gave full vent to his indignation in a volley of incomprehensible Greek. I imagined it went something along the lines of why with a beautiful pool from which the beach could be observed did we feel the need to actually go on it.

Grabbing my arm he marched me along to where the brooms and mops were kept and gave me a dustbin and brush to remove the offending sand. Resuming his admonitions in English, he made it clear this must not happen again. Fearful that it might, I looked for other accommodation possibilities for the following year and so I discovered the wonderfully laid back Nektarios studios. There visitors from all over Europe turned up, and did their own thing, watched over and encouraged by the elderly Greek proprietor who lived in a traditional house next door. Staying there was extremely restful and carefree and so we became annual regulars.

Halfway along the road around the bay I passed Petros's shed. A tall thin very upright man in his late eighties he was sat outside the shed watching the world go by. I waved as I passed, not having time to stop and chat, and he waved back. In the early morning Petros would tend the small section of the plot on which he grew potatoes, chillies, courgettes and tomatoes – his justification for having the shed. In the past I had been given tomatoes by him as he seemed to give away most of what he grew. After his gardening activity, as today, he took out a plastic chair and table and relaxed, often being joined by one or more elderly friends. Following a bread and cheese lunch, wrapped in a kerchief, he retreated inside for an afternoon siesta on a rickety metal bedstead just visible from the open door.

The shed was situated in a key position on a substantial plot of land between two restaurants. The bane of would-be developers, it was Petros's pride and joy. Leaning away from the prevailing Meltemi, the shed heavily sun bleached to an all over light grey was a kind of huge wooden three-dimensional jigsaw constructed out of driftwood, pallets, planks and boxes. In places these were nailed some three or four layers deep which had foiled a few midnight attempts to dismantle it. These walls together with its stout wooden door and rusty padlock also made it impregnable to the small boys who regularly challenged each other to try to gain access.

Shortly after passing Petros's shed I turned left up the narrow lane that meandered through the valley before climbing to the main road just below Kefalos old town. First I came to two traditional houses with white walls and blue paintwork. Shrouded in grape vines and with brightly coloured flowers in pots by the doors, they looked most attractive and had been photographed by me in past years. Then immediately after the lane went through a small olive grove I reached Kos Creative Escapes, Joan and Terry's Art Centre.

'Come in,' said Joan ushering me into the kitchen. 'Is everything OK? I'm really glad you are able to help out.'

'I'm fine,' I replied, 'and looking forward to this. I'm glad of the opportunity to help.'

'That's their lunch packages,' she followed my glance to a large cardboard box on the worktop. 'Can you take charge of those. I've labelled the two gluten free, the dairy free, vegetarian, and the vegan ones and there is a big carton of grapes and bananas from which they can help themselves.'

'Providing meals seems more complicated these days and an increasingly serious responsibility,' I commented. 'So many people seem to have allergies.'

'There have been a few dreadful cases in the news recently of youngsters having life-threatening reactions to what they have eaten so I do worry about it. I definitely don't want anyone becoming ill or even feeling below par because of my food.'

'You have lots of knowledge and experience of the

effects of diet and nutrition and you are very careful so I'm sure that your guests will have no problems,' I sought to reassure her. 'What are they all doing now? Will we be off shortly?' I changed the conversation to a positive subject.

'They are in the studio getting advice about painting at Limonias as it's their first trip out to paint. Yesterday they stayed in the studio and painted seascapes to try to capture the colours of Mediterranean skies and seas and practised calm seas, ripples and waves dashing on the rocks that sort of thing. Ron, our tutor for the week, sold lots of tubes of manganese blue hue, which is a great colour for the seas here, rather different to the usual colour of the sea off Britain. They'll be having coffee break in a minute so I'll be able to introduce you to him.'

Ron turned out to be a slightly built, rather dapper looking man with curly hair, a moustache and a neat beard. When Joan introduced me, smiling enthusiastically, he shook my hand energetically spilling coffee over the top of the mug in his other hand.

'So you are going to drive some of the artists to Limonias for me and then help see they have everything they need. That's great. I hear from our host that you do watercolour painting. I'm sure that if you take heed of the advice I give, when I go around helping individuals, you will learn some extremely valuable tips.'

Somewhat surprised by this, I mumbled 'Well I'm not very good so I could certainly benefit from some tips.'

When I turned the corner at the top of the cliff to start our descent, my passengers greeted the panorama below with appreciative comments.

'What a beautiful view.'

'I like the quaint harbour, I shall enjoy painting that.'

'It's a really pretty peaceful scene. It will be lovely to spend time here.'

'Can't wait to get started,' another said. 'We can choose our subject so I'm going to do that fishing boat.'

As soon as both vans were parked at the bottom of the hill in an area free of scrub, the would-be artists quickly collected their equipment and a camping chair and immediately dispersed.

'Don't go too far away,' John called after them, 'as I might not see where you are and you'll miss out on my help.'

Everyone soon selected and settled into their chosen locations. The exception was one sprightly elderly woman. She lugged a large easel and two over-flowing bags of painting materials from the end of the harbour to the beach, to the little cove behind where the vans were parked, to halfway up the cliff behind the vans, holding up her card window in front of her eyes in search of the perfect composition. Eventually flinging down her easel and bags she collapsed in the scrub. When I went over to her prostrate figure to check on her wellbeing, she declared herself utterly artistically exhausted. On sitting up she stated she would paint whatever she could best see from there, which turned out to be the two mini vans with a sea backdrop. I ensured that she was OK and supplied her with another pot of water as hers had spilt in the scrub.

Afterwards, I went over to where three women friends, who had arrived together, were sitting in a row sketching out a view of the cove where parents were sunbathing while their children were playing in the water.

'Here's some masking fluid,' I handed it to the first of the women. I'd told her that I would look for it once everyone was settled. 'Joan told me there was a box of materials that might be needed in the big van.'

'I wish they could stay still. I just can't get the arms on this little girl jumping up and down in the water to look natural,' the second woman commented.

'Allow me.' Ron suddenly arrived beside us and took her pencil. With a few deft strokes of the pencil the arms were given life and movement.

'The problem,' he said gravely, 'is your pencil. It's a hard HB and you need a soft one like a 3B and you should sharpen it with a knife not a pencil sharpener. Also, I see that you are using an ordinary rubber not a putty rubber. You will ruin your paper.'

On the subject of paper, he turned to where the third woman was looking appreciatively at her efforts having painted a bright blue sky with a few tiny white puffy clouds near the horizon. 'I'm pleased with that,' she said.

'Well I don't know,' said Ron. 'To me it looks as if the sky is painted on blotting paper. What paper are you using?'

'Ur ur Brighouse,' she replied, 'I always use it.'

'Never heard of it. You need good quality paper to get a good result. I suggest you change to a reliable brand and then your skies will improve. You can buy some Waterhouse 300lbs off me, when we get back to the studio, if you like.' Turning to me, 'Could you bring me a bottle of mineral water. This is thirsty work. I'll be with the group over there.' He pointed to where a group of five, who had told me that they knew each other from participating in many of Ron's art holidays, were sitting on the quay focussing on a large blue and white fishing boat where two elderly men were mending their nets. He walked off leaving the creator of the Mediterranean sky somewhat deflated and requiring supportive comments from myself and her two colleagues to persuade her to continue.

As I approached with the mineral water, my experience so far made me rather surprised that Ron was commenting favourably on the painting of one of the younger members of the group. 'Your aerial perspective is perfect, such a lovely hazy background and those strong colours and deep shadows in the foreground really make the boat stand out. I can see you have taken to heart all the valuable instruction on tonal values I've given you over the years. I think …'

Suddenly consternation broke out, as a member of the group in a vivid yellow apron, who was struggling to get a thoroughly stuck lid off one of her paint tubes, inadvertently let go of the brush she was holding. It flicked up in the air, she grabbed at it and nearly caught it but in so doing knocked it up into the air again from where it fell unimpeded into the harbour. Before her horrified gaze it gently bobbed out of reach. 'Oh no! It's my favourite brush. Oh no! What am I going to do? Oh help!' she wailed somewhat disproportionately hysterical.

Ron, with considerable presence of mind rushed over to the fishing boat, hastily procured a piece of netting from the nonplussed net repairers and running down the quay intercepted the brush as it was heading out to sea.

'Oh thank you, thank you. You are so wonderful. How could I have done justice to this holiday without this.' She looked up at him with tears in her eyes as he handed back the rescued brush.

'As you know, I'm here to be of help,' he beamed self indulgently at her.

As he moved off to visit the beach-based artists, the group were effusive in his praise.

'I've been coming on his holidays for over 20 years and you can see why.'

'We always have a wonderful time.'

'I've learnt so much from him, what paint to use, what paper. He's just great.'

'I have never been on anybody else's holiday. I wouldn't go, I wouldn't know what to expect. It would be certain to be a disappointment.'

'Do you remember when we went on his holiday to Sardinia …?'

I left the acolytes to enjoy their memory exchange and also headed off to the beach where camp chairs were dotted around as individuals sought to capture the cliffs, waves and gaily coloured fluttering sun umbrellas.

'Have you seen the colonel?' I asked. Joan had asked me to keep an eye on him because, although he seemed very fit, he was in his late eighties and so she was worried the heat might adversely affect him. 'I thought I saw him setting off in this direction but I now can't see him,' I continued.

'I think you'll find him up the end of the beach, as he kept going when the rest of us settled down here,' said the confident professional artist. She was already well on with her painting, which was quite an abstract but a very atmospheric interpretation of the cliffs and waves. As she had told me over coffee, she lived alone and so enjoyed the companionship of an art holiday. Also, it was a chance to experiment, as the paintings she sold and the commissions that she took on had to be done in the figurative but quirky style for which she had become known.

As I walked up the beach I thought I saw the green canvas of a camp chair abandoned on the sand which, as I got closer, I realised was indeed the case. The colonel, eyes closed was comfortably positioned on a sunbed under an umbrella with his box of art materials unopened by his side. I coughed gently which achieved the desired result as he opened his eyes and looked up at me. 'Haven't you found anything that you'd like to paint?' I enquired smiling at him.

'Beautiful place, lots of possibilities, perhaps after

lunch. At the moment I'm enjoying a creative escape.' He winked at me before closing both eyes in contented repose.

I set off back along the beach. As I passed the recently retired science teacher, who was a relative beginner and hadn't tried painting outside before, I could hear Ron passing on more of his advice. 'You'll never produce anything you are happy with using these paints. They don't contain enough pigment, they're not good quality. Look how chalky and opaque your sea is. I've got some artist quality paints back at the studio that you could buy which will give you proper transparent effects characteristic of watercolour.'

The rest of the morning and the time after lunch passed amazingly quickly but was really tiring. I walked from the cove to the quay and to the beach and back again innumerable times, taking requests for more mineral water, refilled water pots, cling film to create ripple effects, wax crayons to produce sparkle on the waves, sponges to print scrub and seaweed and pieces of plastic card to scrape out rocks. However, the artists were most appreciative and returned to the studio with their paintings and ideas to work on and all seemed very positive about the day.

When I left Joan and Terry's having reported to Joan on how the day had gone, I decided as the timing was right and

I had done enough walking for the day that I would get a lift back to the house with John. I turned left off the lane along the seafront to Kamari square. The expansive dustbowl with a circular concrete plinth off centre and bordered by advertisements of various sizes, colours and states of dilapidation didn't really deserve to be called a square. It acted as a car park for the occasional tourist bus and a store for army tanks when on manoeuvres.

On the corner was Aldi Plus as the big sign on the roof labelled the little supermarket, which not only sold everything the other Kamari supermarkets sold but also sold newspapers for all nationalities. At home John read papers on line but when he was away he regarded it as a treat to have an actual newspaper. Since our first visits to Kefalos the family who ran the shop had always ordered a copy of the Guardian newspaper especially for him. They found his adherence to the Guardian highly amusing and jokingly referred to him as the English Communist.

Having collected his Guardian, I took the path behind the beach where the day's beach activities were drawing to a close. A few sunbathers were continuing to read, top up their tans and get the most out of their five euros investment in a sunbed and umbrella. Pantelis the owner, anxious to be home, hovered around them collapsing the umbrellas and folding up the unoccupied sunbeds.

A young Russian man, obviously very heavily into body building, stood at the water's edge flexing his muscles in various poses and instructing his acquiescent girlfriend on the photos he wanted taking. Pantelis clearly decided to seize the moment and began to lower the couple's umbrella. The Russian, in mid pose realising what was happening, rushed back to his sunbed and lifted Pantelis off the ground while shouting his displeasure at this premature action. Plonked back on his feet and visibly shaken Pantelis hastily reopened the umbrella and the Russian resumed his photo shoot.

The guys at the Everything for Everyone Everyday watersports club in their colourful shorts and T-shirts, which advertised the paragliding, wakeboarding and jet skis on offer, were packing up the enormous banana, sausage and other inflatable edibles to which tourists liked to be strapped and bounced around the bay. At the catamaran hire a group of sailing enthusiasts was drifting into land and pulling the cats up the beach while loudly swapping stories of heavy gusts and near capsizes.

Not far from the Meltemi windsurf hut the line of restaurants backing the beach was broken by the large semi-circular Baystay hotel set around an area of carefully tended and watered grass and a swimming pool. The guests sunbathing there were screened from the wind, and the glances of those like myself walking past, by a glass screen and an oleander hedge.

The sight of the hotel still came as something of a surprise to me as for 15 years or even longer, as no one could quite remember how long, the building – maybe originally designed to be restaurants, studios or shops – had existed as four large multi-storey carpark-like concrete edifices. In the lee of one of these some windsurfers had always set up camp for the summer around an old VW camper van. They had now moved to an area of scrub adjoining the beach on the far side of Meltemi.

As I approached the windsurf hut, the last of the windsurfers were packing up. They staggered bent double up the beach and climbed the steps to the equipment racks carrying their sails on their backs. In their black wet suits and multi-coloured flapping sails they looked like a swarm of ungainly beetles as sudden gusts of wind caused them to lurch sideways and do a few stumbling rebalancing steps before moving forward again. Having thankfully offloaded the sails they returned to the water's edge to make a second trip up the beach with their boards.

Once their equipment was returned and cleaned, the

windsurfers sank gratefully onto the sofas on the new decking. There they were able to share their experiences and to discuss the problems caused by the gaps in the wind as they traversed the bay, the effects of the gusts, the achievement of successful jibes that didn't result in their falling in, the appropriateness or otherwise of the boards that they were recommended and their hopes for better conditions tomorrow.

Feeling somewhat tired after my day's artistically orientated labours, I didn't go and join them. Instead I sat on a rickety wooden seat in the shade of a ghostly looking tree, owing to its branches and twigs being smothered in sand, and waited for John to finish helping stack the sails and boards.

'Hi!' said a voice breaking into my day dreams. 'Good to see you back. How are you?' said a young fair-haired man standing beside me.

'Oh! Andy you made me jump. I've had a really busy day and I think I was almost falling asleep. We are fine and very pleased to be back. How about you?'

'I'm good, really good. It's a surprise to see you so early in the season.'

I explained to him that we were here because we were going to spend the summer in Kefalos. I recounted how this came about and answered his questions about where we were living and what we planned to do.

We had met Andy on our first holiday in Kefalos when he was a waiter at Spiros's restaurant. He came from Bolton and had worked in Athens, Corfu and Crete before settling in Kefalos for the last five years. Each summer he worked in a different restaurant. He may have moved around just to try out and compare different places. However, his cheerful, friendly personality and the way he remembered tourists' names, details and their food preferences made him very popular and additional custom seemed to follow him around. Consequently, it seemed likely he was enticed to move by an increase in wages. When I got onto telling him about the islands we wanted to visit John arrived beside us.

'Hello Andy. How has life been treating you?'

'Pretty well. Especially as at the end of last season Tanya and I were able to rent an apartment in Kefalos old town. The owner said we could stay there as long as we wanted as it was easier to just rent it out to us rather than use it for holiday lets. It's really comfortable and conveniently situated and so much better than having to keep moving each season. Tanya is thrilled with it.'

'Are you still working at Mille Sapori?' asked John.

'No. I enjoyed being there but, as you know I like a

change,' he grinned. This year I'm at Kyrios's. Anyway I must be off as I was just having a quick walk before I go to work. I'll see you around or at Kyrios's.'

'He seems on good form,' commented John.

'Yes and he is still with Tanya.' Tanya was his Romanian girlfriend who had moved in with him a couple of summers ago.

'Well let's go. You can tell me about your day in the car,' said John.

3

Jan and Regi Come to Stay

I spent a couple more days as a driver for, and helping out with, Joan's art group. One day we went to Kardamena where members were asked to choose a beach or cafe scene to paint. On their final day I took them to Kos town where they could choose to either do a painting or explore the town.

Joan was very pleased with the way the first art course of the season had gone. Ron complimented her on the facilities and her organisation and signed up to come and run another course next May. As soon as they learned this, the acolytes immediately booked their places. Apparently others on the course said they also planned to come back but would like to try a different tutor, so could she ensure they were informed of future courses. The professional artist produced a range of increasingly abstract multi-media pictures. Attributing her success to the atmosphere at the centre and the lovely morning and evening light, she booked a fortnight's stay in October when the art programme had finished. The colonel praised it as the most relaxing art course he had ever been on. He left without a finished painting but with an enhanced sense of wellbeing vowing to return.

Tomorrow evening Janice and Reginald were arriving to spend three days with us before taking the once weekly flight from Kos to Crete. Jan had texted me soon after we arrived in Kefalos to ask if they could stay as it seemed a good opportunity for us to meet up. She appreciated it might not be convenient, as we hadn't had long to settle in, but I assured her it would be great to have them to stay and I would really welcome the chance to see her. She was a friend of mine from college days who, when she lived in Newcastle before she married Regi, I used to meet up with regularly. However, in the ten years since she had been married and lived in Brighton I had only seen her a couple of times and had only met Regi briefly on one of these occasions.

On Crete they planned to spend a couple of weeks in Agios Nikolaos and visit Regi's younger brother who was on a year's exchange with an academic from the university at Rethymno. Jan was particularly looking forward to this because, as Regi did a lot of international travelling as part of his post at the University of Sussex and was always busy writing research papers or working on his next book, they seldom took any holiday together.

It was her birthday the day before they were due to leave us and so a present was urgently needed. Fortunately the little pottery in the centre of Kefalos was invaluable on such occasions. In addition to crude wall plaques with neon bright pictures of blue and white houses and windmills, it also sold all sizes and shapes of dishes and plates delicately decorated with traditional island designs.

Back home I had a stack of the fish plates purchased from there. While all in the shape of a fish and in the same pretty blue design they varied in width, depth and fish shape enabling me to gradually build up a matching set by buying one each holiday. Unfortunately, when friends came to dinner, I didn't know how to make enough different kinds of fish starters to display more than a few of my collection at any one time. Jan, I'd decided, would like one of the pottery's small rectangular plates with a wild flower design. They were very attractive and useful, as I'd found, because I also had one on which I put biscuits or chocolates. In addition, it would be easy to pack in her suitcase when travelling around.

I drove into Kefalos and parked at the top of the hill by

the DIY shop, usually very busy, but closed because it was Sunday. As it was a very tiny shop, most of what could be purchased was permanently stored outside. This included a couple of concrete mixers, an essential item for anyone into home improvements, as in Kefalos it seemed anything and everything could be repaired or crafted in concrete. I breathed in as I squeezed Mabel into the remaining space.

There used to be ample parking in this area even with the morning influx of tourists seeking a greater diversity of groceries than that available in Kamari. However, over the winter paving stones were laid in places and piled up in others over much of the parking space combined with the erection of interspersed stone columns. Hopefully, but experience made me pessimistic, these would ultimately be revealed to be part of a grand design and not left overs from another municipal project that remained unfinished. Only by the end of next winter or more realistically several winters, providing those responsible could recall what was intended at the outset, would we know.

The pottery door, with its sample plates including some fish plates hung on each side, was open. As you went in, the room on the right was stacked high with grey unfired, unfinished and damaged pots. The room on the left was the shop with everything currently available on show. There was only one wild flower plate so that made selection easy. Stocks were low as the owner was away visiting relatives. As I hadn't met the two women who were looking after the shop and they were more interested in their conversation than me, the transaction was quickly completed.

Then I popped into Nektarios's supermarket for a few basic food items, some cleaning materials to get the house ready for Jan's arrival and hopefully some navy blue tape to repair John's favourite shorts. This supermarket seemed the Greek equivalent of the post office in the Norfolk village in which I'd lived as a child. Amongst the floor-to-ceiling plastic crates and boxes stacked in higgledy piggledy towers, if you had the time and determination to search, was everything you or anyone else might want or have once wanted. I remember being very surprised when Betty told me that Nektarios was Panayioti's older brother as they were as unalike in appearance and manner as the supermarkets that they ran.

The navy tape eluded both me and Maria, who was serving, and required her to summon her dad Nektarios from the back of the shop. Producing a box of tapes of all colours bar navy he was certain he had some. He'd sold a length to a tourist for the same purpose last May. Three-quarters of an hour and details of everything he'd sold to tourists for repairs later, he ultimately located the missing reel where it had fallen and become wedged between the boxes of paintbrushes and stacks of pink plastic colanders.

As I left, I told myself after this I had earned a coffee and crossed the road to Zephina's, settled myself in a comfy chair in the shade and ordered a cappuccino. The entertainment today was the fish van which was parked on the corner partially blocking the road. Locals chatted while queueing for fish and ignored the vans and vespas tooting at them to move aside.

A successful shopping trip I thought, as I returned to the car and struggled to get it out of the tiny space now further reduced by a large abandoned van with the engine running and doors open but no sign of the owner. I reversed out carefully and drove back down the hill. When I got back to the house it was to find Spiros reclining on a sunlounger on the patio, eyes closed and so most likely asleep but still managing to puff away at a cigarette.

'Hi Spiros,' I called, 'I wasn't expecting you today.'

He jumped, sat up and the cigarette dropped out of his mouth, 'Just resting my eyes, you startled me,' he said reproachfully. 'Look what I've brought you,' he indicated the sunlounger he continued to lie on. Its companion was folded up next to him and a matching umbrella was propped against the door. 'The Acropolis,' he was referring to the first hotel to have been opened on the hillside on the main road up to Kefalos old town, 'has just smartened up its pool area and this morning, when I went round to sort out a plumbing problem, they were putting out their new sunbeds. I offered to take the old ones off their hands for a very generous price and I thought you might be interested in these two.'

'Mmm, well they would make a really good addition to the patio. How much do you want for them?'

He looked offended. 'It's a present, well a loan for you while you are here. Would I take money from you for secondhand sunbeds?' He chuckled, 'But you could show your gratitude by bringing me a beer and some of those cheese things you make.'

I disappeared inside and emerged with a drink for us both and a plate of cheese straws – fortunately I had made some the previous day. John and I really liked cheese straws as an alternative to bread to have with our lunchtime salad or soup. Since I'd also discovered they were popular with the Greek visitors who popped around, most of the time I had some available. While Spiros drank his beer and munched his way through the cheese straws, he updated me on the latest gossip dwelling with enthusiasm on his juiciest new news item about Hector who ran the largest car hire firm in Kefalos. Kidonia, his wife, had found out what seemingly everyone in Kefalos had known from the outset, that he was having an affair with Tina.

Tina was a very attractive Bulgarian less than half his age whom he employed in his Kardamena office and where, apparently, she had considerably contributed to increasing the number of customers. Kidonia had gone unexpectedly to their beach house in Mastihari for some items she had unintentionally left behind at the weekend. There she found Tina, who had used the key Hector had given her to let herself in, waiting for him in the bedroom. Hearing the door open and assuming it was him, Tina had called to him to come on up.

Exactly what happened next in the beach house was a matter of conjecture but on her return home Kidonia had immediately got her brother to change the locks on the beach house and threatened Hector with ruin. As the money that originally had set up the car hire business and maintained its supply of new cars came predominantly from her father, who ran a successful nightclub in Kos town, she had the power to do so.

'Do you think she'll carry out her threat?' I asked.

'Well she is certainly very angry.' He cocked his head to

one side in contemplation. 'I reckon she will make his life hell for a couple of months, keep him guessing about what she is going to do and then when she judges he is sufficiently penitent and she has got him where she wants him, she'll take him back. Yes that is what's most likely to happen, that's what I think.' Having delivered his prediction and finished the refreshments he gave a sigh, closed his eyes and sank back onto the sunbed.

Then almost immediately he leapt to his feet. 'Oh! What is the time? I must be off as I've got some solar lights to collect from that big German resort in Mastahari.' In response to my questioning look he explained, 'Well Germans like to be thought of as green but these lights barely even glowed in the dark. No one could see the paths and someone tripped up and broke his leg and is suing the resort, so the lights are being replaced. I'm going to get them and sell them to the council to put along the extension to the beach walkway.'

'Will they want them if they don't throw any light?'

'Oh yes because they'll cost them a lot less than buying new electric ones and they'll look good during the day. No one goes up there after dark because there is nothing up there, only rocks so they will be perfect.' As I heard his old truck rattling and backfiring its way down the lane, I went inside to get ready the room that Jan and Regi were going to have and make up their bed.

The following evening John and I went to the airport to collect our guests whose plane from Manchester, although it was delayed for what seemed to be the customary two hours for all arrivals, still came in at the unusually civilised hour of eight o'clock. It was great to see Jan again who was looking very well, with her English Rose complexion and her dark brown hair, previously long and pinned up now in a new short bob that really suited her. She certainly looked no older than when we last met. She was pleased to meet up and excited about her forthcoming holiday in Greece.

In appearance Regi was how I remembered him – tall and thin with aquiline features and thick unruly brown hair which hung over his forehead. He was undeniably handsome but for me his features were blighted by what I regarded as a permanent superior snooty look that was accentuated by his adherence to old fashioned style glasses with round lenses.

'Regi you will remember Rosemary and this is her husband John,' Jan introduced us.

'Good to meet you,' John responded. 'Can I help with your bags?' They seemed to have a great deal of luggage.

'Yes thanks,' said Regi. 'I'm afraid that I've brought a

lot of work with me as I've a couple of papers to finish, several journal articles to review and I'm planning my next book.' Enquiring politely about the subject matter of his new book John led the way to the car, as Regi enthusiastically embarked on a description of its intended contents.

'I'm hoping he isn't going to be too busy while we are away. I did try to get him to leave some of this behind,' Jan confided in me, pulling a face as she looked down at the oversized and overfull briefcase that she was carrying. 'I want us to go off exploring. We seldom have time to go out and do things together these days.'

Once sat in the back of the car on the drive to Kamari, Jan and I began updating each other on events. She told me about the birth of her niece and Regi's promotion to professor. I told her about the couple who were renting our home while we were away and our new home and jobs in Kefalos. Meanwhile I was aware that Regi was continuing his explanation of the intended contents of his book with John interjecting with appropriate comments to show interest. Mabel's headlights were far from her best characteristic and so I knew he would be concentrating on the road rather than taking in Regi's information. We seemed to reach the top of the hill, before the road dipped down into Kefalos, incredibly quickly.

As agreed before we left the airport, we parked in a lay-by at the top so Jan and Regi could appreciate the view of Kamari bay lit by moonlight over the sea and around the edges by the brightly coloured lights of the restaurants, cafes and the harbour. When coming to Kos on our annual holiday and arriving in Kefalos in the early hours of the morning, I had always found the lights of the bay an attractive and welcoming sight that reassured us that nothing much had changed during the year. Jan jumped out with enthusiasm to look around, while Regi excused himself saying he would use the opportunity to send a text to a work colleague.

'Oh it is lovely and look at that little chapel all lit up on the island, it's really pretty.' Jan obligingly made all the anticipated right comments. 'I look forward to exploring and seeing it all properly tomorrow. You said you also have a great view from the house?'

'You see the white lights right over the other side of the bay and to the left, well that's the harbour and our house is up the hill behind it. Yes, we are lucky. We think we've got the best view on Kos, probably the best view in … .'

'What's going on down there?' John interrupted pointing immediately below us to where a black pall of smoke was rising slowly from a small but brilliantly glowing red ball of fire.

'Oh no! I do hope it's not another arson attack,' I responded. 'The fire doesn't look big but it looks really intense.'

'Could it be a beach bonfire or a barbecue that's got out of control?' asked Jan.

'I doubt it,' said John. 'After dark there's usually no one down there on the beach.' He went on to explain why we were concerned. 'The week before we arrived here someone set fire to a small windsurfing business on a beach quite close to here and no one knows who did it.'

'Let's go and see if anyone knows what's happened,' I suggested.

As we drove down to the bay, the sight of the fire disappeared under the hillside. When we got down to the corner by the main square, where the road began to run along the water's edge, quite a crowd had gathered looking across the bay to the fire which seemed to be burning less brightly but was issuing enormous amounts of smoke. An acrid smell filled the air, even though the breeze was taking much of it in the opposite direction. Spotting Daryl, one of the speedboat drivers with Bay Sport, John leaned out of the car window to find out what was going on.

It seemed that the small watersports hut at the far end of the beach that housed wakeboards, waterskis and pedalos for tourists to hire had indeed been subject to an arson attack. Apparently it occurred after Dimitri, the elderly owner, as he did every summer evening, had stowed away the equipment in the hut, lined up the pedalos in the sand alongside it and left the hut locked up for the night. When he left, the beach was empty and so no one had seen whoever was responsible for the fire. There was a brief but all-engulfing conflagration, which reduced the hut and its contents to charcoal within minutes, while the pedalos continued to smoulder.

The little business was destroyed almost before anyone was aware the fire had been started and certainly before anyone could get to it to douse the flames with water. The locals, who had rushed to the scene, just watched helplessly. Driven back by the heat they were unable to save anything. The sooty remains of the hut and the blackened distorted pedalos on the sands became another testament to the potential of fire to destroy in an instant livelihoods slowly and painstakingly built up. Speculation as to the identity of the arsonists had started immediately and as we listened gathered momentum.

'I reckon it was his younger brother,' said Daryl. 'He is

an odd guy. He helps Dimitri when he's busy but he doesn't like doing so. He's always moaning about the business that it's too much work and it doesn't make enough money and Dimitri should run it differently.'

'More likely the competition,' chipped in another young man at Daryl's elbow. 'Sure your boss hasn't put you up to it?'

'Could be Konstantinos, rumour has it he is thinking of setting up a water sports centre to go with his waterpark,' suggested a third.

'More likely the Russian mafia,' put forward another. 'It's known they put up the money for the new windsurfing and kitesurfing centre.'

'Known by whom?' questioned an elderly man. 'I'm with Daryl. I think it's his brother.'

The fire on her arrival had certainly provided Jan with a rather dramatic introduction to Kefalos which as far as she was concerned continued when she awoke the following morning. I was in the kitchen at the front of the house preparing fruit salad for breakfast when she came in looking flustered and anxious.

'Is everything alright?' I asked.

'I'm not sure. I think we might be being invaded,' she said. 'Come and look.' We walked into the back where the patio door was open and I followed her gaze. A huge menacing grey naval troop ship filled the doorway. Pointing straight at the house, bows tipped up and open, it was disgorging pairs of soldiers with rifles who were running down the gangway and disappearing up the beach.

'What on earth is going on?' she stared at me wide-eyed. 'Have the Turks arrived?' she asked half fearfully and half joking.

'Oh no, don't worry,' I replied laughing. 'It's the Greek army manoeuvres that take place in Kefalos every year about this time but I can quite understand why they gave you such a fright. I wonder what did Regi think was happening?'

'Oh he hasn't noticed. He is sitting up in bed with his laptop and his headphones on listening to a conference podcast on migration. He can't bear to be interrupted, when he is engaged and concentrating, so I didn't disturb him. So you've seen this before?'

'We first experienced the manoeuvres one afternoon when we were staying at Seagull studios. We were sitting on our balcony and this long procession of tanks came rumbling down the harbour road flattening restaurant menu boards and scattering tourists in their wake. Then this huge carrier approached the shore, like the one there today, and positioned itself at the water's edge. Then each tank with considerable difficulty was reversed on board. It happens every year and it's a most extraordinary sight. I can promise you that, along with the rest of Kefalos, it will provide your entertainment later today.'

She grinned, 'Well it's very reassuring to know it's the Greek army. I'll go and get up and see if Regi has finished his podcast. That looks nice,' she commented as she went past the bowls of chopped banana, grapes, peaches, pears and plums.

'You can get lovely fruit here,' I told her, 'and we like it for breakfast when I can be bothered to prepare it.'

Later that morning I took Jan for a tour of Kefalos old town. John had gone out early to help clean windsurfing boards ready for a new group that were due to arrive later in the day. Regi declined to join us as he was keen to begin reading one of the books he had brought with him. We wandered around the streets, looked at the castle and visited the little local history museum.

In a clothes shop, which I often frequented for bargains, Jan treated herself to a pair of supposedly Giorgio Armani black cropped trousers. She was well pleased with these and wore them when she left to go to Crete. They were only ten euros and in a lovely soft material with pretty patterns in beads and stitching on the back pockets. I had a pair of full length black trousers back at home that I had bought in a sale at the Armani shop in the York Designer Outlet and they had the same metal and material brand labels. Her trousers were a very good copy of authentic Armani, although the care with which they were made suggested that perhaps they might have been genuine – who knows – and Jan wasn't bothered.

We ended up in Zephina's for coffee in order that Jan could experience the appealing pastime of idly chilling out while observing life on the corner. As promised, when we returned past the square Jan saw 20 Greek tanks, somewhat rusty looking and antiquated, and a collection of assorted army trucks all assembled in lines ready, when given the go ahead, to be driven down to the beach for loading.

Loading began in the early evening. The arrival of the tanks under our patio was heralded by the steadily expanding gathering of locals and holidaymakers forming around the Scorpios restaurant from which they bought drinks and positioned chairs in readiness for the anticipated spectacle. We settled down on the patio with our glasses of retsina as the first tanks ponderously rumbled onto the beach and churned through the sand towards the troop carrier.

'I'm surprised those tanks are still in service,' commented Regi. 'They look as if they should be mothballed. I thought the Greeks had spent millions of euros buying the very latest in military equipment from the Germans.'

'I saw a programme about Greece's relationship with the EU and that showed a military march past in Athens,' said John, 'and you are right they had all the latest modern equipment, but I don't think that they sent any out to the Dodecanese.'

'Are they really just going to all charge onto the ship?' asked Jan watching the steadily advancing line of tanks.

'The guys in the ship look like they are trying to get them to change tack,' I responded.

From the opening in the bows of the ship several uniformed figures started running forward gesticulating to the tank drivers to stop moving forward and instead turn around and reverse up the gangway. Since we had first witnessed the army grappling with this not inconsiderable challenge, the council had increased the level of difficulty by installing in the middle of the beach a shower that resembled a large white plastic mushroom, or some 21st century menhir around which scantily clad worshippers performed a water dance.

The way aboard appeared to be led by a very experienced, or very lucky, driver as with much revving to and fro the first tank turned itself around, deftly avoided the mushroom and steadily backed up the ramp until it was swallowed into the bowels of the ship. Two holidaymakers burst into spontaneous clapping, which quickly tailed off as they realised none of the other onlookers were joining them and the locals were giving them 'I wouldn't do that if I were you' looks.

The second tank was having a lot more difficulty getting ready to attempt the required feat. We watched as it sashayed around the mushroom. The more its engines revved, the more it sank in the sand.

'I wouldn't fancy being on that in the desert,' observed Regi. Various military personnel came over to inspect it and shouted instructions at each other and the driver. Eventually the tank stopped digging a hole for itself and crawled backwards towards the ship. Then the driver obviously lost patience and decided to go for it. His tank suddenly shot backwards aiming at the gangway, succeeded in climbing a couple of feet up the ramp before slipping sideways and dropping over the edge with an exceedingly large splash that soaked the instructing personnel. We collapsed in giggles from the safety of the patio, whereas the audience at

Scorpios had to be more circumspect in their amusement or smother their laughter in handkerchiefs.

'We told you it would be good entertainment,' chuckled John.

Tank number three arrived with another very dilapidated tank attached behind it on a long towing pole.

'This should be interesting, how on earth are they going to get that on board,' Jan commented.

They weren't. For about an hour the driver struggled in vain to push the broken-down tank into position. Several times the ancient tank grazed the side of the mushroom which did violent circuitous wobbles before righting itself. The instructions grew ever more voluble and the gestures more agitated but to no avail. It proved to be mission impossible even to get the tank lined up at the bottom of the ramp, let alone move up it and eventually it was towed to the back of the beach and abandoned. The performance continued as darkness fell with the final tanks achieving the manoeuvre by the light of a full moon. However, long before this we had retreated indoors for dinner.

The following morning we were awoken to the sound of a bulldozer on the beach where it was removing the enormous ruts created by the tanks and shovelling the sand back into place. The broken-down tank had obviously been towed away. The shower stood proud having withstood the onslaught and Vangelis was replacing the umbrellas and sunbeds at the water's edge. Soon there was no remaining indication of the previous night's activity.

The final day of Jan's stay and her birthday was tranquil and pleasantly uneventful. Regi sat in the shade on the patio reviewing journal articles. Jan and I began the day lazing on the patio chatting and reminiscing. Jan was very pleased with the wildflower plate, which I gave her at breakfast time, and said that she would like to visit the pottery. When we entered the shop, a potter whom I hadn't seen before, was decorating a large vase with the same wildflower design. The vase was beautiful, with very colourful and intricate detail in the flowers. However, the intended price of 80 euros, and the seeming impossibility of getting it home via Crete unbroken, dissuaded her from buying the plate a companion piece.

In the afternoon we walked around the bay and along the beach path, past Meltemi and further on the sad-looking charred remains of Dimitri's hut. When we reached the ruins of the Christian basilica of Saint Stephen, Jan's reaction was like mine when I first saw them. She was amazed that the pillars and mosaic floors were left open to the elements for children to play on and holidaymakers to scramble over. We sat on one of the walls looking out to Kastri island and watching the windsurfers and sailing boats tacking back and forth in the gentle breeze. We concluded by swimming in my favourite spot behind the ruins, where the water gradually deepened and the sand stretched out to sea and there were no stones to contend with.

'I envy you spending the summer here,' she said. 'This is just perfect.' She sighed appreciatively and tilting her sunhat over her face she stretched out on her beach towel digging her toes into the warm sand.

In the evening we went for a birthday celebration meal to the restaurant on Sunset beach over the other side of the island. We went early so we could watch the sunset from the terrace, while eating our meal, and because she and Regi were being collected by taxi at 4am for their seven o'clock flight to Crete.

It was somewhere we had discovered on our first trip to Kefalos. Back then there was no tarmac road to drive along but only a winding dirt track that seemed to take forever to navigate when returning to Kamari in the dark. The coming of the road greatly increased the restaurant's clientele and its romantic setting made it extremely popular with tourists. However, it was still owned by the family who had set it up and the menu remained unchanged.

We ordered barbecued shrimp for starters and red snapper for our main course because we knew that the fish was always particularly delicious. It was smothered in herbs and seasoning, cooked over the barbecue and served with chips and chopped cucumber and tomatoes.

'That was really tasty, wasn't it Regi?' said Jan. Feeling full and wondering whether we could make space for some baklava, their speciality in the dessert line, we watched the glowing red circle of the sun sink gradually down the sky until it was floating on the sea at the horizon.

'It's just beautiful here and I've had such a …' The insistent ringing tone of Regi's mobile broke into our contented contemplation.

'Do you have to …' Jan began as Regi answered, frowning at her and holding out the flat of his hand, as if stopping traffic.

'Oh yes, I'm sure I could,' he said, as he stood up knocking over his chair and strode over to the steps down to the beach and disappeared out of sight behind the bushes.

'I'm sorry about that,' said Jan. 'As you will have realised his work is really important to him.' She sighed, 'I wish he could just put it to one side while we are on holiday, but never mind. As I was about to say, I've had a great day and I've very much enjoyed our stay with you.'

4

The Sponge Fishers' Island of Kalymnos

We had woken around 7am as usual but I had fallen asleep again. When I woke up properly John wasn't there. I got up, wandered through the sitting room and onto the patio.

'What on earth are you doing?' I exclaimed on seeing John standing on a beach towel with an empty wine bottle at one end. Crossing his outstretched arms in front of him he flicked his head from one shoulder to the other and switched his feet around the bottle. Startled by my question he caught his back foot on the bottle and nearly overbalanced.

'Not the best tack I've ever done,' he laughed. 'I would have fallen in.'

'Is this supposed to be a windsurfing board then?' I pointed at the now crumpled towel.

'Yes, well Otto has a bad cold and so Seb asked me if I

would take his intermediate group and teach them how to tack. I was just experimenting. I thought they might learn quicker if I talked them through what's involved in the manoeuvre and then they practised a bit on land first to get the idea before going out into the bay. Begin to get the footwork into their muscle memory.'

'Sounds logical. I'm sure you will be fine,' I reassured him. 'When you taught water skiing they said you were a good teacher.'

'Hopefully,' he said and looking out to sea added, 'At least the conditions are good. The sea is calm and the wind about 20 knots. Anyway I better be off.'

While I was eating my breakfast on the patio, I had a phone call from Jan who was in good spirits as it seemed that at last she was going to get her wish to have time with Regi to enjoy some exploring and holiday activities. After getting up about 3am and leaving punctually for the airport in their taxi, Jan and Regi experienced the customary delays and finally flew out at ten o'clock. However, they had a smooth flight and were met by Regi's younger brother and his wife who took them to their holiday apartment. Jan reported that they had settled into the apartment which was very comfortable and well equipped and had a lovely view out over the hills. Regi's brother, although also an academic, was apparently less wedded to his work and had promised to take them to his favourite spots on the island.

I had an enjoyable morning working on a painting of an old farmstead that you looked down upon when you drove over the hill to go to Sunset beach. It consisted of a traditional stone house with several adjoining ramshackle animal sheds, which often had goats peaking out through gaps in the walls. The yard was strewn with old farm equipment over and through which chickens pecked and clucked. It was a perfect subject and I had tried hard to do it justice. Depicting the chickens proved a bit difficult but overall I was quite pleased with the result, especially the way in which the sun bleached house stood out against the greens, browns and purples of the hillside and its flowering thyme.

I went inside to make a cup of tea and when I came out again my attention was caught immediately by an unfolding commotion on the beach below. A big pantechnicon was parked on the road alongside the Scorpios restaurant and a team of men were removing multiple boxes and equipment from it. They then carried these along the beach to where a large guy of bouncer like appearance was shouting loudly and gesticulating where he wanted them to be put. I realised this could well be the Russian film crew that were staying at Baystay. According to the staff there, the crew were intending to shoot a few scenes in the locality for a crime drama but no one knew anything about the plot or exactly whereabouts they planned to film.

Another equally intimidating looking individual came down from the pantechnicon and began shouting at Vangelis, seemingly ordering him to clear the beach of his sunbeds and umbrellas and the sunbathers using them. Vangelis started waving his arms in the air in obvious protest, which became increasingly agitated as he started jumping up and down when some of the team began removing the umbrellas from the sunbathers. A few of the sunbathers jumped up, quickly bundled their things into beach bags and hurried off obviously keen to avoid any possible unpleasantness. Others however refused to budge and, as one woman was dragged screaming along the beach hanging onto her umbrella, a fight seemed about to break out between a team member and the tourist he had tipped off his sunbed.

Just as the other male sunbathers seemed to be squaring up ready to join in, a silver sports car screeched to a halt alongside the pantechnicon. At this the team stopped immediately, frozen in whatever they were doing as if participating in a game of statues. The flashily dressed driver, who was clearly the guy in charge, jumped theatrically out over the car door and sauntered down the beach, where with all eyes on him including mine, he obviously asked the bouncer what was going on. On hearing the explanation he reached in his pocket and handed over to Vangelis, from whose change in demeanour, I assumed was more than sufficient cash to cover the hire of his sunbeds and umbrellas. Then he did the rounds of the sunbathers apparently refunding their hire costs with the desired effect that the beach was soon emptied.

The film crew then directed their efforts to putting up an enormous black marquee. The opening to the marquee and the main activity was clearly going to take place on the seaward side and so I could no longer watch what was happening. The entertainment over, I glanced at my watch and realised I'd better get over to Joan and Terry's. They were running a three-day, studio-based mixed media workshop but had an afternoon appointment in Kos town about an exhibition there that they were planning. Therefore they had asked me to go and be on hand in case there were any problems and to serve tea and doughnuts in the break.

In the evening, while as usual we sat eating our dinner on the patio, we kept glancing across at the black marquee. Every few minutes someone would walk around the back of it but obviously the more interesting action was taking place out of sight around the front. Still, John was able to partly satisfy my curiosity by reporting what he had learned about the film crew from Meltemi.

'They are only staying at the Baystay for a couple of nights. They arrived yesterday afternoon and are leaving tomorrow morning.'

'Did you find out anything about the plot of their crime drama?'

'Apparently, it's about a German serial killer who murders women tourists on several of the Dodecanese islands. When he murders a Russian millionairess on Kos the Russian secret police come to the islands, take over the investigation from the Greek police sent from Athens and solve the mystery.'

'Who told you that? It doesn't sound very original.'

'Yiannis. His current girlfriend works as a waitress at Baystay and the director, who is the guy you described with the silver sports car, outlined the plot to the hotel owner who then passed it on to the staff.'

'On my way back from Joan and Terry's,' I said, 'I'm sure that I saw one of the stars of the film walking around the harbour, maybe the millionairess who gets murdered. She was very tall and glamorous and wearing a long dress with lots of jewellery and carrying a small pug so she did rather stand out from the crowd and was getting lots of curious stares.'

At that moment two men appeared struggling with a very heavy and very large light and planted it in the sand at the back of the marquee pointing in our direction.

'I wonder what that's for?' I questioned.

'Perhaps to deter any approaching curious local or tourist,' John replied.

While we didn't find out what it was for, we certainly experienced its effect as once it began to get dark it was switched on and lit up the entire hillside with our house centre stage. Blinking and turning away from the blinding light, we hastily retreated indoors to the living room where the light penetrated cracks in the louvre doors and the shutters making patterns on the stone walls.

Next morning, when I pulled back the doors, all signs of the film crew and the marque were gone and Vangelis was putting out his sunbeds and umbrellas as usual. We were up early as we planned to take the nine o'clock ferry from Mastihari to Kalymnos. We needed to arrive in time to park Mabel and queue for a ticket at the little office at the beach end of the harbour. Then we could make our way along the narrow concrete causeway to the ferry berth at the end vying with the other foot passengers and multiple trucks.

As usual with much revving of engines and shouting of drivers, trucks of fruit and vegetables, building materials and mysterious boxes and crates were fitted into the lower deck of the ferry like pieces of a jigsaw. We walked aboard and climbed the steps to sit in the shade on the top deck, fidgeting on the widely spaced slats of the wooden seats that defied day trippers to sit comfortably. Two middle-aged backpackers wriggled back and forth as they tried various prostate positions in order to catch some sleep during the hour's journey.

The sea was unusually calm with sparkling silver ripples generated by the gentle breeze. It was a perfect day to enjoy a sea trip. We soon left Mastihari behind as we headed for Pothia the capital of Kalymnos. It's hard to believe that it's the fourth largest island in the Dodecanese because, approaching Pothia, which is midway along its south coast, Kalymnos looks deceptively small. However, the island extends way to the north behind the three parallel mountainous limestone ridges that run from north-west to south-east.

The mountains are sunbaked, barren and no longer inhabited and so it is a surprise as the white houses on the shoreline edge of Pothia gradually come into view. When the ferry enters the bay around which the town is built, the vista is really delightful. Houses of pink, yellow and ochre as well as white climb in tiers up the mountainside. Situated high on the cliffs overlooking the town is the monastery of Agios Savvas and a large white cross, which was donated by a former islander who emigrated to Bermuda.

As the ferry comes into its berth, the waterfront is dominated by the church of Agios Nikolaos and an extremely large cream Italian palace style building with a red roof. This has multiple purposes as it houses a museum, police station, customs and a food market. Along the seafront there are various other municipal buildings that were constructed by the Venetians in the 1930s. The Italianisation of the Dodecanese, that followed the 1923 Treaty of Lausanne, consolidated the Italian presence under Mussolini on the islands.

We disembarked and headed off to choose a cafe from the many around the harbour for a second breakfast of coffee and pastries. We walked past the impressive bronze sculptures which emphasised Kalymnos's interdependence with thc sea. These include Jupiter enthroned holding his trident made by the prolific sculptor Michael Kokkinos whose daughter Irene cast the famous mermaid sat on a rock at the entrance to the harbour.

Along the quay were sponge sellers with their trays of natural sponges often with antiquated diving suits displayed alongside their stalls. I stopped at one to buy a small sponge as sponges are very useful for watercolour painting. I like to use one to wet the paper before laying down a wash as it wets it more evenly than using a brush. Sponges are also good for dipping into paint to produce textures and are especially good for creating impressions of leaves and bushes.

The practice on the Dodecanese of diving for sponges dates back to antiquity with their use being mentioned by Homer in the Iliad and the Odyssey. The history of the practice is both fascinating and upsetting. The original naked free divers went out in small boats. The sponges were located using a cylindrical tool with a glass bottom. Then the divers used rocks of up to 15 kilograms in weight in order to reach the seabed some 30 or so metres down. There they would hold their breath and stay for between three and five minutes cutting sponges and gathering them in a special net, but leaving the base of the sponge intact so it could regrow.

In 1865 the introduction of a diving suit – skafandro – meant that the free divers were replaced by divers able to go down to depths of up to 70 metres and spend much longer gathering sponges. The rubber suit had a bronze helmet which was fed with an air supply from the boat up above. Fleets of larger boats with up to fifteen divers took over from the previous small boats and the burgeoning sponge industry made huge profits for the island's merchants. However, as documented by Faith Warn in her book Bitter Sea the risks and accidents associated with these suits resulted in a great many divers suffering decompression sickness from surfacing too quickly causing death, paralysis and serious disabilities. Apparently, the women of Kalymnos distraught at the plight of their menfolk appealed to the Turkish Sultan, who ruled the islands at that time, for help and in 1882 he banned the use of the diving suits. Nevertheless the ban was short-lived because of the extremely negative effect it had on profits.

The next disastrous impact on the sponge industry was wrought by the onset of the two World Wars resulting in it almost disappearing completely as a result of World War II. Many divers left to seek their fortunes, for example by sponge diving in Florida or pearl diving in Australia, and married and settled overseas. The final blow to what was left of the sponge trade came in the 1980s when, as a result of overfishing, pollution and a marine disease, the sponges in the Eastern Mediterranean and the Aegean Sea came very near to extinction.

In recent years, however, sea conditions have improved enabling some natural sponges to be harvested locally in a safe and sustainable way and so business is picking up again. We passed the open doors of the sponge warehouse on the quay where sponges are cleaned, shaped and bleached or dyed. From inside we could hear tourists being instructed in the history of the sponge fishing trade and how for years this was the island's main source of income.

'What about here?' John said stopping in front of a small cafe fenced off from the pavement with plants. There visitors to Pothia were clearly enjoying the kind of fare we wanted to sample. Eating our honey biscuits and halva cake and having coffee, we relaxed for an enjoyable hour. We watched people going to and fro, trucks, taxis and vespas hastening up and down, revving their engines and sounding their horns, creating the ceaseless hustle and bustle that characterises the port of Pothia.

'Look over there,' John said. I followed his gaze to where a small boy was taking a remote control car for a walk along the quay skilfully threading it through the pedestrians. When he drew opposite to us, he sent the car speeding across the road where it narrowly avoided colliding with oncoming vespas before mounting the pavement. Then the boy quickly followed the car, scooped it up and disappeared behind some parked trucks.

'That was a near miss. I could hardly watch,' I said. 'I was really worried his car was going to get crushed or cause an accident.'

'Well I guess we better be moving if we are going to have time to do everything we want to do,' John said.

The plan was to wander through the narrow backstreets. I always enjoyed seeing the old houses of classical Italian design with their big wooden doors, large rectangular shuttered windows and ornate iron balconies – some beautifully restored, some just about maintained and some crumbling. John had his camera with him and was looking for potential shots to post on the website of his local camera club back home. We slowly progressed through the streets and alleys. I stopped to admire a corner house with a circular staircase winding its way up the side and on each step were plants in blue pots with flowers threading through the decorative iron handrail.

'That house is lovely. Can you take a photo of it? Maybe I'll use the photo to paint a picture of it.'

John obliged but then headed up a side alley having spotted a building that offered what he considered more creative possibilities. 'I love the texture of this door with its knots and holes and this wonderful old iron lock.' He photographed it carefully from a range of angles. While doing so a smart black and white cat and three playful kittens jumped onto a decaying window sill and sitting in a row posed helpfully for him. 'That should be a good shot,' he said.

We emerged from the backstreets into a tranquil little square bordered with trees and sat down on a wooden bench under one of them to work out which way to go to find the main shopping street. We knew from past visits this street had shops selling a full range of household and personal items including shoe shops. I was keen to use our trip to Pothia to buy a pair of hiking shoes suitable for walking over rough terrain but cool and light. The street also had elegant art and antique shops which were always interesting to look around.

Almost immediately we sat down we became aware of birds tweeting away above us. Looking up we watched them circling in and out of the branches twittering away. Then focusing on the other trees we saw that each one had a great many small birds flying through and around it. Pothia is at the eastern end of one of the two large flat fertile valleys that transverse the island and doubtless provide corridors for birds. We sat watching and listening in silence fascinated, until four vespas roared into the square and caused the birds to disappear into the top branches where, if they continued singing, their song was drowned out.

Having successfully purchased, as intended, new walking shoes and, as unintended, an attractive old carved wooden plate, both of which were put into John's backpack, we headed off back to the harbour and the bus stop to catch the bus to Vathi. We had been there once before on our second holiday in Kos. We went with an Austrian couple who were staying in the studio next door to us. They hired a 4WD to take over to Kalymnos and tour around the island and invited us to join them. In the morning they took us from Pothia along the valley between the mountains to the west coast where we had stopped for a swim at the lovely sandy beach at Kandouni before continuing up the coast to Emborios for lunch.

Emborios, which is 24 kilometres from Pothia, is the last village on the island at the end of the road. It's a small peaceful picturesque settlement around a sheltered bay with a tree lined narrow sandy beach. A blue and white church with a bell tower gives it an attractive central feature. We chose the Paradise Garden restaurant for lunch which with its idyllic lush garden setting did indeed provide a little oasis paradise in the wilderness of steep bare rocks. This wilderness, as the waiter told us, was becoming a tourist attraction for rock climbers and as we drove back even in the heat of the day we saw tiny figures dangling from the limestone peaks. We then drove to Vathi situated in the other deep valley cutting across the island.

On subsequent visits to Kalymnos we had taken the bus from Pothia to explore more of the west coast, including on one trip taking the boat across the narrow channel to the islet of Telendos, separated from the mainland by a massive earthquake in AD 535. However, we hadn't been back to Vathi. While we had very little time there on this first visit, I remembered Vathi as an attractive place and thought it would be fun to go there for lunch and have a further look around. We were lucky with our timing for the bus, as it came shortly after we arrived at the bus stop. The journey along the rocky coast and over the baked brown hillsides took about 30 minutes.

According to my walking guide of the Dodecanese, you could follow a well-marked path from Pothia and reach Vathi in three and a half hours, that is if, like the author, you are a German hiker. We learned from experience on walks throughout Europe that if we spotted distant figures behind us who rapidly approached, overtook us and disappeared over the horizon, they were German. Apparently the path involved a steep ascent through a barren region without a house, tree or even a chapel. Its sole recommendation was that, 'when you looked back at where you had come you have the feeling that you have accomplished an extraordinary feat.' It didn't appeal to me to break in my new walking shoes by accomplishing an extraordinary feat and so instead we traversed the mountainous ridges by bus. As we approached Vathi, we were able to appreciate the lovely view down onto the trees and fields of the green verdant valley below before arriving at the port.

The houses, shops and cafes of the port were grouped around the end of a steep sided inlet that led out to the sea – very reminiscent of a fjord. We had a leisurely stroll along the quay to see the fishing boats, smart yachts and tourist boats before having a look at the restaurant menus and deciding where to have lunch. Delicious aromas were coming from one with a barbecue and, when John discovered it was serving lamb souvlaki, he was keen to go there. Chicken souvlaki was on many menus but lamb souvlaki, which he particularly liked, was rarely offered. Apparently, according to Spiros, this was because the lamb needed to be marinated well in advance of being grilled to ensure that it was tender.

We selected a table in the shade with a colourful blue

tablecloth to match the blue painted chairs and tables and placed our order. I decided to have vegetarian lasagne made with aubergines, courgettes and lentils, which was also a bit different as the restaurants in Kefalos offered little in the way of vegetarian dishes. While we waited for our food we sipped long drinks of freshly squeezed oranges and speculated, probably quite rightly, that these had been grown in the valley behind us as it was known for its citrous trees.

Our meal took a while to materialise but was delicious. I especially liked the apricopitta with its fresh apricots and ground almond topping, which was also a treat as usually dessert was a choice of Greek yoghurt, baklava or ice cream. We were in no hurry. It was lovely to just rest and watch the fishermen sitting on a nearby boat untangling and mending their nets and the tourists browsing the souvenir shops selecting sponges and shell memorabilia to take home.

Feeling refreshed, we were off to walk around Vathi and see something of the valley. We wandered through the houses admiring the colourful bougainvillea and other climbing plants that we didn't know the names of. We went out of the town along the road through the valley. This initially seemed somewhat risky as it was narrow with stone walls on each side requiring us to press our bodies into the wall when a vehicle approached.

As the walls gave way to verges of sage, thyme and oregano and there were paths off into the farmland we were able to relax and enjoy our walk. We passed fields of vegetables, olive groves and citrous orchards. It grew hotter as the afternoon wore on and so before turning back we sat on a stone bench behind a barn. We were able to enjoy the greenery in total contrast to the encircling barren slopes and the abandoned farm terraces we had seen on parts of the west coast.

By the time we arrived back on the quay in Mastihari, having caught the four o'clock ferry, the sky had clouded over and a stiff breeze was developing. Nevertheless, this was insufficient to do more than create tiny waves which had little impact on the progress of the ferry.

'The weather seems to be changing although the forecast on my phone still shows good weather,' I commented, looking at the sky as we walked back along the jetty to where we had left Mabel.

'At Meltemi they were expecting high winds tomorrow and a possible storm tomorrow night, so perhaps the bad weather is arriving earlier than expected,' John replied.

'If the wind is getting up I'm glad we are back in

Mastihari. Do you remember that really rough crossing we had when we came back on the late ferry?' A few years ago we had gone over to Pothia in the afternoon and stayed to have dinner in the harbour. We had wanted to experience the atmosphere of the town at night and see the cross on the hillside and the monastery lit up before getting the 11pm ferry back.

'Yes, I certainly do. Probably because of the time of night and the fact there were few passengers, we were on a much smaller ferry and it tossed up and down and rolled around in the darkness for what seemed like hours.'

'Mmm, it actually took only half an hour or so longer than usual but it was quite scary with the waves splashing over the gunnels. I wouldn't want another trip like that.'

We got in Mabel which after a few coughs and splutters started up.

'Do you want to get anything here?' John asked. On our way out of Mastihari we would pass a supermarket which was larger and better stocked than the one in Kamari.'

'No, I don't need to get anything, so straight home I think.'

Driving back along the bay at Kefalos it was clear that now a storm was anticipated that night. For their protection the fishing boats and tourist boats were all tied up alongside each other, three and four abreast in order to fit them all inside the harbour walls. A flotilla of yachts, which obviously couldn't get into the harbour, were moored opposite our home sheltering in the lee of the harbour walls and the massive rocks piled around them.

Brilliant white light flashed across the bedroom illuminating its contents. It preceded what canon fire at close range must sound like, with an immediate aftermath of a deep booming rumbling. Startled, but immediately awake, I got up and pulled open the window shutters. Fork lightening ripped through a red tinged sky and heavy black clouds and zigzagged into the sea.

'Wow, look at this.'

'Dramatic stuff, isn't it?' John joined me at the window and we stood together silently watching the storm transforming the usually colourful tranquil bay into a black and white menacing seascape. Sheet lightening flashed on and off across the empty waves.

'I think I'll take some photos,' he said predictably and hurried to get his camera.

'If the power is still on shall I make a cup of tea?' I called to him.

'Might as well because we are not going to get any more sleep until this passes over.'

We sat drinking tea experiencing the threatening *son et lumiere* of Kamari Bay. John with his camera clicked away, adjusting its settings, striving to get the perfect shot to capture the atmosphere.

'You'll have millions of photos to go through.'

'Mmm', agreed John, 'but I should have some good ones, still,' putting down his camera, 'perhaps that will do.'

After about an hour the storm had considerably lessened in intensity with the sheet lightening having retreated to behind the hills to the west of the bay. Occasional flashes arced up into the sky making the headland stand out in black relief. We headed back to bed from where we heard the beginning of the rainfall, a gentle patter at first gathering momentum until for a brief time it drummed heavily on the roof. The rain had been predicted but for the following night and was eagerly awaited by Spiros to resuscitate his olive trees. Theo, our elderly neighbour, who lived at the bottom of the hill and was a keen gardener, would also be pleased to have his fruit trees and vegetables watered.

'Spiros and Theo will be pleased,' I said settling back into the pillows, 'I imagine Theo will have known the rain was coming earlier than expected and will have taken the lids off his storage tanks buried at the back of the garden.'

When we got up the next morning the electricity was off, which came as no surprise as I was amazed it had remained on during the storm. As I discovered when I popped down to Sophia's shop to get some milk, it was unlikely to come back on for some time as the heavy rain had caused a short circuit in the cables running alongside the harbour. The pole holding up these cables was a constant source of concern as at night it fizzed, popped and sparked into the street. Additional equipment to put the damage right was going to have to be brought from Kos town and this was likely to take quite a while to arrive. However, in the shop complaints about the lack of electricity had been supplanted by a more intriguing topic of conversation.

Apparently some time after the storm, Manos's restaurant had burst into flames and rapidly become an inferno that no one could approach to try to check or to salvage anything. By the time the fire engine arrived from Kardamena, the building was reduced to a smoking charred ruin.

Manos blamed the storm, claiming his restaurant must have been struck by lightening or even a ball of fire, such as one that a few years ago had set fire to a bakery near Kos. The Polish youth, who doubled up as a waiter and kitchen assistant, put the blame on the antiquated gas stove, the rings on which apparently regularly flared uncontrollably. The locals, who were all aware that the bank had refused Manos the kind of loan he needed to keep his business running, were quick to speculate on the likelihood that Manos had torched it himself.

Alex, who owned the souvenir shop not far from the harbour, certainly thought that this was the most likely explanation, 'I mean don't you think it was strange that the fire didn't start until after the storm had finished,' he said.

'When we had all gone back to bed apparently, so no one saw it start,' quietly added Athina who was sitting on a chair behind the counter keeping company with Sophia.

Sophia continued, 'Well we know his business was in trouble. This season he has had hardly anyone eating in there. An English couple staying at Seagull studios said they tried it one evening and their souflaki was awful, uncooked but charred not barbecued, and the chicken, if that's what it was, was really stringy, inedible, their verdict.'

'It's definitely suspicious, I expect he is hoping to get some insurance money,' put in Yurgos just entering the shop and guessing the subject under discussion. 'I heard that quite recently he had taken out some massive insurance cover with a firm in Athens.'

'Might give Solomos some ideas,' said Nikolas stirring things as he liked to do. Everyone knew that Yurgos's brother's restaurant was also experiencing problems despite his various innovations to stimulate custom.

'Umm, I don't think Manos will have been insured. I doubt he could afford it,' Sophia interjected quickly before Yurgos, who was glaring at Nikolas, could reply.

'I suppose it could be whoever set fire to Dimitri's watersports hut,' suggested Alex. 'We do seem to have an arsonist amongst us.'

'What can I get you?' Sophia interrupted them by standing up and addressing me and so signalling that for the moment the topic was closed and the speculation was on hold.

By mid afternoon, while the sea remained rough, the wind had eased. We thought that it would be a good time to go to Kohilari beach and visit Lampros at his kitesurfing hut, as owing to the weather he probably wouldn't be particularly busy. He and John had become friends when Lampros was learning to windsurf. However, Lampros soon gave up windsurfing having become converted to kitesurfing. After a couple of years recognising the possibility of making his increasing passion work for him, he started a kitesurfing business. Initially he just rented out equipment to individual holidaymakers and provided instruction himself. However, the business had taken off and he now employed a couple of instructors and serviced windsurfing holidays for several European companies.

Soon after we arrived in Kefalos, John had met him for a drink one evening in order to swap news. He promised that we would go and see the new kitesurf hut that Lampros had built over the winter. Kohilari beach was on the opposite side of the island to Kefalos bay but quite close – just up the hill on the main road and turn left through the scrub and dunes.

When we got to the beach there were five clearly experienced kitesurfers enjoying the swell and jumping and somersaulting over the waves. There was also a couple on the beach struggling to control a kite but otherwise, as anticipated, there was little activity.

'Wow that's quite some hut,' said John as we walked along the beach towards it.

'It's a lot bigger and much more substantial than the previous one,' I agreed.

As we reached the hut Lampros's two dogs, one black and one sandy coloured, got up from the doorway and came wagging to meet us. We obligingly made a fuss of them and John gave them the biscuits he had brought for them.

'Where's your master?' John said to them.

'Coming up the beach,' I replied, as I saw Lampros excuse himself from the couple having shown the man how to practise manipulating the kite.

'Hi,' said Lampros approaching us. He was slim but muscular with sleeked back long bleached hair. He liked to wear the latest in beach gear and ribbed John for digging out the same old beach wear every summer. Today he wore knee length colourful shorts and a stylish black T-shirt advertising his kitesurfing business, 'I see the dogs have given you a welcome. Well, what do you think of my new hut?'

'It looks really good and you built it yourself over the winter?' John queried. 'It looks like it would have been a lot of work.'

'Yes it certainly was hard work and at times I was worried I wouldn't get it done in time for the start of the season but my cousin gave me a hand to finish it off and I'm really pleased with it.' Lampros's cousin, following in his father's footsteps, had a very large herd of goats which browsed on the hills around Kefalos and were often seen on the slopes behind our house. 'Come and see inside.' We followed him into the hut.

'You've got a lot more equipment than you had last

year,' commented John running his eyes over the racks of kites, harnesses and boards.

'The business is doing really well. I've got a lot of company bookings for this season and so I needed more equipment. The experienced kitesurfers expect to have use of the latest boards and kites. I've had to take out a bank loan but, if all goes according to plan, I should soon be able to pay it back.'

Lampros then proceeded enthusiastically to show John his most recent acquisitions. John had done a small amount of kitesurfing encouraged by Lampros and so he understood the basics, although he had decided to stick to windsurfing which he had mastered and much preferred.

Soon they were in deep discussion over the pros and cons of certain items of equipment and so I decided to leave them to it and go for a walk. The dogs chose to accompany me and bounded up and down the sand and in and out of the water. As I passed the man manipulating his kite, it swung around in a circle and did a nose dive into the sand. I smiled sympathetically at the woman who went to pick up the kite. She grinned at me and then rolled her eyes skywards, as if to say how long have I got to stay here doing this?

5

Learning Dodecanese History on Leros

The trickle of windsurfers arriving to hire boards dried up completely, as the wind first turned around and blew on shore making getting started supremely difficult and then died away to nothing rendering even lackadaisical drifting impossible. John suggested that we take the opportunity to visit Leros, which was something he knew I was keen to do, and so begin our exploration of the Dodecanese islands that were new to us.

On the internet I learned that Leros comprises 53 square kilometres and has a deeply indented coastline with large bays and sheltered coves. It has a population around 8,500 and owing to its fertile valleys, which meant many islanders made their living from farming and fishing, it has numerous villages. A flier advertising holidays in Leros described the island as ideal not only for those 'wanting a relaxing break in attractive surroundings' but also 'for those who would like the opportunity to learn more about the history of the

Dodecanese.' Both of these claims sounded like good reasons to visit it.

We caught the nine o'clock ferry from the end of the harbour at Mastihari to Pothia on Kalymnos. Once in Pothia we checked on the times of the Dodecanese Express, as we had been warned these were subject to change outside the main tourist season. Having satisfied ourselves that it was sailing to Agia Marina as anticipated, we bought our tickets from a girl who made her boredom with answering such queries explicit.

Already waiting by the ticket barrier were a plump middle-aged American couple and an elderly English woman, wiry and very tanned with two dogs on leads one painfully trailing a back leg. She was regaling the Americans with her plight. Her home had become a refuge for ill and injured dogs often dumped outside her house because the locals knew she would take care of them. However, she protested angrily that she received no gratitude. Having supplied her with their unwanted pets the Greeks then punished her for the unwelcome noise of the dogs' yapping by throwing glass in her pool and trashing her garden. She was off to Leros because unlike Kalymnos it had a vet. He was going to set the broken leg and castrate the other dog, a bouncy English sheep dog crossed with something woolly, that was wagging cheerfully unaware of the fate awaiting him. In unison with the Americans we nodded sympathetically agreeing the dogs were faultless, some Greeks were intolerable and her situation outrageous.

When we left Pothia on the Express, we relocated ourselves and our bags several times in a vain attempt to avoid being downwind of smokers. Finally we settled near the open door at the back on padded seats which seemed very comfortable compared to the slatted wooden fidget-inducing seats of the ferry from Mastihari to Pothia. We marvelled at the rocky cliffs and the barrenness of the mountains of Kalymnos, as the twin-hulled Express, apparently once capable of going at 50 kilometres an hour, chugged slowly but steadily along the Kalymnos coastline to Agia Marina on Leros.

Agia Marina looked enchanting, quite a picture-postcard-perfect kind of place. The entrance was guarded by the fortress of Brouzi and above it the impressive Pantelios castle. This was built by the Knights of Saint John at the top of Pitiki hill about two hundred metres above sea level, after they took over the island in 1314. The Knights of Saint John were a medieval Catholic military order with their origins and original headquarters in Jerusalem. However, after the conquest of the Holy Land by Islamic forces they moved their headquarters to Rhodes in 1310. They governed the Dodecanese islands including Leros until 1522 when the Ottoman Turks under Suleiman the Magnificent came to dominate the whole of the Aegean.

Traditional one and two storey square pastel coloured houses climbed up the brown rocky hillside. They formed a picturesque arc around the waterfront with a carefully preserved old windmill jutting out into the water to form a centrepiece. The little harbour provided mooring for fishing vessels of all shapes and sizes with the larger ones, which sported a tangle of ropes, nets buoys and stacks of wooden boxes on their decks, suggesting that they engaged in fishing further afield and in deeper waters.

We enthusiastically disembarked and headed for the tourist information portacabin in search of a map but, as was usually the case, it was closed. Instead we collected a predatory studio owner lying in wait for tourists with bags in need of accommodation. The swarthy individual was determined that we should rent his studio. We accelerated our steps to outpace him but naively followed his directions to another tourist information site in the town. This turned out to be his shop. As we stood outside pondering on the possibility of it having the desired information, he screeched alongside us in his car, jumped out and resumed his verbal onslaught.

We took refuge in the shop next door where we bought a map and easily resisted the altogether gentler marketing techniques of the attractive young shop assistant. Nevertheless, she convinced us that Alinda was definitely the place to stay, if not in her expensive sounding studio. We set off to walk around the bay to reach it. Fortified by seafood pasta at an overpriced taverna, which had the best harbour view imaginable through the open loo window, we reached Alinda with its wide choice of empty studios.

Kidonia's studios, built in her back garden, were our choice owing to their proximity to the beach but quiet location away from the vespa route around the bay. Kidonia, a tall masculine stern-faced woman summoned to her front door by John's knock, looked extremely displeased at the prospect of clients. However, she agreed to show us a studio. Once inside our delight at the attractive well-equipped studio at a reasonable price softened her features and she became almost welcoming. Having satisfactorily secured holiday accommodation of our own choosing, we dumped our bags and headed to the beach for a cooling swim.

In contrast to Kos parts of Leros, such as Krithoni, which spreads up the hill between Alinda and Agia Marina, exude affluence. It has many large houses including modernised and extended traditional Greek houses, renovated grand Italian style houses dating from the Italian occupation and new houses in various styles. Most are adorned with grapes, bougainvillea and other climbing plants and set in colourful well-tended gardens.

Tourist development appears to have been kept under control with holiday accommodation, shops selling the usual beach ware and souvenirs and the provision of hire craft, tours etc mainly confined to Alinda. Apparently in August, Leros is very popular with Greek holidaymakers from Athens, as there are direct flights from there to the island's airport.

As we discovered on our walk that evening, the streets of Agia Marina and Platinos, the old town that adjoins it, contain inviting attractively arranged craft, antique and furniture shops which presumably are particularly appealing to the mainland clientele. Paintings on driftwood of ships and religious icons seemed characteristic of the island. We debated which one of several depicting sailing boats we should buy to hang up at Kefalos. However, to the disappointment of the helpful and chatty shopkeeper, who seemed sure he'd made a sale, ultimately we decided against it. Neither of us wanted to carry the driftwood back to the studio. John didn't like my suggestions of where we might hang it in our Kefalos home and asked what I planned to do with it when we left.

Considering it's a small island with few roads, many of the island's inhabitants own stylish new cars. These they paraded at top speed on the road around the bay from the harbour to the far side of Alinda accelerating at the sight of pedestrians. Hurtling back and forth and in and out of the cars are young men and, not so young men who really should know better, on motorbikes doing wheelies over the bumps and ruts in the road and vespa riders convinced of their immortality.

Over lunch in a beachside cafe in Alinda, I had overheard a small group of tourists sighing over the restaurants that they might be able to visit but for 'that road.' Returning from enjoying pizza sitting at a table on the beach with the water almost lapping at our feet, walking along 'that road' back to Kidonia's, given the manic behaviour of the drivers and the lack of a pavement, did indeed prove a death-defying experience.

'No problem really,' said John, 'as long as you always face the oncoming traffic. I'll lead the way.'

'Fine if the oncoming traffic can see you,' I responded.

In several places the buildings and walls jutted out at

right angles into the road necessitating listening carefully for a gap in the traffic, body flattened against the wall, and then darting around the corner. After narrowly avoiding being squashed flat by an articulated lorry, John yielded to my preferred survival strategy of zig-zagging backwards and forwards across the road to as least ensure we could see the cause of our likely demise.

Having miraculously arrived back at the studio unscathed, undaunted John pronounced that in order to make the most of our visit to the island tomorrow we should hire bicycles, as we had done in various other holiday locations. He pointed out that in Ancient Greek *leros* means flat and smooth and so it shouldn't involve too much hard pedalling. That decision made the night a restless one for me as I had nightmares of being hospitalised by everything from one of the tourists in the restaurant riding vengefully round the bay on a quad bike to the largest articulated lorry ever seen on the island.

In the morning we went to the bike hire shop by the beach and hired bikes for the day. Unusually for hire bikes, they had quite reasonable gears and brakes, both of which were needed as, contrary to its name, Leros turned out to be quite hilly.

We began our explorations by crossing the island on the

high road to Lakki on the opposite southwest coast, as we wanted to see the harbour there which is exceptionally deep and reputed to be the the largest natural harbour in the Mediterranean. Surrounded by hills the enclosed bay has a narrow mouth only five hundred metres wide and so it looks like a massive lake, which was why it was called Porto Lago by the Italians.

The town of Lakki was created by the Italians in the 1930s, after Italy defeated Turkey on Rhodes and took over the Dodecanese islands, until 1943. During that period the Italians sought to transform Leros into an important sea and air base and many military facilities were built across the island.

Lakki was conceived as a new model town to house the 7,500 or so civilian dependants of the nearby Italian navel base. Built essentially in Mussolini's Rationalist style, a kind of fascist quasi Art Deco with Bauhaus influence, this was dubbed Stream Line Modern in Leros. The restored cinema building was reputed to be a good example of the style and so we were curious to see it. We found the cinema on a corner where a side street joined the main road. It was a rectangular building with a bold semi-circular front and steps up to the entrance. The building adjoining it, which was built at the same time, stretched to the next corner with a repeating pattern of alternate circular and rectangular windows.

'I like the cinema,' said John. 'I think it's interesting, especially the window shapes above the entrance. The repetition of the windows on the next door building is effective too.'

'It's helped by being newly painted and the way the colour outlines the shapes. It does make me think Art Deco.'

'It's a pity the islanders don't have the finance to restore more of the buildings and make the town more like the original intention. It could be quite a tourist attraction.'

'Yes it could be but maybe they don't want reminders of the occupation.'

At one time possibly Lakki was impressive but now, while a few buildings had been restored, they were mostly decaying, in some cases still bomb damaged and largely unoccupied. The wide streets and monumental but plain buildings were originally intended to be enlivened and humanised with trees and parks. Apparently two other residential areas were built in a similar style – Saubadia in Italy and Weissenhof in Germany. Lakki seemed rather devoid of life and activity and somewhat depressing and so we decided to move on.

It was easy pleasant pedalling along the road around the harbour. We could look across at the modern port area where the larger ferries and the container ships call and watch the sprinkling of holiday yachts sailing to and fro in the gentle breeze. We decided to continue on the wide road along the waterfront stopping only to look at the monument on the beach to the torpedo boat Vasilissa Olga.

'The Vasilissa Olga, the Italian flagship which was sunk by the Germans, was the first casualty of the Battle of Leros,' said John authoritatively having obviously studied the free tourist pamphlet we picked up in the restaurant the previous evening. 'If you look over to the marina, well that used to be the dock for the torpedo boats.'

'Interesting, you wouldn't realise that now. I expect we will learn more about it in the Tunnel Museum.' We had planned to visit the museum which is in a restored military tunnel once part of the Italian system of tunnels and underground arsenals.

Two or three kilometres further on through a pine forest we entered Merikia and there we found the Tunnel Museum. It is full of exhibits collected from around the island such as military hardware, uniforms, maps of the various military installations, documents etc but with little provided by way of explanation we couldn't learn much from them. However, at the end of the tunnel in a small darkened seating area, we watched a fascinating short film with archive footage on the Battle of Leros.

Italy surrendered to the Allies in 1943 and in the autumn of the same year at the Battle of Leros the Germans defeated the British and Italian troops after the heavy and continuous bombardment of the island. We had seen a sign in Agia Marina to the British War Cemetery for those who died when the British forces were unable to hold on to Leros, Kos and Kalymnos which they had taken after the Italian surrender. When we left the museum, we had lunch in a nearby sandwich bar and discussed what we had learned.

'It must have been very difficult for the Greeks on these islands having to live under Italian control,' I said.

'Yes, at first life continued much the same as it always had but gradually the occupation became more and more fascist and repressive,' John added.

'Remember how Theo said as a child he had to learn to speak Italian because the Greek language and history were forbidden in school.'

'Then we know how they suffered under the Germans. It must have been terrifying during the bombing of Leros.'

'In this guide,' John produced the pamphlet from his

camera case. 'It says that the island was liberated from the Germans in 1945.' He read, 'on the 9th May the Dodecanese islands were handed over to the British and the Greeks.'

'I didn't realise that we kind of occupied the islands,' I said surprised to learn this.

'Yes apparently for two years, and then in March 1948 Leros and the other Dodecanese islands were returned to Greece.'

'It's not surprising by the time the islands were fully liberated so many people had had enough and lost so much that they emigrated to America, Canada and Australia.'

'Yes it explains why so many of the locals in Kefalos have relatives in Canada.'

When we got back on our bikes, we returned around the lake the way that we had come and then took the road to Xerokambos, the last village on the southern tip of the island. We cycled through the old industrial zone at Temenia with relics such as the building of the Public Electricity Company and the gasworks. Then on into Lepida, where on the right behind a high fence and hidden in the trees were the buildings of the notorious psychiatric hospital with which Leros is negatively associated.

Originally built to house Italian hydroplanes in 1957,

the converted warehouses were used to institutionalise those with serious mental illness brought from congested psychiatric hospitals in other parts of Greece. In 1989 there was a major scandal when the British press exposed the conditions in which they were being held and necessitated change. Albeit slowly, wards were shut and the patients moved elsewhere or provided with support and reintroduced into the community. Finally in 1997 the hospital was closed.

Unfortunately, recently the site has once again become associated with suffering and hardship. Increasingly refugees and economic migrants from Syria, Iraq, Afghanistan and other war and climate stricken zones have been arriving on the Dodecanese islands and those arriving on Leros are housed in these dilapidated and unsuitable buildings.

We descended into Xerokambos which is set back from the head of a long seemingly landlocked inlet out to sea. By contrast to the area we had left, it was an attractive well-kept little community with a shop, taverna and rooms to rent. The fertile surroundings with gardens growing vegetables, flowers, palm trees orange trees and pomegranates were a welcome relief from the somewhat dreary road from Lakki and the surrounding barren mountainsides. It also had a little beach backed by tamarisk trees where we briefly stopped for a rest in the shade.

Then we headed off up the dirt track where we came across the white and red chapel of Panagia Kavouromana which was built into the cliff. The chapel was open so we went in and were surprised by the unusual icon depicting Mary and baby Jesus encircled by a crab. Kidonia, who contrary to our first impression was very helpful, told us later that the chapel's name meant Mary of the Crab.

We decided to keep going up the track to see what else was up there. The answer was nothing specific apart from a few ruined buildings. One of these we ventured inside and thought that because of its shape and size it had probably once been one of the many military barracks situated on the island. Now though it was empty and crumbling and solely occupied by goats, who were startled to receive visitors. However, we were glad that we had continued along the promontory because it provided a truly breathtaking view out to sea over three small islands and the northern tip of Kalymnos. We got off our bikes and sat enjoying the peace and the beauty of the place.

'Well I guess we better get going again although it's lovely here. Where next?' I asked.

'We'll go to Gournas bay. The map has sun umbrella

signs there so that means there's a beach and perhaps we'll have a swim. To get there we need to go back to Lakki and then take a left to Drimonas.'

When we got to Drimonas, before going down to the beach, we popped into a shop to buy Fantas, which we particularly like when we are hot and thirsty. Then John decided he would like to cool off with a quick swim, but I decided I couldn't be bothered and would just paddle in the shallows, drink my Fanta and chill out in the shade.

'I feel better for that,' he said towelling himself down. 'When I've dried out and finished my drink, we'll carry on along the road around the bay to Kokall, have a final look around there and then we'll be able to take a short route back to Alinda.'

Near Kokall we discovered the enchanting little chapel of Agios Isidorous with its whitewashed walls and red roof. It was built on a rocky outcrop quite a long way out into the north side of Gournas bay and joined to the beach by a low concrete causeway. The water was very still so we were able easily to walk out to it. It was locked so we couldn't go in but sitting on the wall that surrounded it was like sitting in the cockpit of a boat. We spent a pleasant 20 minutes just watching the seagulls flying around and two fishermen in a boat nearby untangling and repairing their nets.

That evening a waiter in the restaurant where we had dinner, on learning that we had visited the chapel, told us the legend of how it came into being. According to legend, a fisherman, who had only one hand, found an icon caught in his net which he gave back to the Orthodox church. In return his hand was restored by the Virgin Mary and he built the chapel to show his gratitude. The chapel provided a fitting finale to an excellent day's exploring. The road back was busy but mostly downhill and we arrived back in Alinda to give the bikes back about 6.30pm.

After our previous quite strenuous day, the next morning we planned to have a lie in followed by a leisurely time reading on the balcony. This turned out to be a good plan as we had a disturbed night. At 3am we were suddenly woken up by a powerful light beaming down on us from a lamp fixed on the wall opposite the bed.

'Oh goodness. What's going on? What's happening?' I said in shock.

'Don't worry' replied John. 'Nothing's happening. We just seemed to have acquired our own private searchlight.'

'Given much of the history of Leros, I thought I was about to be interrogated. Can we turn it off?'

'Yes but I'm not sure how, there doesn't appear to be a switch,' he examined the wall where the light was fixed.

'Hang on let's put the other lights on,' he went over to the door flicked on the switch and nothing happened. 'Oh they're not working.'

'Do you think there's been a power cut and this is an emergency light which comes on if that happens?'

'Good thinking, that's probably it, but it's a stupid idea if it wakes you up in the night and you can't turn it off.' He continued hunting around unsuccessfully for a switch that we hadn't previously spotted.

'There's a fuse box in the corner of the kitchen can you pull the fuse out or something?'

This was what John did and fumbled his way back into bed in the dark having been blinded by the searchlight. In the night, although the problem was solved, we were left very wide awake and actually poured ourselves a glass of wine and chatted for a while before we managed to get back to sleep. Next morning the power was restored and when the fuse was put back the light stayed off. We vowed to remove the fuse on the remaining nights to prevent a repetition of the experience if another power cut occurred.

After breakfast, when we were out on the balcony and I'd just opened up the novel I was reading, I heard my mobile ringing from inside. 'Hello,' I said picking it up off the table.

'Hi it's Jan.'

'Hi how is the holiday going?'

'Well it isn't, which is why I'm ringing.'

"Oh no! What's happened?'

'Regi left yesterday to go to Taiwan. His Head of Department at the Uni, who was going out there to do a lecture tour and then teach a course for the next six weeks, had a stroke. He is now in hospital and so they asked Regi if he would stand in for him. Well it's right up Regi's street and he loves such opportunities so he said yes straightaway. He didn't even consult me. He flew to London yesterday, is at home at the moment getting organised and will fly out to Taipei tomorrow.'

'Wow! What surprising news. How disappointing for you. You were so looking forward to your holiday. What are you going to do? You obviously decided not to go back home with him.'

'No I didn't see any point in going home. I was really upset and annoyed at the thought of our holiday ending so abruptly. Regi's brother said that I could stay on with them and I will for two or three days but then I thought that I'd like to be independent and do my own thing. I thought that I'd come back to Kos, stay in a hotel in Kos town for two or three days because I've been reading about it on the internet and it looks an interesting place. Then I'll rent a studio or something until Regi returns. Do you think that I could do this in Kefalos as it seems a very relaxed friendly place? Would you help me to find somewhere to stay?'

'I'm sure you could find a studio there and of course I'll help you. It'll be good to have the chance to spend a bit more time together.'

'Oh thanks that's great. I really want to make the most of this trip. I haven't had such an adventure for years. I'll let you know when I've booked the plane to Kos and fixed up a hotel.'

'Yes do that and I'll come and collect you from Kos town when you are ready. When John and I get back to Kefalos I'll see what accommodation is available.'

'Thanks again. I'm really grateful. I'll keep you posted.'

John had been listening to my side of the conversation. 'So Jan is coming to stay in Kefalos,' he said. 'I wonder what Regi thinks about that.'

'Well Jan is so fed up with him at the moment I don't think she cares what he will think.'

When we went out, I was glad we were exploring on foot rather than biking, as apart from initially feeling rather tired, after so much time in the saddle I was left with a bruised bottom for the next couple of days. We walked along the waterfront at Alinda where tourists were sunbathing, swimming and having coffee. Afterwards we went on to the harbour in Agia Marina and watched the day trippers going off to Kalymnos and Patmos. Then we wandered through the alleys and backstreets of Platanos to further enjoy the antique and craft shops. It was a busy area with locals going in and out of the government offices and attending to their work and business.

More or less by accident we came upon the large church of Agia Paraskevis, apparently once the island's metropolitan cathedral, and found the beginning of the stepped path that leads from the town up the hillside to Pantelios castle. The castle, as we came to realise through our explorations was, like many of the Dodecanese castles and churches, built on the site of an ancient acropolis. It was well kept and had obviously been subject to considerable renovations in recent years but the various plastic signboards were blank as the information to go on them had yet to be written and posted. However, the panoramic view from the hilltop was spectacular. You could look out over Platanos, Agia Marina and across the bay to Alinda or look in the opposite direction over Pandeli and out to sea.

'It's quite hard work walking up here but it's definitely

worth it for the view,' I observed.

'Just right for taking a panorama,' said John taking out his camera and working out the vista where he would start and stop to get the scene he wanted.

After taking in and recording the view, we had a brief look in the 14th century church of the Panagia with its paintings and golden icon screen but gave the ecclesiastical museum housed in a new building next door a miss. We preferred to head down through more backstreets to the fishing village of Pandeli.

We thought Pandeli a very appealing place with its white houses set against the backdrop of the brown hillside and the line of traditional windmills along the ridge. Unlike Alinda, its harbour is sheltered from the Meltemi. It was crammed full of colourful fishing boats and yachts of all kinds. We had decided that Pandeli would be a good place to treat ourselves to a fish lunch.

Outside one beachside restaurant between posts octopuses were hanging out to dry on lines. These were covered with hornets and so definitely extremely off-putting. After some deliberation over the menus on offer we chose the one that advertised a mixed fish platter for two and was well away from the octopuses. When our meal arrived on a large metal plate it had pieces of swordfish, fried squid, a large red snapper and grilled prawns decorated with slices of lemon and accompanied by a Greek salad and a basket of chips. It looked delicious and it was.

'That was excellent,' said John. 'Just what I fancied but now I feel very full.'

'Me too,' I agreed. I don't think we'll want to go out for dinner tonight.'

'I feel too full to move so I think we'll just sit here and have a coffee then we better try and walk off the effects of our lunch.'

'If we walk around that headland we'll come to Vromolithos beach so we could go and have a look at that,' I suggested.

'Good idea but look at it and sit on it is all I can do. I couldn't go swimming this afternoon I'd just sink,' and so sit on the beach and chill out was exactly what we did.

The following day we woke up to a windy day with a lot of grey cloud but at least this made it cooler for walking. We hadn't seen anything of the north of Leros and so we decided to take the 10.37am bus to Plefoutis, the last stop going north. We waited for the bus at the bus shelter outside a cafe on the road to the airport. Several elderly men were also waiting for it and a young German couple with a little boy, maybe five years old. Before the bus came into view, we heard it coming as the horn was sounded loudly at every bend. This obviously amused the little boy who grinning joined in calling 'toot toot' and when he got in the bus toot tooted at the driver.

'You like my horn,' said the thickset Greek laughing and tooting the horn. 'Here you have a go,' he invited the child, who happily accepted his offer sounding the horn continuously as the bus set off. The houses along the main road eventually gave way to local industry and ultimately to barren hillsides of scrub and low trees with the occasional tall eucalyptus by the roadside.

The bus took us past the tiny airstrip that was rather exaggeratedly called an airport and from there around the very sheltered harbour of Ormos Partheni. Next we passed an army camp which, like the one on Kos, had rows of jeeps, rusty tanks, ambulances and the usual crossed out camera 'no photo' signs. Then we came to an enormous dry dock for yachts housing lots of expensive looking boats. Leros certainly seemed to attract sailing enthusiasts of all kinds. Finally we drove up the hill and around into Plefoutis, where the bus terminated and the few remaining occupants including us and the driver got out.

Plefoutis was a pleasant place but with little to see. There were a few houses dotted around the hillside and a chapel up on the left. Several wooden and concrete jetties provided mooring for fishing vessels and little motor boats. The beach, which was rather narrow and stony, was shaded by an arc of trees. It sported the customary shower and single changing cubicle which seemed to be a feature of beaches on Leros. Looking around didn't take long. There was a cafe opposite the main part of the beach and the bus driver was sat outside having a coffee. We decided to ask him if he would give us a lift back up the hill to the fork in the road from where we could walk to Agia Kioura – the end of the road and the northernmost point of Leros. The driver agreed and said he would be leaving in ten minutes.

This was a good decision as it was an attractive walk along the narrow dusty road with views first over Partheni bay and then Plefouti bay. Agia Kioura was a small place but with lots of activity particularly by the little fishing jetty and the nearby helipad. Meanwhile, across the other side of the harbour nearer to the open sea, a container ship was unloading.

We wandered over to the chapel which was large and unlocked. Inside on the walls were beautiful paintings done by political prisoners in 1968 for which reason the chapel is now a protected monument. During the 1967–1974 Greek military dictatorship known as The Regime of the Colonels, vast numbers of political prisoners from all walks of life were detained in the warehouses of the old Italian barracks at Patheni, which we had driven through in the bus, and at Lakki.

While the circumstances were totally different, visiting this chapel brought to mind for me the chapel that we visited on Orkney which Italian prisoners of war had built out of two Nissen huts. Inside they created a beautiful rood screen and an altar painting of Mary and baby Jesus.

On our walk back to Plefoutis the wind suddenly really strengthened battering us with some very strong gusts. As we entered the village we thought that we would find somewhere where we could go inside to get out of the wind and have a leisurely lunch. We went into what turned out to be a very large restaurant suggesting that maybe in peak periods it catered for coach parties. A sour grumpy looking woman brought us the menu and, as we suggested what we would like, it soon became apparent that most of the seeming possibilities were unavailable.

We settled on a couple of omelettes which had to be plain because they were out of mushrooms and cheese and no they couldn't do chips or salad. She scowled at us for making such an unreasonable request. As she went into the kitchen, she slammed the two menus back down on the pile.

While we were waiting the German couple with the small boy who tried out the bus hooter came in. Discovering little was available they decided to order a portion of anything that could be produced. As anticipated, when the omelettes arrived they were exceptionally skinny with no trimmings. However, despite its meagre nature lunch did turn out to be leisurely, as it took an hour to arrive even if it took very little time to actually eat it. We left the Germans still waiting for their food but from their body language guessed that they might soon decide to give up and depart.

We returned to the bus stop by the beach and tooting away the bus appeared punctually at 2.30pm. However, the driver got out to have another leisurely coffee and to swap news with some elderly inhabitants playing draughts. We chatted to an English couple, who told us that they were on their yacht, which was moored in the bay to shelter from the wind.

We decided to get off the bus again at Kamara and walk down to Gournas bay where we had cycled a couple of days ago. When we got there we found the sea in the bay was surprisingly rough. Whereas previously we had walked with ease over to the chapel, on this occasion we were disappointed to find that the little chapel of Agia Isidoros was totally inaccessible, as waves were crashing over and around the causeway.

We thought that we would walk along the tree-lined beach road, and then go up the hill and through to Alinda on a different route to that which we had taken when cycling. We were surprised to find that the whole of the bay area we subsequently walked through was being developed with large private houses being built and ornamental gardens being planted. On our way up the hill, for sale were two smart new traditional style houses with beautiful little landscaped gardens complete with twee mini windmills. However, their view over the bay was likely to be short-lived as between them and the sea was a large vacant plot 'right for development'. All along the upper road were large expensive looking individually designed houses with wrought iron balconies, arches, patios, terraces and pools.

When we got back to Alinda we decided to go in a shop and reward ourselves with an ice cream. Having both chosen a choc ice on a stick we sat on the wall delineating the beach from the road. We had no sooner sat down than the youth, who had eyed us up and down from the back of the shop, approached us and started shouting at us in a mixture of Greek and English. At first we wondered what was his problem but then recognising the odd English word we realised he was trying to get us to hire a motorbike. We shook our heads vehemently repeating, 'No, no, we are going home tomorrow,' but he simply yelled louder.

Just as we decided to take ourselves and our ice creams elsewhere, another English couple appeared and he immediately transferred his attention to them. To our astonishment his aggressive sales technique apparently worked, as they allowed him to herd them into the shop. Whether or not they did hire a motorbike we will never know, as ice creams eaten, we set off back to Kidonia's. However, we were sure that if we wanted to hire a motorbike he would be the last person from whom we would get one.

That evening the wind appeared to have dropped, which pleased us because it meant we could have our last dinner in a restaurant with tables on the beach. Across the bay coloured lights lit up the castle. It was lovely sitting there under the stars, which in the clear Greek sky always seemed more numerous, larger and brighter than at home. It was a romantic conclusion to our stay in Leros which had been very enjoyable and extremely informative. Our memories would be of an island with particularly beautiful and tranquil bays, interesting chapels and a past and recent troubled history with which the islanders had to live and move forward from.

6

Climbing Mount Dikeos

John announced purposefully, 'So we will definitely climb the peak today.'

'Well, we said we would and it's a good day to do it, hardly any wind,' I responded. 'This morning we are going to watch Theo and Eleni make bread and have lunch with them but we will be back in plenty of time to go to Zia this afternoon.'

The peak that he referred to was the peak of the Dikeos mountains that we could see from the house. These mountains form the backbone of Kos, a largely flat island. They rise steeply from the sea in the south and gently come down to the water in the north. We had embarked on the 550 metres ascent from the village of Zia to the chapel on the peak during our first holiday on Kos and then on every subsequent visit threatened to do it again. However, we always used the heat, the wind or all the other things we wanted to do in the time available as excuses to prevaricate.

When we did the ascent the first time we had set off early in the morning. However, by the time that we came down again the temperature was in the thirties. This time we proposed to go late in the day when it was cooler.

Theo and Eleni were an elderly couple in their mid eighties who liked to bake bread for themselves, family members and friends on a Saturday. They were our nearest neighbours as their house was situated just off the track at the bottom of the hill. I often popped in for a chat when I was passing and they always gave me either eggs, fruit, preserves or bread if they had been baking. After a few visits, realising this was always going to happen, I ensured that I had something to give them in return. Yesterday I had been baking in readiness for our visit and so I put into my shopping bag the cheese straws and iced chocolate buns that I had baked to take with us.

Their home was a beautifully kept traditional house built of stone and painted white with a gnarled wooden front door and turquoise blue shutters at the two small square windows. Adjoining one side of the house was the large bake oven with a tall chimney where the couple worked together to bake bread. Set apart on the other side was their shower room and toilet joined to the main house by a wooden roof which provided a wide shady area where they liked to sit and rest in the afternoon. Along the front of the house metal poles set in a low surrounding stone wall supported an overhead trellis covered in a large vine, the ancient stems of which twined around the poles. On one corner the positioning of a tall aerial enabled them to watch television, which was how they liked to spend their evenings. On the opposite corner was a large chimney where in winter they lit wood fires to make their home cosy.

A lean-to tin shelter at the back of the house provided protection for Theo's ancient moped. Most days he used this to go up into Kefalos old town to get provisions and visit his two daughters, his grandchildren and their families. They regularly tried to persuade the couple to move into a modern house in town. However, Theo and Eleni were too fond of their house to move. Theo, who had been a fisherman all his working life, wanted to remain living close to the sea. When he retired, he had bought the house and the large plot on which it was situated from the sale of his fishing boat.

When we arrived at their house Theo was propping up a branch of the large bread fruit tree that grew by the path at the entrance to the garden.

'As these bread fruit ripen they get large and heavy,' he explained. 'This branch is rather weak and I don't want it to break and spoil the shape of the tree.' He knocked in further the post that was supporting the branch. 'That will do it,' he said. Theo had an enviable garden surrounding his property. At the back of the house he cultivated a large vegetable patch growing zucchinis, potatoes, marrows and bushes of brightly coloured orange chillies and behind this he had an avocado tree and several lemon trees.

At the side of the house were three more trellises growing the tiny local grapes from which Eleni made grape preserve and raisins and a small olive grove in which scrapped and scratched their extremely free range chickens. The whole garden area was surrounded by a typical Greek style fence made up of a multiplicity of metal poles, bedsteads, palettes etc all roped and wired together to keep out Lampros's cousin's goats. When the clanging of the huge metal bells they wore around their necks indicated that goats were approaching, Theo aimed a few of the readily available rocks at them and they soon scattered back up the hillside.

Eleni came out of the kitchen where she had been preparing the dough. She invited us to sit down in the shade at the front of the house under the vine and have a glass of her homemade lemonade. When she went inside to fetch the lemonade, Theo showed us the long-handled wooden spatula-like paddles and wire wracks hung in permanent readiness on the house wall by the oven. He had built a fire in the cavernous bake oven built onto the side of the house and now proceeded to stoke and coax it until the flames roared into a red furnace. While he did this, Eleni went back in the kitchen to put the final decorative touches to the many waiting loaves. She brought out a flat basket of these and showed us how she made patterns in what would form into crusts and sprinkled them with sesame seeds.

When the flames had died down Eleni, with a scarf draped over her head to protect her face from the hot steam, took charge of the oven. She cleaned and further increased the heat in the oven by dipping a large cloth into a bucket of water and swishing it over the hot embers on the end of one of the long wooden paddles. When she was satisfied the oven was ready, she sent Theo to fetch the other baskets of bread and carefully loaded the loaves one at a time onto the paddle and placed them in the oven.

When all were fitted inside, Theo briefly fastened the door letting the heat begin to do its work. Once the loaves had begun to bake the door was opened again and Elena kept watch over them as the oven slowly cooled and to her practised eye their crusts revealed them to be ready. Then they were placed to cool on the wire wracks in the kitchen filling the air with the comforting, nutty, yeasty aroma that only such home-made bread cooked to perfection can yield.

Then Theo fetched a tray with a large bowl of salad and various accompaniments to the bread for us to have for lunch. Cutting through the thick patterned crust of the warm loaf of bread, Eleni scattered sesame seeds over the table and revealed the loaf's soft honey coloured interior. She cut lots of thick slices and invited us to help ourselves. John followed Theo's lead and made his initial slices into a sandwich with goat's cheese and green olives while I coated my slices with butter and ate them with a helping of salad.

'Mmm,' John murmured in appreciation taking a large bite out of his sandwich. 'Your bread is really excellent,' he said to Eleni.

'It is delicious,' I said, 'particularly when you can eat it while it is still warm.'

'Well I have had years of practice,' she laughed, clearly pleased to be complimented on her bread making.

We all made second sandwiches of combinations of the salad, cheese, olives and ham. Then for dessert we each had one of the buns that I'd brought. Afterwards we sat chatting until her niece arrived with her son and new baby daughter. We admired the smiling baby and then, as more family members arrived, it seemed appropriate to take our leave after thanking Theo and Eleni for showing us their bread making and giving us such an enjoyable lunch.

When we got back we got organised to go and climb the peak.

'I'd like to stay up there to watch the sun go down and perhaps get some good photos in the golden hour before sunset,' John suggested.

'Hmm, I don't know,' I said doubtfully, 'I think we need to leave the top half an hour or so before sunset. Then watch the sun go down and take those photos on the way back because we don't know how long the descent will take. I'd hate to have to follow the path in the dark, especially through the pine woods.'

'I'm sure the path will be well-marked and clear enough, you worry too much but…,' he paused. 'Well, I don't really fancy driving on that track from the footpath to Zia in the dark so perhaps you are right,' he agreed somewhat reluctantly. 'Let's leave here at three to make sure to give ourselves plenty of time. We need to allow for losing time if we have any problems accessing the dirt track behind Zia in Mabel,' he continued.

Behind Zia, stone steps led upwards through the houses to a wide dirt track that climbed gently through the pine woods as it skirted around the mountain.

'I guess it's cheating a bit as we walked all the way from Zia the last time, but it will be good to cut out the track and start walking from where the footpath begins. Do you think Mabel can cope with the potholes and get up that sandy slope?' I questioned.

'She'll be fine, I'll take it steady. It's no worse than the track down to Hilandriou Beach,' he said to reassure me. This was a beach that we sometimes visited on the peninsula beyond Kefalos. We liked it because it was wild and usually deserted as it was difficult to access.

'Yes well, we've nearly been stuck in the sandy bit there several times,' I reminded him. 'Remember there was that German couple who were stuck and we had to help to push their car out.'

In the event John took the sandy slope at a run and Mabel made it surprisingly easily. We drove past a couple of chapels, then a couple of farms. We were held up for a while at the first farm while a young woman finished feeding her chickens in the middle of the track. Then at the second an elderly man was having a lot of trouble persuading his handsome but unruly mule to go where he wanted rather than where it wanted. The broken rope around its neck, which the man was trying to grab hold of, suggested it might have escaped. Fortunately the position of

Mabel in the middle of the track acted as a mule barrier and, as the mule swung around to head off up the track again, the man grabbed the rope and tugged the mule back into his yard.

When we reached the faded red metal arrow, which we knew indicated the start of the footpath, we parked Mabel, got out and checked we had everything we wanted and set off. Propped on the arrow was a curved stick of pine which someone had almost certainly used to assist them in their passage up and down the mountain. 'Good idea,' I thought to myself seeing all the stones and rocks littering the path and decided that I would similarly make use of it.

'It was very helpful of someone to leave this stick where it could be seen,' I said picking it up.

The path zigzagged its way steadily up through the woods, the trees providing welcome dappled shade from the sun and a pleasant aroma of pine. After several stops for a brief rest and a drink of water, we emerged from the trees onto the mountainside, which being brown and barren was in strong contrast to the woods. We progressed upwards along the narrow stony path guided by very faded red dots and arrows to a ridge where we could see the peak that we were aiming for.

'Oh it's further away than I thought,' I said with the

realisation that the peak was on the ridge of the next mountain not at the top of the slope that we were on.

'Yes,' replied John. 'I remember it now. We've got to follow the path downhill here, and then in the corner we should find a path going up again.'

We found it easily enough and then climbed steeply through the rocks and rubble stopping to admire the view out over the salt flats and the north coast of Kos to Kalymnos and its neighbouring tiny barren island of Pserimos. Somewhat out of breath, we reached the top. This was marked by a simple white cross and characteristically by a tiny blue and white chapel. We stood getting our breath back looking out across the narrow strip of sea separating Kos from the Turkish coast.

'Turkey is really clear today and it looks so close,' John said. 'You can see why the Syrian refugees try to get here.'

When we went to Kos in 2014 the refugees arriving in small boats camped in colourful pop-up tents all along the waterfront and the children played freely around them. The locals were sympathetic to their plight and helped out with accommodation and food. In Kefalos Angela had a basket in the bakery where she collected toys for the children. However, as the number of refugees arriving increased and it became clear that this was going to be a longstanding issue that would be extremely difficult to resolve, the locals became concerned about the impact on their livelihoods and the tourist industry.

A detention centre was constructed outside Pyli and the refugees and asylum seekers were moved there. Originally intended for around eight hundred migrants it soon became overcrowded and conditions deteriorated, especially as some refugees were brought there to relieve the pressure on the other islands. Those detained there, while they can move around the island, cannot leave it. They have to wait for their claims to be processed and this can take over a year and there is no guarantee that they will ever ultimately be able to travel to their desired destination. We thought about their desperate situation as we gazed at the white buildings of Bodrum and its outlying settlements and the narrow Turkish peninsula of Resadiye.

'Let's go in the chapel and see if there are any books of signatures,' John broke the silence. He was keen to see if the book we had signed when we first did this climb was still there. Perhaps unsurprisingly it wasn't, as the little chapel had had many visitors since then. We signed in the current book under an entry made by a family from Florence. Most of those climbing the peak in recent months were Italian.

We accepted the book's invitation to add a comment. We commented favourably on the tranquility of the place and the view and negatively on the pile of plastic bottles, beakers and plates outside the chapel door – probably left there from a festival. A few metres from the chapel, perching on a rocky outcrop, we were at the peak's highest point from where we could see Nisyros, Tilos and Halki bathed in a golden haze as the sun was sinking lower in the sky.

John got out his camera. 'I must take a panorama of this although the sun is still rather bright.' He clicked away trying several attempts with different settings.

'Before we go back I'd like to find the refuge that Spiros mentioned when we told him we planned to come up here,' I said.

'I think I caught a glimpse of it just down there below the chapel,' he indicated back along the ridge. We found the refuge hut tucked into the rock but, as it was locked, we were glad we weren't in need of shelter. However, there were three little wooden stools outside of it and so we sat down overlooking Zia appreciating the view in the golden hour approaching sunset.

'It's magnificent up here on such a lovely evening.'

'We're really lucky that it's so still,' I agreed,

remembering how previously we had been buffeted by the wind which had made standing at the highest point a precarious balancing act.

Going down was much quicker than we had allowed for, even though the rocks, loose earth and stones on the path meant our feet needed to be placed with care. As anticipated, my borrowed stick came in very useful and prevented me from slithering over on several occasions. Just before re-entering the trees, we paused on the slope for John to photograph the beautiful blue and white church of Lagoudi lit up by the evening light against a backdrop of sea and the mountains of Kalymnos. By the time we drove into Zia, it was well into the blue hour – the time after sunset beloved by photographers, when the sky has a blue tinge which tints all beneath it.

Most of the tourists had left so it was easy to find a parking place. The balcony in Zia, which faces west, is well known for having an uninterrupted view of the sun setting over the sea. Coach loads of tourists are ferried up the narrow winding roads to the village to observe this phenomenon and hopefully to spend some money in the plethora of tourist shops and stalls selling holiday clothing, souvenirs, sweets and vast quantities of herbs. I wanted to buy some herbs for making souvlaki and then we were going to have dinner before driving home.

'This is the life,' I said as I sipped my glass of cool white wine, breathed in the warm scented air and looked at the lights twinkling down the mountainside. We were sitting on the patio of a traditional Greek restaurant situated at the edge of Zia having ordered our dinner.

'It's remarkably quiet once the coaches have left,' John remarked.

'I was thinking about that Greek evening we had here the first time we came to Kefalos. Do you remember it?' I asked.

'Yes we joined Seagull studios' Zia night tour. I noticed the restaurant we were taken to is still there with its rows of chairs and tables, but clearly nothing is happening there tonight.'

'I wonder if they still do the same line dancing and plate spinning and crashing bit. I've never really understood the point of breaking lots of plates but I like the line dancing to traditional music. One thing that I really did enjoy about Seagull studios was doing line dancing after the Saturday night barbecue. Mitsos the barman was really good at it,' I reflected.

'He did wonderful lamb souvlaki on those evenings. I always look for it on the restaurant menus but none of them seem to do it.'

'You were able to have it at Vathi,' I reminded him.

'True and that was pretty good, if not quite up to Mitsos's standard.'

'One meatballs in tomato sauce with rice,' the waiter arrived with two steaming plates. 'That's his,' I interjected.

'One lemon chicken in the pot, which must be for the lady.' Smiling, he put the brown casserole pot down in front of me. 'Enjoy your meal.'

'Umm, smells good, I'm hungry,' I said.

'It tastes good,' said John already tucking into his meatballs. 'What are your plans for tomorrow. You are planning to meet Jan aren't you?'

'We agreed to meet outside the bookshop in Eleftherias square because she knows where that is as she went in to buy a map of Kos. We'll go and have lunch somewhere and after that we'll fetch Mabel and drive to the hotel where she is staying to pick up her case. Then we'll come back to Kefalos and I'll take her up to the old town to see the flat.'

'You think she'll be happy with it.'

'Oh I think so. I described it to her and she thought that it sounded ideal.'

'When he showed you around the flat, did Spiros tell you how it came to be empty as most accommodation is booked up this time of year.'

'Yes it's usually a long term rather than a holiday let. The young woman who was renting it worked at the airport and she was unexpectedly offered a job at Athens airport. As she really fancied living in Athens, she accepted straightaway. The owner was about to advertise the vacancy when I asked Spiros if he knew anywhere that Jan could rent particularly in Kefalos old town. Jan had said that she would particularly like to stay there as it would be more interesting than renting a holiday studio. It was fortuitous timing.'

The following day I was in good time to meet Jan, having successfully parked Mabel in the nearest carpark to the town centre of the several on the main road on the way into Kos. I ambled up one of the streets into town looking in the windows of the modern shops at the expensive clothes. Several had sales of boots and woolly jumpers which, as it was so hot, I didn't imagine would encourage many buyers. I thought how clothes in stores often didn't reflect the time of year. In England if you didn't buy any summer clothes that you might want at the beginning of the season, by the time it warmed up or you were about to go away on holiday, shorts and other such items were often difficult to come by.

When I got to the bookshop Jan was already there looking cool and relaxed in a pretty sundress and straw hat.

'Hi. You are looking very well,' I greeted her. 'I really like your dress.'

'Thanks, I'm feeling good and enjoying doing as I please. I bought this dress yesterday in the market. Do you go shopping there?'

'Yes I have several times, though not yet this year. There are masses of stalls and a great variety of items for sale but it's particularly good for summer clothes.'

'I admit I also bought three tops and a pair of trousers. They are really fine thin cotton. The equivalents at home are always linen or such thick heavy cotton. I really enjoyed browsing around. I was there for ages. Regi would have had a fit. He would never have let me spend all that time there,' she sighed.

'In your wandering around have you spotted anywhere in particular that you would like to try out for lunch?'

'There is a very pretty looking Greek restaurant down a backstreet leading off Platanos square. You know that's the square with the enormous propped up tree under which Hippocrates was supposed to have taught. I wonder if he did.'

'Possibly, he was a native of Kos. It's a nice idea and

gives a bit of added interest to the tree. You lead the way,' I replied.

Having fortunately got the last available table, decided to have pastitsio and Greek salad and placed our order, I asked her about her stay in Kos town.

'I've had a lovely time. The first day I just wandered around the town and explored the backstreets and the ruins. The second day I went to Lambi beach, hired a sunbed and umbrella and chilled out reading the novel I brought from home and hadn't got around to starting. Then yesterday I went to the Asklepion. There was a leaflet on it in the hotel saying that it's the most renowned Ancient Greek medical sanctuary in Greece so thought I ought to go as I'm here. I have to admit that I'm not particularly interested in Greek antiquities but actually I really enjoyed it. All the ruined buildings are identified and there's a lot to see. Also, its location on the hillside among the pines and cypresses is lovely and there are wonderful views of the town and the Turkish coast. It's quite amazing. Have you been?'

'Yes, the second time we had a holiday here we went to see it. I remember being impressed by its huge staircase and terraces, and like you enjoyed the views. However, I've forgotten its history apart from the fact Hippocrates was supposed to have founded it in the 5th century BC, although the ruins all date from much later.'

'Regi would have liked the Asklepion but in his usual way he would have ensured that we did it to death. He would have insisted on identifying and inspecting every tiny aspect of the ruins to be absolutely sure he hadn't missed anything. Also, while doing so he would doubtless have pontificated about the ancient Greeks' role in Kos, as if he were an expert, and I would have had to listen to it all,' she said with a vehemence that rather took me aback.

'Do you know how he is doing in Taiwan?' was the only response I could think of.

'He has done several lectures at the University in Taipei, which apparently were extremely well received. As a result, after he has completed the lecture tour and taught the course, they want him to go back and do two or three more weeks working with their PhD students.'

'Goodness does that mean he is going to be in Taiwan all summer.'

'At least three months it would seem but don't worry,' she said observing my look of anxious surprise. 'I hardly see anything of him when he is at home because he is always either at work or working at home shut in his study. He hates to be disturbed so I practically have to book an appointment to speak to him. If I put my head round the door to tell him something and he is reading, on his computer or on the phone, he just glares at me and does fly swotting gestures to tell me to go away. I have really had enough of being treated that way. I'm sorry that our holiday together didn't work out as planned but, although he doesn't know it yet, that was his last chance,' she stated decisively. 'I plan to spend the next couple of months in Kos doing my own thing for a change and I'll use the time to decide what to do when we both get back home. Oh good here's our lunch.'

She concluded confiding about Regi as the waiter brought two large and delicious looking plates of food. I realised from their stay with us that they seemed rather distant from each other but I hadn't realised just how far they had drifted apart.

In the car on the way back to Kefalos, Jan elaborated describing how depressing her life with Regi had become and how she despaired of their marriage. She explained how increasingly she felt more like a housekeeper than a wife, as he seemed to take her completely for granted. He assumed that she would do all the household chores, the cooking and anything and everything he required to support him but never expressed any appreciation for what she did for him or showed any concern about her interests or the quality of her life. She made it abundantly clear to me that she was thoroughly fed up with him. She said that she was in a deep trough and envisaged her holiday in Kos as the first step to climbing out of it.

As Jan and I had both anticipated, she really liked the flat in Kefalos old town. It was on the top floor of a renovated two storey building, which was well situated in a quiet back street that ran parallel to the main street. It had a tiny kitchen but it was well equipped with a modern cooker, fridge freezer and washing machine. She was particularly pleased to see the latter as she hadn't liked to ask Regi's brother if she could do her washing and said all her clothes could do with a rinse through. The kitchen led into a large airy lounge/dining room with a balcony over the street. The single bedroom was also a good size and had a balcony over a tiny alley.

'It's perfect,' she said, 'on the one hand it's really central so I will feel part of the town's life but on the other hand it seems fairly quiet. The decor is really bright and cheerful and I love the balconies. I think that I'm going to enjoy staying here. Also, I'd like to rent a car and it looks like it will be OK to park it in the street.'

'Yes it will.' I was able to assure her this, as Spiros had told me that previous occupants had parked below the flat.

'Should I hire one from where you got Mabel?'

'We got Mabel from Explore and it's very cheap probably because no one else wanted it and perhaps because each year we got our car for the holidays from them. Still, they are expensive. We always had to be ready to haggle, know the airport price for car rental and stress our loyalty to them to get a competitive price. Also, until last year they used to have an office in Kefalos but now the nearest one is in Kardamena. I think it might be easier and you would do better to try Budget.'

'Is Budget based here and you think that they will be cheaper?'

'Yes. Budget is by Kamari bay not far from the harbour. They only started up at the beginning of last year so are very keen to attract customers and, as you want the car for several weeks, I think you could get a good price. They have a very tiny forecourt because of where the office is situated, but they have plenty of different cars to choose from parked at the owner's home on the way to Limonias.'

'Good, right I'll try them first and I'll use your strategy of finding out, before I go to see them, what the cheapest car on hire from the airport would cost.' She looked at her watch, 'Goodness look at the time, the afternoon has gone quickly, should we go and do the shopping?'

I had said that we would wander around the town together and I would show her my favourite shops and she could buy in some initial provisions. We visited the butcher where I liked to buy our meat and she bought one of his lamb pies. Next we went to the bakery and I introduced her to Angela, and Jan bought some of of the popular honey buns. Then we went to Panayioti's supermarket where, like me, Jan was amazed at the organisation and creativity of his shelves and displays. When we passed it, I also pointed out his brother Nektarios's shop for absolutely anything and everything else you might possibly need.

We got back laden with purchases and had a coffee and honey bun on her lounge balcony to christen it and celebrate her occupancy. Then I left her with the pleasurable task of unpacking her case and shopping and deciding which cupboards should be used for which items.

7

Pilgrimage to Patmos

I awoke exactly at seven o'clock when the alarm was set to go off but didn't. The reason was a Kamari power cut which during our holidays we had learned was a regular occurrence. This meant that I couldn't have my usual cup of tea in bed to help me to wake up and get ready for the day's activity. Nevertheless, it didn't affect my mood. I was excited, as first thing we were off to Patmos – the island much visited through the ages by pilgrims because Saint John the theologian had written the Book of Revelation when he had been exiled there between AD 95 and 97.

We drove to Mastihari, left Mabel on the parking area near the harbour and caught the 9am ferry to Kalymnos. As we were choosing a place to sit out on deck, we were joined by Andy and Tanya.

'Hi. Are you like us having a day out on Kalymnos?' asked Andy.

'Not today,' I replied. 'Even better we are going to get the ferry to Patmos and spend a few days exploring it.'

'Good idea. You'll enjoy yourselves. The first year I was in Kefalos I went there and wandered around the old town and visited the famous cave and the monastery of Saint John. It was fun and really interesting.'

'What about you?' I asked.

'We are going to do some shopping and have lunch out,' said Tanya. 'I really like Pothia's busy bustling atmosphere and I think it's better for shopping than Kos town, particularly for household items.'

After swapping stories of our trips to Kalymnos, Andy surprised us by telling us about the project that he and Tanya had just embarked upon and were clearly very thrilled about.

'We feel so lucky because I was able to get a bank loan and I've just purchased an empty shop in Kefalos old town which I'm going to run as a bar. I plan to have Greek music nights, quiz nights for Brits and discos, all sorts.'

'That sounds great but a big project, quite an undertaking,' I said.

'Will the building require a lot of work to get it ready?' asked John.

'Yes it will but it's all very doable. I'll have to convert it for its new use and redecorate it completely but it's structurally sound which is the main thing. I'm doing a bit of reorganising of it now and experimenting with a few ideas but I haven't much time because I'm really busy at Kyrios's. Over the winter I'll be able to work on it properly.'

'I'll be able to help him then,' added Tanya enthusiastically. 'I've done a lot of decorating back home in the past and at the end of the season I'll give up my job at Baystay.'

'Where exactly is the shop?' questioned John.

'Just around the corner on the right hand side before you get to the school. Go and have a look at it, then next year when of course you must come to my bar you'll see what a transformation we've accomplished,' he said laughingly.

On arrival in Pothia, we said goodbye to Andy and Tanya and went to the cafe on the waterfront that we had discovered on our day trip to the island. There we had a second breakfast of very welcome coffee and pastries while we waited for the 11.35 ferry to Patmos. The sea was extremely calm and so our ferry journeys were very smooth.

When the boat called in at Agia Marina on Leros, we

enjoyed briefly seeing the familiar sights again. When we got to the tiny island of Lipsi we were curious to see what it was like, wondering if perhaps we should have had a couple of days there. The port, and the main village named Lipsi like the island, looked very inviting. The village was set in an enormous enclosed circular bay but from what we could see of the island it looked fairly flat and very barren. Other than visiting the beaches, which were supposed to be good, beyond the town of Lipsi there didn't seem much to explore.

Twenty-five minutes later we arrived in the port of Scala on Patmos. Above Scala the white, cube-shaped houses of Chora climbed the hillside and above the old village the famous fortress monastery of Saint John towered over the southern end of the ridge. We were surprised to find how busy the port was, as it was bustling with ferries and tourist boats plus motor boats that were bringing tourists to and from cruise ships moored outside the harbour.

Over the far side of the harbour there were also lots of people wandering around the marina. This was filled with yachts, some of which were very large and looked luxurious and all packed in, sterns tied against the jetty. We realised that Patmos had long been a place of pilgrimage but we hadn't appreciated just how important a tourist destination it had become, although fortunately as it turned out, this was predominantly in and around Scala and Chora. As we alighted in the harbour, and stood amidst revving vespas and trucks and the coaches which were loading and unloading day trippers, we realised that the area could be a crowded and rather noisy place to stay. While we looked forward to exploring it, we thought we would rather find accommodation somewhere more peaceful.

Unusually the tourist office was open but then there were certainly plenty of potential customers. From the possibilities suggested to us Meloi a little way up the coast to the north sounded the kind of place that we would like and so we took a taxi ride there. As we had hoped, Meloi turned out to be small, pretty and tranquil. We went in the beach taverna to enquire about accommodation. The waiter told us we needed to see Irini who owned the plot next door on which there were two houses for rent, one of which was available. He popped out to fetch her and she took us to a traditional single storey whitewashed house right on the beach. She unlocked the door with a large rusty key ushering us in, then leaving us to look around and decide if we wanted to stay.

When we first went in I was rather put off by its musty

smell but this soon disappeared once the door and windows were opened. The house turned out to be spacious, comfortable and authentically traditional. The walls were extremely thick which kept it cool and, when the wooden shutters were closed, provided effective soundproofing blocking out the rural sounds of donkeys braying, dogs barking, cats fighting and cockerels crowing. The wooden beamed ceilings were high, further adding to the cool airy feel.

The house had wonderful ancient wooden doors and windows with dark ornate wooden pelmets from which hung heavy lace curtains. In the living room there was an assortment of wooden tables and wicker chairs, wooden cupboards and chests of drawers on which were ornaments and photographs. An extremely long wooden sofa with straw stuffed cushions, which looked as if it could seat all the members of a large family, had an ornate wooden back which matched the pelmets. The walls were hung with mirrors in ornamental wooden surrounds, portraits and religious prints.

'This house is really lovely,' I said. 'Do you think it belongs to Irini's family?'

'Quite likely, we can ask when we get a suitable opportunity,' replied John. 'We were really lucky it was available and that she was at home.'

'I feel more like a guest of the family that once must have lived here than a holidaymaker renting accommodation,' I added, reflecting on how welcoming the house felt.

The kitchen consisted of a rusty sink under the window, which was an oblong hole fitted with mosquito netting, an open wall cupboard, a small calor gas burner and a fridge. However, this was fine as we didn't plan on doing any cooking and it had the one necessity, a fridge. In the bedroom we were amused by the double bed which was a massive metal construction with the head and foot sloping down to meet each other. Rather surprisingly the bedside table was an antique round wooden pedestal table exactly like the one we had in our bedroom back in England.

The bathroom was typical of Greek bathrooms we had encountered, both ancient and modern. It had a sink and a toilet and a shower pointing out into the room so that everything got soaked when you had a shower, making it essential to remember to remove your towel and the loo roll before doing so. The Greeks clearly had their version of wet rooms well before they became trendy in England.

The first day of our stay, we had breakfast on our patio which was large, shaded by two small tamarisk trees and only separated from the beach by its narrow patio wall. It was the ideal place to start the day. Just as we were putting our cups and plates outside on the wooden table I heard an announcement over a loudspeaker. Although I didn't understand what was being said, I guessed it was a van of some kind, hopefully one selling fruit. I went to find out and was pleased to discover that a melon van had come into the area behind the house.

The owner of the taverna and Irini were buying melons and so I bought two for us and cut one up straightaway to add to our breakfast of cereal, yoghurt and honey. As soon as we sat down at the patio table, we were joined by the pretty young ginger and white tabby cat that had walked in the house to introduce herself the previous evening. She alternately prowled around the table rubbing her body against our legs and sat on the wall purring. When we had eaten, I gave her a saucer of milk. Then, by way of thanks, she posed on the wall turning her head from one side to the other, as if saying to John who was taking her photo, 'Do ensure that you take me from my best angle.'

After breakfast, we were keen to explore and so set off on foot to walk the couple of kilometres into Scala. Once there an elderly woman doing her shopping pointed out to us the route to the monastery, which was up some steps past the supermarket that she had just come out of. As we climbed, we could see the harbour immediately below with boats of all kinds and sizes going to and fro and then more and more of the island became laid out before us.

Patmos is shaped like three islands in a line joined together by two narrow strips of land – the smallest in the south and the largest in the north with Scala and Chora located on the central one. Smaller than Leros it covers 34 square kilometres but like Leros, it has numerous wide bays and little islets. The resident population is about three thousand and while the majority live in and around Scala and Chora the island has numerous small villages, a testament to the one-time importance of farming.

At the top of the steps we came out on the road and turned right. About halfway to Chora we reached the Cave of the Apocalypse. It was no longer open to the elements, as in the 11th century a chapel was built over the cave and another in the 17th century.

'I'd like to go in here,' I said to John.

'I know it's important to Christianity,' he replied, 'but do you know why?'

'Yes, it's where the apostle John the Evangelist is reported to have heard the voice of God from a fissure in the rock. He dictated what he heard to his disciple Prohoros and this became the Book of Revelation, the final book of the New Testament.'

We went in the chapel and inside you could see the original shape and roof of the cave. With its dim interior, fresco of Christ speaking to Saint John and incense burners hanging from the ceiling, it certainly conjured up an intense sense of spirituality and history. Everyone stood in silence absorbing the atmosphere until three young German girls entered giggling over their mobile phones, one of which was ringing out breaking the silence.

On their departure the silence and the sense of mysticism was restored. A woman went and kissed the recess in the rock where Saint John was reputed to have rested his head at night. For her this was obviously a very profound experience and we were moved by her action and emotion.

When we left the cave we took the old track up through the trees heading for the monastery of Saint John. However, somewhere we went wrong and ended up at the back of a private garden. We couldn't see a way forward and so we returned the way we had come until we found the broad steps that took us up and past the Patmiada. This is a collection of white surprisingly modern looking buildings that form the famous theological seminary created in 1713.

We went to the end of the steps and then zigzagged through the narrow streets and alleys with their many shops full of religious paraphernalia – crosses, paintings, plaques – until we came to the fortress monastery of Saint John.

Looked up at from below the well-maintained monastery was undoubtedly impressive with its huge grey brown crenellated walls, imposing towers, powerful buttresses and open belfry arches housing the five bells. We went through the entrance and paused inside to read the notice drawing our attention to the space above the main gate. The notice informed us that this was where the monks had a boiler on a platform so that they could pour boiling water and oil on invaders. While no doubt necessary to protect themselves, it did seem rather un-monk-like behaviour.

'Before we look round,' I suggested, 'let's find somewhere to sit where we can read the brochure about the monastery that I found in the bedroom drawer.'

We sat on a concrete seat in the main courtyard and I retrieved the brochure from the front pocket of John's rucksack. From this we learned that the monastery was created by Christodoulos in the 11th century on the highest point in Chora. As was usually the case, it was built on a site of importance to the Ancient Greeks, that of the temple to the goddess Artemis. Initially there were few inhabitants on the island apart from the monks and craftsmen that Christodoulos brought with him from Crete and Asia Minor. However, the monks needed a workforce, particularly for agriculture, and so settlers and their families were encouraged to come and work there. From the late 13th century onwards the promise of security provided by the massive monastery walls led to the spread of the village outside the fortifications.

With its courtyards built on five different levels and adorned with pot plants, its five chapels, arcades, arches and colonnades, we found the monastery very attractive. Extensions over time to house the growing community meant the styles of the interior architecture were very diverse. We climbed up onto the roof near the highest point of the monastery by the three bells but disappointingly you couldn't see the view for the tall ramparts. We visited the heavily ornate gold Byzantine church which contains the marble tomb of Christodoulos, the refectory with its built in long stone tables and the monks' kitchen. However, the extensive library, which we would have liked to visit was shut to the public. As the monastery didn't close until 1.30pm, we had time to absorb the atmosphere and watch a monk in his long black robes toll the 1pm bell.

When we left we walked down the opposite side of the hill to Scala through a churchyard and lots of twisting picturesque streets of well-cared for houses and tiny squares. Despite the destruction brought about by earthquakes and the demolition of buildings by the Italians during the 1930s, the houses were attractively homogenous. Most of them were tall with rectangular windows and interesting wooden doors and reflected the fact that they dated from the 17th century when Chora was at the height of its prosperity.

Some of the grandest properties had belonged to shipowners who accumulated wealth through trade. One house was in the process of being renovated and workmen were removing damaged stonework and stacking it in the panniers of two mules. Clearly only mules could be used to remove rubble and carry building materials up and down the narrow, steep, stepped and cobbled alleys.

Eventually we found ourselves back in tourist land again and took advantage of this to have lunch in a restaurant with wonderful views. I had a very nice cheese omelette but John had a weird rubbery chicken souvlaki for which he compensated by having a large baklava.

After we had eaten, the restaurant owner showed us the way to walk to Grikos. We went along the street to the main road, which we crossed, and took a dirt track that after a few hundred metres became a monopati of large stones. It went down the hillside curving near the bottom to reveal Grikos bay to the right. Contrary to our expectations from the tourist information, the part of Grikos in which we arrived was a quiet sleepy place.

We walked to the large stony beach and sat on a wooden pallet that was resting on the stones. Almost immediately a large and rather aggressive man appeared from nowhere and demanded five euros if we wanted to sit on his pallet. We told him sorry but we didn't and so we got up and moved on. We walked the length of the beach and then back around the bay to the centre, where as originally anticipated there were holidaymakers sunbathing, tourist shops and cafes. We had a hasty Fanta at one of the cafes and then went off to find the bus stop to get the 4.45pm bus back to Scala. The bus didn't take the coast road as we expected but instead took the back road up to Chora and then down to Scala. From there we walked back to Meloi satisfied that we had had a very successful day's exploring and learned about the importance of Patmos to Christian pilgrims.

In the evening we ate on the vine covered terrace of the beach taverna as we had done the previous evening. It was a convenient, welcoming and friendly taverna. The previous evening we found out that the owner Manolis, whom we had initially asked about accommodation, was Irini's nephew. We had also chatted to the young waitress Evgenia who served us. She had told us about the beaches and how the one at Lampi on the north coast was her favourite. Creatures of habit, we sat at the same table as the previous evening and were greeted by Evgenia as she brought us the menu.

'Have you had a good day?' she enquired smiling.

'Excellent,' we chorused in unison.

'So where have you been?'

'We have done the tourist trail but we found it very interesting,' I said.

'We have been to the Cave of the Apocalypse, looked around the streets of Chora, visited the monastery of Saint John and then walked down to Grikos bay,' elaborated John.

'You have fitted in a lot. I also like walking around Chora. The houses are so grand and lovely,' responded Evgenia. 'Well as you have had such a full day, I think that you must be hungry. What are you going to have?'

'What do you recommend today?'

'I think the youvetsi or the moussaka.'

'I'll have the moussaka,' I said. 'It's my favourite,' and John opted for the youvetsi – beef baked with pasta.

After an early night and another leisurely breakfast on our patio and making a fuss of our resident tabby cat, we were ready to see more of Patmos. We decided we would walk to Kampos and Lampi in the north of Patmos and visit Evgenia's favourite beach.

We walked past the field behind the house, where the four donkeys that we had discovered the previous evening were standing in the shade. The largest and darkest brown one with a white band around his nose came trotting over to the wall to say hello. He seemed very gentle and friendly. I stroked his nose, which he seemed to like, and John took a photo of us. After this we passed the campsite, reportedly the only one on the island, which was probably why it seemed very popular. Then we went by the hotel before joining the main road.

We encountered very little traffic as we walked the four kilometres or so through the countryside to the village of Kampos. On the way there were a few cultivated fields but mostly the land lay parched and idle. The square in the centre of Kampos was on a wide crossroads with a restaurant on one side and a church and a small shop on the other, all of which appeared deserted. We took the right hand fork, which dropped down to Kampos bay.

We met a mule train of four mules coming up from the

seafront. One was carrying a mattress and the other three were laden with what looked like bedding. When we reached the sea, the road followed the bay around to the left. However, we decided to go along the beach, where there were several tiny fishing boats pulled up on the sand and a few others moored in the shallows. At the far end of the beach past the empty sunbeds, was a watersports hut.

We checked out with the young guy sitting inside what the water skis were like and I could see John was definitely interested. He enjoys having a ski when the opportunity presents itself. Unfortunately there was no possibility of such an opportunity on this occasion, because that morning the ski boat and its driver had failed to appear and it seemed very unlikely that he was going to do so.

We decided to have a brief sit on the beach and then walk on to Lampi. I thought an ice cream would be nice as I could see there was a kiosk advertising refreshments. However, John pointed out that the lid of the freezer standing alongside the kiosk was propped open and on closer investigation, as he pessimistically prophesied, the freezer was empty so no ice creams were forthcoming.

We slowly climbed up the hill to the little hamlet of Christos with its scattered white houses and rather dilapidated looking farms. Christos was interesting to us because it was where our young waitress had told us that she was born and brought up. Her father had been a farmer but the increasingly hot dry summers made for such difficult growing conditions the family moved to Scala. He now worked at the harbour and her mother, like Evgenia, was a waitress. At the top of the rise before the road descended to the sea, rather surprisingly, there was a restaurant. However, my hopes that this might produce an ice cream were soon dashed as we entered and realised that the freezer there was also empty.

'We don't get in ice cream until July when we have visitors wanting it.' The waiter supplied the explanation for the dearth of ice cream.

We headed down the zig-zagging road to the beach looking unsuccessfully for shortcuts through the scrub to cut off the corners. At the bottom, we walked onto the pebble beach reputedly of many colours and discussed if this was a deserved reputation.

'There are certainly lots of smooth, round, different types of pebbles,' said John, 'but I don't think they are particularly colourful.'

Heading down to the water I replied, 'If you look at them where they've been washed by the waves they have more colours. They do look better when they are wet.'

'True but I don't think they are any more colourful than the ones on the beach at home.'

There was a fish taverna called The Dolphin with tables set out on the shingle and we decided that this would be a lovely place to have lunch. I had a tuna salad and John had a gilt head sea bream, which he thought sounded exotic and indeed both dishes were very good. Disappointingly, as it seemed that nowhere in the locality stocked ice cream in May, I wasn't able to have one for dessert. Settling for a cup of Nescafe instead, we sat watching the waves and, as the sky was very clear, we could see the distant mountains of western Samos. Afterwards we walked back up to Kampos. There we caught the 2.30pm bus to Scala. In Scala we passed half an hour in an ice cream parlour – no shortages of ice cream there – while waiting for the bus up to Chora.

Once again we enjoyed the magnificent view from the top but this time it was much more meaningful, as we were aware of the layout of the north east of the island. We matched the coastline to the map that we had bought when we first arrived in Patmos. We could recognise Meloi bay and Kampos bay and see the headland that we intended to explore the next day. John had planned a circular walk for us, as Manolis had told us there was a path along the cliffs from Kampos to Meloi. Having thoroughly taken in the view and photographed the panorama, we reluctantly decided it was time we went. We found the old stone monopati and walked back into Scala and then back to Meloi.

As we went past the taverna on the way back to the house Irini came out. 'Hello. Have you had a good day?' she enquired.

'Yes, we have had a lovely day thanks.' I said.

'We've been to Kampos bay and Lampi bay,' John added.

'Lampi bay is very nice, the stones are so pretty,' responded Irini. Did you get a bus there?'

'No, we walked but afterwards we got a bus back to Scala from Kampos,' he explained.

'Then we took the bus up to Chora as we wanted to have another chance to enjoy the wonderful view from the top,' I told her.

'You certainly seem to have done a lot. I think now you must be ready for a rest.'

'Yes, we are going to sit on the patio and have a glass of wine. I love sitting on the patio looking at the beach and the sea,' I said.

'When I lived there, I too used to like to sit on the patio

and watch the waves and the birds.'

'So once it was your home. We did wonder.'

'Yes I lived there as a child, well until I got married, and then Nikos and I had our present house built. My parents continued to live there until my mum died. Then my dad went to live with my older sister in Grikos but that was several years ago now.'

'Are the photographs of your family?' John asked.

'Yes the large one hanging on the wall is of my parents and the one on the chest of drawers is of me and my husband when we were much younger. The other photos are also of members of the family.'

'The photos make us feel like family guests. We are really enjoying staying there. We think it's a lovely house,' I said with enthusiasm.

'Yes it is, but I prefer my house with a large modern kitchen and a nice bathroom,' she laughed.

On the morning of our last full day we had an early not-so-leisurely breakfast on the patio because we wanted to make the most of it. However, tabby cat still arrived for her saucer of milk. By nine o'clock we were on our way saying good morning to the donkeys, observing the early morning activities at the campsite and going past the hotel, where the occupants didn't yet appear to have surfaced.

Contrary to the previous day, when we reached the main road, almost immediately we turned right and headed down a gradually sloping lane to Agriolivado. An old monopati ran alongside the lane but we decided it was easier to walk on the tarmac than negotiate its cobbles. We left the lane and took a narrow sandy track to the edge of the bay but clearly this wasn't the best route to get to the beach. We found ourselves with a shoulder high stone wall on one side and the water's edge on the other. In order to reach the beach we had to clamber through the branches of tamarisk trees and over rocks. However, the beach was worth our effort as it was wide and sandy – real sand not just earth or pebbles.

We walked around the bay on the beach. Empty sunbeds awaited sun seeking tourists but the only person we saw was a solitary fisherman who was sat untangling his fishing line. We planned to walk up and over the headland path to get some height to enjoy the view and to look down on Kampos bay, where we had been the previous day. To achieve this required further considerable scrambling over rocks.

From the top of the headland, we were rewarded by a view back over Agriolivado bay that was stunning. The sea was azure blue and brilliantly shimmering around the tiny island in the bay with its little chapel to Saint Thekla. It all looked quite magical. Looking back across the bay, perched on the cliff edge, we could see the Seagull taverna that Irini had told us about and recommended for lunch. Behind it across the water, but unmistakable in the heat haze, was the dark shape of the monastery of Saint John.

As we continued walking over the headland the white chapel of Agios Nikolaos and the nearby hotel complex on the edge of Kampos bay soon came into view. At the point where we reached a wall and a cattle stall, we could see all the little resort below us and beyond the brown hills dotted with trees of the north east peninsula. After mentally tracing where we had walked the previous day, we turned around and made our way back to Agriolivado beach.

Renegotiating the rocks we watched a fisherman in a wetsuit trying unsuccessfully, at least while we were watching, to spear fish with a small harpoon. Walking back along the sand we saw that four tourists were now installed on the sunbeds and applying suntan oil. The fisherman, who had been sorting out his line, had cast it into the water and was standing patiently waiting for a catch. We looked around for a suitable spot to encamp. We considered hiring sunbeds but decided it wasn't worth it for an hour or so and instead found a pleasant place to sit under a tamarisk tree.

John decided to have a swim and go snorkelling around the rocks and so he got out his snorkel and goggles. I took out my novel, propped his rucksack against the tree and lent back comfortably. It was nice to have my head in the shade but I stretched out my legs enjoying the warmth of the sun on them and the sand between my toes. I did read a few pages but I spent more time just looking at the islet and the sparkling sea. Unaware of time passing, I was just appreciating the moment.

When John returned he declared that, as he anticipated, the deeper water around the rocks was a brilliant place to go snorkelling. While we didn't see either of the two fishermen catch any fish, John told me he had seen a large number of them. There were shoals of long thin grey ones and plenty of more interesting brightly coloured ones, especially two kinds of bright red fish, some small yellow ones and one large green grey one. After he had sat in the sun long enough to get totally dry, we decided it was time to go to the Seagull taverna for lunch.

From the extensive display of photographs and information in the kitchen area of the taverna, we discovered that it had been a house for two hundred years and a taverna for twenty years. We chose a table on the terrace and ordered chick pea patties, tzatziki and salad which was served with some delicious freshly made bread. While we were waiting for our meal we sat sipping our freshly squeezed orange juice and admiring the beautiful view of the cliffs, the bay and out to sea.

'This,' I said, 'is definitely holidaying in the Dodecanese at its best.'

I took out my phone and positioned myself to take his photo against the scenic backdrop and noticed I had a text message from Jan. Having taken his photo I sat down again and read the message.

'Jan has got a job,' I announced surprised.

'That's unexpected. What is she doing?'

'Hiring out cars presumably as she is working three days a week at the Budget office. She noticed an ad for the job on the office wall when she hired her car and got to thinking that it might be interesting and quite fun as it's only part-time. She went in a few days later to discuss what the job involved and decided to take it. She says that she'll tell me more when we get back.'

We left the taverna by a track which took us past where two men were coating a newly built chapel with concrete rendering. Given the abundance of chapels dotted everywhere, building another in the middle of nowhere seemed unnecessary and we wondered who would be paying for it. We continued on the track which led down to a tiny beach. Annoyingly, then we were faced with a tall wire fence barring any access to the headland in front of us.

Two rather portly middle aged Greek men were slowly heading in our direction and so we waited for them to reach us and explained that we were looking for the footpath. Much scratching of heads and animated discussion in Greek led to them concluding that the path was now impassable owing to the intended building of a new road. While we realised they could well be right, because Manolis had told us many of the old paths on Patmos had become lost through the island's development, we were a bit sceptical because they didn't look like they were into walking.

We went back up the path we had come down on until we found a higher track going in the right direction. We took this optimistically but after ten minutes it petered out onto a wide straw strewn terrace. Here a peacefully grazing, sleek, brown horse carried on munching and totally ignored us. We turned back again and had just decided that we were going to have to return to Meloi on the road, when John noticed a tiny cairn of small stones marking what seemed like a goat path through the thyme, sage and prickly scrub. We took it and amazingly it turned out to be what was needed, as it led us behind some isolated houses and onto a very narrow lane which ultimately joined the back road into Meloi.

On the final morning we sat having breakfast on the patio reflecting on how quickly the time had gone on our visit to Patmos. We played with tabby cat and told her that she would soon be entertaining new residents. We walked around the village and visited the chapel on the hillside behind us that we hadn't got around to doing before. We said goodbye to the donkeys and I told the one with the white band on his nose that he was lovely and I would miss him. I wondered unrealistically whether I might get a donkey when we returned to England.

We sat on the hillside and watched a cruise ship put down two tenders and, once they were stowed with passengers, head for Scala. Then we went for a final swim in Meloi bay before showering and packing our things back in the rucksacks and going for a light lunch at the taverna. We said goodbye to Manolis and Evgenia and then Irini called us a taxi and we were off to Scala for our ferry journeys back to Kos. Sadly on this occasion our pilgrimage to Patmos was over.

8

The Feud

The morning after our return from Patmos, I went up to Kefalos old town to stock up on groceries from Panayioti's supermarket and afterwards to call in on Jan to find out more about her job at Budget car hire. After we settled down with our coffee on her lounge balcony, she satisfied my curiosity by giving me more details on how this came about.

'Last Thursday, the day you went to Patmos, I decided that I would really like a job of some kind to give me something else to do and an opportunity to meet people. I only wanted it to be part-time as I'd still like plenty of space to relax on the beach and go exploring. I thought maybe I might be a waitress but when I enquired in a few restaurants, they either didn't need any more staff or they needed someone to work full-time.'

I responded giving my view that working in a restaurant wouldn't have suited her. 'I guess that would have involved doing really long hours. The restaurants here have to make as much as they can during the holiday season to keep everyone going when they are closed during the winter months.'

'Yes. I really didn't want to be tied down like that,' she replied. 'Then I thought, perhaps I should call in at Budget and see whether the job that I'd seen advertised when I hired the car was still available and, if so, find out more about it. I noticed the job ad on the wall but I didn't read it fully, as at that stage I hadn't thought of finding any work. Anyway I went in and Sandra, who works there, explained that they needed someone to look after the desk for three afternoons a week and a couple of evenings which meant hiring out cars to customers and answering the phone. Then on Saturday to help get cars to, and collect cars from, the airport as that is when a lot of holidaymakers arrive and leave.'

Jan continued, 'She made it all sound interesting and not too demanding so I told her it seemed just what I wanted. She said she thought that Andreas would be happy for me to take the job, but obviously I would need to discuss it with him, so could I come back in the evening when he would be in the office. I did and, after we discussed at some length what would be involved, he offered me the job and I took it. He was particularly pleased when I told him that I spoke Italian. I told him that because I'd noticed quite a few Italians holidaying in Kefalos, guessed some might want to hire cars and thought it could prove useful.'

'When do you start?'

'I already have. I started on Saturday evening. I went backwards and forwards delivering four cars to the airport and fetching three back. Then when I took the final one I had to wait at the airport until Elias, Andreas's father, came and collected me.'

'Was it easy to find the cars to bring back? I know there's usually quite a lot of hire cars parked there.'

'One took a bit of finding as it was right at the edge of the parking area and not with the other hire cars, but Sandra warned me if at first I couldn't see it, not to panic but just walk up and down the rows until I found it, which I did. Also, I had Elias's number to ring if I really had a problem. I was a bit anxious but I managed OK and having done it once I won't be so worried again.'

'I'm most impressed. I think it's very adventurous of you to take this job.'

'Yes I must admit I think so too as I'm not normally so bold.'

'When are you in the office, have you done that yet?'

'Monday, Wednesday and Friday. I was there yesterday but I mainly observed what went on. Andreas showed me what to do and what forms to fill in if someone comes in to hire a car. Also, I answered a few phone calls. Sandra will work with me tomorrow and Friday and from then I'll usually be on my own, although Andreas will be around quite a bit and I can always contact him if I need help.'

'What's Andreas look like. I don't know that I've seen him?'

'Early forties probably, tall and slim, thick dark wavy hair, very brown, aquiline features, stereotypically Greek looking, really attractive actually.'

'Attractive, could be dangerous,' I teased.

'No way,' she blushed.

'So you think he'll be OK to work for.'

'He certainly seems very pleasant and straightforward. Sandra says he's nice and she has worked there since Budget opened, so we'll see.'

'Is Sandra English or is that just the English equivalent of her name?'

'She is Scottish from Melrose. She met her Greek partner when she was on holiday here a couple of years ago. He works in the Post Office, here in town.'

'In that case I can guess who he is,' I responded. 'I don't know him but I've been served by him when I've gone in there. Have you told Regi?' I couldn't resist asking.

'No, not yet. I will of course, but I know he won't like it and will try to talk me out of it. I feel really pleased to have got the job and I just don't want to argue about it.'

'I can't see there is any rush to tell him,' I said reassuringly. 'If all goes well and I'm sure that it will, you'll have much more to tell him if you leave it a bit and you will be able to make it all sound very positive. Anyway, look at the time. I better go. I'm due at Joan and Terry's this afternoon to meet the current tutor and take some of his group to the basilica ruins where they can sit and paint Kastri island.'

Wishing Jan luck with her job I left and went straight home, unpacked my shopping and put it away. Then I ate a cheese sandwich in haste and drove to Joan and Terry's.

'How is it going?' I asked Joan when I entered the kitchen, as I knew this was a first at her centre for this particular tutor.

'Really well. Judging from the conversation over lunch they all enjoyed this morning and found it really helpful.'

'That's good, what were they doing?'

'Well the course is mainly aimed at beginners or

certainly those who are inexperienced at painting *en plein air*. This morning he did a demonstration painting of Kastri island. He had a big photo of it up on a screen and, as he produced a painting based on it, he talked them through his composition decisions, the colours he was mixing and the techniques he was using.'

'Sounds like an interesting and helpful start,' I responded rather wishing that I could have seen it too.

'Also he gave them all a drawing of Kastri island that he did yesterday before they arrived. If they don't want to draw the scene from scratch they can copy his or reproduce it using trace down paper, so that they are all ready to make the most of this afternoon. Anyway come and meet them all.'

Peter the tutor was a thickset, blonde haired man in his thirties with a smiley countenance. As Joan had said, the group seemed very positive, friendly and talkative. In fact Peter the tutor had to chide them gently to get them to stop chatting and get their things together ready to leave. It only took six or seven minutes to drive to the ruins but it would have taken too long and been too far for them to carry their art equipment. They were astonished at the extent and condition of the ancient Christian basilica of Saint Stephen and enthused at the iconic view of Kastri island.

'If ruins like these were in England, they'd be fenced off and you'd be charged entrance.'

'At home near us there are just bumps in the ground where apparently there was a medieval village. There are plaques to read but nothing to see and you have to pay to get in.'

A woman pointed to her feet and bent down to brush some of the sand away on the ground and take a closer look. 'It's amazing what good condition these ruins are in given no one looks after them and they're exposed to the elements. Just look at the remains of this mosaic floor.'

'The view of the island from here is just beautiful. What a great place to sit and paint.'

The group members proceeded to climb around the ruins to explore and to look from the highest point to the beach over the other side and then to decide on a suitable viewpoint and find a piece of the remaining basilica wall or a column to provide shade. Eventually everyone was settled and Peter went around helping them to get started and, specifically for those using the trace down paper, to remind them to put the correct side against their watercolour paper. Even so, two would-be artists, who were very excited to embark on the challenge, got it wrong. This meant that they discovered having carefully traced Peter's picture they had nothing to show for their efforts and had to start again – a frustrating experience anyone who has used trace down paper can empathise with.

I assumed the role that I'd become accustomed to of fetching and carrying water to drink and water for paint pots. Then supplying items individuals had forgotten but subsequently wanted, such as masking tape, soap with which to coat brushes before using masking fluid, pencils, putty rubbers, and even a palette for one participant. Having taken ages to decide where to sit and to lay out her materials, she realised that she had left her palette in the bedroom.

The group worked hard at the task displaying considerable concentration. Everyone had the same focus and were using the same techniques and colour mixes but even so the emerging paintings were fascinatingly different.

'The island is so picturesque especially with its little blue and white chapel. I hope that I've managed to do it justice,' the young woman, who had admired the mosaic floor, said to me as I refilled her jam jar with clean water.

'I think your painting has turned out well,' I was able to respond honestly. 'The rocky outcrop is especially realistic and not easy to capture. You must be pleased with it.'

'Uhm I am quite. The sea might be better but on balance

I'm pretty happy with it. Have you ever been on the island?'

'Yes, on one holiday we hired a sailing dinghy and sailed over there and moored up,' I replied.

'You have all done really well but it's time to pack up now.' Peter was walking among the group calling time on their activity. 'Sorry but you'll have to stop now. There'll be time this evening after dinner, if you want it, for you to finish your paintings.'

When I got home I was greeted by John and Spiros relaxing on the patio having a beer. John grinned at me 'Spiros has brought you a present.'

'Hi Spiros, good to see you. Is John kidding me?'

'Absolutely not. I've brought you a present for the garden. I've brought you a statue of Aphrodite.'

'Oh, er uhm. That's really kind of you,' I said trying to sound positive but imagining some enormous female form in stone that would overpower the garden. I went over to him, 'I hope that it's only a small one Spiros as there isn't much space left now.'

'Don't worry it's very small and delicate.' He beamed confidently at me. 'I know you will like it.'

He put down his beer and returned to his truck to retrieve it. When the sacking protecting it was unwrapped, it turned out to be about three foot high and very carefully carved. Tucked neatly into the base of the oleander at one side of the garden, it added interest and looked most attractive. I was genuinely pleased with it.

'You are right Spiros, I do like it. It's a perfect addition to the garden. Where did it come from?'

'A hotel on the outskirts of Kos town is being refurbished and I took them a delivery of new sunbeds. They thought that when the new swimming pool was built and the patio modernised the statue wouldn't fit in. I agreed with them that this was definitely the case and I offered to do them a favour and take it away.'

'Didn't they want you to pay something for it.'

'No. I'd got them the sunbeds at an excellent price and they didn't want the statue and so no, it hasn't cost anything.'

'Well that's brilliant, thanks Spiros.'

Changing the subject Spiros delivered the latest local news. 'As you've been away on Patmos, you probably haven't heard about Manos?'

'No we haven't. Is it to do with his restaurant burning down?'

'Indeed, on Saturday he was arrested,' Spiros declared with a dramatic pause before specifying arrested.

'Does that mean he deliberately set fire to his restaurant

as Yurgos and some of the others suspected?' I asked.

'Yes, like they thought, it turned out that a couple of months before the fire he had insured it for a lot more than it was worth. He didn't set fire to it himself, but paid a teenage cousin of his to do it so he could make sure that he was seen drinking in Bertie's at the time it happened.'

'How did the police find out because it's several weeks ago now and so Manos must have thought he was going to get away with it?' said John.

'His cousin was boasting about it to some friends, who then told some other lads who also passed it on and so the story came out. Apparently the cousin was grilled by the police in case it was him who had set fire to Georgio's and Dimitri's water sports businesses but they concluded quite rightly in my view that these two fires were unrelated to the fire at the restaurant.'

'Well that's solved the mystery of one fire,' said John

'We rely on you Spiros to keep us up to speed with what is going on.'

A couple of days later as I had a free morning I walked to Joy's tourist office. I'd promised John that I would give Joy the memory stick on which he had saved a number of photos of Kastri island, Kos old town, Limonias and other local places. She was going to look through them and choose any that she wanted to use on her website, or on the additional posters she was planning to get made to brighten up the office walls and hopefully interest clients in taking excursions around Kefalos.

Joy had opened her Joyful Tours travel agency at the beginning of last summer. She knew what she wanted to do because for the five years since she married Mikos, the owner of a bar in Kefalos old town, she had worked for an agency near the harbour in Kardamena. When she worked there she developed lots of ideas about additional local excursions and trips to the other islands. Her employer wasn't interested in her suggestions. He made it clear he didn't want to take advantage of new possibilities and seemed totally against making any changes.

Certain she could do better and be more client-centred, efficient and creative, she became increasingly keen to set up her own tour business in Kefalos. However, she had had to wait patiently in order to find somewhere for an office that was appropriately situated to be seen by tourists. When she heard that the owner of a motorbike and quad bike hire firm was thinking of closing down, she quickly approached the owner of the premises on the waterfront and negotiated a lease.

'How is business?' I enquired as I walked in the door.

No visitors were in the office but that wasn't unusual for late morning, as potential clients were either out on trips or on the beach.

'Pretty good,' she said getting up from behind her desk, which faced the open doorway so that she could look out and see the passersby. Her movement led to the appearance of an attractive, smooth-coated young dog shaking the rag bone in his mouth and inviting her to a tug of war.

'Who is this?' I asked.

'This is Bonzo, that's what I've decided to call him. When I went to Kalymnos last week to get material for my new curtains,' she pointed to the window, 'I bumped into Jane. She had just got off the ferry with several dogs that she had taken to be checked out at the vets in Leros. Apparently she had gone out one morning and found Bonzo tied to a post in her garden. The locals all know she takes in stray and unwanted dogs and so someone had left him there.'

'It's quite a coincidence but I'm sure we have met her. She was waiting for the ferry to Leros at the same time as us and had a couple of dogs with her that she was taking to the vets and so we got chatting. Is Jane elderly, tanned and very fit looking?'

'She is and, as you have met her, you'll appreciate how

I came to get Bonzo.'

'He is lovely,' I said tugging on his bone so he growled delightedly.

'He is,' she said, 'and so friendly so I don't think he has ever been ill-treated. Jane asked around to check that he hadn't just got lost but no one recognised or claimed him. In Kalymnos he looked up at me with his big brown eyes and licked me on the knee and I couldn't resist him. I'd been thinking for a while that I'd like a dog so here he is.'

He threw his bone in the air and jumped on it sending the rope attached to his collar and anchored to the wall banging against the chairs and tables.

'Bonzo calm down,' she laughed and patted his head and tickled his ears. 'I have to have him on a rope so he can potter in and out but can't go in the road. I give him a long walk at home in the morning and Mikos takes him out in the evening.'

'I've brought you the photos John's taken,' I said handing her the memory stick.

'Oh thanks, that's great,' she replied. 'I want to put some new excursions on my website. It's a shame though but I think I'm going to have to alter my Antimachia trip which is a pity as it was going well.'

'When I last saw you, you said it was very popular.'

'Yes, those who went on it said it appealed because it didn't leave too early, there was lots to see and the traditional restaurant in Mastihari gave them a really good lunch.'

'That all sounds very positive, so what's the problem?' I asked.

'The problem is with the first place they go to, the Antimachia castle, which they really liked. You know how impressive the battlements are as you drive up to it, and walking around them inside you get wonderful views of the surrounding area and out to sea over Kardamena.'

'Yeh. I'll never forget the first time we saw it. We had no idea it was there. We had hired a car and were just taking little side roads and tracks off the main road to see more of the island. We went around a corner and there it was this massive castle with amazing semi-circular fortifications.'

'It's an impressive place and my groups really enjoyed spending time there, either exploring and looking at the chapels or just sitting on the walls admiring the views.'

'We were quite excited when we explored it that first time,' I told her. 'There was no one there and the huge area within the walls was very overgrown but really pretty with wild flowers and ancient olive trees. It was as if we were the first people to have discovered it since it was abandoned. We've been back lots of times but, unfortunately, the atmosphere isn't the same since EU money was used to clear the ground inside and build those toilets right in the middle, which as they are not connected to a water supply are just rubbish dumps. It's a real shame but why are you having a problem with it?'

'Well the last two times we have been, there were these two guys dressed in white sheets who, I think, were trying to look like they belonged to the Order of the Knights of Saint John who had the castle built. At first they stood by that big wooden kiosk at the entrance, which is another EU aberration, and asked us all for a fee to go in. Then, when they didn't get one, they continually went from one person to another pestering everyone to hire them as guides or pay them to tell the history of a particular chapel or fortification.'

'How annoying. What did you do?'

'There wasn't much we could do. On each of those last two visits we had to leave earlier than planned to get away from them, and so for the time being I've decided it would be better not to go to the castle. However, if I leave out the castle, I need a replacement because we go from there to Antimachia to see the traditional house and the windmill and those alone won't give enough variety to the trip and occupy the morning.'

'Are there any places practising local crafts in the town or nearby that you could visit and have a demonstration, like the pottery in Kefalos?'

'No not really. There's an interesting speciality Greek herb and spice shop but the evening trip to Zia covers that.'

The mention of herbs made me think of the thyme honey business run by Sophia's daughter Ionna. She and her husband had a large shop selling honey that also housed a bakery which made a range of different flavoured baklavas and other Greek desserts that used honey. 'What about Ionna's place?' I suggested. 'It's quite near Antimachia and she speaks excellent English and could talk about their beehives and honey production or honey in Greek cooking or whatever.'

'Mhm, yes possibly, thanks for that, it might be a possibility. I'll sound her out on it. I need to hurry up and come up with something,' she said just as a couple of elderly tourists entered the office and were greeted enthusiastically by Bonzo, tired of sitting quietly.

'Hello doggy,' said the woman patting him on the head. 'What a cute dog.'

'We've come to ask about trips to Nisyros,' her husband went over to Joy.

'Certainly,' she replied. 'We do day trips by boat and then take you by coach to different parts of the island or you can go and stay there for three nights. It's a very attractive and interesting island.'

'I'll catch up with you later,' I said to Joy and, 'I was just going. I'm sure that you'll enjoy Nisyros,' to the couple. 'Bye Bonzo.'

Walking back home from Joy's office, I reflected some more on our visits to Antimachia when we first came to Kos and smiled to myself as I recalled our introduction to the windmill on her tour. Nowadays the outside has been renovated and the milling machinery totally overhauled. While it still grinds flour, it is predominantly a museum and tourist attraction. However, back then it looked rather dilapidated but nevertheless very quaint and interesting. Attracted by the sight of its unusual, to our eyes, triangular white sails arranged in a circle going round and round, we got out of the car and went to take a closer look. An elderly man and woman, perhaps the parents of the current owner as it has been in the same family for four generations, stood in the open doorway and beckoned us in to look around.

The ground floor was clearly their living quarters, the intermediate floor was for storing wheat and bags of flour and the top floor housed the machinery, which powered by the turning sails was in operation. From this floor, the woman pushed John up a ladder until his head went through the hole in the wooden roof. At first he thought she was doing this so he could admire the view, but she kept on pushing him up through the hole till he was afraid she was going to push him out of the mill altogether.

I watched this in growing alarm until the man touched my arm, pointed to John's camera that I was clutching, and gesticulated that I should go outside and take a photo. Relieved and amused, I shouted up to John to let him know that what was happening wasn't the precursor to homicide but the provision of a unique photo opportunity. We still have that snapshot in one of our holiday albums.

I ambled along the seafront thinking how lucky we were to be staying here all summer this year instead of a couple of weeks. We were having a really interesting and enjoyable time and so I imagined that we would have a lot more colourful memories by the time we went home. It was a beautiful day with clear blue sky and a stiff off-shore breeze. There were several catamarans out and lots of windsurfers were whizzing back and forth. When I reached Petros's shed I called 'Kalispera' to him and waved. He was sitting outside his shed but today he wasn't alone as Vasilas was sitting alongside him. Sometimes Vasilas's grandson looked after the sunbeds for him and I guessed that was what was happening today. They waved back at me.

As I approached the turn to the left for the track up the hill, I became aware of the laboured sound of an engine accompanied by extremely loud rattling and clattering. This didn't concern me because during the daytime the harbour and surrounding area were often filled with such noises. I rounded the sharp bend where, shortly after leaving the road, the track begins its ascent up the hill. Then I stopped aghast. A huge tip-up lorry was backing up and manoeuvring into position in the middle of the track. Anticipating what was coming next, open-mouthed I watched incredulously as the back of the lorry slowly raised and sent its load of dirt, rubble and large concrete blocks crashing onto the track.

'What are you doing?' I shouted helplessly, my voice drowned out by the whine of the engine and the cascading earth and rocks. As the dust slowly cleared, it revealed the way up to the house to be totally blocked by a haphazard, jagged wall of debris. Having accomplished his task, the driver stopped craning backwards out of the cab window and turning around noticed me fanning the dust out of my eyes.

'You going up there,' he smiled cheerily.

'Doesn't look like it, does it,' I responded.

'No, well that's the idea.'

'Whose idea?'

'Ah ha,' he grinned. 'Must be off, more work to do,' and with a wave he scrunched into forward gear and lurched off uprooting an oleander as he misjudged the corner.

I stood contemplating the 'wall' in front of me noticing a section of rather attractive mosaic tiles through which projected a length of pipe with a brass tap on the end. 'Could this once have been someone's bathroom?' I wondered. With a sheer crumbling rock face on one side of the track and a considerable drop into an olive grove on the other, circumventing the blockage just wasn't an option. I could have attempted to climb over the top but to do so also seemed unwise. If I dislodged part of the heap I might end up pinned down by a lump of concrete. There seemed nothing for it but to go back down to the harbour, walk along the beach to where it was possible to take a windy goat path through the prickly scrub and up the other side of the hill to the bottom of the garden.

I'd been home an hour or so and was brushing the patio and watering the bougainvillea and the pelargoniums that I had planted recently, when a very hot perspiring Spiros made an appearance in the garden. I'd been unable to concentrate on doing anything more creative or complicated than patio tidying for wondering about the reasons for the blocked track and what might happen next. I'd phoned John to alert him to the problem so he could leave the car on the harbour and, like I had done, take the goat path.

Spiros stumbled onto the patio puffing hard and wiping his brow with his sleeve. He sank onto the nearest chair. 'I've, I've, huh, huh come up, huh, from the beach,' he gasped an unnecessary explanation.

'You've seen what's happened to the track then?'

He nodded an affirmative. After gulping down a glass of water, finding his hanky to wipe his face and taking the time this took to get his breath back, he embarked on the story of the feud resulting in the blockade.

Stephanos, the owner of the olive grove below us, also claimed ownership of much of the hillside including the track. However, the latter was the subject of a long running disagreement between him and Leonidas the owner of our house. At the very end of the track close to the bottom of the garden, reputedly was the temple of Diana – well at least according to an official brown sign of the kind that marks such antiquities. There was nothing to see but a small pile of loose stones in the tiny overgrown site enclosed by rusty wire. However, traditionally there had always been a footpath to the temple that anyone was entitled to use.

Five or six years ago Leonidas had bulldozed into the hillside to make the track wide enough to get a car up to the house. Stephanos objected from the outset and complained to the council, who tut tutted sympathetically but did nothing, and so periodically he had made his annoyance known in the form of various obstructive fences made of tree branches, wire and old bedsteads. However, more recently the situation had worsened considerably.

Leonidas, on the death of his uncle, had been left a plot of land much higher up the hill where his uncle had once kept goats. Leonidas decided to build a house on it for his daughter when she married. In order to allow lorries to access the site he had widened the bottom of the track still further and cut a new track across the hillside to his plot. Stephanos was now locked in another major dispute with him over who owned what and the rubble blockade constituted his most effective protest to date.

'It's been going on for years,' beamed Spiros 'there just isn't an answer to it.'

'Well, will the rubble get shifted?' I asked despairingly, envisaging having to climb up and down the goat path to go anywhere and also lug groceries and other purchases up it. It would be hopeless.

'Oh could take months even years,' said Spiros vaguely, looking sad. However, on observing the upsetting effect on me of this statement, he broke into laughter and said, 'no, not really, sorry, don't worry. Word has probably already got to Leonidas and he won't stand for it. He'll have a digger down to clear a way through before the end of the week I bet.'

'Oh do you think so, what a relief. I couldn't imagine how we would manage just using the goat path.'

Spiros had only been gone for ten minutes when John appeared at the end of the garden. Having not seen the blockade he suggested we walk down from the house to look at it. We rounded the hill and 'Heaven help us,' John gasped, when confronted by the monstrous pile. 'Is that a toilet in amongst those rocks?' he enquired.

'Mmm, more than likely,' I confirmed, 'as part of a bathroom wall is on the other side.'

'What can we do? What did Spiros suggest?'

'Oh he was very upbeat as usual. He said Leonidas wouldn't stand for it and would get a digger to shift it really quickly.'

'Let's hope so,' said John, 'but it'll take a bit of doing.'

We retraced our steps back to the house and sat down despondently on the patio.

'There's nothing we can do, well certainly not at the moment, so let's do something positive to cheer ourselves up,' I suggested.

John agreed and thought that, as he was back quite early, we should go and do 'Angela's walk', so called by us after Angela who worked in the bakery and had originally recommended it to us. The circular walk out the back of Kefalos old town took about one and a half hours. It involved walking on the track up the hill through the wind turbines and following goat paths through a valley lined with juniper bushes and out into an open area of scrub, that sloped gently down to the rocky shoreline. Then there was another track that led past farms and cultivated fields back to the starting point.

When we reached a derelict farmhouse we sat on the cracked steps and absorbed the atmosphere. I leaned back against the bleached wooden doorpost, and stretched out my legs in front of me.

'It's lovely here. Look at the pink cistus and those tall yellow verbascum, they're so pretty. The air is full of the scent of sage, thyme and oregano and it's just so peaceful.'

The valley was totally sheltered from the strong winds that powered the wind turbines up on the hill and the silence was only disturbed by the rasping of the cicadas and the chattering of the little birds hidden in the leaves of the gnarled old tree behind the building.

'It's so green I think there must be water quite near to the surface.'

'Perhaps in winter there's a stream along the bottom of the valley,' suggested John.

'It certainly looks quite fertile,' I agreed.

In front of me was a large, flat patch of once tilled land, still free of scrub, that must have been used to grow vegetables. Alongside the house a smaller dwelling provided a byre in which to house a cow and goats in winter. The blue front door lay forlorn and broken at the side of the steps, but inside the stone and reed roof still kept the sun and rain out of the spacious but single room that comprised the house. It was easy to imagine a family's belongings stored in the wall alcoves and on the brick shelves and a fire burning cheerfully in the blackened hearth with the smoke billowing out of the ample chimney.

However, overly romantic images of what it might have been like to live there were quashed with the acknowledgement that the whole family had to share the one room with no personal space and no privacy. John sat down again beside me having got up to peer in the huge bake oven on the side of the house and speculate on how many loaves might have been fitted into it.

'I wonder how long ago the farm was abandoned,' he said. 'It doesn't feel as if it was that long ago but I suppose abandoned buildings don't deteriorate in this climate as fast as they do at home. I wonder whether relatives of those that farmed here still live in Kefalos,' he concluded.

We sat enjoying the golden light that marked the approach of evening for a little while longer before pulling each other to our feet, crossing what had once been the garden and setting off diagonally across the side of the valley on a goat path. We paused to admire the onset of sunset over the sea and to try unsuccessfully to coax a couple of small kid goats to come and say hello. Far too timid they preferred to chew on a young juniper bush and stare at us through the twigs. Then we increased our gait past the working farms to where we had left our car parked by the disused factory. We encountered lots more goats but saw no one apart from a hunter with his rifle slung over his shoulder riding his scooter in search of game, which as it was out of season he shouldn't be doing. His three dogs grateful for the exercise ran alternately in front of the scooter and behind him.

As we were driving back along the harbour I spotted Betty coming out of Aldi Plus and waved to her. Realising who was waving, she shook her hands above her head and ran after the car in a clear indication that she wanted us to stop. We pulled over and waited for her.

'I'm glad I've caught you as I was going to ring you this evening because I've some really good news. Anna and Alistair are going to get married in Kefalos.'

'Oh that's really great. It certainly is good news,' I responded. 'I'm not surprised you're so pleased but how did they come to make the decision?'

Betty explained, 'In Anna's last phone call she was telling me how she planned to give all the guests colourful umbrellas which would look pretty in the photos and they could use if it rained. Well after this, I was worrying about how disastrous it would be if everyone got soaked and her dress got wet and muddy, and I got to thinking what if I could persuade her and Alistair to come here with their wedding guests and have the ceremony on Kastri island. She could have exactly the service she wanted with Scottish traditions, although perhaps we could incorporate a few Greek touches, but good weather would surely be assured and Kastri island would make a lovely setting. I had to work quite hard to convince her how much better it would be and wondered afterwards whether I'd done the right thing, after all it's her wedding.'

'What did Alistair think?' I interjected.

'Well his view was what led her to change her mind and she seems very happy about it now and busy revising her plans. To my surprise I found I had an ally in Alistair. He could see lots of advantages in having the wedding here, not least that some of his relatives, whom he is not too keen on, wouldn't want to come because they don't like leaving Scotland. Also, I think he too was concerned about what would happen if it poured with rain and we all got soaked. I don't think he was reassured by Anna's claim that this wouldn't matter because in Scotland you don't worry about the weather, you just carry on regardless.'

'I can understand why you are relieved. Do you know where they will hold the reception?'

'Not yet, she and Alistair are going to come out for a long weekend in a couple of weeks time and they will go round and visit some possible restaurants and hotels and then they can choose.'

'It will be interesting to hear where they choose.'

'I'll keep you posted,' she promised before we headed off to park by the harbour and climb up the cliff to get home.

Fortunately, as was generally the case in relation to local matters, Spiros was absolutely right about Leonidas's reaction to the rubble blockade. The gossip in the shops the following day recounted the rage with which the news was received by Leonidas, who immediately went to see what had been done for himself. Two days later, mid-morning, I again heard the sound of a straining engine and clattering rocks. Hoping fervently that the rubble was being removed and not added to, I hastened to see what was happening. Rounding the corner to my immense relief I witnessed a large digger loading rubble and bits of bathroom back onto the same tip-up truck as had dumped it. Having ascertained the blockade was definitely going, I retreated back to the house to avoid being covered in dust as the wind was blowing it in my direction.

Spiros, also keen to check on the situation was around the minute the track was clear and he could drive up it again.

'I told you that Leonidas wouldn't allow Stephanos to get away with it,' he said. 'I bet Stephanos now regrets what he did and is wishing he hadn't done it,' he chuckled.

'Oh no what's happened now?' I asked correctly anticipating revenge.

'Well he got the driver to upend his truck over the wall around Stephanos's house and now all the rubble is in his yard. He can hardly get in his front door. Can you imagine?'

'I can,' I responded. 'It sounds horrendous but won't they get into trouble with the council or the police. I mean, surely you can't just go around dumping rubble on people's property?'

Spiros paused thoughtfully, then grinned. 'Well Stephanos phoned the police in Kos town but they told him they were far too busy dealing with refugees and preparing for an anti-austerity march to get involved in rubble wars and he would have to sort it out for himself.'

'So they won't do anything,' I questioned.

'No, no, they probably are busy, but the deputy police chief is Leonidas's cousin so Stephanos should have known he wouldn't get anywhere.'

'What will he do?' I asked.

'He'll just have to get the rubble shifted again.'

'Not back here I hope.'

'I don't think you need worry. He'll try and find another way of getting his own back on Leonidas. Good business for the tip-up truck driver though,' Spiros added with a wink.

9

Volcanoes and Natural Saunas on Nisyros

On Thursday morning we were woken up at 6am by heavy rain pelting down on the roof and the sound of the wind gusting around the house and whistling through crevices in the door and window frames.

'Goodness the weather sounds horrendous. We weren't expecting this were we?' I exclaimed.

'Not really, Otto did say that they were having storms in Athens but the forecast was that they wouldn't reach here,' John replied as he got out of bed to pull back the louvre doors to look out. 'The wind really is stirring up the sea. It was flat calm last night but it's pretty rough now.'

We both stood watching the waves breaking on the beach below. A catamaran that had been moored a little way out was tossing up and down with its mast swaying around and the tangled rigging dipping in and out of the water.

'Oh I hope that it's not going to be like this all day

because it will stop us going to Nisyros tomorrow,' I said dismayed.

'Hopefully not, but hmm, we'll just have to see,' John replied.

The next day we had planned to go to nearby Nisyros, a volcanic island and being only 41 square kilometres one of the smallest inhabited islands in the Dodecanese. Joy had fixed up some accommodation for us on the recommendation of a friend of hers, who owned a shop not far from the harbour in the capital Mandraki. We had been on a day trip to the island from Kefalos on our first Kos holiday but subsequently, although we had promised ourselves that we would, we hadn't got around to going back.

On that first visit, like most day-trippers, on arrival at the harbour we had been taken by coach to see the massive circular Stefanos volcanic crater, which with a radius of 180 metres occupies almost all the centre of the island. We climbed down from the rim onto the floor of the caldera. I remembered wandering around avoiding the pools of hot bubbling mud and feeling the intense heat burning through the soles of my sandals, praying that the earth I was standing on wouldn't collapse. The volcano was last active in 1888 but it felt as if it could erupt into life at any minute.

Afterwards we only had time for a brief look around the seafront of Mandraki and then it was time to take the boat back. Although fine and sunny on that occasion, I recalled that the sea had seemed rough particularly on the return trip. However, we were in the little Kefalos I which only took about eight passengers, whereas Kefalos II, which we had booked to go on this time, was much bigger.

After breakfast John ventured out in the strengthening winds and still pouring rain to find out, if as we feared, the boat would not be going to Nisyros tomorrow. When he returned he reported that Kefalos II was being moved from its mooring on the pier to inside the harbour walls and would definitely not be leaving the harbour tomorrow. He described how waves were crashing over the bay road and splashing the fronts of the restaurants but he had dodged getting too soaked and managed to reach Joy's office. She had phoned through to a tour office in Kardamena and booked us tickets on a larger and more powerful boat that the tour operator was sure would be going to Nisyros as usual.

Fortunately for us, we awoke on Friday to a beautiful morning with the wind little more than a stiff breeze. As planned with John, Joy picked us up at 8am from the chapel at the bottom of the hill.

'Hi how are you doing? You are lucky, it's going to be a lovely day so the boat trip should be fine.'

'Thanks so much for taking us to Kardamena and fixing us up with the boat from there,' I said as we got in the car.

'No problem, we just have to take the couple of my customers that I told John about to Mastihari.'

As we passed Sophia's supermarket it prompted me to ask, 'How have the trips to Ionna's honey business gone down with the holidaymakers on your Antimachia tours? Ionna told me she really enjoyed talking to them and showing them around and that she had sold lots of honey products from the shop.'

'Pretty well. Most found it interesting and thought she was very friendly and spoke excellent English so they could easily understand what she was telling them. One or two thought the tour spent a bit too long there but I think the timing was about right.'

We collected the elderly Belgium couple from her office. They were going on a Joyful Tour to Kalymnos and so after she had dropped them off on the quay at Mastihari, where they joined the rest of the tour goers, she took us to the harbour at Kardamena.

The boat left promptly at 9.30am and we arrived at Mandraki, which is about 13 kilometres away, an hour later.

Mandraki as well as being the island's capital and main port is home to about seven hundred of the island's around one thousand inhabitants. We easily found the souvenir shop in the old square in front of the town hall, where Joy's friend worked, and introduced ourselves to her. She told us that as the two Italian newly weds, who had rented the house were still there, Georgia the owner apologised for the delay to our moving in and asked if we could come back later. We assured her that we would be very happy to go exploring and arranged to return to meet Georgia and be taken to the house at 3pm. We left our bags in the shop and set off.

We found Mandraki to be a maze of narrow paved streets climbing up the hillside with sets of steps leading up and more steps leading back down. In front of the houses, on corners and at the top of flights of steps, we found delightful little open areas decorated by traditional designs of fish, dolphins and flowers depicted in small white and black pebbles. The closely packed houses had brown or blue painted wooden shutters, pots of flowers outside their doors and wooden balconies enhanced with climbing vines and bougainvillea. We thought them extremely attractive and took lots of photos.

Eventually, when back at sea level and feeling like a rest and beginning to get rather hungry, we stopped for a lunch of tuna salad and ice cream at a cafe overlooking the sea. After this we just had time to pop in a tour office to see if there was a bus to Pali that we could catch in the morning. Pali is a small fishing village four kilometres away, where we planned to start the walk to Emborios described in our walking map of Nisyros. Then from Emborios we were going to take footpaths back to Mandraki. Consequently, we were very pleased to be assured that there would be a yellow mini-bus leaving at 10am from the harbour. Then we returned to the shop where Georgia was waiting for us.

'I've got the car outside,' she said. 'It's quite a demanding walk up to the house because it's on the top level and also I want to stop at my home to collect clean linen.'

She drove past the harbour and ascended the levels via a winding road, stopping about halfway up at her house. This had a pretty garden which I commented on when she returned to the car with the linen. I also told her how we had enjoyed walking around the backstreets.

'We had no idea that Mandraki would be so attractive. We were surprised by the many beautifully kept houses.'

'We like welcoming tourists to Mandraki but we didn't want the town to be spoilt by tourist developments which has happened on a number of the other islands. Strict laws govern renovations and developments and this has ensured the town has kept its character. We are very happy about this. The inhabitants of Mandraki are very proud of it.'

'Well we are certainly very impressed by it.'

We were also shortly to be very impressed by her house where we were going to stay. Apparently, it had only been rented out since the beginning of May. It was a recently renovated old three storey house in pointed up volcanic stone and wood. Tucked into the cliff it had a tiny walled garden with a bougainvillea climbing up the corner but, as the garden was in full sun, it was probably too hot to sit out in during the afternoon.

The interior of the house was really lovely. It had beautiful wooden floors and beamed ceilings and the kitchen was fitted out with pale green, antique style, wooden units made by her husband, who was a carpenter and furniture maker. The bedroom had an unusual four poster bed and a fitted wardrobe all along one wall which had different kinds of blossom painted on each door. The upstairs windows all had wooden shutters which pleased John because he liked the bedroom to be really dark at night. The woodwork throughout was just magnificent. I particularly liked the door of the broom cupboard under the stairs, which had a tree in full blossom painted on it and the carved wooden front door with its climbing vine motif.

We had a brief siesta in the house but wanting to see as much as possible of the island on our weekend there, we soon decided to go out again.

'Let's go and see the Paleokastro,' I suggested. 'As we are on the top level of Mandraki we probably won't have to do too much climbing to get to it.'

'Good idea. Do we know anything about it?'

'Not really. The information on the back of the map says it's a really ancient fortress, 7th century BC but it doesn't say who built it.'

We headed towards the Kastro on the road and then came to an old monopati with a sign indicating that it went to the castle. We took the monopati and soon arrived at what was a very impressive defensive bastion with its black walls built of massive blocks of volcanic rock. We walked around the outside until we came to a wide intact archway. Just inside was a huge staircase leading up to the top of the walls.

'Come on,' said John starting up the steps. 'I bet there's a great view up there.'

'It looks a bit vertiginous,' I replied hesitantly, as there wasn't a handrail on the open side of the steps. Still they were very wide and so I quickly followed not looking down over the side.

From the top of the walls we could see that we had the castle and its environs completely to ourselves. As John anticipated we did indeed have a fantastic view. The town of Mandraki was laid out before us with our house in clear sight. Over the sea we could see Kos, and the island of Yali, which we had passed close by in the boat from Kardamena. From the boat we had seen the quarry which seemed to have devoured much of the island. Apparently it exports pumice stone all around the world and brings considerable wealth to Nisyros.

We sat there taking in the view and watching the sky with its warm and increasingly orange glow as sunset approached. Inside the castle there wasn't really anything further to see, as there were virtually no markings indicating how it might have been laid out.

'Have you any thoughts about where we might go for dinner?' I asked.

'According to a drawing on the wall in the tour office there's a big square called Platia Ilikiomeni, somewhere in the middle of Mandraki which has several restaurants. I thought that we would go to there. I'm surprised that we didn't come upon it when we were exploring this morning.'

We retraced our steps along the monopati but, when we came to the road to our house, we took the first flight of steps downhill. On the way down a group of elderly locals were sitting on a wall chatting and so we asked them for directions to the square which was then easily located.

The square was full of tables making it quite difficult to work out which tables belonged to which restaurants and what any difference in those restaurants might be. Consequently, we hovered in the middle debating whether and where to sit. When approached by one of the Lachanikos waiters, we were persuaded to sit down in the centre by the trunk of a truly massive fiscus tree. John, thinking the name Lachanikos might have some relationship to vegetables given *lachanika* is Greek for vegetable, suggested that this restaurant would be a good choice for me and indeed it did have a number of vegetarian dishes. However, Lachanikos turned out to be the surname of Marcos, the owner of the restaurant.

I chose chickpea patties flavoured with dill and a Greek salad that unusually also came with carrot and celery. John opted for lamb stew. The square soon got increasingly busy but with as many, if not more, locals than tourists. It seemed that, like us on our first visit to the island, the majority of tourists had departed by four o'clock. The staff at

Lachanikos proved to be very friendly and over coffee we chatted to Marcos. He told us that he had a goat farm near the Evangelista monastery which, as we were planning to go walking, we would be sure to see because several of the old paths converged there. When he learned that we had never eaten goat, he sought to persuade John that he should definitely try it.

The next day we were at the harbour for the 10am bus, which contrary to the assurances of the girl in the tourist office, failed to materialise. As we stood disappointed and wondering about our next move, a man turned up, set up a desk and was selling volcano excursion tickets. He saw us waiting for the non-existent bus and asked us if we had a problem. We explained and he told us if we were prepared to wait he would get us a ride to Pali.

Thirty minutes later we boarded a coach and joined a group of Polish day-trippers, who were going to the volcano. As instructed by our rescuer, the driver set us down above Pali where a side road down to the harbour left the road to the crater. Feeling very grateful for the way things had turned out, we strolled cheerfully down the road until we saw a set of steps straight down to the harbour which we took to cut off a lengthy corner.

We had an interesting wander around looking at the

flashy yachts and colourful fishing boats. We walked onto the long concrete pier to watch a smart looking blue and white fishing boat equipped with radar and piled high with nets and buoys come in and moor up. Once the boat was secure the three fisherman began unloading their catch onto the quay. While they did so, a three-wheeler van towing a trailer with a large set of scales drew alongside. We asked the men what the fish were and found out that they were red snapper. We told them we had enjoyed grilled snapper on several occasions but hadn't seen them freshly caught before. Then John asked if he could take some photographs and they jokingly agreed holding up some large specimens. He took lots of photos of them setting up their scales on the quay and proceeding to weigh the fish.

'It's really interesting here but, as we have a long way to go, I think that we had better move on,' I said as the men concluded sorting the snappers.

'Yes you're right,' John replied placing his camera back in its bag and putting it over his shoulder. Taking out the walking map he consulted the instructions.

'We need to walk along the street parallel to this one and look out for a left turn through the village. This will then become the monopati that we need to start the walk.'

As is all too often the case, finding the beginning of a

walk can prove frustratingly tricky. Consequently we wandered back and forth on the street not knowing how far along it we should find the desired left turn. Eventually after taking an early left turn that took us into a neglected garden, we found the monopati up through an alley with houses on each side. It continued uphill as a series of wide stone steps between crumbling stone walls and shaded by ancient trees. Ultimately we reached a white wall of large stones that marked the boundary of the old town and where we paused to look at the view of Pali and the pumice island.

At this point the steps increasingly disintegrated into piles of rubble until we reached the road at the top. We crossed over and found the footpath heading towards Emborios. It was rather overgrown but clearly marked with red dots. The map showed that the path climbed beyond Emborios and so, if we wanted to get there, we needed to leave the monopati but the problem was at what point.

'We should be leaving this path or we are going to miss Emborios,' said John. 'The directions say that we should keep going uphill until we reach a footpath going beneath a chapel. There is supposed to be an old mule track that we can follow which will take us to the footpath.'

'Do you think that we might have missed it or maybe it's completely overgrown?' I speculated.

'The mule track off was supposed to be marked with a red arrow which I've been looking out for but I haven't seen one. Still I reckon the chapel mentioned must be that chapel we can see over there. Then off that footpath we should find another stepped path up to Emborios. I think we may have to just head for the chapel.'

'Well I hope that we don't get lost,' I said but agreed, 'you're right we can see where we should be heading.'

Having come to the decision to go cross country we left the path and set off across open grassland. This was easy walking but then we found ourselves slithering and struggling through a wide area of loose pumice. Just as we had lost sight of the chapel in the bend of the hill and were beginning to lose confidence in our strategy, we thankfully came across the gulley mentioned on the map. As instructed, we walked along the side of it and took the path at its head. This quickly brought us to the road and a landmark water tank which meant that we were back on track.

What followed was a very hot sweaty climb up a stepped monopati to Emborios but at least, while a number of the steps had disintegrated, it was clear where we needed to go. On the way up we encountered two unusually lethargic Germans laying down under an oak tree.

'Hello,' one called propping himself up on his elbow. 'Are you going to Emborios?'

'Hopefully,' I replied. 'Are you?'

'When we have had a rest and cooled down. Where have you come from?'

'We are staying in Mandraki but we've walked from Pali.'

'We have walked from Pali too, but we are staying there.'

'Did you have any problems finding the way to this monopati because we did?' asked John.

'No, because at the top of the steps out of Pali we just walked along the road until we came to the beginning of it. Our walking book said that you needed a pioneering spirit and long trousers to take the footpaths and, as we are not feeling adventurous today and we are wearing shorts, we thought we would take the easy route.'

'Probably a wise decision. Our shorts didn't cause us any problems, except in a few places, but we did feel like pioneers at times,' said John.

'Yes and we had to scramble across this big area of loose pumice stones which was hard work,' I added. 'You won't have minded missing that.'

'Well enjoy your rest. I think we will get going again,'

John said as he turned to resume heading up the steps.

'Perhaps we will see you in Emborios,' added the other German as he pulled his hat down over his eyes.

We climbed steadily up to where the monopati came out on the road into Emborios, only stopping to talk to, and pat the nose of, a gentle lonely looking donkey. I felt really sorry for him. He seemed so pleased with our attention and there were no other animals or any sign of human habitation to provide him with some company. He reminded me of the donkey I'd befriended in Patmos.

Almost immediately on the right on the outskirts of Emborios was the natural sauna in a grotto that was mentioned on our map. Out of its white painted stone entrance gushed masses of boiling steam. It felt tremendously hot as we approached and so we weren't inclined to linger.

Natural saunas are a fascinating feature of Nisyros and have been used there since Roman times. Close to Mandraki by a small marina are the buildings of the municipal baths of Loutra constructed at the beginning of the 20th century. Once they formed a luxurious resort housing up to three hundred people who came to experience the curative powers of the hot sulphurous waters. Apart from one end building, where in faded grandeur you can still bathe in the mineral waters, the buildings are derelict. Also to the east of Pali there are the ruins of the Pantelides baths. Built in 1910 this was an even grander spa resort utilising the hot springs and it attracted a great many visitors from all around the Mediterranean. However, when its owner died 18 years later, it too deteriorated into ruins.

The crumbling buildings of Emborios stretched up the mountainside above us. Obviously it was once a large village before it was abandoned after the earthquake in 1933. We had been told that now some of the houses are being done up by wealthy Athenians and foreigners. Certainly, as we climbed the steps into the village and went along the narrow alley between the buildings, there were plenty of signs of repair work being undertaken. However, we didn't encounter any actual workmen and there were little signs of anyone living there apart from lots of contented looking cats dozing in the shade.

The taverna Baltani had been recommended to us for lunch. It wasn't difficult to find as it was the only taverna and was next to the nicely restored blue and white church with its pretty layered bell tower. We entered the taverna and went through to the back terrace which had a truly magnificent view over the Stefanos crater. Thirsty after all the climbing, we quickly downed two welcome Fantas and ordered our lunch. I decided on a cheese omelette and John had stuffed squid. When we were on the ubiquitous Nescafe and mini baklavas another customer came in and took the table beside us and ordered a beer and a moussaka.

'Wow! What a view,' he said to us as he tipped back on his chair and stretched out.

'It certainly is, the village seems to be perched right on the edge of the crater,' John replied.

'Is this the first time you have been here?' the customer, who seemed keen to chat, asked.

'Yes we have just walked here on the footpaths from Pali.'

'How long did it take you? I've come from Pali as well but I biked up the road.'

'That must have been hard work and hot,' I joined in. 'It took us about three hours to walk but we stopped to take lots of photos.'

'It certainly was hot but I'm used to cycling in all conditions as I do triathlons. I brought my road bike from Switzerland and I'm using it to explore the islands. It's easy to take on the ferries.'

'We often hire bikes on holiday,' said John, 'but we are definitely not up to tackling mountain biking.'

'Did you see the steam bath on the edge of the village?'

I said. 'We thought that was interesting. Apparently, some of the houses had natural saunas in their basements.'

'I like to have a sauna but I'm not sure I'd want a volcanic one in my house. Did you see it?' asked the cyclist.

'Yes, it was really hot. I think you would be scalded if you tried to go in,' I responded.

At that moment his lunch arrived and so we wished him enjoyable cycling and took our leave, as we weren't sure how easy it would be to find our way back to Mandraki. We climbed the steps to the upper village where several of the ruined houses were well on the way to being restored. However, we still saw no one working on, or living in, them. We left the top of the village by a path high above the valley. Several metres along it a goat, or perhaps birds, sent an avalanche of small rocks hurtling down in front of us from the peak above. The rocks narrowly missed John who, as is customary, was in the lead.

We quickened our pace and hastened along the path with more rocks raining down behind us. When we felt confident that we were not in danger of being pelted by any more, we stopped to enjoy the fabulous view. We could look back at the white houses of Emborios, in front of us up the mountainside to a white walled cemetery and to our left across the wide valley. Initially the narrow path was decorated with the tall white flowers of foxtail lilies. Then the hillside became barren and the path ran beside some strange looking grey volcanic rocks punctuated with holes.

Rounding the final peak on the walk we could see the sea and Yali, Kos and Kalymnos. From then on the walking became easier and the way clearly marked. When we came to an abandoned farmhouse on the terraced hillside we stopped to take a look inside. It had stone walls with recesses in for cupboards and stone shelves and even the remains of a stone ceiling. It also had stone arches in the centre, which we learned later were a feature of traditional Nisyros buildings in order to give them extra strength to withstand earth tremors. We also observed earth packed between the stones in the walls to give them flexibility and prevent the walls from cracking if shaken.

Soon after leaving the farmhouse we crossed an attractive flat green area of holm oaks and olives and walked through buttercups, poppies, and past cistus bushes covered in pink flowers. Next we passed through an extremely decrepit farmyard and along a narrow path between fences until, as anticipated by Marcos, we arrived at the impressive but closed Evangelista monastery. There we sat and rested under its huge terebinth tree.

Afterwards, we alternated between sections of monopati along agricultural terraces and stretches of road in order to arrive back in Mandraki. By rather surprising coincidence, when we happened to be on the road, Marcos probably going to see to his goats came towards us on his scooter and waved as he went past. In the evening we returned to his restaurant and as creatures of habit, we sat down at the same table that we had occupied the previous evening.

'Did you enjoy your walk? Where had you been?' Marcos enquired.

'We had a wonderful walk along old monopatis and mule tracks. We went to Emborios from Pali and then from Emborios back to Mandaki,' I told him proud of our achievement. 'We were on the final homeward stretch when we saw you.'

'You certainly walked a long way but I'm sure you enjoyed Emborios. The views are spectacular from there. Did you have lunch in Baltani looking out over the crater? Most visitors do.'

We took this as an invitation to describe the highlights of our most enjoyable day and our meal at Baltani.

'But after all that exercise you will be hungry again now I hope.'

'Yes,' said John, 'Definitely.'

'Well you must have goat as you said that you have never tried it. It's excellent. I must persuade you.'

'OK you have, as you highly recommend it,' said John smiling.

'And you as well,' he turned to me.

'No, I don't think so. I'd like to have your vegetarian moussaka.'

'Very good choice too. It's my wife's recipe. A lot of English visitors are vegetarians and they all compliment her on her moussaka.'

After we had eaten, over a glass of local wine, which tasted much better than expected, we discussed our plans for another walk the next day. We thought we would first go to Nikia to have a look around. Nikia is a hill village on the east side of the Stefanos crater about 14 kilometres from Mandraki. From there we planned to walk down into the crater and then take a different route out and back above the coast to Mandraki. Marcos came to find out our plans and so we asked him if there was a bus to Nikia, and if there was, how likely was it that it would turn up.

Next morning there was no chance of oversleeping as the Greek Orthodox service and Mass boomed out loudly from the monastery of Our Lady Spiliani. The monastery looks extremely picturesque. Lit up at night, painted white and tucked in the corner of the ruins of the 14th century castle built by the Knights of Saint John, it is perched high on a cliff overlooking Mandraki.

After a leisurely breakfast we were in good time for the 10am bus to Nikia which arrived punctually as promised by Marcos. Nikia with its blue and white houses clinging to the crater rim turned out to be very picturesque and, unlike Enborios, bustling with inhabitants. We enjoyed wandering through the narrow stepped alleys decorated with pots of red, pink and orange pelargoniums. The round central square of Platia Porta in front of the church paved with a circular pebble mosaic was a meeting place for locals and tourists alike. A viewpoint from it showed the entirety of the enormous barren crater with its steep sulphur stained walls and floor pockmarked from fumaroles. Across the other side of the crater, we watched the tour buses come and go.

First, however, before making our descent we decided to make a detour. From behind the bus stop we took the path down to see the monastery of Agios Ioannis Theologis. Well before we arrived we could hear signs of socialising. Locals were sat around tables in the monastery yard drinking coffee and eating snacks. The priest in the centre was addressing them. Obviously he was doing so in a very entertaining way because everyone was laughing. One group smiled at us and gestured for us to join them which we did – would that we could speak Greek. We learned from one of them that the previous evening there had been a festival service at the monastery and partying, prior to clearing up, had resumed in the morning. As the priest was happy for us to do so, John took some photos. Then we participated in the convivial atmosphere until a small group stood up and stacked their chairs and so we decided to retrace our steps back to the village.

Back in Nikia we found a quiet cafe with tables in the shade. Opposite, in the sun outside a taverna, some British tourists sat drinking beer and chatting with their tour guide until their coach arrived and off they went to their next stop. We had lemonade, Greek salad and traditional rice pudding made by the waiter's mum. Such rice pudding was a favourite of John's from his student days in Greece and he often sought unsuccessfully to find some and so he waxed lyrical to the waiter about this unanticipated delight. Over lunch a ping from my phone alerted me to the fact that I had a text message from Joy in response to the one that I sent her saying how much we liked the accommodation that she had organised for us.

'Joy is really pleased that we like the house and are

having a good trip,' I told John.

I also told him about the contents of an email from Jan that I'd just read.

'Jan says that she is feeling pleased with herself because Andreas has complimented her on her handling of an incident. Apparently a hire car reversed into the parked motorbike hired from Budget by a young couple. They were very upset because it had knocked the bike over and damaged it and then speeded off. They managed to note the hire company the car came from but didn't get the car registration. Jan calmed them down and reassured them about the insurance they had taken out with Budget. Also through contacting the other hire firm, she found out who had caused the damage as when the car was returned the back was scratched and had a slight dent. Jan is really enjoying her job,' I concluded. 'It seems to be doing wonders for her confidence. She is going to come round when we're back and tell me more.'

Refreshed, it was time for us to climb down into the crater. Back behind the bus stop again, we found the steps that led to the zigzag trail to the crater floor. The path down through the scrub was well marked and we made speedy progress until, when were nearly at the bottom, it disappeared in dead vegetation, cinders and stones. The further we headed down, the more the unpleasant bad egg smell of sulphur rising up toward us got stronger and stronger.

As we crossed the crater floor the last tourist bus was leaving, and so we congratulated ourselves on our perfect timing because now we were the only ones there. We walked over the crater floor as we had done so many years earlier and marvelled again at its massive size and circular walls. However, we thought that there was much reduced volcanic activity. There was less steam escaping from the fissures and cracks and none of the scary bubbling mud pools that we remembered and of which we had taken photos.

'The map shows a trail to the Polyvotis crater which is over there,' John pointed. 'I suggest we go and take a look at it.'

'Good idea. We didn't see that when we were here before,' I replied.

We took the narrow trail up out of the Stefanos crater and towards the Polyvotis crater. As we approached, we could see lots of steam escaping from three of its crevices and its surface was covered in purple, pink, green and yellow colouration.

'Oh! er.' A sudden hissing as steam spurted out of a vent

made me jump. 'There's much more volcanic activity here,' I said.

When we had seen enough of the activity of the Polyvotis crater, we climbed back down, circumvented the now deserted admission booth and walked around the left of the Stefanos crater until we picked up a wide track far under Nikia. From there we started the long slog up the hillside which was featureless apart from rocks and the odd cactus. The mid afternoon sun was exceedingly hot making us feel weary and dehydrated. Eventually we reached the top of the ridge and soon after we were extremely pleased to see the pretty blue and white Stavros monastery.

We sat on a stone bench in the chapel courtyard sipping water and appreciating its cool shade for nearly an hour after which we were reenergised and ready to move on. We started the trek down the dirt track to Mandraki in the late afternoon sunlight. The sea below us was shimmering brilliantly and we could clearly see the nearer three islands and just make out the distant island of Astypalia in the heat haze. The dirt track seemed to go on forever but eventually it took us to the monopati that led down from the castle to the road past our house.

It was past eight o'clock before we got to Lachanikos for dinner and recounted to Marcos our day's explorations.

'You caught the bus to Nikia?' asked Marcos.

'Yes and it was bang on time,' said John.

'We enjoyed looking around Nikia, like Mandraki it has some very pretty alleys and Platia Porta is very attractive,' I added.

'Did you take the trail down into the crater?'

'Yes, but first we went to the monastery perched on the hillside and found lots of locals enjoying a gathering there.'

'They would have had a festival there the evening before. I don't know which one that would be. Their main festival day is in September. The crater is quite a sight don't you think?'

'Yes it's amazing but we've seen it once before years ago. We also went to the Polyvotis crater because we hadn't been there before.'

'Do you know the story of Polyvotis. Did you hear him groaning?'

'No, but do tell us about him and why he is groaning.'

'Well he was a giant that angered Poseidon, who in revenge tore a huge rock from the island of Kos and crushed the giant to death with it. The sound of the cauldron bubbling beneath the crater is poor old Polyvotis groaning.'

'Well he wasn't groaning today, probably just as well as that would be scary,' I grinned.

'Well where to tomorrow?'

'Back to Kos I'm afraid,' said John. 'We have the morning here first, so we thought we'd take a closer look at the little monastery of Panagia Spiliana.'

'Your visit has been too short. There are lots more walks you could do. You haven't climbed the peak and you get great views from up there.'

'We've really loved Nisyros. We'd no idea from our day visit how fascinating it would be and so good for walking. We will definitely come back some time,' John assured him.

'Make sure that you do and that you come here for dinner, best eating place in Nisyros.' He winked at us, as he turned to see to a family who were considering where to sit.

As promised in her email, Jan called around at the house the afternoon after we got back from Nisyros. We sat on the patio and I told her about our trip and how much we enjoyed it before giving way to my curiosity and reminding her that she had promised to tell me more about how her job was going.

'I really like it,' she enthused. 'I enjoy chatting to customers about their holidays when they are booking their cars. It's very sociable which I find a major plus. Back in England working on editing from home most of the time, I was getting too used to just being alone and I don't think that was good for me.'

'In your email about the young couple and the damaged motorbike you sounded really confident about the way you are handling everything.'

'Well,' she paused. 'I was anxious at first that I'd do something wrong or forget something important but Sandra was really helpful showing me what to do and at first when I was on my own Andreas's dad popped in a couple of times to make sure that I was OK.'

'Have you been able to use your Italian?' I asked remembering that she had said that Andreas thought her knowledge of the language would be useful.

'Yes quite a bit, which I was glad about. We have had four Italian couples come in and they were pleased that I could speak their language. They all hired cars so,' she laughed, 'it may well have been good for business. Andreas is really delighted that he has just got a contract with In Paradise which has lots of English and Italian guests and he says, if I'd like to, I can take a turn with Sandra looking after the desk there which might be fun.'

'I remember a couple of years ago when Explore had a contract with a hotel complex near Tigaki, which enabled them to have a hire desk in the reception. Elias told me that he paid a lot for this but it had brought them a lot of business. However, he discovered through a friend, whose sister was a cleaner there, that three of the other cleaners in the pay of the Best Deal hire firm based in Kos town were touting for business and offering potential customers car rental at a cheaper price. To try to put a stop to the clandestine rentals, he rang the owner of Best Deal several times pointing out what he paid for the privilege of having a rental base in reception and he also complained to the manager of the hotel. Nevertheless, the touting for business continued so eventually in desperation he sanctioned his father's suggestion to solve the problem the old fashioned way. His dad took the oldest car in the fleet and reversed into one of the waiting hire cars severely denting first the driver's door and then the passenger door. The next day the cars were gone, seemingly proving the effectiveness of traditional Greek methods over negotiations to remove competition.'

'Goodness didn't Best Deal go to the police?' she asked wide-eyed.

'Apparently not, perhaps there was more to the story, or maybe there were reasons the police turned a blind eye.'

'Well I hope Andreas doesn't have similar problems with In Paradise because I doubt he would resort to such extreme tactics.'

'I'm really glad that the job is working out so well and you are enjoying it. Have you told Regi about it yet?' I asked suspecting she might not have done.

'Yes I have. He phoned me from Taiwan a couple of days ago and so I thought that I mustn't leave it any longer, I'd better tell him. I really expected that he would be annoyed because I'd gone ahead with the job without consulting him but amazingly he wasn't bothered. To be honest, while I was glad he didn't make a fuss and start criticising me as I expected, it was kind of upsetting that he didn't seem that interested.'

'That does seem surprising from what you've told me about him,' I agreed. 'Did he ask you anything about what the job involved or who you were working with?'

'No, not really. He mainly wanted to talk about how well the course he is teaching is going. Also, about how he has started working on a research proposal with a couple of the professors in the department where he is based, and how optimistic they are that they will get funding from the university and the Taiwanese government.'

'Well I'm glad you've told him and he didn't react negatively, as it means you can enjoy your job not worrying about what he thinks. You told me Sandra said that Andreas was good to work for. Do you see much of him?'

'He is away quite a lot delivering and collecting cars and negotiating new business. However, he does tend to come in most afternoons and works in the back on the paperwork.'

'Well do you have much to do with him and what do you think of him that's what I want to know,' I admitted smiling at her. 'After all you said you thought him attractive.'

'In the afternoon, when it's quiet and he feels like a break from admin, he usually makes us a drink and we have a chat over it. A couple of days ago, when it was time for me to go, he said he felt like a walk and was going to close up the office and go and take the footpath up the peak behind where you live. He said you get a great view of Kamari from the top and asked me if I'd like to go with him.'

'John and I have done that walk several times and the view is lovely. Did you go with him?'

'Yes. While I was saying to him that I liked the idea, I was thinking that I shouldn't go really but I enjoy his company and I told myself what harm would it do and it would be fun.'

'And was it?'

'Yes it was very much so. When I go walking with

Regi, which isn't very often, he likes to walk quickly so I either have to half run to keep up or, what usually happens is, I follow several metres or so behind him. Andreas walked at my speed. He identified the bird song we heard walking up through the woods and pointed out wild flowers to me. When we reached the little chapel on the way up he knew where the door key is kept and he opened it for me so I could go inside. When we walked past a lot of rusty remains he told me about the mine that was once there. He didn't lecture at me like Regi would have done. He just wanted to tell me things to make the walk interesting for me. Then when we reached the end of the path, we sat looking over the harbour and he told me about his childhood in Kefalos and I told him about growing up on my parents' sheep farm in Northumberland. I think that we were both reluctant to leave and walk back down.'

'You sound really happy describing your time with Andreas,' I said observing how her face lit up when she spoke about him.

'I wanted to tell you about it because he said that next week he would like to drive me to the end of the road on the peninsula and then we could take the footpath to the place overlooking Skinou bay and take a picnic. I responded that would be really nice because I want to go and to see more of him but do you think it was sensible of me?' she asked.

'Well I'm not sure I'd describe it as sensible but it might be right for the two of you. It depends on what sort of relationship you want with him, just a friend or something more. I mean he isn't married or living with anyone and so there is no problem there but, if you encourage him to think you want him to be more than a friend, it could be difficult and embarrassing if you subsequently change your mind and have to cool it.'

'I admit I'm really attracted to him and believe he feels the same way about me. To be truthful I want to spend time with him and get closer to him,' she said somewhat defiantly. 'I know I should feel guilty because of Regi but I just don't. I don't think that there is any chance of Regi being unfaithful to me while he is in Taiwan so I haven't that as an excuse. However, I'm quite sure he won't miss me either or even give me much thought.'

'Maybe the easiest and the best thing to do is to take it slowly with Andreas, let him determine the nature of your relationship and if, and how it develops, and just see what happens,' I advised, suspecting that this was what the newly independent Jan would do anyway.

10

In and Out of Paradise

The alarm peeped away in increasingly piercing and insistent tones. I put out a hand to silence it, but miscalculated its whereabouts and knocked the protesting alarm off the narrow stool acting as a bedside table. The alarm rolled under the bed from where a muffled peep continued. Cursing it through a yawn I went down on my knees to rescue it, dusted off some fluff and returned it to its rightful place on the stool. We had been out late the previous evening having gone to Sunset beach for dinner with Betty and Mike and then gone back to their place for coffee. John needed to go out early to Kos town to collect some sails that had been repaired and I wanted plenty of time to get ready to go to meet Julia an old college friend.

Recently divorced from her fourth husband, Julia was staying at the newly opened In Paradise resort in order, as she put it, to restore her equilibrium and decide the future direction of her life. I hadn't seen her during the three years of her latest marriage because she was seldom in England. Her exceedingly wealthy ex-husband made his millions selling cement to the United Arab Emirates, the need for which wasn't difficult to imagine judging from the vast numbers of unfinished skyscrapers we had witnessed there on a recent working trip. The last time I had heard from her, some eighteen months ago, she claimed to be living the dream in Dubai, where shopping was to die for and the parties out of this world. I wondered what had ended the dream and brought her to Kos, but was aware from experience that I would know the answer in every detail by the end of my visit.

Julia, tall and dark, sophisticated and statuesque, had always been surrounded by attentive males as she searched continually for the right man. Each boyfriend, partner and husband had been richer and handsomer than the one before and the relationships shorter lasting, as she discovered previously undetected flaws in their personalities or she simply became bored and wanted to move on.

While being five foot three inches blonde and not in the least imposing, I knew there was no way I could compete. Still, I was slim and people told me that I was young looking for my age and, as usual, wanted to meet her looking my best. Having been up late the previous night wasn't a good start but once I had had a shower and washed my hair I should hopefully see an improvement. However, the odds were further stacked against me. Having vigorously shampooed my hair the shower spluttered, dripped and died. 'Oh sod it! How could it?' I pointlessly turned the dial back and forth, knowing with a sinking heart that the water probably wouldn't return for two or three hours. When the water went through phases of total unreliability, I kept buckets and saucepans of it on standby for such predicaments. However, lately the water had been well behaved and I was unprepared.

Fortunately, we had just restocked with bottled water, as the water from the mains supply, even when well behaved, was usually the colour and consistency of insufficiently stirred powdered milk. Safe to drink when boiled, it contained myriads of white particles in suspension which floated unappetisingly to the top of tea and coffee.

I dripped my way to the kitchen, eyes stinging from shampoo, and returned with four bottles of still water with which I doused myself. I was thankful that John was out because he certainly would have been outraged. He continuously moaned about having to buy bottled water and the damage to the environment done by the stacks of plastic bottles as nothing on the island was recycled. An hour later, hair dry with a little carefully applied make up and in my smartest shorts and a new Armani top, which probably wasn't really Armani because of the tourist shop it came from, I was ready to meet my glamorous friend.

At about half past nine I set off in Mabel who unusually cooperative started straightaway. While there wasn't a breath of wind, there was still a little coolness left in the morning air but it was obviously going to be a very hot day. Inland lots of tiny thin clouds hung motionless in the sky. Over the bay, a pale washed-out sky disappeared into the silvery haze which lay delicately over the water obscuring Nisyros and the mountain. The last of the colourful little fishing vessels made lines in the glass top sea as they chugged into the harbour to unload their catch.

Along the harbour road tourists were heading purposefully to the beach and restaurant owners were sweeping their forecourts and rearranging the tables and chairs. Dodging in and out of the parked cars and large restaurant boards advertising variants on gargantuan English breakfasts, I swerved to avoid a meandering truck overflowing with melons. On automatic pilot the driver was facing backwards out of the window continuing a conversation with some men fishing from the pavement.

Going slowly I became increasingly aware of a strong

smokey smell. As I passed Petros's plot I glanced over to his shed to see if it was open and he was there. Without thinking I braked and incurred an indignant toot from the car behind as I took in the totally unexpected fact that his shed was a charred heap. What could have happened to the shed? I questioned myself. Surely no arsonist would want to set fire to it. When I came back I would have to find out.

I speeded up once on the main road out of Kefalos and wondered why there was a veritable queue of traffic coming in the opposite direction. Was something out of the ordinary going on in Kefalos we didn't know about? Round the next bend was the answer – roadworks! I jammed on the brakes to stop behind the white tourist car in front of me, brought to a halt by a road worker jumping riskily in front of it holding a red wooden baton. Up ahead nothing was happening. 'Oh no!' I said aloud.

Greek roadworks were a new experience for me and judging from the number of potholes were an infrequent occurrence. 'Why now, why here?' I correctly anticipated I was in for a lengthy wait. Coming towards me an ancient and very rusty old lorry appeared spraying tar from its underneath. Gathering speed alarmingly as it advanced, I was glad I wasn't in the car in front as it lurched to a halt centimetres from the tourist's bonnet. It reversed drunkenly back and charged again, a process repeated five times until the whole road was thickly coated with pungent smelling tar.

Next an equally rusty but painfully slow moving lorry took its turn to go backwards and forwards dumping intermittent piles of gravel. Behind that followed a bulldozer to spread the gravel and finally an ancient steam roller clanked back and forth. By this time there was a long tailback of traffic. Tourists were leaving their cars to discuss and take photos of the process.

'Now if this was England, they would have done one side of the road at a time so the traffic could still get through.'

'Well, it ain't mate, you've nothing to be in a rush for have you?'

'No, but suppose I was going to the airport.'

The driver of the bus immediately behind me with Terrific Turkish Tours on the side obviously was in a hurry. Probably he wanted to catch the ferry to Bodrum from Kos town so that his passengers could embark on a terrific tour. He indicated his displeasure by periodic bouts of extreme tooting. An elderly Greek waiting in an old van at the other end of the roadworks obviously decided he wasn't prepared to sit there any longer. He set his van to climb precariously up the bank, after which he proceeded to bounce along the field past where I sat waiting and disappeared out of sight in my rear view mirror.

'Bloody nutter,' muttered one of the onlookers.

'Oh, can we do that dad?' asked his son obviously impressed.

'How is he going to get back down on the road again?' asked someone else, observing that the gradient of the bank grew increasingly steep.

'He might get stuck in the field,' said a woman a trifle anxiously.

'Well serve him bloody right, bloody nutter.'

'He'll be a local so I'm sure he'll know a way out,' laughed one of the photographers returning down the line to his car.

While this conversation was going on, the more impatient and intrepid scooter and quad bike riders began skidding along the verge bouncing through the scrub and stones. At last after three quarters of an hour learning how Greek islanders repair their roads and watching the antics of those refusing to be further delayed, I got through the roadworks.

Fifteen minutes later I arrived at Bubble beach so named because, at various places in the shallow sea, volcanic activity deep below the sea floor causes hot air bubbles to rise and pop on the surface. A fence and high hedges surrounded the extensive In Paradise resort situated on the high cliffs overlooking the bay and so effectively closed it off to the public. Splendid ornamental portals marked the entrance across which there were barriers manned by security guards.

I left the car in the carpark outside, walked over to the barrier and announced that I was there to visit an inmate and friend. I was told to wait by the barrier for her to come and get me. I was looking forward to seeing Julia and to looking around the resort. At night on the far side of Kamari bay, the bright lights of In Paradise shone out like a small city, so I was definitely curious to see what it was like.

Extraordinarily for the islands, where an amazingly lengthy timespan was normally required to build even the most modest of houses and expat pensioners despaired of experiencing their dream retirement homes within their lifetime, the resort had been completed within its two-year schedule. Its speedy completion had been received with considerable shock and some antagonism in Kefalos. It was correctly anticipated that there would be little additional employment for local people and that few visitors to the all-inclusive resort would venture to Kefalos. To make matters worse, a major holiday company that filled the local studios with tourists on package deals pulled out cancelling their contracts in favour of working with the more administratively straightforward and lucrative In Paradise.

However, much to their welcome surprise the resort brought unanticipated business to the owners of the small blocks of inexpensive studios with no view, pools, bars or other facilities that previously had to rely for custom on backpackers and returning regulars. They found their studios provided cheap homes for the Eastern European workforce and they were full for the summer season and beyond. Three times a day the resort minibus could be seen by Kamari harbour collecting and discharging those beginning and ending their shifts. These workers also bought their provisions from the local supermarkets and so for some small businesses the resort came to be viewed in a more positive light. The owners of the more up-market studios discovered their clientele were less loyal than expected and had to search for new European markets notably from Russia and the Czech republic.

After ten minutes, just as I was beginning to wonder if the security guards had failed to contact Julia, a large golf buggy topped by a colonial style canopy whizzed into view. The driver, Isadora Duncan style, wore a large hat and sunglasses and had a long silk scarf flowing out behind her. The buggy jerked to a stop and she jumped out and hugged me.

'Thanks for coming, it's great to see you,' she enthused. 'You are looking good, Greece must suit you.' She hugged me again.

I returned the compliment as my friend looked stunning as usual. The intervening years, when we didn't see each other, counted for nothing in terms of how we interacted with one another. As was the case with my group of other college friends, while we inevitably got older and our lives crisscrossed in diverse directions, the nature of our relationships with each other continued unchanged.

'Sorry, I had to wait five minutes for them to bring me a buggy. It's far too hot to walk but you can go everywhere by buggy,' she explained. 'You'll see it's beautiful here. It has absolutely everything. Hop in and I'll give you a quick tour before we go and have a coffee in my apartment. Then I'll tell you all about my new wonderful man.' As the buggy purred off, she enthused, 'it's just fantastic. There are a thousand people staying here but you would never know, it's so incredibly spacious and quiet.'

We wound our way past souvenir shops, perfumeries, elegant boutiques and cafes and restaurants catering for all nationalities and tastes. We sped past two enormous blue pools on different levels, one offering the possibility of floating in peace and quiet and the other pulsating to disco music with the opportunity to take part in competitive events.

'These are the family villas here,' she gesticulated, urging the buggy to go past them as fast as possible. 'Over there,' she pointed to some apartments on the far side of a vast expanse of lawn and gardens, 'is the quiet zone. Adults who stay there can avoid contact with children and teenagers,' she added approvingly.

'Is that where you are?' I asked.

'Oh no. No, I'm staying in the luxury zone. It's a bit further on and as you'll see the apartments there are truly fabulous and have the best sea views on the site.'

'That is the conference centre and the big building here is the gym,' she said as we skirted an ultramodern building of glass, wood and metal that looked as if it should house contemporary works of art. 'It's fantastically equipped I went there this morning.'

'That doesn't sound like you,' I teased, as Julia, who was blessed with a stunning figure, had always avoided all forms of physical exercise.

'Well,' she retorted, 'Things are changing. There is this

new research, you see, that shows that if you participate in virtual exercise you can get toned and lose weight while you lie down and relax. It is just great. This morning I lay on a water bed and did an hour and a half of virtual pilates, zumba and weights. Then I had a head and body massage, actual not virtual and I must say I really feel the better for it. In fact I think I might do it again tomorrow. Right, look, we are here,' she said steering the buggy into a covered buggy port just as I had convinced myself I was in some kind of Hollywood theme park.

We entered the cool air-conditioned interior of the apartment and I followed her into the large immaculate lounge with its deep cream leather sofas and stylish hard wood and stainless steel furniture. A large picture window facing the sea perfectly framed the island of Nisyros now emerging from the haze that had hidden it earlier. She picked up the phone, 'I'll ring for coffee, cappuccinos?' she enquired.

'Mmm, please and a croissant would be nice.' I imagined what had become a rare treat since moving to Kefalos would be readily available here. 'I didn't have time for breakfast.'

She followed my gaze to the end of the lounge where a fully equipped kitchen with split level cooker and microwave was visible off the open-plan dining area. 'Oh there's no need to use the kitchen. You can order or go out for food and drink here 24/7 but the apartment wouldn't be complete without one. In luxury accommodation you expect everything you would have at home.'

Sipping my cappuccino, I asked the inevitable, 'Well, what happened with George and how come you are here?'

She gave a very deep sigh. 'As you know we were living in this beautiful penthouse flat with a wonderful view of the Arabian Gulf. It was above the most amazingly brilliant shopping mall selling every designer label you've ever imagined. It was just the most wonderful place to live. We gave marvellous parties and, if there was an important event, we were always invited. I had lots of friends, like the wives of the business men George worked with and other women in the English community there. I just loved it. I really was happy. I thought this is it. This time I am really settled. Then I just couldn't believe it when one day George came back from a meeting and announced his next concrete-based project was in Papua New Guinea and we were going to live in Port Moresby. Well all I knew about Papua New Guinea was it had rainforests and headhunters so I told him straightaway I certainly wasn't going there.'

She went on to recall the countless arguments she and

George had had through the two months before he left. 'He kept on about how a wife's place is by her husband's side supporting him wherever he chooses to go. Well not in the jungle kilometres away from anywhere. How chauvinist is that?' She described how incredulous she was when she discovered George was not the man she thought he was but old fashioned, dull and boring. He was obsessed with concrete and, when she told him he must choose between her and concrete, to her total chagrin he had chosen concrete.

She had stayed on in Dubai for a while but found life there as a woman on her own had lost much of its appeal as the party invitations dried up. The friends she had made seemed to become increasingly busy and unable to meet up. Shopping lost its appeal, when opportunities to show off purchases became increasingly limited, and so she moved back to her London home and filed for a divorce.

'I was just so depressed and exhausted with it all. I didn't know what to do next. Then I went to dinner at Margo's and she introduced me to this marvellous man. He's just wonderful, so attractive, such fun and really rich. He owns this place.'

'He owns In Paradise,' I repeated suitably surprised, 'so that is why you are here.'

'Exactly, that's why I'm here. He said that a holiday in Greece would be a chance for me to rest, relax and get over the stress of everything and I could give him insider feedback on what it was like to stay here.'

'Who is he? Is he German?' I asked as most of Kos island's all-inclusive resorts seemed to be German.

'No, he is called Dimitri Symios and he is Greek and he comes from Athens. He comes from an old established family and his older brother is a politician in the Greek government and his younger brother is a lawyer. He owns a number of resorts in both the Cyclades and the Dodecanese islands but this is his largest and newest one and he is really excited about it. He wants it to become the best resort anywhere and he is using it to trial ideas that he can incorporate into the resort he is planning for the Cape Verde islands. He says it's time he moved beyond developments in Greece.'

'Well, I imagine the chance of him developing a resort in Port Moresby is fairly remote so you should be safe,' I mused grinning.

'Definitely,' she laughed.

'How long are you staying here?' I asked.

'Well Dimitri is going to join me here next week and we are going to stay on together for a couple of days. He has several things to see to. Setting up another bank of solar panels was one thing he mentioned. Then he is having his private yacht brought to Kos harbour and we are going cruising, which I'm really looking forward to as he says it's a really sumptuous yacht with a big crew.'

'Sounds great,' I agreed thinking Julia had an amazing talent for swopping men and glamorous life styles.

The rest of the morning passed quickly and extremely pleasantly. Julia quizzed me on life in Kefalos and I learned more of George's failings, the barriers he was presenting to the divorce and the infinite possibilities offered by a more permanent association with Dimitri. Then we went to the exclusive Diet Corner cafe and dined on consommé and tomatoes stuffed with green beans and broccoli. There I and several other diners found our gaze and taste buds stimulated by the wafting aromas of pizzas and pastas from the Italian restaurant situated alongside. It all was obviously too much for one overweight, intending-to-diet couple who, having eaten their calorie-free salad, treated it as a starter and moved across for chef's special pizzas with multiple toppings.

After lunch we changed into our swim things in Julia's sumptuous bedroom with its wet room off one side and a walk-in closet off the other. 'I said to Stefanos, he is the publicity officer here whom Dimitri told to see I had everything I needed. I said to Stefanos I love this wardrobe but because of the 20 kilo weight limit for luggage I've virtually nothing to put in it. He told me apparently women just adore the walk-in wardrobe and are happy to imagine what it would be like filled with clothes. Well I thought that sounded pretty stupid.' I agreed with her envisaging my meagre collection of shorts and T-shirts hung up in one end of the vast space.

'Anyway,' she continued, 'I said to Stefanos that my imagination wasn't up to the challenge so he said to just choose what I'd like to hang in the closet from the shops in In Paradise and Dimitri would pay.' She threw open the door to reveal summer tops, dresses, shorts and trousers grouped according to colour. 'It's great when you have the clothes to fill it isn't it?'

Julia and I spent the afternoon sitting in the shade on the swinging sofas by her apartment's private pool and, between dips to cool down, swopped news of the fortunes of those who had been in college with us. Brightly coloured flowerbeds adorned the pool patio and like all the flowerbeds in the resort soaker hoses were arranged in lines 15 centimetres apart in the earth to ensure the flowers continually looked their best. Recalling my water shortage crisis that morning I pointed this out to Julia in a rather jaundiced manner, speculating on the vast amounts of water the hoses must waste, only to be rebuked and told that of course the resort had its own water supply.

'Oh well, fair enough,' I admitted. While I privately thought that I would soon get bored with the insulated unreal lifestyle offered by the resort, some aspects of living In Paradise, such as the plentiful supply of water, I could easily become accustomed to – well probably several aspects if I'm honest – although I had little use for the walk-in closet.

Arriving back in Kefalos, I called in at Meltemi in case John was about to finish work and might like a lift home. On the beach in front of the hut a group of beginners was being shown the windsurfing basics by Alain and practising managing the sails on land.

'You've just missed him,' Otto said from behind the counter as I arrived in front of the hut. 'He's gone to Kardamena with Seb to fetch the other motor boat that has been repaired. Have you had a good day? He said that you were meeting an old friend at In Paradise.'

At this invitation I recounted something of my day and the surprising facilities the resort had but added that I didn't see anyone windsurfing, although there was a trolley of boards on the beach.

'Yes they've got quite a bit of the latest equipment and in fact asked me if I would go and do some instructing for them, but it's not really my scene and anyway I'm too busy here.'

When I drove around the bay to the house it was on new tarmac and, as I stopped outside Sophia's to get some milk, I could see the lorries, bulldozer and steamroller parked alongside the chapel.

'I got held up this morning going to Bubble beach when the road outside Kefalos was being resurfaced,' I explained to Sophia. 'I expect they are going to do the road up to Kefalos tomorrow.'

'It certainly needs it.'

'I imagine it was a bit inconvenient when they did the Bay road because you would have to drive all the way up to Kefalos and back down the other side to get from one end of Kamari to the other.'

'Yes it did cause a bit of chaos,' she giggled, 'and protests from Zephyros and the sunbathers on Cavos beach.'

'Oh why?' I asked enquiringly.

'Well the tar lorry was going too fast and hit the railings and dripped tar onto the beach. Fortunately, most of the sunbathers had moved nearer to the sea when the work started in anticipation of possible problems and so they avoided the tar but it damaged some of Zephyros's umbrellas. As you can imagine, he was irate and was shouting and swearing at the driver. Then he and the remaining sunbathers got pelted with gravel. Savas, who owns one of the nearby restaurants, said he was sure the driver of the bulldozer did it on purpose.'

Changing the subject because I wanted to find out what had happened to Petros's shed I said, 'When I set off this morning, I got a shock when I saw that Petros's shed had burned down. Do you know what happened. Is he alright?'

'Yes he is but very upset,' replied Sophia. 'A neighbour warned him that his shed had been on fire in the night and he went down to it first thing in the morning but he couldn't salvage anything.'

'That's really awful because his shed means so much to him. How did it happen?'

'Whoever set fire to it soused it in petrol and ensured it was completely destroyed. Well you can imagine how all that old wood would have burned and being so dry as well.'

'Do you know who did it? Do they think it's the arsonist?'

'Whoever did it would no doubt like us to think that it's

the arsonist. However, it's much more likely to be Adonis as he has been trying to buy the plot from Petros for years but I doubt we'll ever be able to find out.'

'Who is Adonis? I asked. 'We haven't come across him.'

'He owns the Sunshine studios halfway up the hill on the road up to Kefalos.'

'The very smart studios with their own restaurant and swimming pool,' I questioned guessing the ones she meant.

'Yes that's right,' Sophia confirmed and went on to explain, 'Well Adonis would like to develop another similar set up right on the bay front. He wants to build on Petros's plot. Owing to its choice location, it would attract other holidaymakers in to use the pool and to eat there. He has tried to buy it but Petros didn't want to sell.'

'You think that now he has lost his hut Adonis thinks that Petros will give in to pressure and let him buy it.'

'I'm sure he does but Petros is popular in the village. We will ensure that Adonis doesn't bully him into doing something he doesn't want to do. Petros has never done anything to upset anyone. When he was younger he went out of his way to help a lot of us and we don't forget. Even now he is always generous giving away the vegetables he grows.'

'Yes,' I agreed. 'When he learned we were here for the summer, he even called me in and gave me tomatoes and aubergines.'

'Apparently Spiros, who is good at getting things done, and some of the other men are discussing the possibility of building him a new shed as soon as possible.

'Oh, that sounds an excellent idea,' I said pleased to learn Petros was being supported and seemed likely to get a replacement shed.

11

Cycling, Sailing and a Birthday Meal

While the sun was hot on my back, the off sea breeze had a freshness about it cooling my face as I tended my ever-expanding patio garden. I was keen that it should look at its best for the forthcoming visitors. Our closest friends from Norfolk and their three children, with whom we generally went away on holiday in the summer, were arriving that night. I was looking forward to sharing my Mediterranean garden with Colin and Carol who were keen gardeners.

When we moved in to our little house, the back yard had nothing in it apart from an upturned oil drum. However, it was shaded by a magnificent vine which rendered its upgrade to patio status extremely promising. The vine's thick trunk spiralled around the doorpost and a myriad of thickly leaved branches wove in and out the overhead supporting network of metal poles and wooden beams. The bougainvillea that grew through and around the vine now sported bright purple flowers which I thought very pretty. After I had expressed a wish to turn the empty yard, into a patio with pots, Spiros had supplied me with a number of quite large, very large and extremely large empty paint tins and some sacks of soil.

'Punch a hole in the bottom of these and paint them up and they will be beautiful for your plants,' he beamed.

He got the tins from his brother who worked in a bar in the summer but turned painter and decorator in the winter and the soil from a house that had just had an area dug out to accommodate a swimming pool. As I painted the tins in traditional Greek blue and planted them with red, pink and white pelargoniums and green and yellow phormiums, gradually the cracked concrete slabs disappeared under luscious greenery and brightly coloured flowers.

I bought the plants from the garden van that called around Kefalos once every two weeks. I guessed that I was one of the van's best customers although I knew that the driver also did well supplying plants to several retired English couples with recently constructed, if as yet unfinished, new houses. The van would come up the hill and hoot outside the house and if I wasn't about, assured of a sale, would wait for me to appear.

The van like some Gardeners' World float in a

horticultural festival was a truly amazing sight. It zigzagged drunkenly along owing to the effects of the wind in its foliage as the cargo of banana plants, palms, rose bushes and tall sunflowers swished rhythmically from side to side. The pots of geraniums bounced precariously on the cab roof and the vines and bougainvillea festooning the sides threatened to entangle the unsuspecting who failed to step back in time. Hoes, rakes and other tools stacked on the passenger seat stuck out of the cab window.

I completed watering the plants, clipped off some of the oleander threatening to hide Aphrodite completely and straightened the patio furniture. In addition to the sun loungers acquired from Spiros, the oil drum was now the base of a teak driftwood table and the white plastic chairs of which the island seemed to have a cheap never-ending supply provided seating around it for us and visitors. I surveyed the transformation of the yard into a patio with considerable satisfaction. I was sure that our friends would approve.

Given the imminent arrival of our visitors, my main task that morning was to go and do a massive shop in order to have plenty of food in. However, first I planned to meet Jan for a coffee at Zephina's.

'Zephina definitely does the best cappuccinos in

Kefalos,' I said as I scooped up a teaspoon of chocolate flakes floating on the cream.

'Last week Angela and I went for afternoon tea at Bettys 2,' said Jan. 'I'd told Angela how you and Betty had become friends when you were here on holiday and how you had introduced me to her. Angela said that she really liked Betty's cafe and that we should go there one day for afternoon tea and so we did last Thursday. Betty was very welcoming and because the cafe was fairly quiet, as apparently there are no coach parties on Thursday, she came and joined us.'

'What did you have? Her scones are particularly delicious.'

'Yes they are. Angela said she was never that bothered about scones when she lived in Wales but now she regards them as a real treat. We had egg and cress sandwiches and sausage rolls followed by Betty's fruit scones with jam and cream and then finished off with a slice of chocolate cake. I can tell you I didn't need any dinner that evening,' she said suggesting the resulting bloated stomach.

'No I imagine you didn't. Betty's slices of cake are enormous. Did she tell you about the plans for her daughter's wedding?'

'Yes she is obviously thrilled that Anna and Alistair are

getting married on Kastri island. I agree with her that it will provide a really romantic setting. Apparently they were over a couple of weeks ago to make arrangements and to visit possible places for the reception and decided on Dionysus.'

'Yes Betty told me that was their choice and I think it's a good one,' I commented. 'It's very spacious, has plenty of seating and a good dance floor.'

'Betty said the only major decision left now is where to go for their honeymoon. She said they were spoilt for choice but thought Anna would particularly like to go to Rhodes. Have you ever been to Rhodes?' Jan asked.

'No, I haven't. John had a holiday there with a girlfriend before I met him but I've never been there.'

'Will you take the opportunity to go this summer while you are here?'

'Probably not because it's not an island we have planned to visit as we like the smaller less touristy ones. Halki is the next one we want to go to.'

'I particularly liked the sound of Patmos when you told me about it,' Jan said adding, 'When I told Andreas this I discovered that he has relatives there. When he was a child he often went there with his parents to stay with his uncle. He has offered to take me there,' she said blushing.

'Will you go?' I asked and wasn't at all surprised at her affirmative answer. Since the picnic above Skinou bay with Andreas she had been seeing him after work and had been on several more outings with him.

'Yes. I didn't really stop to give it much consideration. I just told him that would be great.'

'Have you said much to him about Regi?' I couldn't help asking.

'No more than I felt I needed to but I have told Andreas that being with him is so positive and different from how I feel about my life with Regi. We get on so well and enjoy sharing experiences. I let him know that Regi and I have been drifting apart, which is certainly the case, and my staying in Kefalos is a trial separation. I know that's a bit of an exaggeration because that's not how Regi sees it but it's becoming a reality for me.'

Before I could find out more about Jan and Andreas's plans for visiting Patmos, we were assailed by 'Hi! Hi you two. Can I join you?' and became aware of Joan waving at us from across the road.

'Of course,' 'Yes do,' we beckoned her over.

'How's the drawing course going?' I asked knowing that this week she was putting on a drawing course for beginners.

She flopped down in a chair opposite us sighing, 'Well, hmm, just about OK I suppose. I've left Terry in charge this morning as I wanted to go to the bank and Nektarios's. His shop is just amazing. I wanted some suction hooks to stick on the windows to hang the mobiles that next week's craft class are going to make. I didn't really think he would have any but, as he is so resourceful, I imagined he might suggest an alternative I could use but he had a box full. They took a bit of finding though,' she laughed.

'It's a great shop,' Jan agreed. 'Every time I think of something else that I could do with I go to Nektarios's and nine times out of ten he has got what I want but tell us more about the drawing course. I've often thought that I'd like to learn to draw. I think it must be very satisfying to be able to record places you've been with pencil sketches.'

'You don't sound too happy with the course,' I added.

'I expected it was going to help course members to do simple graphite sketches, like those Jan probably has in mind. Hopefully it will but the tutor seems really hung up on perspective from zero to multi-point and his demos are a bit technical and complicated for beginners. Some of them were looking really perplexed by the end of yesterday,' she grimaced.

I would like to have heard more but looking at my

watch I realised that I needed to go. I explained that with our friends coming to stay I had lots of groceries to get, followed by some cooking when I got back, and so I had better get on with my shopping. I left them discussing what ideally they would expect from a beginner's drawing course.

John and I planned to meet our visitors off the plane from Manchester, which was due to arrive at Kos airport at the customary antisocial hour of two in the morning. However, like most English visitors to Kos, who arrived bleary eyed from their night flights, the exciting anticipation of arriving for a holiday would keep exhaustion at bay until we had met up and brought them back to the house.

We couldn't all get into Mabel plus their luggage and so we had arranged with Elias from Explore to leave a car at the airport for them. We turned off the Kos road and took the dirt track short cut into the airport. Elias had told us the number of the hire car and so we headed to the wide expanse of tarmac where the hire firms parked their cars. After walking up and down the rows three times – the first time, ambling together chatting with cursory glances from side to side. The second time, one behind the other, we scrutinised every vehicle reading all the 'Welcome back

Derek,' 'Shit, good to see you Wayne,' 'Go, go, go Flo'
signs. The third time we marched around impatiently with
John muttering 'Where the fuck is it?' as we concluded
wherever it was, it wasn't where we had expected it to be.

John always extolled the virtues of arriving anywhere
and everywhere early and practised what he preached,
especially when arriving at stations, ferry terminals and
airports. As this was not a virtue shared by me, he never
missed an opportunity to stress its benefits.

'See how important it is to get to airports early,'
emphasised John. 'Yeh, but it's not as if we're going
anywhere,' I grumbled.

'Remember that time in Spain we'd have been
scuppered if we hadn't been early.'

On that occasion he'd been right I conceded. We were
returning home from a walking holiday in the mountains in
Spain blissfully unaware that we were living in our own
personal time zone while the rest of Spain had put its clocks
forward an hour. Panic ensued at the entrance to Malaga
airport when we encountered our first clock for days.
However, owing to John's customary insistence that we
should be mega early, and after progressing through the
baggage checkin and security at unprecedented speed, we
had just made our flight.

'Yeh, but this is different,' I rejoined. We split up and going in opposite directions circumnavigated the airport without success.

'He can't have forgotten. I only reminded him this afternoon,' said John.

'The airport's really full. He probably had a job finding somewhere to leave it,' I replied. We set off around again but this time when we met up John was running towards me.

'It's OK it's over here. It's practically parked in a bush, no wonder we couldn't find it. We better get in the airport, they could already have landed.'

We weaved our way through the queues of package company tourists radiating out from the doors in all directions, as they waiting patiently on the pavement outside the building to be allowed in in batches for security screening. Once in the large hall, where more queues snaked to and fro to the baggage check in, we both groaned in chorus as we looked up at the arrivals board and registered that the plane from Manchester for which we were waiting was an hour late.

'There can be advantages to getting to airports late,' I muttered. 'Like not having to hang around here for an hour.'

'Oh shut up moaning,' was the dismissive response.

'Let's go and sit over there.'

We watched the advance of the shuffling queues and in the absence of any other diversion in the early hours in Kos airport played Spot the Tourist – the tourist with the silliest shorts, the oldest tourist, the most ostentatious tourist, the tourist child in the trendiest designer gear – you get the idea. The time until the announcement of the plane's arrival passed remarkably quickly.

Our friends emerged from the arrivals hall in single file in order of reverse seniority. Nick age seven shouting 'There they are,' hampered by a large canvas bag staggered towards us to give us both a big hug. Michael age twelve slowly followed. An extraordinarily avid reader since the age of four, he was trying to read a book while dragging his enormous suitcase. He yanked at it when it got caught in an immovable object, the leg of the most ostentatious tourist. With amazingly quick reactions, she pushed his book to one side, thrust her finger under his nose and told him in explicit terms what fate ought to befall thoughtless idiots who didn't look where they were going.

Next, walking past her brother with a disdainful air and carefully steering her similarly enormous suitcase, while trying not to drop a variety of jackets and a large red glittery shoulder bag, was his fourteen-year-old sister Amy.

'We are here,' she announced. 'Oh I hate flying. I've just had the most noxious five hours imprisoned between Michael stuck in his book all the time and this old man who was snoring, just gross.' Following our gaze, she added 'Don't know what's happened to Mum and Dad. Dad's case burst open during the flight and he's been trying to find his shoes, too embarrassing.'

At that moment a smiling Carol strode over to us followed by Colin pushing a trolley stacked with cases on top of which were a pile of clothes and one shoe. 'Were they really only coming for a week,' I wondered. Still I had plenty of previous experience of their preference for travelling heavy. It was great to see them. Hugs and kisses were exchanged all round with the exception of Amy whose scowl succeeded in warding off any such welcoming embraces.

Having arrived at the hire car partially hidden in the prickly bush, John with the air of one accustomed to such situations, indicated to us to stand back. 'The key will be in a magnetic box under here,' he said authoritatively. Having our attention he took a small torch from his pocket, switched it on and lowered himself gingerly onto the ground. Trying to keep his legs out of contact with the bush, he swivelled his head under the front passenger side of the car catching his ear on the chassis. 'Ow!' After several minutes of grovelling, he emerged without the key.

'It's probably further back,' he predicted, prostrating himself in the dust for a second time, swearing as sharp thorns from the bush caught his arm. But it wasn't. At that moment, Carol screwing her eyes up to see through the driver's window commented, 'I think there's a key in the ignition and the driver's door has been left unlocked,' she added helpfully as she opened it.

'I don't think Elias would be happy if he realised the car had been left unlocked,' said John, 'but I'm really glad there isn't a problem. I'll go and bring our car over and let's get the cars loaded up.'

Back at the house, as both cars were unloaded, the luggage pile in the living room grew upwards and outwards over the floor.

'I think that's about it,' said Colin surveying the heap with satisfaction. Carol and Colin were having the tiny spare room where the two twin beds were aligned along opposite walls with their brass bedheads just fitting under the window. The only other furniture the room could accommodate was a little wooden chest between the beds and so not much of the heap could be relocated there. Amy was going to sleep on the large comfy sofa in the living room and the two boys were camping on the patio under the vines on sunbeds.

'All you need for tonight are your washbags and night things,' Carol instructed the three of them. 'Everything else can wait until the morning. I'm looking forward to a shower. I feel horrible, really sweaty and sticky.' She began rummaging for her canvas bag.

'What's this one? Whose is this? Goodness! It's heavy, no wonder we were over the weight limit.' Colin explained they had exceeded the 20 kilos each that they had paid for with the plane ticket and had to pay extra at the check-in desk – something of a sore point. As no one moved to claim the large grey bag, Carol unzipped it and with an expression, first incredulous and then exasperated, took out a bicycle inner tube, a foot pump, a cycle repair kit, a small pannier and a first aid box.

'What on earth have we brought these for?' she demanded. Amy and Michael with 'I simply can't imagine,' 'nothing to do with us,' expressions looked hard at Nick.

After a long pause, 'We absolutely always bring these things when we stay with John and Rosemary,' said Nick, adding with some justification, 'You always keep telling us whatever else we mustn't forget them.'

Over the past three years they had always come to stay

plus bicycles and we had gone on cycling expeditions along forest and off-road trails.

'Did you bring this bag then?' questioned Carol.

'Well not exactly,' Nick mumbled.

'Well how did it get here?' she asked crossly.

'I added it to the pile in the kitchen when you were packing,' he admitted, 'so you wouldn't forget it,' he whined.

'But we haven't brought our bicycles,' she reasoned.

'Well you said that we could hire some. We always go cycling with John and Rosemary. We can hire bikes can't we?' His voice trembling he looked tired and near to tears.

'I'm sure we can,' I replied. 'Our friend Spiros will see to it.'

At six o'clock in the morning the privileged occupants of the house were woken by loud shouts and banging from the underprivileged encamped on the patio.

'It's raining, Mum it's raining' wailed Nick, 'big drops of rain and my bed's getting wet. Dad said it didn't rain in Greece.'

'Then bring it in like I'm doing,' said Michael trying to drag his sunbed and tousled bedding through one of the patio doors. His sheets caught on the bolts and the little mattress swung through ninety degrees blocking the doorway. 'Mum my bed's getting soaked and Michael's is stuck in the doorway. We need help,' Nick wailed in a higher key as Michael tried to shake his bed free.

'What are you two doing in here? This is my room, go away, it's not time to get up,' Amy lifted her head up from the sofa, glared at them and collapsed back again on her pillow.

'What's on earth is going on?' Colin asked yawning and peering blearily from the bedroom doorway.

'It's raining,' explained Michael somewhat unnecessarily, as the rain could now be heard pounding on the flat extension roof, 'and as usual Nick is making a fuss.'

'It's alright for you, your bed is indoors, well most of it is but mine is ...Mum.'

'It's OK we'll soon get you sorted,' responded Colin now sufficiently awake to take in the scene. Jumping into action to help Michael unblock the doorway, he caught his foot in the previous night's abandoned inner tube, executed a spectacular crash into the coffee table and went sprawling across the sofa.

'Aah! Dad get off what are you doing?' Amy squawked from the sofa.

The crash succeeded in summoning Carol, John and I to survey the scene and come to the rescue. Colin was hauled upright and his knees and the coffee table surveyed for damage. Colin's right knee looked very red and as if it might swell up and so I went to get some ice cubes to put on it but the solid wooden table remained unscathed. The rain had stopped as abruptly as it started and the sun was coming out and so the beds were taken back outside where they rapidly dried out. Fortunately, as was usually the case at that time of year there was no more rain that week. The boys delighted in their bedroom under the stars, which twinkled brightly in the clear night sky and, consulting Google, they tried to identify them.

The week of their stay unfolded in a happy and relaxed manner for both them and us. They enjoyed spending time on the beach and John taught Michael and Amy the basics of windsurfing. Amy proved unexpectedly keen wishing to impress a lad of her own age who was also a beginner. As a result she became rather good at it and consequently rightly pleased with herself.

One day they went to Kos town to experience the history and culture of the Asklepion and do some shopping in the market. Carol and Amy returned with a range of summer outfits. They all took a day trip to Nisyros with Joyful Tours from which Nick returned most impressed with the sulphurous smells and unusual colours of the crater. While there they went to Lachanikos for lunch and passed on our regards to Marcos.

We also had a very successful day cycling around Tigaki. Spiros negotiated for us to borrow bikes from a hotel there. We cycled around Alyki, a former salt pan, which as usual was dried up in mid summer but in winter is a wetland visited by flamingoes. Then we took the coast road to a beach on the edge of Kos town where we had lunch before cycling back. John's rear tyre gradually went down and needed to be pumped up a couple of times and so Nick feeling vindicated pointed out we would have had serious problems if he hadn't brought the pump.

Their last day was Michael's birthday, which everyone was in agreement should be spent doing his favourite activities of reading, swimming and sailing. We took a picnic to Mastihari and encamped for the day on the beach away from the crowds in the shade of some carefully selected scrubby trees.

The process of finding a suitable spot took a prolonged physical, mental and emotional toll of us all. We struggled further and further from the car park, first along the boardwalk behind the beach and then the sandy path beyond, carrying everything required for each individual to have a successful day on the beach – sunbeds, a collapsible table, a first aid kit, bags of towels, swimming things, goggles and snorkels, camera equipment, a cricket set, bags of food and a veritable bagged up library of books. All of this plus Jules, an enormous inflatable dolphin that Nick had instantly been enamoured with on the second day with us and on which he had spent all his holiday money.

'What about here?' said John hopefully as we went past the windsurf hire shed which offered him the possibility of windsurfing talk with its occupants.

'Far too many people,' responded Carol, 'and the Germans have already taken all the best shade.'

'What about here then?' said John rather less hopefully, as we were about to round the rocks where the windsurfing fraternity would be hidden from sight preventing him from studying their choice of boards, sails and jumping techniques even through the magnifying lens of his digital camera.

'Nowhere decent to sit,' said Carol. 'It's too stoney and there's too many of those prickly bushes.'

'I'm sure there'll be a nice bay around the next corner,' said Colin.

As we reached the next bay, Amy immediately noticed five tanned teenage Greek boys lounging, drinking and smoking in the dunes. 'Umm, here is just great,' she said dropping her load.

'Definitely not here,' said Carol.

'Oh why, what's wrong with here?' protested Amy. 'It's cool. My arms ache and I absolutely cannot go any further.'

'No not here, but we'll definitely stop around the next corner,' promised Colin.

We didn't because the next little bay revealed a group of very elderly nudists prostrate on the sand. Probably used to such intrusions, they remained immobile and seemingly unmoved while we weaved through and past them. They appeared not to register Nick's loud demands to know why were they undressed, what had happened to their clothes and were they streakers? Nor to hear Micheal's ageist rejoinder, 'Don't be an idiot, do they look capable of streaking anywhere.'

'Please just ssh,' said Carol hurrying onward.

Fortunately, unbelievably, the next bay turned out to be perfect with golden sand, trees for shade and uninhabited. We all sank gratefully down on the sand. We drifted through the rest of the morning and early afternoon in a tranquil haze of well-being alternately reading, dipping in the sea to cool down and chilling out watching the seagulls dipping and soaring against the backdrop of brilliant blue sky and the rocky brown and grey hillsides of Kalymnos.

Fortified by our lunch of crisps, ham rolls, stuffed vine leaves, cheese pies and honey buns from Angela's bakery, we felt sufficiently energised to respond positively to Nick's pleas to play cricket. However, while in mid-summer on the North Norfolk coast, games of beach cricket get the blood circulating and prevent the onset of hypothermia, in Kos ten minutes in the hot sun is more than enough.

'The sand is scorching my feet, so I have to keep moving,' said Michael jigging up and down, 'but it means I'm ready to run for a catch.'

'Ugh, I'm dissolving in sweat can I field from under a tree?' moaned Amy.

'Hang on a minute,' I said applying more suntan lotion to my shoulders as the ball hit me in the stomach to the chorus of 'Oh catch it,' which I didn't.

'Michael run and get that,' said John the wicket keeper as Carol's ball went wide yet again.

'It's these glasses,' said Carol, who was holding sunglasses on over her ordinary glasses as she ran up to bowl. When Michael's catch finally brought Nick's innings to a close, Colin patted Nick on the shoulder in a congratulatory fashion. 'You are too good for us, we concede defeat.'

Ignoring Nick's protests, we retreated back to the trees and resumed our former spiral of much less demanding activities, until Michael announced he had finished Lord of the Rings so it was time to go sailing. It was getting a bit late in the afternoon and there wasn't much wind but as Colin and John had promised to take Michael sailing the three of them trudged off back to the windsurfers' hut to hire a dingy. Meanwhile the four of us waited, staring out to sea, for them to come into view. About three-quarters of an hour later a small dinghy was sighted.

'Is that them?' I asked.

'Uhm think so,' said Carol.

'Why are they sailing backwards?' enquired Nick.

At that moment they were indeed going backwards though not actually sailing just simply bobbing up and down on the gentle waves. The sail hung idly giving only the occasional desultory flutter. Colin pumping vigorously away at the tiller got the dinghy facing forward again, whence it slowly, very slowly, drifted across the section of sea in front of us and exited left around the corner.

'Where is Daddy taking them?' Nick asked anxiously.

'To the end of the island and beyond. Africa, Turkey, Spain, whatever is out there,' Amy replied.

'How are they going to get back?' Nick looked tearful.

'Shall we go to the windsurfers and see what they suggest?' I said.

'Good idea,' said Carol. 'It's time we made a move anyway but can we manage all this stuff?'

We found that we could, just about. Dropping and retrieving items as we went, grumbling and cajoling we staggered back to the windsurfers' hut.

'No need for worrying,' laughed the tall tanned German well aware of what had happened. 'They will just drift and drift until they reach the place where the beach sticks out and then they will drift aground, pull the boat up the beach and walk back.'

'They are not going to Africa then,' Nick sought reassurance.'

'No, no, they will land back in Kos.'

'What will happen to the boat?' asked Amy.

'When Yugen gets back with the jeep we'll take the trailer to get it.'

'Does this happen often,' I asked.

'Well, if the wind drops it can.'

'How long will it take them to get back?' asked Carol, thinking about how we had planned to go out for a meal to celebrate Michael's birthday.

'Over an hour, maybe an hour and a half.'

'If they are going to be such ages let's go and get an ice cream,' suggested Amy, 'and a cappuccino' I added.

'A lager would be good too,' put in Carol.

'You see it's Michael's birthday,' Nick explained to the windsurfer, 'so he is going out to eat spaghetti. That's his best food.'

'If they are still walking back when we fetch the boat we will give them a lift. Don't worry there will be plenty of time for spaghetti.' After we had been sat in the cafe for an hour and were on our second round of ice cream, cappuccino and lager, the would-be sailors turned hikers arrived.

Owing to the vast numbers of tourists that flock to Kos from June to mid-September, there were plenty of possibilities for Michael's birthday dinner. However, although there were lots of different restaurants, most served up virtually the same fare of traditional Greek dishes, pasta to cater for the Italians and vast quantities of chips with everything to satisfy the British. Our choice for the evening was Georgio's kitchen described by its owner in a huge illuminated sign on the roof as 'a gastrognomes delight.'

Georgio's restaurant was a family business which had been run by him for 20 years and his father before him and as we knew from our frequent visits was excellent value for money. Georgio's wife did the cooking, helped in the evening by her daughter who taught in the local primary school. Georgio warmly welcomed clients thanking them with repetitive gusto for patronising his restaurant. On arrival, when taking orders and on their departure he enthused, 'Thank you very, very, very, very, very, much.'

Throughout the evening he chatted to the visitors, shouted instructions to the rest of the family, took verbally and remembered everyone's order and hurtled back and forth between the kitchen and the tables with brimming plates of food. His eldest son, who used to help with waiting, was in his first year at university in Athens so his middle son now filled that role assisted by his younger brother who was only about two years older than Nick.

Georgio's was among the numerous restaurants situated between the beach and the road up the hill out of Kefalos. It consisted of a smart traditional white house with blue painted door and shutters where the cooking took place. In front of this was a wooden roofed patio with conservatory style walls on two sides to protect customers from the elements on windy nights and a second trellised patio hung with vines.

We selected a patio table facing the sea from where we

could observe activity along the harbour road but out of the wind and away from the vines. We had learned from miserable past experience that the vines were home to droves of mosquitoes. These are capable of descending on unsuspecting diners and transforming perfectly acceptable looking legs into ones covered in unsightly extremely itchy red lumps which took days to fade and calm down.

We debated the pros and cons of what to have. In addition to the labelled pictures of meals faded to uniform pink mounds on platters, the menu chalked on the board outside offered the additional delights of 'roast lamp', 'grilled coat,' 'vegetarian friendly sausages' and 'backed potatoes' as a welcome alternative to chips.

Michael, who had decided on what he wanted before he arrived, immediately announced his choice of chicken and spaghetti. John opted for his favourite dish at Georgio's of pastistio with rice instead of chips. After trying to identify any distinguishing features of the photographed meals and changing her mind at least six times Amy decided to try it as well. Colin and I chose snapper barbecued in herbs and always delicious, although buried under mounds of tomato and cucumber chunks, the rather impoverished but universal Kefalos interpretation of Greek salad. Nick was adamant that he wanted 'scrumpled eggs on toast' and

Carol, after considerable deliberation, decided it would probably be unwise to rely on the friendliness of the sausages to vegetarians and instead chose tomatoes stuffed with herbs and rice.

As was the case with most of the popular restaurants the ratio of staff to tourists meant service was slow or exceedingly slow, but as long as you weren't extremely hungry what did it matter. Sipping a drink, chewing on some homemade bread, enjoying the balmy Mediterranean evening and the sound of the waves lapping the shore was lovely and relaxing, especially so when shared with friends.

It appeared likely we were in for quite a wait as over half the tables were already taken by a mix of English and Italian couples and a large Greek family group. Michael took out a novel he'd been given for his birthday, Nick took out his crayons and sketchbook to work on his drawing of a sailing boat going backwards – that is until Georgio clipped over the striped red plastic tablecloth a clean paper one decorated with a blue map of Kos and tourist sights. Nick thought that this would be greatly improved with the addition of colour and set about colouring it in. Amy was kept entertained watching the middle son hoping to catch his eye. John and I chatted with Carol and Colin about their holiday, the effects of Brexit and life in general.

'What's that restaurant like? Has it got a bad reputation?' Colin suddenly interrupted John's animated chairbound description of how to do a front to back toehold when waterskiing.

'Why, where, which one?' John let go of his toe and swivelled his chair back round so he could see the front of the restaurant to which Colin was referring.

'People keep going up to the steps and then turning round and leaving,' Colin explained.

We watched a couple hasten away and after a couple of minutes three more people stopped to look at the menu. A man appeared in front of them gesticulating inside the restaurant and pointing vigorously at items on the menu. Shaking their heads the threesome hurried off. Two more couples ambled past. With alacrity the man jumped down the steps and intercepted them. As they made to move away, he took hold of the arm of the woman at the back of the group and appeared to be propelling her up the steps, that is until the burly individual in the lead rounded on him pushing him in the chest backwards through the door.

'What on earth's going on?' Colin questioned. Michael stopped reading, Nick stopped colouring and Amy transferred her gaze from the waiter to the restaurant down the road.

'Oh I know,' I said, recognition dawning. 'Katrina Spiros's wife was telling me all about this and Zephina mentioned it too.'

From the gossip in the village I had learned that Solomos the restaurant owner had a cousin Nikos in Hania in Crete, who had recently opened a restaurant which was doing remarkably well. Seeking the secrets of his success, Solomos was told by his cousin that the waiter he employed to act as a front man was excellent at persuading potential clients that his restaurant was the best place to eat. In fact he stressed, the frontman would never take no for an answer.

Nikos couldn't believe such a practice didn't exist in Kefalos, insisting that all the restaurants in Hania employed someone out front and that it was essential to generate customers. He was adamant that such an employee would make an immediate positive impact on his cousin's takings. Judging from our vantage point, he was indeed making an impact. However, the frontman's growing desperation to recruit custom was leading to increasingly intrusive efforts to get passing tourists inside and appeared to be having the opposite effect on customer relations to that desired.

Solomos had not been able keep his enthusiasm for the practice to himself. The news that an experienced waiter from Crete was about to fly in to assume the frontman role had spread quickly around Kefalos causing considerable curiosity and not a little consternation among the restaurant owners. They speculated as to the outcome, whether and when they might have to follow his example and worried about which family member could be spared from cooking or waiting to stand outside.

The accosted English foursome mounted the steps into Georgio's just as our meals arrived and we tucked in. The woman was complaining to her companion that she was suffering from a twisted arm and the burly man, clearly her husband, was boasting to his friend that any more of that and he would have 'knocked his fucking head off.' Nick looked up wide-eyed from his 'scrumpled egg.'

'Would he really have knocked his fucking head off Mummy?'

'Quite possibly, by the look of him,' said Carol, 'but you don't use language like that.'

'Ohh but …'

'No buts,' said Carol. 'Eat your dinner.'

Fortunately the worries of the Kefalos restaurant owners were short-lived. A few days after the meal at Geogio's, Solomos experienced a total decrease in customers as tourists crossed over the road to avoid walking in front of the restaurant and being tackled by the frontman. He was sent back to Crete and Solomos's disgruntled family ceased contact with their Cretan cousin.

When Georgio learned it was Michael's birthday, he beamed and announced that he had exactly what was needed to conclude such a birthday meal and disappeared into the back of the kitchen. He was gone for what seemed rather a long time and so we were getting a bit apprehensive as to what to expect. Then he returned bearing aloft a lemon drizzle cake piped with cream and a sparkler stuck in the top. Singing what presumably was the Greek equivalent of 'Happy birthday to you' or something similar he put it down in front of Michael.

Everyone in the restaurant clapped and Michael turned from pink to red to puce. However, entering into the spirit of the occasion he stood up, waved the sparkler and took a bow amidst another round of clapping, but on calls of 'speech,' muttered, 'not likely,' and sat down hurriedly. We cut ourselves generous slices of lemon cake and agreed with Georgio that it was definitely what was needed and a fitting end to Michael's birthday and their stay with us.

12

Discovering Turtles

When I arrived at her house, I found Eleni hanging out the washing. One of the great things about Greek weather is that washing dries so quickly, in contrast to England where it can hang outside for hours and still be damp. Alternatively it might have dried but before being taken indoors a sudden shower saturates it again.

'Hello Eleni. How are you doing?'

'Apart from a little backache,' she put her hand on her lower back as she bent down gingerly to pick up a wet shirt from the wash basket, 'I'm good,' she said. 'The last time I saw you, you were excited about having your friends from England to stay. How did that go?'

'Really well. We had a lovely time and they really enjoyed themselves.'

'Where did they go?'

'Well they went to Kos town of course to look around,

do some shopping and visit the Asklepion.'

'It's many years since I went there. I think there is a lot more information provided about the ruins now so it all means more. Were they impressed with it?'

'Definitely. It is an amazing place. There are these books called Horrible Histories that Michael used to love when he was younger and he knew lots about Ancient Greece from those and so he was especially interested in it.'

'Did they like Kefalos?'

'Yes they did. They spent lots of time relaxing on the beach near the ruins and going swimming and John taught Michael and Amy to windsurf. It was really fun. What about you? What's been happening with you?' I asked.

'Well nothing good. I must admit I've been feeling very depressed. Last week I went to Antonis's funeral and I still just can't get it out of my mind. His death was just so tragic and I'm so sad for his parents. They were very proud of him and he was such a handsome lovely boy. He was only fifteen, such a waste of a young life. They are just devastated. I don't know how they are going to cope. It is so hard for them.'

I explained to Eleni that John and I didn't know Antonis or his parents but we had learned of the accident from Antonis's uncle Andoni. When Colin and family had left us, we went for an Italian meal in the Sapori restaurant where Andoni is a waiter. He wasn't his usual joking self so we enquired after his health and with tears welling up in his eyes he told us the horrific story of what had occurred. He described how the accident happened when Antonis had been helping his elder brother to tile the flat roof of his parents' house so they could make better use of the space. Antonis had a long metal pole to use as a rule to ensure the tiles were laid in straight lines. Standing up for a break, he forgot about the bundle of power lines drooping over the house and caught the end of the pole on one of the cables. He instantly received such a powerful electric shock that it killed him.

'We were so horrified by what he told us. We have often commented how dangerous the cables look drooping over the houses but we didn't know of anyone who had been harmed by them. It is just dreadful. You went to the funeral, that must have been very upsetting.'

'It was really difficult and I can't stop thinking about it but the funeral service was a beautiful service. The priest is a family friend and knew Antonis really well and so the service was very personal and extremely moving.' Eleni led me to sit with her on the sofa in the shade of the wooden roof. Then tearfully she described in detail the funeral service which took place in the large church of the Presentation of the Holy Mother in the centre of Kefalos old town, the procession to the cemetery on the edge of town and the burial ceremony.

Walking back up the hill I reflected on how desperately sad Antonis's death was and how unnecessary. It was such a dreadful end to his life and emphasised the threat to life posed by the power lines which dangled haphazardly over the town and its surroundings. As Eleni said, the locals regularly talked about the dangers posed by the cables and complained about them to the council and the authorities in Kos town but nothing ever appeared to be done.

The next day we woke to cooler conditions with numerous white puffy clouds scudding across the sky. We felt like doing something positive and as the weather seemed just right for walking we decided to do the walk to Paleo Pili that Spiros had told us about and take a picnic lunch. Paleo Pili is one of my favourite places on Kos and has been since we came across it by accident on our first visit to the island. We were bumping along the backroads in our hire car and came to a flat area by a stream and shaded by trees. As at that point the pot-holey road turned into an even more pot-holey dirt track, it seemed a good place to leave the car and get out and stretch our legs.

On the other side of the stream we found the steep stone path that climbs up through the tall pines to the deserted village of Paleo Pili. As we ascended our sense of anticipation grew, which was more than fulfilled when we got to its idyllic location. Hidden in the hills and forest in the centre of the island, the village was situated to keep its occupants safe from marauding pirates. Comprised of many stone dwellings, now ruins in various states of dilapidation and only inhabited by wandering goats, in its hey day it was obviously large and thriving.

The tall 12th century Byzantine castle merges indistinguishably into the jutting outcrop of grey and brown rock on which it is situated. It afforded those on lookout with uninterrupted views of the northern coast and the strait between Kos and Kalymnos. When we first discovered Paleo Pili, before the advent of EU money to develop the site and its accompanying regulations for health and safety, we also enjoyed this magnificent view.

Back then it was possible to climb the crumbling stone steps up inside the tower, pausing on the way up to stare down into the blackness of the gaping holes in the floors to gain glimpses of hidden vaults and chapels. We were entranced by the mysteriousness of what we could see and imagine, while horrified at the possibility of falling into the void. Then almost reaching the top we could perch on the stonework and look through an archway out to sea and over Kalymnos and imagine the lives of those who had trodden those stairs in previous centuries.

The villagers could receive early warning of any potential dangers and must have felt secure in their well disguised location. However, in the early 19th century the village was devastated by outbreaks of cholera which, as the death toll grew, gave rise to increasing panic causing those surviving to abandon their homes in 1830 and move to the coast in an attempt to escape. It might be imagined that the trauma of those times would somehow live on in the atmosphere, but there is no sense of past suffering in Paleo Pili – rather it is a place of serene beauty and tranquility.

While we had been to Paleo Pili each time we went to Kos, we had always driven there and parked on the flat space by the stream before taking the stone path up to the village. We had never done the walk we were about to embark on. We had been surprised to read, when browsing through a tourist guide in the bookshop in Kos town, that Kos was the home of large turtles. As we had never seen one we were extremely sceptical as to whether this was still the case. We put this to Spiros the next time we saw him.

He was incredulous that we could doubt their existence.

'Of course Kos has turtles. You are telling me you've never seen one.'

'Well where can we go to see one?' we challenged him.

'The old path from Pyli to Paleo Pili,' he retorted. 'That is the best place to see turtles. If you take that and don't see one, well more than one, on that walk then you must go around with your eyes closed.'

We drove to the newer village of Pyli, which with modern houses springing up around its outskirts is developing rapidly, but it still preserves its attractive old village square. We left the car near the fountain that has quenched the thirst of the local inhabitants for five hundred years. John topped up his water bottle from it claiming it was good to be able to drink natural spring water for a change instead of bottled water. I would have liked to have had a coffee in one of the cafes around the square but John was eager to get going. 'Come on,' he urged. 'Have you got everything? It must be this way.' He set off at a fast pace.

As directed by Spiros, we walked uphill from the village square looking out for signs to the Heroon of Charmylos and as he instructed we went straight on at the second sign. We were quite curious to see the chapel built over the tomb of Charmylos a mythological hero-king. His large tomb had reputedly once consisted of twelve crypts each with recesses for graves, although subsequent buildings, including the chapel, had used materials from the tomb in their construction. However, much tramping up and down and retracing of footsteps failed to reveal it.

Blaming Spiros for the inadequacy of his directions, we eventually admitted defeat and gave up the search. We agreed it didn't matter, because like many of the historic sights on Kos marked with brown signs it was probably no more than a pile of stones, which to other than the trained eye of a specialist in Grecian archaeological antiquities would be quite indistinguishable from all the other surrounding piles of stones. Contrary to our expectations, a more sustained search on another occasion did enable us to find and enter the dark interior of the tiny chapel tendered with care by its elderly custodians.

Leaving Pyli we found the fork in the road by an olive grove that Spiros had mentioned but instead of one path leading uphill there were three.

'Well which one of these do you think we should take?' said John irritably. 'I wonder how long it is since Spiros did this walk.'

'Possibly never, I think Spiros prefers his truck to walking,' I said, thinking that I'd never actually seen him go anywhere on foot. 'Let's take this one.' I liked the look of the well-trodden path snaking through the olive grove.

We opted for that but when we emerged on the other side of the olive grove, while we were sure we were heading in the right direction, we failed to find the dirt road we were supposed to take to climb the hilltop.

'Oh it doesn't matter,' said John impatiently. 'We don't need the road, we know we need to get to the top of the hill,' and he set off upwards over the scrub.

'Slow down, it's really prickly.' I tried to pick my way through the low thorny bushes to incur minimum damage to my legs. 'Ouch! I don't think much of this.' I stopped to extricate a thorn from my ankle.

'Oh John look.' As I stood up and looked along the scrub, I spotted our first turtle. It was a very small one, probably only a year or so old. Its shiny light brown shell with a lighter brown frilly edge was divided by dark markings into squares, each with a central dark dot. It was the size of the back of my hand. The turtle's head moved from side to side seemingly eyeing us up and down.

'Look at the dark markings on his shell. He's lovely. He's just like Henry.'

Back at our home in England Henry had been a visiting tortoise for the week up to Christmas in order that a friend of ours could keep his purchase a secret and give the tortoise to his wife as a surprise Christmas present. As Henry needed to be kept warm to stop him from hibernating he lived in our bathroom, that being the warmest room in the house in his special tortoise box with sleeping quarters and run. You could watch him while sitting on the loo so during his stay we learned quite a lot about tortoise behaviour and food preferences.

Henry was particularly partial to dandelion leaves. While all too plentiful in our garden for most of the year, they were in somewhat short supply in midwinter so he had to accept carrot tops as an occasional substitute. Sitting among the stones, prickles and twigs there didn't seem much greenery around for Henry II but he seemed happy enough. Giving us a final look over and obviously deciding we were not the bearers of dandelions or anything else of interest to turtles, he trotted off with surprising speed for a creature famed for its slow pace.

Below us to our left, in a dip in the hills, an army depot came into view with a few soldiers patrolling around the usual neat rows of rusty tanks and assorted old trucks. As we approached the tall sturdy wire perimeter fence, we found alongside it a dirt road winding around the hillside.

'Good,' said John. 'We are back on track, the next thing

to look out for is a narrow path off to the right which will lead us up to the ruins of an old house.'

We were congratulating ourselves on having found the path, which dipped appealingly through the oleander bushes with their bright pink flowers, when we turned a corner and found our way barred by an unanticipated impenetrable wire, iron stake and bedstead fence. The Greeks of the Dodecanese, and maybe the inhabitants of rural Greece in general, have a very creative approach to recycling items of ironmongery as fences. The metal bedhead gate of this one still replete with brass knobs was firmly wired shut. As climbing over, under or around it wasn't an option and wire cutters were not part of our hiking kit, there was nothing for it but to set to work untangling the wire. The untangling seemed and probably did take ages and, as the wire was thick and resistant to bending, generated sore fingers and further harsh criticisms of Spiros's credentials as a hiking guide. Also, when we had passed through the gate, we felt a duty to make at least a half-hearted attempt to retangle it.

Having done sufficient retangling to satisfy our consciences, we rounded the next bend. What was ahead caused a loud synchronised 'Oh no!', followed by various expletives as we were faced with a wood and wire contraption in amongst the oleander bushes. Spiros had warned us about having to pass through this but it had come sooner than anticipated. However, fortunately the wire on this improvised gate was much thinner and more brittle and so considerably easier to undo. While I was working on it, John wandered off for a rest on some rocks. Out of the corner of my eye, I saw him half lower himself onto a rock before shooting upright again. He hurried over to me.

'Come and look at this,' he said quietly. I followed him over to where a coiled up snake brownish gold in colour with distinctive scales and a faint zigzag stripe along its back was seemingly having a nap in the shade of the rocks amidst a pile of bleached goat bones.

'Ooh it's quite big do you think it's poisonous? Could it be a type of adder?' I whispered.

Not used to seeing snakes in the wild we stood in awe of it. At that moment sensing our presence it woke up, uncoiled in a very unhurried manner and slowly slithered off between the rocks. It was several centimetres in girth and a metre or more long. Later Spiros informed us that from our description it was probably a female sand viper – females have less obvious markings than males. This seemed very likely as, despite their name, sand vipers don't live in sand but on dry rocky hillsides with sparse vegetation like the one we were exploring.

We learned later by putting sand viper into Google that the three sub species of sand viper are the most dangerous of European mainland vipers because of the toxicity of their venom. Fortunately, however, like the one we saw, sand vipers are generally rather lethargic creatures and not aggressive unless provoked and we certainly had no intention of provoking it.

We followed the path that became little more than a goat track up the increasingly barren hillside towards the ruined house that Spiros had described as a landmark. However, before the house came into view the path appeared to end at the base of a rocky overhang. Walking around the rocky outcrop we confirmed that indeed it had ended. While surveying the overhang trying to decide which face would be the least difficult to scramble up, we came upon a really big turtle. He peered up at us from out of his dusty brown shell, which had enormous greyish blobs in each darkly delineated segment. He kept quite still as if used to posing for the photographs that John was extremely keen to take. The only problem was that behind him below us was the army camp now in full view which meant that we were in full view of the guards.

'One of the them might look up and think we are photographing their camp,' I warned.

Realising that might mean trouble, John got down on his knees and hurriedly took his photos. On Kos, signs depicting cameras with a line through marked all approaches to any kind of army or army connected installation. 'Mmm, hurry up I think one of the guards is looking up here,' I said before helpfully reminding him of how once on holiday he had nearly had his camera confiscated by the French army. He had stopped the car in a country lane to take a picture of a parked army ambulance because it was just like the one in his French dinky toy collection. However, the French soldiers were unimpressed by his explanation.

Having found a way up the overhang, John pulled me up onto the top of the final piece of rock to be scaled and there before us was the ruined house. It was unusually large and quite imposing, as the tessellated tops to its walls, narrow window openings and position made it resemble a small castle. Most of its walls were intact, although its rooms were now only occupied by goats. The older wiser ones were snoozing inside in the shade while the kids, goat bells clanging, practised their footwork and jumping skills clambering onto and leaping off what was left of the roof.

We sat for a while watching them admiring their variation in size, colour and facial expressions and laughing at their antics. We could also look across the olive groves and brown plains to the tourist resort of Tigaki and the sands of Alyki where we had gone cycling with our friends from home. Beyond the coast and out to sea we could see the barren hills of Kalymnos, slightly blurred by the developing heat haze as the day warmed up, and to the right of it the rocky islet of Pserimos.

'The view from here really is superb,' I sighed appreciatively. 'I wonder who built this house. I guess they too must have loved the view. It's not at all like the usual farm dwellings. I wonder when and why the owners left.'

'It's very isolated. The ground is dry and stoney. It would have been hard to make a living here,' John speculated. 'You know the rise of tourism caused numerous families to leave their hill farms and seek an easier way of life on the coast.'

'Whoever they were they must have been really upset to leave. Maybe the last people to live here were an elderly couple and they couldn't manage. Perhaps one of them died and the other couldn't cope all alone. I think the house has a sad tale to tell.'

Reluctant to leave such an enigmatic place, eventually we set off on a goat path which merged with lots of other goat paths to form a clear track lined with kermes oaks up to our next landmark, another much smaller ruin. Then we scrambled over rocky terrain to reach the required third set of ruins. However, from there the vista of stones and scrub stretched upwards and outwards with no sign of any path. As you do in such circumstances, we sat, had a drink of water and debated what next. We knew the direction we needed to go in to find Paleo Pili and so we decided to make our way over the hill to the left.

Spiros had assured us that by now, up above on the right, we would see the chapel of St George in a groove in the rocks. However, although we kept hopefully surveying the hilltops we didn't get to see it. At the top of the incline we had chosen to head for, we were a bit surprised to find a dirt road. Behind us this appeared to come to a rather puzzling dead end in some rocks but along it ahead of us we could see the farmstead Spiros had told us would indicate we were soon to enter the area of Paleo Pili.

Beyond the farmstead a low stone wall ran beside the road. As we stopped to look at the castle ruins, which were now clearly in view, we could hear lots of rustling in the undergrowth on the other side of the wall.

'What's causing that?' John said. We peered over and saw two turtles walking side by side at fast turtle speed through the long grass along the edge of the field.

'Look at the size of these two!' I exclaimed. 'They are even bigger than the other one and I thought that was big.' Leaning on the wall, we watched them until they disappeared under a bush. Then acknowledging that, never mind the reliability of his directions, Spiros was definely right that this was a good walk for seeing turtles, we continued to Paleo Pili.

'I'm starving so I'm glad we've reached Paleo Pili.' said John. 'Shall we find a doorstep for a picnic spot?'

We walked across the piece of flat ground by the stream that served as a car park – two hire cars were there – and we began the familiar steep climb up to the village on the wide gently sloping stone steps. About halfway up, marking the beginning of the village is a tiny chapel with a large bell. There we passed the tourists shouting and joking on the way back to their hire cars. 'Good,' I thought selfishly as Paleo Pili is best enjoyed with the silence broken only by the sound of goats and goat bells.

We continued our climb past ruined dwellings up to the centre of the village. There we found a suitable picnic spot under some pine trees on a wall adjoining one of the larger ruined houses. In front of us in a clearing that was perhaps once a carefully tended olive grove, goats sat in the shade of the remaining gnarled old trees, or munched away at the prickly undergrowth. One curious goat with a pristine long straight white coat, fluffy white tail and an aristocratic black and white face, climbed up on our wall to get a better look at us. John tried to tempt him over with a piece of roll but he remained aloof. Our cheese rolls, which we felt that we had well and truly earned, tasted really good even if the bread was rather chewy. Post noon, Kos rolls take on an increasingly tougher texture becoming inedibly leathery by evening.

We were just on our pudding of overheated KitKats with juicy tangerines to take away the sticky sweetness, when another very large turtle plodded purposefully past us and disappeared behind the wall. This really did surprise us. How come we had never seen a turtle here before? We had visited Paleo Pili each time we came on holiday and always sat soaking up the atmosphere of this unique place, yet we hadn't seen a turtle. However, as we now realised, clearly it must be home to lots of them.

We lazed in the shade unwilling to move and, when we decided that move we must, we went to inspect progress on the renovation of the chapel of the Hypapanti. The chapel situated in a broad courtyard of very uneven stone slabs is a large rectangular building with a domed stone roof at the back and a flat walled roof at the front suggesting that once it was more than one storey high. The piles of building materials and drooping wire and orange tape that made a vague attempt to cordon off the area around the chapel all looked much the same as they had the previous three years. The exception was that the chapel now had smart new solid wooden double doors between the white pillars supporting its arched entrance. To our disgust these doors were firmly locked meaning that we could no longer venture into the cool dark interior.

We said goodbye to the goats. For a while they followed us at a safe distance and watched curiously as we scrambled over the rocks and ruined walls to the path back down. About 50 metres above the parking area, we took the old paved path to visit the chapel of Agios Basileios.

Halfway along, while as customary there were no workmen to be seen, there were signs of their intentions to repair and widen the path. A concrete mixer on its side straddled the path and piles of stone and bags of cement mix barred the way. Circumventing these we reached the chapel with its gleaming white walls and blue roof and were pleased that the doors were still open to passers-by. Its brightly painted gold embossed altar shone out into the darkness and the arrangements of religious icons, plastic flowers and candles revealed the love and the care with which it was tended. Emerging back into the light we sat on the plastic chairs in the shady seated area to the side and finished off the last two tangerines of our lunch.

In the past we had always retraced our footsteps to the parking area and our hire car. However, on this occasion we were assured by Spiros that we could take footpaths and tracks to Amaniou and from there take the road back to new Pyli. The military occupation of the surrounding terrain between Amaniou and Pyli made any further cross-country excursions highly inadvisable.

The dirt track leading downhill from the shady area almost immediately deteriorated into a very overgrown footpath across a field. Here in the middle of the path shuffling through the dead grass and prickly scrub we encountered two more exceedingly large turtles bringing the turtle count to seven. The path led into the side of an olive grove before becoming totally swamped in thorns and thicket. We found a gap in the rusty wire fence around the olive grove and crawled through onto a dirt road.

Very soon this road metamorphosed into a street of smart new houses and pretty gardens which marked the edge of Amaniou. A friendly brown and white dog of mixed parentage stood in the entrance of one of them and barked and wagged hopefully. John went over to say hello and played with him, until my desire for a Fanta got the better of me, and I dragged him off in search of a taverna.

On joining the main road through the village we went into the first and possibly the only taverna in Amaniou. Climbing the steps from the road onto a little balcony supporting a couple of chairs and tables, we entered a large room empty except for a small bar and a very large fridge at one end.

'Looks closed to me,' I said. 'Oh and I'm dying for a drink. Is it worth knocking on the bar or shouting or something to let them know we are here?'

A short stocky figure appeared behind us, 'Kalispera, how can I help you?' he asked.

'Two orange Fantas if you have them,' John enquired not over hopefully.

'But of course,' he grinned and his eyes twinkled. 'Have a seat.'

He pulled out a balcony chair and indicated for us to sit down as he retraced his steps back to the other end of the balcony and into the door of the house. We sat down appreciating the shade and the opportunity to rest our legs. When he reappeared he put the glasses and Fantas in front of us and sat down for a chat. John particularly likes his drinks ice cold, especially when he is hot, and so on picking up the bottle of warm Fanta and looking over at the fridge, 'Any chance of a cold one or some ice?' he asked.

'No I'm afraid not, but this is much better for you. My father, and he is 104 years old so he knows how to keep healthy, doesn't believe in serving cold drinks. He says that giving hot tourists cold drinks is doing them no favours. It's really bad for the blood pressure so you are far better just enjoying your Fanta as it is.'

As we drank our warm Fantas and watched the cars winding their way through the narrow street, we learned about Sofos's life. As a young man, he had been a singer and violinist in Kos town and had gone to Australia in his thirties to see more of the world and earn a better living. He travelled around Australia playing in bars and working as a bricklayer until he met his wife, whose family were from Rhodes.

He settled in Sydney and there he bought an old shop and converted it into a taverna. He and his wife provided Greek food and entertainment there for 20 years. He reminisced how they worked hard and the taverna became very popular, being especially lively at the weekends when it would get really crowded. However, eventually he and his wife grew tired of the demanding routine and increasingly they missed the islands.

Now they had been back on Kos for over ten years and were glad that they had decided to return to his birthplace, where he had bought the taverna in which we sat. Although he didn't say so, it seemed he was now more or less retired as the taverna had little for sale. However, old habits die hard so he obviously didn't want to turn down two keen customers. Well rested, we bade farewell to Sofos and agreed that next time we found ourselves in Ameniou we would look him up and have further healthier warm Fantas. Discussing Sofos's interesting life, we soon covered the short distance by road back to where we had left the car.

We decided to extend our enjoyable day by going out for a meal and chose to go to Kyrios's. As there are so many restaurants to choose from we had only been there once this summer and we were disappointed that Andy hadn't been there.

Kyrios's restaurant was reached by a short track off the main road and was situated alongside a couple of small newly built, but as yet unoccupied, shops in the midst of several sets of studios. Although the area around it had changed in recent years, the restaurant was very well established. Its tables were in a large very sheltered outside area which made it particularly popular on windy evenings. It was made additionally welcoming by a variety of large pot plants and coloured lights hanging from the beams that supported climbing plants. Greek programmes with the sound turned off played continuously on a large television screen fixed on the outside of the kitchen wall.

Kyrios circulated chatting to customers and giving his views on any political items portrayed on the silent news. His view that the islands would be much better served by Greece leaving the EU and coming out of the euro were frequently stated and widely known. His wife did the cooking and his daughter and Andy took orders and waited on the tables. We entered and were greeted by Kyrios and chose a table away from the attractive but potentially mosquito ridden pot plants. He gave us the menu which, although it remained more or less the same from one year to the next, usually had a few dishes that were different from elsewhere.

As soon as he spotted us Andy came to say hello and take our order.

'This is our second visit here,' John said. 'We missed you last time.'

'That will have been when Tanya and I went to the barbecue put on by Baystay for their staff. They have to work very long hours through July and August so the barbecue is to thank them and show that their loyalty is appreciated. It was a good evening. Have you decided what you will have?'

'I had grilled snapper last time which was very nice but I'd like to try something different. What do you suggest?' I said.

'I remember,' he said addressing me, 'you would often have a vegetarian option if there was one. I can recommend the cheese and onion pie with stuffed tomatoes.' Then turning to John he said, 'You liked a steak if one was on the menu. Unfortunately we don't do steaks here but the beef stifado is excellent.'

'I will go with your recommendation,' I said. 'What do you think John?'

'Yes I'm very happy to try the beef stifado.'

When we had finished our meal, which was excellent as Andy had promised, he brought us the bill. Then, as everyone was settled and served, we were able to tell him that the next time we were in the old town, after we had seen him and Tanya on the ferry, we had been to look at his future bar.

'Well what do you think?' he asked expectantly.

'It looks really promising. It's certainly in a central location,' John said. 'Anyone there shopping will notice it.'

'I think it's an attractive building from the outside

especially with the arch shaped windows,' I commented.

'I want it to look appealing so visitors to Kefalos want to go in.'

'When we looked through the windows we thought it looked bigger inside than we expected,' John added.

'Yes it's quite spacious inside which will allow me to have seating at the bar, as well as tables and chairs, and provide a raised area for musicians to use. Roll on winter so I can get on with it.'

'Well we can't agree with that sentiment but we certainly wish you all the best with it,' said John, 'and we will definitely be customers.'

'It's living the dream,' he grinned. 'I'm really excited about it and so is Tanya. Well better crack on,' he said and headed for the kitchen.

13

Walking and Walkers in Tilos

This week promised to be an especially enjoyable one because on Monday we were going to Tilos. I had always wanted to go there because it was reputed to have some really good footpaths and to be protective of its wildlife.

First, however, on Sunday afternoon Kamari bay was having a party to hand over his new shed to Petros and to celebrate its completion. The shed's construction had involved a range of donations of component parts from a couple of windows from a renovated hotel summerhouse to the decking provided by Meltemi, as when they made their decked sitting area in front of the hut they had several strips left over. However, although composed of a range of materials, the shed had been put together with considerable care and was much more substantial than the one that it replaced. Items of furniture had also been donated to make up for those destroyed, including a deep mattress from the

Baystay for Petros to use for his afternoon nap on his extremely blackened but now cleaned up bedstead.

Everyone, who could make time to do so, was there. We all took food – I made chicken pasta salad and some chocolate crunch – and we arranged it on the trestle tables erected by the side of the shed. All the contributions made a really large and delicious looking spread. Spiros opened the party by making a speech thanking everyone for coming and for their help in building the shed. Then with a flourish he presented Petros with a key to the large lock on the door. We all cheered and clapped and Petros overcome with emotion struggled to keep back the tears as he put the key in the lock, opened the door and went inside.

He was in the shed for quite a while, and so we were all getting a bit worried as to whether the occasion was proving too much for him, but then he emerged all smiles and enthusiastically thanked everyone. Spiros christened the shed with a bottle of something fizzy and invited us to tuck into the party food which we did with enthusiasm. While we ate we were entertained by a young couple related to Spiros, who played their guitars and sang. Afterwards those who needed to get back to work left but the rest of us reluctant to break up the social occasion continued to sit and chat for a while longer.

Graham and Terry went to join Seb and Otto and Andreas went to have a word with Petros and admire the shed. This provided Joan, Angela and I with the opportunity to find out from Jan how her trip to Patmos with Andreas had gone.

'We had a brilliant time. I really enjoyed myself,' she responded enthusiastically. 'It's a lovely island.'

'I'm sure that's not the main reason you enjoyed it so much,' Joan teased.

'True enough,' Jan grinned at us, 'but I really did like Patmos.'

'Where did you stay?' I asked.

'Well Alexis, the uncle he told me about, is in his seventies now and lives in a little cottage near the village of Lampi, which I think you told me that you and John walked to. His daughter Ourania lives just down the road from him and her husband has combined his own farm with that of Alexis and runs both of them. Andreas had told them that we hadn't known each other that long and so Andreas stayed with Alexis and I stayed with Ourania.'

'How did that work out?' Angela asked.

'Really well. I had Ourania's daughter's room as she is working in Athens. Ourania also has a son but he is still at home as he is at secondary school. Alexis had the opportunity to have Andreas to himself for some of the time and he obviously enjoyed that. They were all really nice. By the way they treated me, I got the impression that Andreas had told them that I was important to him.'

'What did you do? Did you get to see much of the island?' questioned Joan.

'Yes, although we only had three full days there, Andreas showed me around and so I think that I got quite a feel for the island.'

'Tell me where you went, probably some of the same places as us,' I said.

'Well the first day in we just walked around the farm, chatted to Andreas's uncle and visited Andreas's cousin who also works on the farm. Andreas said he felt he should visit his cousin as they always got on extremely well but hadn't seen each other for ages.'

'When we were on Patmos,' I recounted, 'several people commented to us that climate change was making it increasingly difficult to make a living from farming and we did think that the countryside looked really parched.'

'Yes, that's what Alexis told me. He said that increasingly people were giving up trying to farm and looking for other employment, particularly tourism, to make a living. Forty years or so ago he said that they used to grow wheat and vegetables but now his son-in-law mainly keeps goats.'

'Did you go to the monastery of Saint John?' asked Angela. 'I imagine you did. I found it really impressive and there was so much to see.'

'Yes we did. We took the bus into Skala and like you,' she looked at me, 'we went to the Cave of the Apocalypse and then walked to the monastery of Saint John. Andreas said that they both were so important to the history and prosperity of the island they were a must visit but I assured him that I really wanted to see them. I loved the mystical atmosphere of the cave and found the history of the monastery fascinating and the fact that it wasn't just a museum but there were still monks living there. We spent the afternoon on the beach at Petra and then had dinner in a very quaint little traditional Greek restaurant in Chora. The next day we borrowed Alexis's car and did a tour of the middle and north of Patmos and on the last day we went to the beach at Psili Ammos. Have you been there?' she asked Angela and I.

We both responded that we hadn't. 'I don't know where it is,' I said.

'It's right down the South. We went there because Andreas has a friend there with a very smart yacht which he lent us. We didn't sail it but just motored around the peninsula and moored in a bay.'

'You would have seen the views of Kalymnos then.'

'Yes with the blue sky, the different colours in the sea and the contrasting stark brown mountains it was really beautiful.'

At that moment Andreas rejoined us. 'Petros is thrilled with his shed,' he said. He thinks that it's a great improvement on what was there. It's quite an amazing construction,' he laughed.

'I've been telling them about our trip to Patmos and how much I enjoyed it,' said Jan.

'We did have a good time didn't we?' he looked tenderly at Jan. Then turning to us, 'Well I hope you'll excuse me but I'm going to have to take her away now, as this evening we are going to a friend's barbecue in Marmari. It's his birthday.'

Jan gathered up her handbag and the cardigan that she might need later and Andreas picked up the bag in which she had brought her contribution to the food and they left with our wishes that they should have an enjoyable evening.

'I think Andreas is in love with her,' confidently stated Angela.

'Could be, the way he looks at her,' agreed Joan.

'Well she admits that she is very keen on him,' I added.

'When they are together you can really sense the connection between them,' commented Joan. 'I wonder how far their relationship has gone.'

'Well they stayed in separate houses and so they didn't sleep together on Patmos,' said Angela.

'No, but they had time alone together on the yacht,' I pointed out.

'Uhm, well you told us how unhappy she has been with her husband and so good luck to them. Let's hope everything works out,' said Joan bringing to a close our speculation as to the progress of their relationship.

Early next morning, as planned, John and I took a bus to Kos town. We had decided to catch the bus rather than leave Mabel in a Kos car park. The bus takes around an hour and 15 minutes, as it goes to Mastichari and then picks up and drops passengers on the back road from there to Kos.

In Kos harbour we boarded the ferry to Tilos, which first called in at Mandraki on Nisyros. The turn around was quick as the ferry rapidly disgorged its foot passengers and assorted vehicles. I leaned on the stern rail and watched the white buildings of Mandraki diminish in size and evaporate into the heat haze. The ferry chugged alongside the rocks and cliffs of the island's mountainous rim. As we knew from our stay there, Nisyros has little in the way of beaches. The ferry, having semi-circled the island, headed out across the sea to our destination of Livadia.

I returned to the cabin with its large screen TV on which anxious looking politicians addressed the debt crisis issues to rows of empty seats. Taking my novel out of my bag I settled down beside John, who buried in his newspaper merely grunted an acknowledgement of my presence.

When movement outside suggested we were approaching Livadia, we both went out to be greeted by the beautiful wide bay in which nestled the sheltered port. Having walked out of the ferry's hull and onto the quay, taking care to avoid being run over by disembarking vans, cars and mopeds all revving impatiently, our eyes were drawn to a large noticeboard. This proclaimed the island to be a special protected area for nature according to an EU directive. Apparently it harbours around four hundred plant species and over a hundred types of birds including birds of prey such as the Bonelli's eagle, Eleonora's falcon and the long-legged buzzard. The bird life, especially the possibility of seeing an eagle, had been one of the island's main attractions for us along with its reputation for being very good for walking. We looked at the pictures of the birds of prey, read their descriptions and tried to memorise what they looked like.

On Kos, once the shooting season started, we were accustomed to being woken up by gunfire on the mountain behind us and seeing men with guns in trucks or on scooters heading for the hills. Spiros told us that when he was young there had been eagles on Kos but that they had long since disappeared. We were impressed that the residents of Tilos cared sufficiently about their island's wildlife that they supported their mayor when he introduced a hunting ban. We were rather less impressed, when later on in our stay, the friendly and informative curator of the paleontology museum in the town hall in Megalo Chorio told us the ban arose from the need for self-preservation. Apparently they kept mistakenly shooting each other, which owing to our Kos experiences came as no surprise to us.

We bought ice creams from the supermarket and were attracted by its tray of large delicious looking grapefruit. We thought that they looked ideal for taking on our walks and vowed to stock up once we had found some accommodation. We sat on a wall by the white and blue Art Deco police station built like similar buildings on other Dodecanese islands during the Italian rule in the early 20th century. We discussed our strategy for finding somewhere to stay and where that somewhere might be situated.

On the cliffs behind us to our right, smart white hotel apartments occupied a key position overlooking the harbour and the bay – definitely out of our price range. Ahead behind the quaint old Italian style harbour building the town climbed the cliffs. No doubt some of the houses hugging the narrow streets contained rooms and studios to let, but these seemed likely to be noisy. I thought it would be really nice to stay on the waterfront somewhere along the paralia – promenade – and that was where after a couple of hours wandering, inquiring in supermarkets and restaurants and negotiating, we found just the accommodation to suit our needs and our budget.

We visited and rejected possibilities on a continuum from a scruffy room in the backstreets to a splendid but overpriced studio overlooking the beach. The owner of the apartment we took ultimately happened to walk past us when, offering apologies, we were hastening from the overpriced studio. Immediately recognising an opportunity for customers, he approached us to explain that he had an apartment only a short walk further along the paralia. As we felt we were running out of options, we dutifully followed him.

The apartment's position in a seafront building but at

the back with a distant view of the hills and Livadia's ruined castle and an immediate one of the town's waste and recycling bins ensured that it was only 25 euros a night, a very good price. Moreover, it was new, and apart from the immediate view, had much to commend it. The bright clean kitchenette was well equipped with adjacent to it a smart new black wood dining table and matching chairs.

However, our initial excitement at seeing the large cooker soon dissipated on reading the notice proclaiming it dangerous to use with the exception of two of the hobs – the usual Dodecanese cooking facility. Nevertheless, the shower room was spacious with water that, at least while we were there, flowed continuously. Best of all there was air-conditioning that quietly and efficiently cooled the apartment. The benefits of the latter luxury were very much appreciated. We soon came to realise that the waterfront of Tilos teemed with mosquitoes rendering it necessary at all times of day and night, whatever the temperature, to keep all doors and windows tightly shut.

We used the plastic chairs and table provided at the front to have breakfast by the beach and in so doing met the American tourists occupying the front apartment. Feeling rather smug we listened to their complaints of exorbitant rates, lack of air conditioning and mosquito bites. Then fortified and ready for the day's exploration, we set off to find the ruined town of Mikro Chorio, which means small village. This was founded in the 15th century by the Knights of Saint John but apparently by the late 1960s had become completely abandoned.

We passed the tourist office situated on the waterfront just before the harbour. As it had been shut when we arrived, we were surprised to find it open. We decided to go in but inside was very little information apart from that already obtained from the harbour noticeboard. However, we picked up a timetable for the local bus that on leaving Livadia circumnavigated Megalo Chorio, meaning big village, which is the capital of Tilos. It then went on to the tiny port of Agios Antonios and Eristos beach several times a day. John explained to the smartly dressed young man in charge of the office our intention to walk to Mikro Chorio.

'Many people do this,' he observed. 'It's an ideal walk.' However, when pressed to identify which street we should take in order to locate the old monopati leading to the village, it was soon obvious that he hadn't a clue. Initially he suggested heading towards Livadia's castle, the antiquity just visible over the rubbish dump from our apartment. Then, when we pointed out from the map, which we had purchased from the supermarket the previous evening, that this would have us heading in the wrong direction, he took our map and looked studiously at it from various angles. Adopting a deep in thought pose, he then appeared to have an 'aha' moment and lead us out of the tourist office and pointed across the bay to where we could see a path snaking round the headland. 'That will be it,' he said.

'Afraid not,' we said shaking our heads but thanked him anyway.

We headed through the town and took a street going uphill, then climbed some steps and found a footpath.

'This is the right direction. It will be up here somewhere,' said John with convincing certainty, between chunters about people in tourist offices who couldn't read maps and who didn't know their locality. However, to our dismay the footpath led onto the main road to Megalo Chorio and for an extremely hot 20 minutes we walked back and forth along the unshaded asphalt looking for something that might be a footpath. Eventually, as the road bent steeply back on itself, we could see the old monopati on the bank above us going straight ahead.

'Great now we should be OK,' I said pleased to be on the lovely old path through the hillside. 'Let's sit under this tree and have a drink.'

We passed the water bottle between us and rested

comfortably in the shade while John studied the map. When we stood up to walk on, I felt a sharp prick on the back of my thigh as a hornet buzzed around me and flew off. I realised that I'd probably been stung by it. However, it had stung me through my shorts and didn't feel particularly painful when it happened and so, not wishing to introduce anything negative into such a potentially delightful excursion, I didn't mention it.

The narrow path dipped, straightened and climbed until we found ourselves once again back on the main road but this time we could see the monopati continuing over the other side of it. Soon after at the point where we crossed a cement road, the path disappeared into piles of stones, ruined walls and terraces. In the seemingly not particularly near distance, we had our first sight of the ruins of Mikro Chorio. Unfortunately these rose steeply and inaccessibly from a gorge between us and the village.

While debating our next step, two figures emerged from the gorge and strode towards us. Anticipating that they were returning from the village, we walked towards them. Tall, skinny, scantily clad and heavily tanned with well-worn hiking boots and hiking poles, this elderly couple were clearly serious walkers.

Correctly interpreting our questioning looks, the woman

responded, 'It's no good, you can't find your way across going down there.' She pointed back where they'd come from. 'The path has totally disappeared. It's hard work climbing over all the stones and although it doesn't look so bad from here the rocks on the side of the gorge are really steep and slippery.'

'We had to give up so now we are going up the road,' said her companion. Quickly concluding that if they couldn't make it we certainly couldn't, we asked them about their alternative route.

'The cement road you've just crossed bends around to the right and then goes all the way there,' said the man.

We learned from them that this road had been constructed to enable buses to get through, as one of the ruined houses had been restored and turned into a bar. On weekend evenings in the summer months, the village became a large discotheque and youngsters danced among the ruins. There they could party till dawn disturbing no one but the ghosts of more opulent times. Having delivered this information and sucking heavily at the tube leading from the water bottle strapped to his side, the man strode off.

'Must go,' the woman gave an apologetic smile and scuttled after him.

Intending to follow in their footsteps up the cement road

we waited for them to disappear from view. We sat on a large rock admiring the multitude of grey stone ruins rising in terraces up to a small mediaeval castle. It looked to us very much as if it had once been a macro rather than a micro village and we were keen to explore it fully.

The cement road provided a steady but easy climb to the entrance of the village, where we were faced by layers of identical windowless and roofless houses grouped around a magnificent renovated church. This with its white walls and new red roof stood out boldly against the grey rocky backdrop. Climbing up the steps into the village and taking the twisty paths through the ruins, we found ourselves outside the closed and deserted bar.

We decided to avail ourselves of a couple of plastic chairs in the shade of its walls and make it our picnic spot. We sat eating our sandwiches and grapefruit purchased from the supermarket and tried to imagine what life there might have been like during the times when the village was thriving and vibrant. During the Crusades being sheltered from the sea it would have been valued for its safety from pirates and its extensive hillside terraces farmed to feed the local people. Our contemplations were soon interrupted by three friendly purring pussy cats. Looking plump, furry and cared for, they just seemed to want some attention, which we were happy to give them.

After lunch we pottered around the empty ruined streets. It seemed strange that such a large community of occupants of what must have been a very picturesque and established village should have decided to abandon their homes. However, we knew that as the threat from pirates waned, many villagers began to move from the hills to the coast and the flat area of Livadia – the name which means meadows. This migration steadily continued and when in 1948 the island became part of Greece again the remaining villagers left.

We climbed up to the castle built by the Knights of Saint John in order to admire the view over the barren hills and out to sea. Below it we discovered another smaller church. There peering through the rectangular opening in the top of the locked metal door, as we became accustomed to the darkness, we found ourselves looking eye to eye with saints depicted in some very old frescos. Then climbing down over collapsed steps and through narrow streets we reached the edge of the village and what must have been a huge millstone for grinding corn.

After leaving the ruins of Mikro Chorio we had decided to head for Lethra Bay, which had glittered at us through the hills from the top of the village. A well-defined stone path through the fields and kermes oaks led us from the ruins below the mill stone back yet again to the Megalo Chorio road. We crossed over and picked up a track beside a dry river bed. This took us to a charming old stone fountain that, unlike others we found on Tilos, still gushed water and was continuing to assuage the thirst of passers by.

From there we climbed down into a ravine and scrambled over and between boulders, through and under oleander bushes, until hot and dishevelled we emerged at the beach. Avoiding the goat droppings we rested on a wall under the second largest olive tree. A young hiker, engrossed in a book, had claimed the best stone wall perch under the biggest tree. There, as we often did on our island walks, we indulged in the enjoyable pastime of goat watching. A band of multi-coloured and multi-sized goats provided our entertainment doing three, two and one-legged balancing acts on the walls to see which could reach the highest leaves of a nearby tree.

Having cooled down and decided against swimming in the inviting water owing to the uninviting large stones and sharp pebbles that made up Lethra beach, we set off up the hill to find the headland path back to Livadia. This was easily done as the high path was wide and well maintained and afforded magnificent views back over Lethra bay and down to tiny inaccessible bays and our next destination, the Red Sand beach.

I removed a couple of ill-placed pebbles and wriggled around to form the red gritty sand into a more comfortable dip to sit in and leaned back against a flat rock. It had been a relatively easy but very slow descent to Kokkini Paralia, the Red Sand beach, following the cairns and picking our way through pebbles and prickly undergrowth. Although now late in the afternoon, the descent was a must for John.

As a student hitching in Crete, he had suffered sunstroke, dehydration and, with repetitions of the story, near certain death owing to a dogged and obsessive determination to press on and on in search of the extraordinary phenomenon of a red sand beach. Such a beach he had never witnessed previously and wasn't on that occasion destined to witness. He never found it, probably because it was insufficiently red to match his expectations, or because in his semi-delirious state he stumbled past it. However, the sand on this Tilos beach was indisputably red, especially in the deep bronze glow of the early evening sun, if for purists a bit on the gritty and pebbly side rather than fine and soft.

John walked enthusiastically up and down photographing the beach and its sand from all angles, trying to best capture its redness. Unfortunately, this task was rendered somewhat difficult because we were sharing the phenomenon with two very active extrovert nudists seemingly on acid. They moved up and they moved down and they moved along the beach in continual motion doing exercises or exorcisms whatever, splashing in and out of the sea and running into my averted gaze and John's camera lens. However, unlike the nudists, after an energetic day's exploring I appreciated an opportunity to recline statically in nature's armchair.

Having made the most of the experience and taken sufficient pictures of the red sand to make up for his youthful disappointment and to convince sceptics of its redness, John pronounced it was time to go. With the sun going down emphasising the redness of the beach and rendering the headland path high above us in shadow, we left the prancing nudists and began the slow climb up through the stones and the prickly scrub to the headland path back to Livadia.

The little port town of Livadia was delightful in the early evening and at nightfall. There was immense pleasure to be had in ambling through the streets, dining outside and relaxing in the square enveloped in the gentle warm Mediterranean air. This climactic novelty was never likely to lose its appeal for those of us all too accustomed to shivering in sweaters on miserable English summer evenings at the barbecues of friends determined to eat *al fresco* no matter what.

Each evening seemed a joyous occasion as shopkeepers left their counters and sat outside their shops. Friends and neighbours joined them lining the streets with their plastic chairs to swop gossip and debate the issues of the day. Banter passed back and forth across the streets drawing in the tourists as they sashayed down the middle. The restaurants were bustling, especially the popular ones, as to a tourist the sight of a full restaurant serves as a recommendation for the cuisine and an invitation to enter.

On our first night, using this selection criterion, we had discovered the Acropol, an obviously extremely popular restaurant just along the waterfront from our apartment. We found their dish of pork medallions in honey and cream was truly delicious and so we had booked a table there for this our second night and also for our last night. After enjoying lamb fricassee followed by peach compote and the restaurant's special ice cream, John announced he had just received a surprising text message from Daryl. It said that they planned to use the photo of him doing a toehold on his trick ski to make a poster advertising water ski possibilities.

'I would have thought they would have wanted a photo of a young person probably on a wake board for an advert,' he said, though obviously pleased at the news.

'Well it is a really good action shot and a bit unusual so it might attract more attention,' I suggested positively.

After eating, locals and tourists alike gravitated to the main square for coffee and ouzo and to observe life go by, and go by again, in fact go by numerous times owing to the small size of the town. As we found out, if prepared to wait, you were practically guaranteed to come across those encountered during the day's explorations and be able to continue any conversation started earlier.

We headed to the square after dinner because I wanted to get something from the pharmacy for my hornet sting, as during the day my thigh had swollen until the swelling was threatening to engulf my knee and was creeping up my left buttock. The pharmacist was very sympathetic and very unsurprised. It seemed that each night would see a few tourists with the same problem in the queue for his attention, alongside those with the usual upset stomachs, sprained ankles, sunburn etc. The aggressive hornets of Tilos seemed to have it in for tourists or maybe the locals had become immune to their particular brand of poison. Ointment was prescribed to rub on to cool down the skin and reduce the redness while antihistamine tablets were to be taken to bring down the swelling.

I considered a cappuccino was required in order that I could take the first tablets. Crossing the square to the quaint bar seemingly beloved by the island's visitors, we met the elderly couple who had told us the way to Micro Chorio.

'Did you go to the village?' asked the elderly woman, her appearance transformed in a blue silk dress and glittery sandals.

'Yes we did thanks and we found it really interesting,' I replied. 'We walked all around the streets, looked at the renovated church and climbed up to the castle. We spent quite a while there.'

'We had a quick look around but Nigel,' she gestured towards her husband now moving across the square, 'was keen to take the path from below the castle to the Cave of Harkadhio so we couldn't stop for too long.'

'That sounds like you had a long walk.'

'Yes, it was quite a distance because from there we walked to Megalo Chorio but we did get the bus back. Oh must go,' she said as her husband disappeared into a shop and she hastened after him.

We sank into the bar's comfy chairs under the trees and ordered cappuccinos. These were authentically made with frothy milk on top, rather than Greek island style with squirted cream, but they were extremely small and jaw-droppingly expensive. Much better value was the competing street side cafe with hard seats, unsuitable for those with swollen bottoms, on the other side of the square.

On future evenings my prescription having returned my bottom to normal, although the swelling on my leg took much longer to go, we observed life in the square from the opposite direction. We patronised the cafe alongside the more cost-conscious inhabitants of Tilos while drinking our Nescafe and enjoying exceptionally sticky baklavas.

At 10.20am the following morning we were back in the square waiting for the bus to Megalo Chorio, the island's capital. From our bench under the trees we observed tourists mainly wearing hiking boots and backpacks, ranging from the minuscule to the simply enormous, converge on the square from every street and alley.

'I wonder what size bus it is going to be. There looks like there are rather a lot of us,' I observed.

'I don't think they will have bendy buses here,' retorted John referring to the monstrous purple buses that caused blockages and traffic jams in the narrow streets of York.

'Well in that case I think we need to get nearer to the bus stop as it's going to be quite a free for all when the bus turns up,' I predicted.

We left our spot in the shade and moved to the pavement. At only a few minutes after half past ten, its departure time, the bus turned up tooting loudly to announce its arrival. Without actually quite resorting to pushing and shoving each other out of the way, the tourists aimed for one of the two open doors, leaning and straining, elbows and sticks to the fore to lever themselves inside.

Thwack! A large rucksack wielded by a tall thin gangly man hit me on the side of the head, while his panting companion dug her left elbow into my ribs to help to get herself up the bus steps. Arms bent and sticking horizontally out from my body, I prevented anyone else from getting past me and ensured that I was next to get on the bus. It quite took me back to my daily 30-kilometre journey to and from secondary school, where to ensure I got a seat on the way home, I had perfected this manoeuvre.

Triumphant, John and I found ourselves standing in the aisle in the centre of the bus wedged between the gangly rucksack man and an Australian couple. As with a grinding clash of gears and an outburst of tooting we drove off, a few timid tourists could be seen retracing their footsteps back from the square but clearly most potential passengers had succeeded in squashing themselves aboard. With another burst of loud tooting, the bus departed groaning and swaying under its heavy load.

The bus climbed up the hill, going past Micro Chorio to the left where we had been yesterday and continued inland on the only road until we arrived in Megalo Chorio. Passing cars in the very narrow main street required considerable skill and appeared to involve all the elders of the village. Making the most of the day's excitement, they ran backwards and forwards and leapt up and down shouting directions, thereby adding considerably to the complexity of the challenge facing the bus driver.

When we eventually reached the bus stop at the end of the street, we alighted and walked back past the shops until we found the zig-zagging path up to the ruins of the castle of the Knights of Saint John perched on a crag high above the town. The climb up was slow and hot and got slower and hotter, as approaching the top, the stone steps and the hill's rocky outcrop merged together making it difficult to determine the intended way up. Although between gasps for air I disputed John's claim that the view from the top would be worth our efforts, it certainly was. We could see in detail Megalo Chorio laid out before us and in the other direction at the foot of the hill, situated on the coast the village of Agios Antonios.

A substantial intact arch in the walls of the medieval citadel led us into the centre of the ruins. There we were able to enter a temple and, when our eyes grew accustomed to the dark, we could see some uninspiring murals which dated from the 16th century. Apparently the inspiring silver adorned icons, belonging to an ancient Greek temple on the same site, had been moved elsewhere. Going out into the light we found a place under the walls to sit in the shade and decide what to do next.

Leaving the castle by going through the arch we made our way back down, a great deal easier and quicker to achieve than going up. Once down again we bought Fantas from the supermarket and looked for somewhere to sit and eat our picnic lunch. We headed for the church but were disappointed as it wasn't situated in the hoped for square. However, nearby, up some steps we found a bench under a tree alongside an attractive white building. When two tourists came out, from their conversation we realised the building was the City Hall which houses findings from the excavation of the Cave of Harkadhio. The significance of this cave, to which the two sprightly elderly walkers had walked from Micro Chorio, was about to be revealed.

'Just fancy pygmy elephants living on Tilos many thousands of years ago.'

'I thought all elephants were large, the notion of pygmy ones is fascinating.'

We are not particularly interested in palaeontology but pygmy elephants sounded a must see. Consequently, John popped in straightaway to make sure that based on our past experience the exhibition wasn't about to shut and told the curator that we would come in the minute that we had finished our sandwiches. This we did and it proved very interesting and worthwhile.

The curator, who was really nice and helpful, explained how the excavations in the cave had revealed the bones from 30 pygmy elephants. The elephants probably originated from Africa and had lived on the island since prehistoric times. The species would have diminished in size because of the limited food resources on Tilos until they were only about one and a half metres in height. The elephants that were found in the cave were clearly sheltering there and during the volcanic eruptions of Santorini or Nisyros they had died and been covered in ash. She showed us bones, teeth and tusks of two of them – an adult and a baby – and explained how these helped to produce the depictions of their skeletons in the exhibition.

She also told us about the cemetery dating from the Hellenistic period found on both sides of the road to the west of Agios Antonios, the coastal village we had looked down upon from the castle. All the bodies buried there were young people – a fact that remained a puzzle as to why this should be the case. Maybe the two skulls that she showed us, which had been drilled into in order to let out the evil spirits, held a clue. On the subject of human skeletons she also told us that the petrified remains of three sailors from the 5th century BC were visible in the tessellated rocks on the beach. We had thought that we might take the footpath to Agios Antonios and this gruesome history clinched John's intention to do so.

The curator told us that to find the path we must go up past the church and continue up until we came upon it on the left. We did this and with her directions we found it easily. The path was pleasant and gently made its way downhill. On the coast it was surprisingly windy and the sea was quite rough.

Agios Antonios consisted of a few houses and a couple of restaurants alongside the harbour, which even in the afternoon was full of activity. We bought an ice cream and sat on the waterfront watching some fishermen mending their nets, while some others were trying with limited success to repair a boat's engine and a couple more were sat on the quay gutting fish. Afterwards we walked along the beach to look for a place to swim and possible evidence of skeletons. However, as the wind blew sand continually in our faces, the waves crashed on the rocks and there were no signs of petrified sailors, we decided that we would prefer to flag down the 2.30pm bus and go to Eristos bay instead, the island's main beach.

Situated on the opposite side of the island we anticipated it would be sheltered and indeed it was very tranquil. Moreover we almost had the whole beach to ourselves. John found some rocks up the far end to snorkel around and look for interesting fish. I decided that I didn't want to swim. Instead, noticing an old car seat under the terebinth trees which lined the back of the beach, I sat in comfort reading my book and in truth snoozing a little until John returned. Then we caught the 4.30pm bus back, which returned first to Agios Antonios and then to Megalo Chorio, before taking us back to Livadia.

The next day was Sunday, which presented us with the opportunity to take the once weekly 11am bus to the monastery of Saint Panteleimonas on the island's northwest coast. From there we planned to find the footpath to Agios Antonios where we could catch a bus back to Livadia. As had happened on the previous day, when the time approached 11 o'clock, potential bus travellers appeared from all sides of the square. The as yet uninitiated formed an orderly queue in front of the pastry shop, while those aware of the impending free-for-all tried to position themselves near to where the bus doors might be when it stopped to pick us up.

Bang on time loud tooting announced the arrival of the bus and all but the polite and fainthearted surged forward into the fray. This time we managed to get on the back seat of the bus alongside a friendly elderly woman and her disabled husband. He was determined to see the monastery and in such circumstances felt justified in using his two sticks and seeming frailty to protect him during the onslaught.

His wife told us that they had once been on holiday in Tilos years before and had enjoyed a trip to the monastery and really wanted to repeat the experience. When younger they had been keen walkers and she told us if we had time we should do the walk from Livadia to Ghera because it was very scenic and so she was sure that we would enjoy it. I was able to say to her that we had one more day and her recommendation sounded ideal for it.

The road to the monastery climbed and climbed up the barren cliffside and the bus went slower and slower. The engine groaned and wailed in protest as the sheer drop to the sea below got more and more intimidating. Consequently it was something of a relief to reach the end of the road near the top of the hill. There we alighted from the bus in front of a very well preserved entrance arch to what is a very picturesque fortress monastery built in the 15th century. No longer inhabited, the 25th July is its most important date as from that date it hosts a three day festival to celebrate Saint Panteleimonas.

We walked through the arch into a delightful cobbled courtyard shaded by trees and vines and furnished with a spring fed fountain and pots of herbs and flowers. Doing our tourist bit we went into the dark atmospheric Byzantine church and, as our eyes became accustomed to it, duly admired the murals and the famous carvings on the iconostasis – altar back, for those of us that didn't know this before. Then we climbed the stone steps to the wooden arcade over the medieval cells and out onto the roof. From there we looked out onto the tower and over the pebble mosaic passageways and the roofs of the little red tiled circular chapels.

Returning to the courtyard, we thought that we should start our walk back. We left by the lower cafe area but stopped to bid goodbye to the couple we met on the bus. Having looked around they told us that they were pleased to find the monastery had undergone major renovations and so was in much better repair than on their first visit. We left them comfortably ensconced in a shady corner for their half an hour wait for the bus to return to Livadia.

We walked a little way back along the road and easily found the clear path up the hill marked by a large, totally empty so uninformative, information board. We climbed steadily up the good path enjoying the views over the rocky seascape until we reached a narrow ridge. At the point where the path started its descent over the other side were the dilapidated ruins of an old stone chapel and a couple of benches. This seemed a good spot to eat our lunch and just as we had finished it we were joined by two walkers, who turned out to be an Italian and a German, with the same idea in mind.

'Have you also come from the monastery?' John enquired.

'Yes we are staying in Agios Antonios and we walked there first thing this morning and now we are on our way back,' replied the Italian. 'What about you?'

'We also went there this morning but on the weekly bus as we are staying in Livadia,' John responded.

'We stayed in Livadia a couple of years ago. It's a very attractive place and rather more lively than Agios Antonios but we are only here for a couple of days and then we are off to Halki,' said the German.

'We have spent several summers exploring Greek islands and we particularly like the Dodecanese,' the Italian added.

'The islands are changing though and not always for the best,' added his companion. 'Some of the tourist developments on Kos and Rhodes are dreadful. They spring up anywhere and everywhere and they have no character,' said the German.

'We have seen lots of examples where the Greeks have taken EU money supposedly to preserve traditional communities and historic buildings but they've squandered the funds and never finished the work, just created a mess,' complained his companion.

'Here apparently a new museum has been built near the Cave of Harkadhio to house the pygmy elephant exhibits but there was insufficient money to finish it so now goats are the only ones using it.' The German gave a local example to make his point.

'Yes, unfortunately we have seen examples of this happening,' I reluctantly agreed, thinking particularly of Paleo Pili and the castle of Antimachia on Kos.

'I feel sorry for the youngsters though,' said the German. 'Half at least of the Greeks under the age of 25 have no job and no prospects of getting one. The Greek economy is a disaster and their tax system corrupt and inefficient.'

'We know several Greek families on Kos who were proud of the fact their children were able to go into teaching or nursing on the island or in business in Athens, but with the cutbacks they have lost their jobs and had to return home and work in the family restaurant or shop. At least the family business provides them with employment but it's hard to make enough for everyone to live on,' I explained.

'Also they point out that increased tax reduces their profits unless they pass the increased costs onto customers, which they are trying not to do as the tourist trade is vital to the islands,' John added.

'Well arguably their parents' and grandparents' generation are to blame. They weren't prepared to work hard to improve their living standards and they kept corrupt politicians in power until the crisis hit. Nowhere else in Europe could people retire at 50 with a pension,' criticised the German.

'True, but it's perhaps unsurprising that the Greeks accepted what was on offer from the state, no questions asked. Now of course their pensions have been cut several times, 40 per cent or more, so they are not enough to live on,' I pointed out.

'It's not the people's fault that the politicians and investment bankers signed up to the euro when economically Greece was not not in a fit state to join the EU on its terms,' John offered in the Greeks' defence.

'They were proud to be part of the EU and join the front ranks of the European nations and so to stay there I'm afraid they must end corruption at all levels, pay their taxes and put up with austerity. They will emerge stronger eventually,' the German concluded emphatically as he stood up to go.

'Interesting talking to you,' said the Italian. 'Enjoy the rest of your holiday.'

'And you,' we replied in unison.

'I was afraid that was going to get a bit heavy. I'm glad they didn't get onto Brexit,' I said relieved as they disappeared down the hill.

Initially the descent to Agios Antonios involved slithering through rocks, loose stones and red earth but ultimately became a gentle winding path shaded in part by towering rocky outcrops above us and profusely decorated with white foxtail lilies. Lower down we passed empty green signposts on which scribblers suggested distances to their home towns. John was amused at the one where the two prongs of the signpost, that pointed in the direction from which we had come and to where we were heading, had been variously labelled God 1 and God 2 and so he decided to record it with a photo.

From then on the path became much clearer. It passed through an olive grove and a windswept tree arch, which appealed to me and so I asked John to take a photo of me standing under it, before we arrived at the road into Agios Antonios by the walled and locked Kamariani monastery.

On our last day we planned to potter around the harbour and the square in the morning and then after lunch to walk to the abandoned village of Ghera, as suggested by our companions on the bus. No buses were needed for this excursion as we simply came out of the house and turned right up the paralia. We walked past all the beachfront studios and past a renovated stone chapel. Then we started climbing past the Faros taverna and had a close up look at the tiny fishing harbour of Agios Stephanos, with its long concrete jetty, which we had viewed at a distance from outside our studio.

At the top of the hill were some rather swish studios and a line of parked cars that the tourists staying there would need if they wanted a trip into town that didn't involve a tiring climb in order to return. Looking back before rounding the headland gave a beautiful view of the bay and Livadia nestled at the base of surrounding hills.

A little further along the track was the pretty blue and white chapel of Agios Ioannis. It was open and so we went inside. As we had found with many such chapels, its altar, incense burners and paintings of saints were carefully tended. It was a totally still, extremely hot day and so reluctant to set off again, we sat on the stone ledge in the shade of the front of the building where we were soon joined by a pair of Norwegians.

'Where are you from?' one asked in a friendly enquiring tone. We explained from near York in England but currently from Kos.

'You are lucky to have the summer to explore these islands. We have found Tilos very good for walking. Have you done much walking? We understand the English dislike walking. All the walkers on Tilos are Norwegians.'

'We enjoy walking though nothing too demanding. You see more when you are walking and it's very enjoyable,' responded John. 'There seem to be walkers in Tilos from all over Europe, including quite a few from England, but you are the first Norwegians that we have met.'

'You will meet more. It's definitely the case that all the walkers here are Norwegians,' he said repeating his extraordinary claim.

They sat sharing a bottle of water until it was almost finished and then stood up and announced 'Well we will be off now. We are going to Ghera.'

'Do they really think all the walkers here are Norwegian? It seems an odd claim,' I said as they disappeared from view.

'I don't know, perhaps,' John shrugged. 'Well as they didn't have a rucksack, they obviously didn't have a map or any more water, so it's hard to believe that they are particularly experienced walkers.'

Leaving the chapel we followed a renovated paved way. This led zigzagging upwards with cliffs towering above us, sheer drops on the seaward side and magnificent views back towards the chapel and out to sea. At a fork we followed the instructions on our map and turned left going over a small ravine filled with oleanders with colourful pink flowers. Then as predicted we came to an abandoned farmstead, which as usual was occupied by goats. The older more sensible ones stood in the shade but three younger ones were having jumping competitions off the walls.

While we stood still watching the playful goats, John nudged me to follow his gaze towards where a huge grey lizard with striped horizontal markings and skin like chain mail was basking in the sun on a rock. As we walked onward, the bays below with fantastic green, turquoise and navy blue water looked beautiful and appealing. There was an inviting path down to a black pebble beach but we decided that in the heat climbing back up would be too exhausting and so we continued on into Ghera. At the edge of the village we met the Norwegians heading back.

'I wouldn't bother to look around Ghera. It's of no interest,' said the one who had chatted to us before.

'There's nothing there. It's not worth a visit,' added his friend as they walked off.

'Do you think maybe they believed Ghera was an inhabited village,' speculated John.

'Umm, quite possibly, because that might be why they were so disparaging about it even though it's in a such a beautiful location.'

'Also it would explain why they didn't have more water with them, perhaps they thought they would be able to buy drinks.'

Ghera had obviously been a thriving village at one time because there were several rows of square grey stone houses all facing the sea. Like those in Micro Chorio, they had been abandoned in the 1960s but were generally in better condition. While they had no doors or windows many still had roofs. Perhaps it was too far to Livadia to carry the roofing materials.

Surrounding the village were a number of trees and we selected a large olive tree to sit under and eat our grapefruit and biscuits. Terracing stretched up the sunbaked brown hillsides suggesting the importance agriculture must have had to the village in its heyday. Enjoying the tranquillity and the aromas of hot crushed thyme, sage and chamomile we felt very content. We were reluctant to leave such an attractive place but eventually decided we better get back to pack and tidy up.

On our return between Ghera and the path down to the beach we were incredibly lucky and very surprised to see close up a pair of Bonelli's eagles. We knew that we were in their kind of territory as they like dry open landscapes in the mountains and nest in cliffs and caves but we didn't expect to see them. We first spotted the pair when they were well below us gliding elegantly on the air currents. They spiralled around and around, moving steadily upwards until they went by us at our level and then circled above our heads.

From the poster on the harbour we recognised them instantly with their whitish breasts, dark wings with shallow fingers and tails with a dark band at the tip. John took photos both as a memento and so we could match them up to pictures on the internet and find out more information about them. They had an impressive wingspan which we discovered later could measure up to 160cms for a male and 180cms for a female. Apparently in the wild they can live up to 32 years and they stay together as a couple outside of the breeding season. They took their name from the Italian ornithologist Franco Andrea Bonelli who identified them. We were thrilled with our sighting as we knew there were only four pairs on Tilos and they are fairly rare throughout Greece. It provided a wonderful finale to our walking trips on Tilos and emphasised how much more you were likely to see if exploring on foot.

14

A Greek Wedding Scottish Style

I stood on the patio looking at the calm sea and the blue sky dotted with the odd white puffy cloud moving slowly across it in the gentle breeze. Doubtless at Meltemi they would be wishing for the wind to get up. However, there would be no windsurfing activity for John today, as we were guests at the long awaited and much planned for wedding of Mike and Betty's daughter Anna to Alistair.

It was a typically perfect summer's day although later it would be very hot. The wedding was a great opportunity to dress up and I was really looking forward to doing so. There were very few occasions requiring anything smarter than shorts. I was glad that I'd decided to bring with me a dress that I'd bought in a sale the previous autumn and had hardly worn. It was a pretty pale green flowery dress with a lovely full skirt of midi length which I thought would be perfect. I'd packed it just in case I needed to dress up but wasn't expecting to do so. John certainly hadn't anticipated the need to look smart and so had to go to Kardamena to search out a lightweight linen jacket to upgrade his tidiest looking shirt and trousers.

Around 10am along with the 30 or so guests – friends and family of the bride and groom from Scotland and England and Greek and English residents of Kefalos – we lined the track to the beach opposite Kastri island, where the wedding was to take place, to wait for Anna and her father. They were due to arrive in the pony and trap which in the evenings ferried tourists around the bay or up into Kefalos town. We didn't have long to wait before we heard the sound of the pony's hoofs on the track. Someone began clapping and everyone joined in. Mike jumped out smiling and went to assist Anna to alight, which she did with care so as not to catch her dress on the side of the trap.

'Oh doesn't she look radiant,' said a female guest that I didn't know, turning to me.

'Yes, she certainly does,' I agreed adding, 'and her dress is beautiful.'

'I love the way her hair is piled up with flowers pinned in it,' said a teenage girl who was probably the woman's daughter.

Anna shook out the lace tiers of her dress and took

Mike's arm. They promenaded slowly down the beach to the water's edge and we all followed. There, in readiness, was the rowing boat in which Mike was going to row them both over to the island. As Betty had told me, this had been part of the plan if they had got married on the Scottish island and Anna was particularly keen to adhere to it.

Having tuned up his bagpipes, the piper who, when he retired from his role in a regimental band, had moved to Kefalos began to play a Scottish reel. Smiling happily Anna stepped into the rowing boat which had been pulled up onto the beach and was being held steady by Alistair's friends. They were at the ready to push the boat back into the water as soon as Mike was aboard. Unfortunately, owing to their undue enthusiasm resulting in less than perfect timing, the little boat was sent off fractionally before Mike jumped into it. This left him splashing around in water up to his knees before diving headfirst over the side of the boat and landing at the feet of the bride. Laughing she waved at us and we all waved back, as Mike picked himself off the bottom of the boat, grasped the oars and made ready to row across to the island.

'Oh no, oh no, he is going to capsize,' I muttered under my breath and grasped John's arm at the sight of Mike leaning precariously over the side of the rowing boat.

Having let go of an oar to adjust his sitting position, it immediately slid with unanticipated ease out of the rollick and floated slowly but seemingly deliberately out of reach. Anna, sitting in the stern, had turned to wave her small bouquet of brightly coloured flowers to all of us gathered on the shore. She was obviously blissfully unaware of the potential impending disaster.

Stirring the water vehemently with the other oar, Mike proceeded to set the boat off in a dizzying circular motion so that Anna stopped waving to grab the gunwales and steady herself, nearly dropping her bouquet in the water. As Mike leaned out over the side still further straining hopelessly after the out-of-reach oar, there was a noticeably loud gasp from all of us watching. The guest, who had spoken to me earlier, put her hands to her eyes and looked away. Her daughter started giggling in nervous anticipation. The bagpipes serenading the occasion ceased with a strangled whine as the piper, also rightly concerned, caught his breath.

Fortunately, Yiannis obviously sharing our thought processes and fears and activated by the whine of the pipes ran into the water, jumped into his speed boat and was quickly to the rescue retrieving the rapidly disappearing oar and returning it to Anna's dad. Mike gratefully reseated himself and set off on a zig-zag course to Kastri island. Clearly rowing practice hadn't been included in the pre-event rehearsals. The piper, looking embarrassed, resumed with gusto his rendition of the reel.

Once father and daughter had clambered out of the boat and stood safely on the flat rocks at the base of the island, Alistair's friends whistled loudly and spontaneous applause broke out from the assembled wedding party and an ever increasingly large gathering of onlooking tourists. It was then the turn of the wedding guests including us and the groom, who had arrived unnoticed during the potential disaster, to get into a flotilla of small boats, fortunately propelled by engines not oars, to travel over to the island for the service.

When we landed, as previously instructed we put up our colourful parasols. We had been given these to serve a dual role as sunshades against the hot midday sun and attractive enhancements to the wedding photos, especially as they were in the six different colours of the bridesmaids' mini-dresses. After a lengthy photoshoot of the bride and groom proceeding through the arch of parasols, which the photographer insisted was repeated three times, we made the short rocky climb up to where the ceremony was to take place.

In front of the tiny blue and white chapel, under the craggy tower of rock that characterised the island, was a suitable area of flat ground. There the humanist minister from the groom's native Glasgow was adjusting her make-up and adding some lipstick in preparation for her central role.

A few guests in fashionable exceedingly high heels managed to achieve the climb although with considerable difficulty. However, the best man's wife having lost a stiletto heel to a crevice in the rocks was doing her best to pull off the heel on the other shoe to avoid continuing with a lop-sided gait. The bridesmaids experienced no such problems. They were all wearing hiking shoes with tartan laces chosen to ensure that there were no stumbles and strained ankles and to reflect the bride and groom's enthusiasm for climbing Scottish Munros.

The cobalt blue sky provided a backdrop to the scene and all around the island the turquoise sea, darkening to navy blue in the distance, was lit up with bright dancing sparkles of light as the sun caught its ripples. It was undoubtedly a lovely setting for the occasion. We assembled in a horseshoe around the minister, who stood behind the picnic table altar on which were placed the contributory props for the ceremony.

She began by introducing herself and key members of the wedding party, such as the friends of Anna who were the bridesmaids, and the best man Alistair's close friend. Then the ceremony got under way with poems read by Anna's godparents which spoke of enduring love, the valuable gift of marriage and the hopes of those assembled that they would enjoy a long and happy life together.

Throughout the poems the antics of the photographer proved something of a distraction. Bent on getting the perfect viewpoint to take a shot of the scene he kept striding backwards and forwards and climbing up rocks on which he perched precariously. Anticipating another potential calamity, our gaze left the couple to watch him thinking that he might overbalance, until that is Mike climbed up beside him and instructed him to stay put.

After the poems followed some Scottish wedding traditions, which John and I were unaware of and which was probably the case for the majority of the guests as we watched intently. First, as an acknowledgement of their original intention to marry on Inchcailloch island, the bride and groom had each brought scoops of sand from different sides of that island. As Anna and Alistair poured their sand, which the minister explained represented their individuality, into a jar the contents mixed together.

This symbolised the new inter-relationship of their lives and led neatly into the part of the ceremony where the wedding vows were exchanged. As first Alistair, and then Anna, answered 'I do' to the promise to love, respect and always be there for each other, Betty fished in her handbag for tissues to dab her eyes. Anna borrowing the words of an unknown author declared, 'In all of creation you are the one whom I cherish most. The one with whom I hope to share my life, its joys, its sorrows, its accomplishments, its challenges, while building our dreams together and growing everyday in the love that makes us one.'

At this Betty could no longer hold back the tears and so Mike put his arm around her shoulders and provided a large white hankie with which to mop her eyes. However, she was soon smiling again as the couple cemented their vows in the traditional Scottish manner of handfasting.

The minister explained, 'The term "handfasting" derives from the old Norse words "hand-festa" meaning to strike a bargain by joining hands.'

'That is where the expression "tying the knot" originated,' a tall Scot in a kilt announced in a loud voice seemingly to show off his knowledge. 'Shhhhh' was the united response, not wanting the spell to be broken. The minister bound the hands of the couple with a scarf in the tartan of Alistair's family. Then grinning at each other and with a joyful shout they thrust their hands in the air each holding an end of the scarf in the middle of which was a large knot.

'I wonder how many times they practised that,' whispered John.

Then to cement the promises that they had made Anna and Alistair exchanged rings. Before they did so, everyone was invited to participate in the ceremony by warming the rings with their fingers and by making a wish for the couple's marriage. Everyone happily accepted the invitation, with the best man setting an example by vigorously rubbing the rings and looking skywards with closed eyes while mouthing his silent good wish.

However, the rings were passed from guest to guest with some haste. It seemed we were all terrified of dropping one. Certainly, I had visions of the embarrassment of holding up the ceremony while scrabbling around among the sand and rocks trying to locate a dropped ring. I fantasised as to what would happen if one was lost, perhaps carried off by a seagull, but imagined the minister could continue with the one remaining or even improvise, although perhaps that might be regarded as a bad omen.

Fortunately, no such mishaps occurred. Instead in turn

Alistair and Anna placed a ring on each other's finger repeating, 'I give you this ring as a token of my love for you and as a constant reminder of the promises we have made today.' After which the minister pronounced them husband and wife and turning to Alistair declared, 'Alistair you may kiss the bride.' As Alistair obliged, we all clapped and cheered.

When Betty had shown me a printout of all that was planned, she said that she was worried that the guests might think it a bit cringeworthy. Also, she admitted that Mike thought it was a bit over the top but had acknowledged that, unlike Anna and her future husband, he was just not romantic. However, as the ceremony unfolded for real and the sincerity of the contributions and the happiness of the young couple were emphatically apparent, all aspects of the ceremony fitted well together and seemed totally appropriate and very moving.

When it drew to a close, at first no one moved, as if reluctant to acknowledge it was over. After a significant pause Mike broke the silence by announcing that, as soon as they could be unpacked from the cooler bags, champagne and snacks would be offered around by the bridesmaids.

Once everyone had a glass of champagne in their hands the best man proposed a toast to the newly weds and we all raised our glasses chorusing in unison our good wishes for their future. As we enjoyed the champagne and Betty's delicious canapés, sandwiches and miniature cakes, the guests mingled with each other and shared their perceptions of the unusual and memorable ceremony.

I found it fun chatting together and getting to meet some of the family members that Betty had told me about. The woman with her daughter, who had spoken to me on the beach, turned out to be Betty's younger sister Sally. I'd met her older sister several times because she was unmarried and regularly came out for short stays with Betty during the summer, but this was the first time Sally had visited Kefalos.

The knowledgeable Scot was Alistair's uncle Hamish, whom John discovered was a history teacher at a large secondary school in Glasgow. As he, like John, was a keen photographer, they discussed the challenges of taking wedding photographs, especially of the bride in her dazzling white dress, on such a bright sunny day in order to avoid blown highlights and capture the details of the lace on her dress. Having exhausted this topic they swapped ideas on which aspects of the ceremony and from what angles they would have taken the photographs had these been their responsibility.

The bridesmaids were also very interesting to talk to. While handing out the refreshments they recalled how they had each come to know Anna from school, college, working abroad and sharing a flat.

'Hello, I see you've met Sally.' Betty came over towards us.

'Yes we were standing alongside each other on the beach while waiting for Anna to arrive, but I've only just found out that she is your sister.'

'Sally has probably told you that it's her first visit here but she is going to stay with us for a few days holiday before flying home.'

'I wish my husband could have come too,' said Sally. 'It's a shame that he had to miss such a special occasion but he is a garden designer and he is always really busy in the summer.'

'It was a beautiful ceremony Betty,' I said. 'I've never been to a Humanist wedding before but I thought it was highly original and simply lovely.'

'I'm just so relieved that everything went according to plan. I thought it should do, as Anna and Alistair put so much thought into it and apparently the minister was really helpful, but you just never know whether at the last minute something is going to go wrong. Somehow we nearly left one of the freezer bags of food by the car. One of the tourists, who had been watching, spotted it as she returned to her scooter. She came rushing down the beach with it shouting to us, so we were able to quickly turn the boat around and go and collect it.'

'The refreshments were excellent, everyone seemed to be really enjoying them,' I commented.

'It was a nice idea to stay on the island for a while and have a social get together,' Sally added.

As the sun was getting higher and hotter, it was time to leave the island. Prompted by the best man we again raised our parasols to make an archway. The couple walked through the archway smiling at us, while the photographer and the male guests including John and Hamish took advantage of the final opportunity to take colourful photos. The couple then moved away from the chapel back down the slope to the rowing boat, which was vigorously propelled back to the beach by Alistair. Once Anna and Alistair reached the shore the small flotilla that had brought us to to the island came back to collect everyone.

John and I then went home to cool down and relax in readiness for the wedding reception in the evening at Dionysus. The reception as anticipated was extremely entertaining and enjoyable. Spiros had been put in charge of the evening. In his element, he welcomed everyone and told them at which tables they would find their place label. After the three course meal of shrimp souvlaki, moussaka – lamb or vegetarian – and fruit salad layered with different flavours of ice cream came the traditional speeches with everyone laughing at, although not necessarily understanding owing to his Glaswegian accent, the best man's jokes.

Anna and Alistair announced the start of the dancing by doing a waltz with lots of intricate moves that they had learned specially for the occasion which earned our admiration. Then it was the turn of everyone to dance to a ceilidh provided by a Scottish band flown out as a present from Alistair's parents. This caused much hilarity, as despite very clear instructions from the organiser, various individuals whirled in the wrong direction, or at the wrong time or with the wrong person. When everyone was totally out of breath came the cutting of the magnificent cake made by Betty. Then with Spiros as compere, there was dancing to a disco until midnight.

The next day feeling rather the worse for wear we got up late. After lunch John went off to Meltemi and I awaited a visit from Joy, who had phoned to ask if she could pop round. While she thought that it would be good to have a chat she also wanted an excuse to leave Maria, who she was training as her assistant, to experience managing the office on her own for a couple of hours. Her arrival was announced by Bonzo, who having come up the cliff path from the beach, bounded across the garden to woof hello followed several minutes later by Joy.

'As soon as we started up the path he disappeared but I guessed he knew where we were going,' she said as she sat down on the patio.

I patted Bonzo's head and gave him a couple of the biscuits I had at the ready which he crunched down at speed. 'He is looking really good,' I said admiring his shiny coat.

'He is becoming quite obedient too,' she replied. 'When he has taken him for his morning walk, Mikos spends a bit of time training him and it has really paid off.'

'I'm very pleased to hear this Bonzo,' I addressed him and handed over another biscuit. 'That's it though or your mum will accuse me of trying to make you fat.'

'As you haven't been out this morning, you won't have heard the latest,' Joy said clearly keen to update me.

'Oh no, I haven't, what's that?'

'In the early hours of this morning someone set fire to Konstantinos's waterpark.'

'Really, a second fire at Paradise,' I said, surprised the arsonist had gone back there. 'Did they catch whoever did it?'

'No it was something of a repeat of when Georgio's windsurfing hut burned down,' she recounted what had happened. 'A holidaymaker in the hotel who couldn't sleep, looked out of his window about three o'clock in the morning, saw the flames and rang down to the night porter who called the police. They arrived surprisingly quickly, as they had been dealing with a drunken disturbance in Kardamena, but they were too late to catch whoever did it. Hearing the police car coming down the cliff road, he sped off in a boat.'

'Was there much damage?'

'Apparently quite a bit, but because he was disturbed nothing like there might have been. The little entrance hut was destroyed but none of the attractions. The big tunnel slide and the bouncy pier had been soaked in petrol but fortunately he didn't have time to set fire to them. The hotel called Konstantinos and he and one of his workers came and washed them down.'

'It's a real worry for all those with businesses on the beaches,' I reflected. 'I imagine John will have heard about it at Meltemi. They were concerned after the other fires, although they are lucky to be near to the road and some restaurants and so they are less likely to be a target.'

'Now you tell me all about the other happening yesterday, the wedding. If I hadn't been taking a tour around Kos town, I would have joined you all on the beach to see them go over to the island,' Joy said changing the subject. Happy to oblige, I described the ceremony in detail beginning with how Anna's dad nearly capsized the boat.

'Kastri island is a a lovely setting for a wedding,' Joy commented. 'I think there may be quite a lot more weddings on the island in the future. There is a new company called Celebrations in Kefalos old town that have done up that empty shop by the school and they've an advert in the window promoting weddings on the island.'

'Oh really, that's interesting. I haven't seen that,' I told her.

'It's only just opened but I looked them up on the internet and found that they've also got a website targeting British couples. As increasing numbers of people like to go abroad for their weddings and they are also advertising events to renew vows, I think it could prove quite popular.'

'Next time I'm on my laptop I'll have to have a look,' I said. 'That reminds me that I meant to tell you that your website looks pretty good now. I looked at it the other day.'

'I'm very pleased with it. I paid this guy who owns a computer business in Kos town to redo it. He is a friend of Angela's partner and she recommended him to me. He's done a good job and the website looks much more professional now so that should be helpful in promoting my tours for next year.'

She then turned the conversation to Jan and Andreas quizzing me about their relationship, as she had seen them out together in the evening and Angela had told her about their trip to Patmos.

15

Halki's Venetian Mansions and Traditional Kyfis

It was Thursday in the first week of September and we were off on the Dodecanese ferry from Kos town to the island of Halki – or Chalki – which is 16 kilometres west of Rhodes. Only 28 square kilometres in size it is the smallest inhabited island of the Dodecanese. The majority of the population that live there all year round number about three hundred and are concentrated in the port village of Imborios.

We finished packing, had breakfast and walked to the square for the 10am bus to Kos town. In town we had a leisurely lunch before walking to the harbour. As the ferry was starting from there, we were able to get on it half an hour before it left at 2pm. It called first at Nisyros and then at Tilos and at both we enjoyed seeing the familiar landmarks once again and looking out for sight of the paths that we had walked previously.

The port of Imborios on Halki is extremely attractive and as soon as I saw it I knew that I would enjoy wandering around its alleys. Its Italian style two-storey houses painted in white and pastel colours – particularly, cream, ochre and strawberry pink – are arranged on the hillside in rows around the bay with some going right down to the water's edge. Their fronts are symmetrical with tall rectangular windows and doors, many have balconies and most have red tile roofs. They are very noticeable against the grey brown barren slopes capped by three traditional stone windmills up on the ridge.

In the bookshop in the square in Kos where John bought a newspaper, while he was queuing to pay, I looked up Halki in a book about the Greek islands. In the short entry on it, I read that independent travellers should avoid Halki as all the accommodation is taken up by those on package holidays. We hoped this wouldn't be the case in September.

When we got off the ferry there were no touts trying to recruit for studios, which we thought was possibly a bad sign. Nevertheless, amazingly there was a tourist office, which had opened for the arrival of the ferry, and this had information on available accommodation. Anne, who had moved to Halki from England and worked in the office over the summer, suggested we might like one of two apartments in a traditional Italian style house on the hillside overlooking the harbour. It had once belonged to a Venetian captain and this historical association gave it added appeal.

She closed up her office, as it seemed we were the only customers, and took us to view our potential accommodation. We decided on the apartment that had the largest balcony accessed via the kitchen/dining room which also had stairs up to a little mezzanine floor. The big windows with their wide window seats looked out over the harbour and the old town and had large shutters, which John heartily approved of as he liked our bedroom to be quiet and dark at night. The house had air conditioning but it wasn't needed because of the high ceilings and the open windows, which gave a cooling through draught.

We had a leisurely start to the next day enjoying the novelty of our villa, eating our breakfast on the balcony and watching the activity in the harbour. Afterwards we went for a walk over the hill behind the house, past the three renovated traditional windmills but still requiring sails and an army hut with its gun seemingly aimed at Rhodes. Then we wandered along the concrete road south to Ftenaya, a pebble cove bordered with trees that grew back into a valley between the hills.

There were some sheds in the cove housing chickens

and geese. While we were watching these clucking and hissing around, John spotted a very large black scaly lizard, which he considered required photographing to add to his growing lizard photo collection. We then took the clearly signed footpath back to Imborios. We passed some new very expensive looking apartments, which were closed up, presumably because the main tourist season had ended.

On our way to the harbour we went through a street with some lovely traditional Greek houses. John took a photo of a wonderful old wooden door with interesting swirly grained panels covered in knots and a blue glass window in the top half with an ornamental wrought iron protector.

'You taking this photo reminds me of a postcard I bought in Crete which depicted eight different old wooden doors. Perhaps you could collect photos of Greek doors as well as lizards,' I suggested.

The next street that we found ourselves in was a contrasting one of tall Venetian mansions decorated with pink and purple bougainvillea and other climbing plants. When we reached the harbour, two large tourist boats from Rhodes were arriving. As they weaved through the moored fishing boats, they sent these bobbing up and down in their wake. The tourists surged off and mostly headed along the broad waterfront where the cafes and restaurants were located.

We decided to go back up to the top of the town for a close look at the clock tower, which is reputedly the tallest freestanding clock tower in the Dodecanese. This didn't seem too outstanding an achievement as I doubt there are many competitors. The clock on the tower said twenty past four, which we thought was a temporary malfunction, until Anne enlightened us that the locals prevented it from working because they found its loud chimes exceedingly annoying.

The clock tower was next to the white two-storey town hall which had an unusual neoclassical front and an interesting history. It had been built in 1933 as a boys' school with funds from former Halki residents who had moved to America. It seemed incredible that in the 19th century the island had three thousand or more inhabitants. Apparently they began moving away following the decline of the sponge fishing industry, which like on Kalymnos had been crucial to the island's economy. Throughout the 20th century depopulation continued as islanders sought jobs and a different way of life elsewhere.

We also went to see the church of Agios Nikolaos built in 1861 that had an attractive bell tower built of tiers of columns and – you have guessed it – was reputedly the tallest bell tower in the Dodecanese.

'They don't look very safe,' I commented on the two young men balanced on very flimsy looking scaffolding painting the tiers of columns. 'Despite the supposed height of this tower, it doesn't seem much attention has been paid to their health and safety.'

'True but they don't seem bothered,' John replied as we watched one flick paint from his brush on the other who retaliated in like mode and they both laughed.

I found the black and white pebble mosaic squares and yards very appealing. We had seen these in several of the Dodecanese islands, especially in Mandraki and Nikia on Nisyros. Turning my eyes from up the tower to below my feet, I thought that Agios Nikolaos had a particularly attractive mosaic courtyard. After studying this, we walked back through the streets and down to the end of the bay where the smart renovated houses had their waterfront patios and steps down into the water. While we stood admiring them, a couple of occupants walked out of their door and just plopped into the water and swam off.

'Just like having a massive swimming pool in your garden,' commented John. 'If we were staying here I'd have an early morning swim every day.'

'I'm not so sure about that,' I retorted as John wasn't keen on getting up early, 'but it is very convenient if you like swimming,' I agreed.

Next we decided to join the Rhodes day-trippers and have lunch at a cafe on the harbour. We found a table in the shade and ordered taramasalata, cheese balls, tuna salad and bread rolls. While we ate, we watched two fishermen mending their nets on a large fishing boat, three men unloading crates and boxes from a cargo boat onto a truck and tourists ambling around enjoying the atmosphere.

'Should we get the map out and see where we might walk later this afternoon?' I asked. As had become customary, we had bought a hiking map from a souvenir shop on the waterfront. John took the map out of his rucksack and opened it out on the table.

'We could take this path, which goes past a basilica and then along the cliff road to Kania, and we could come back via an inland road so making it a circular trip,' he suggested tracing the route with his finger.

'Sounds good to me, I like circular trips where we can do them,' I said in support of the idea. 'Where on the map is the castle and the old abandoned town of Chorio that we plan to go to tomorrow?' John showed me. 'Are we going to walk there because it doesn't look that far?'

'We might or we might take the bus, as if you look at the contours it's all uphill to get there,' he said.

'The contour lines are really close together practically everywhere apart from the area in the far east of the island,' I observed.

'Which means I suppose, that you'd like to do a walk there', he grinned. Over a Nescafe, we studied the map further for possible walks and then we went back to the villa for a midday siesta.

Keen to explore more, by mid-afternoon we were ready to venture out to visit Kania. We walked to the northern end of Imborios and climbed the stoney hillside until below us we saw the path marked on our map to the ruined basilica. We scrambled down to this and from the basilica we followed cairns of small stones over a dip in the hillside to the fish farm that bred sea bream.

Then to continue, we had no choice but to pick our way through extremely prickly scrub in order to get around the lengthy perimeter wire fence encircling the fish farm's sheds and busy quay. Eventually we found a makeshift gate of poles and wire, which we were able to go through and so thankfully get on the other side of the fence. From there it was easy walking along a concrete road that took us to the delightful little Kania beach with its jetty, sunbeds, shady trees and mobile canteen.

We bought a lemonade from the canteen and sat under a tree observing the scene. Four rather large tourists were clearly trying to negotiate a lift back to Imborios in a tiny blue and white fishing boat. Ultimately, obviously successful, they climbed aboard practically submerging the boat's gunnels underwater.

'I hope they don't sink going round the cape,' I observed.

'I'm sure they'll be fine but the helmsman is certainly taking his boat out to sea exceedingly slowly so maybe he's a bit worried,' John replied.

If we had wanted to, there were no other fishing boats for us to hitch a lift back with, and so after enjoying the tranquility of having the beach to ourselves, we set off to return on the road. This took us through a brief green area of juniper bushes providing relief from the brown landscape. There we came upon a group of baby goats playing chasing in an enclosure watched over by a goatherd. He waved at us as we stopped to watch them and we waved back. Where we joined the main road on the edge of Imborios we had views of the road up to Chorio. This was sufficiently steep to make us decide that we would definitely take the bus to go there. From our vantage point we could also see over to the island's main beach, the sandy Pondamos beach to the south west of Halki.

The evening was totally still and very hazy making the hillsides look particularly grey, stark and jagged. Their solitary trees stood out black in outline against the strips of sunset orange filtering across the sky. The tourist office was open and so we decided to go in to see Anne and report on our day. When we told her about the walk to Kania and our plans for walking the next day, she suggested that we might like to go and talk to Clive.

Clive was an elderly man who lived in Imborios, knew the island extremely well and could advise us on walks. She said that he had walked all the paths and in the high season organised walking tours for those wanting to explore on foot. We responded that he sounded like an interesting and useful person to talk to and so she gave us directions to his home. When we left her office the whole sky had turned brilliant red, the sea was a darker red in tone and the islets darker still. It was a breathtaking sunset.

In the morning we were down on the harbour waiting for the 10.45am mini bus having been to the bakery to buy cheese pies, frankfurter rolls and cinnamon slices for lunch. When the mini bus arrived it was driven by a young Greek man who had spent time in England working in Manchester airport and as a result spoke excellent English.

The trip to Chorio went via Pondamous Beach and took about 15 minutes. However, it cut down considerably the amount of uphill walking. We drove past a new chapel and, as when we had been in Patmos we were surprised another was deemed necessary, especially as the driver said there were three hundred chapels on the island – one for each inhabitant – but perhaps he was kidding.

We got out of the mini bus on the corner from where we looked up at the Knights of Saint John castle. It still looked as if we had quite a climb to reach it but, although it was very hot, there were lots of clouds in the sky and some of the walk was in the shade of the mountainside.

We set off on a concrete path which soon split up in various directions to go to a number of chapels. These paths formed something of a maze halfway up and made it difficult to locate the zigzag path and then the steps needed to get up to the castle. The driver had warned us of this, telling us that various renovations had been ongoing but as it seemed was all too often the case the money for these, which had been provided by the EU, had run out. Eventually we reached a short section of wooden ladder steps and we entered the castle ruin through the tower keep. The castle was wide but not particularly deep reflecting the cliff top on which it was perched.

'Wow the views from here are spectacular,' said John.

'You can see everything in Imborios really well and Trachea beach immediately below us,' I said, impressed by the scene in front of me.

'I like that interesting island shaped promontory over there, that definitely deserves a photograph.'

'We can also see Cape Mirtos at the far south west end of Halki. As is usually the case, it's definitely worth the climb for this view.'

After John had taken the photos that he wanted and we had admired the view for a while longer, we withdrew to the shade provided by the church of Saint Nicholas situated within the castle walls. Its frescos, long exposed to the elements, were now protected by a new roof. We were amused by the upside down icon to the right of the entrance. We found out later that this was thought to have come about because the stone on which it was painted was transported to the church from somewhere else.

When we had cooled down we took the walkway around the outer walls and looked inland over the area to the Palarniotis monastery where we intended to walk next. When we set off we soon came to a new house, where a man was putting up a wire fence around his plot. Soon after we passed several other plots where it seemed houses were in the process of being built. Perhaps Chorio, like Emborios on Nisyros, was starting to be repopulated.

We came to a building that had once been a school and another that in the tourist season functioned as a cafe. We easily found the start of the hiking trail marked on the map, although it shortly emerged onto the road by the concrete way we had walked along earlier. Soon after we hit the first problem. We came to a chapel and the red and blue markers indicated that the trail should go through the chapel yard but the gate was padlocked and the wire fence impenetrable. It was baking hot as now the sky was cloudless and the air totally still.

I sat in the shade of a wall while John, unwilling to be defeated, looked unsuccessfully for a way under or around the wire. There wasn't one and so we had to give up trying to follow the trail. After a pause for a drink of water and discussion we decided to walk along the road to where another concrete road led to our intended destination of Palarniotis monastery.

We walked past a big tree but ignored its inviting shade. Then we came to a small one-time settlement with deserted animal pens, stone terracing and ruined stone houses. At the end of the road John undid the rope holding shut a large metal gate and we walked up towards the monastery enjoying different vistas of Imborios and views back up to the castle. When we reached the square, white, well-kept monastery building we were confronted by more high wire fencing and a broad metal gate with spikes along the top.

'Oh how frustrating. Looks like there is absolutely no way we are going to get in there,' I quickly concluded.

We looked disconsolately at the unyielding wire separating us from the shade under the numerous trees around the monastery.

'See that new path,' John pointed through the gate. 'It must be the one built by volunteers to the monastery chapel, but I'm not sure of the point of their labours if you can't get to walk on it,' said John crossly.

Reluctantly we retraced our steps in the searing heat. This was turning out to be the hottest walk of any that we had done on the Dodecanese islands. Still, we were about to have an upturn in our fortunes. Back along the main road below the monastery we found a small delightful white chapel built into the hillside, with its bell housed alongside in a separate little tower built of four columns.

'Do you think it's only that rock up against the door that's keeping it shut and if we move it we could go in,' I questioned hopefully.

John moved the rock and the door swung open and in we went.

'Look one wall and half the roof are formed from a cave in the rock,' he said.

'I expect that's why it's lovely and cool in here,' I replied adding, 'It reminds me of the chapel called Mary of the Crab that we went in on Leros.'

'Why don't we sit on these two little prayer stools and eat our lunch,' he suggested.

'Excellent idea.' I sat down and took out the cheese pies and passed him one.

'Umm, they're really good,' he commented admitting, 'I'm actually quite hungry.'

We soon devoured our tasty provisions from the bakery, washed down with a carton of fruit juice to make a change from water. As we ate our lunch and cooled down we watched a large beetle hurrying back and forth as if he was looking for something he had lost. John offered him a crumb from his cinnamon slice but he just continued scurrying around and ignored it. Eventually we agreed to leave our refuge. We pushed the rock back against the chapel door and returned along the road to Imborios.

We did a tiny bit of the original path from Chorio to Imborios. The path went along below the castle but part of it had been dug up in front of where another new house was being built. A bit further on, a red and blue marker appeared before a wide gap in the dry stone wall that ran alongside the road. We could see the old path about five metres below us in an olive grove but by then we had lost our enthusiasm for monopatis and decided to keep on the road. No cars passed us but on the outskirts of Imborios there were places where rusty old cars had been dumped.

As we got lower down we could also see Pondamos beach. We decided to stop off there and went to the taverna for ice creams. We had the last two cornets leaving the taverna freezer empty. This reminded us of our quest for ice creams on Patmos. The waitress told us we were lucky as stocks generally ran out before September and they wouldn't be replenished until next year. The taverna was a lively cheerful place with an appealing menagerie of two nice brown dogs, one smooth haired and one rough haired, the usual pussycats and two black and white rabbits hopping around on a raised circle around the tree growing within the taverna.

Several holidaymakers were splashing each other at the water's edge and some others were jumping off a small yacht and swimming around it as it bobbed gently at anchor close to the shore. We thought that we would at least cool our feet by having a paddle which we did. John was amused by the two dogs as they decided to join us and splashed back and forth in and out of the water.

On our way back we decided to go and visit Clive, whom Anne had told us about, to see if he had any suggestions about where we might walk tomorrow. Clive had an interesting and attractive old stone house. It was two storey but wide and deep rather than tall. Stone steps on each side led to the first floor that had a magnificent balcony with an ornamental stone balustrade right across the front.

John went up the steps and called out 'Hello, does Clive live here?' several times until Clive appeared. He was very friendly and welcomed us into his small study/sitting room. He made us a cup of tea and we talked about the island which was somewhere he had come to know and love. As Anne had said, he had walked all the old paths. He said that unfortunately increasingly, as on the other islands, the building of new homes and concrete roads was making the monopatis impassable. He thought this a shame not only because he regretted their loss but also because the paths could be used to attract those like ourselves who enjoyed exploring on foot.

We told him we thought we might get a bus to the

monastery of Saint John the next day and asked him about walking around there.

'It's a good area for walking. I suggest that you do the walk to the old village of Kefali. You can see lots of evidence of the old settlement there with its terraces and traditional Halki stone houses, kyfis they are called. Also, there is the ruined Byzantine chapel of Agio Pelaghia.'

We showed him our map and the walk was clearly marked on it. 'In places the path is quite indistinct,' he said 'but you won't get lost and there are no wire fences or other barriers to contend with. I think you'll find it interesting.'

'I notice there's another walk from the monastery to the Burning Cave. We won't have time to do it, but when I saw it on the map I wondered what is the significance of the cave?' I enquired.

'It is a huge cave with a very tragic history. There women and children from Halki died at the hands of Admiral Francesco Morosini. He was head of the Venetian fleet that sailed to occupy Halki in 1658. The Halkians had warned the Ottomans that his fleet was heading for Rhodes. In revenge he had a huge bonfire of wood from a nearby almond grove lit in the entrance of the cave and the smoke suffocated all those taking refuge in it. As legend has it, you can still see smoke drifting out from the cave entrance,'

Clive explained.

'That's a really sad story, I don't think you would want to go there would you?' John addressed me.

'No that's horrific, I would definitely prefer to go to Kefali.'

Clive then asked us where we were staying and we got to talk about the architecture in Imborios. He told us how he had been a mariner for years but when he retired from the sea he bought his house in order to retire in Halki. He said the house was in very good condition and apart from fixing the roof he had needed to do very little to it. We said we thought that it looked really attractive. I told him I particularly liked the long stone balcony. John commented that the wooden doors and shutters looked in good shape supporting his opinion that the wood used years ago lasted so much longer than the modern wood used in homes today.

Clive offered to show us around and we were certainly interested to see more. Behind the study was his dining room. It ran the width of the house and had a long table set for the dinner party he was holding that evening. Alongside his study was a little bedroom that he used when he had guests to stay. Upstairs, although the ceilings were lower, in style the bedrooms in his house were reminiscent of the rooms in our apartment. While enjoying chatting to him and looking around his house, we were mindful of the fact he probably had more to do to prepare for his dinner party and so we thanked him for his hospitality and took our leave.

The next morning we stocked up again with food from the bakery for a picnic – pizza slices, bacon pastries and apple and cinnamon pie. Then we caught the 10.45am bus to the monastery. It was running a bit late and so we got to the monastery shortly after 11.15am. The road climbed steeply up beyond Chorio and there were some sheer drops down to the sea on the left hand side.

The bus dropped us off at the attractive entrance to the monastery. It was painted the usual blue and white and had a bell in each of the two alcoves on either side of the wrought iron gates which were under an arch topped with a mosaic. Cells in an L shape with closed doors and shuttered windows bordered the yard. There were no monks to use these nowadays and the monastery only really came to life on the 29th August, its festival day.

In the centre of the yard under the branches of a huge tree was a small chapel. On the far side two taps over a large stone trough provided water. Under the tree a trestle table and chairs provided a shady place for refreshments. A meagre list of possibilities alongside a serving hatch suggested ouzo, retzina, Fanta and cake were sometimes available but today this was firmly closed up.

The bus driver appeared in the yard obviously having parked the bus somewhere outside the gates. A scrawny elderly man and his plump smiling wife came out of the monastery to greet him. Then she went in and returned with a coffee for him. She was wearing a thick black print dress, cardigan and grey woollen knee socks all of which looked very hot given the temperature, although perhaps it was chilly in the monastery. The driver had told us that they looked after the place and were the only ones living there. I thought they must have a rather lonely existence and so I wasn't surprised that they both sat chatting animatedly with him as he drank his coffee.

Following Clive's directions, we climbed the steps out of the back of the monastery. There we found the red earth path and set off at a brisk pace. We saw the fork with the alternative path on which we were to return and, as advised, kept to the right hand one. However, it soon dwindled into stones and scrub. Looking around everywhere along the tops of the old terracing there were strips of red earth which seemed like possible paths. We could see the old agricultural settlement of Vokolia down to our left, which on our return we would pass through. We scrambled ahead and down over the terraces, rocks and scrub. It was hot as there was no shade and virtually no breeze although we could look down the slopes of the open landscape to the sea. The scrambling was quite hard work with prickles constantly sticking through our socks and sandals and puncturing our feet.

Eventually, when we were getting really tired of the difficult terrain, we got to a flat area with some remains of houses that were thick with goat droppings and with bones – hopefully also from goats not dehydrated hikers. However, these ruins indicative of one-time inhabitants served as encouragement by hinting that we might be on course for our intended destination.

After crossing this area and more dodging of prickles, tripping over stones and balancing on rocks, we came upon dry stone walls and then what had clearly once been a substantial settlement. There were the ruins of numerous stone kyfis and exploring these we easily located the remains of the tiny ancient Byzantine chapel of Aghia Pelaghia. Nearby we also found a well and two threshing floors built with large stones.

'I'm really pleased that we managed to find the abandoned village of Kafali. I was beginning to think we might not,' I said.

'Clive told us we would find it so I wouldn't have given

up,' John replied.

'I wonder what that old round tower over there was,' I pointed to the tower built on a rocky outcrop.

'I don't know, probably a look out tower for spotting enemies or pirates.'

We stood looking over a large thick dry rock wall to the slopes going down to the sea and tried to imagine what it must have been like to live in such a harsh isolated place.

'I can't see signs of any more settlements,' said John 'so I think this must be the end point of our walk.'

We found a distinct path back and it took us straight to the old agricultural settlement of Vokolia, which had rusty farming gear scattered around and sheep or goat skins piled on a wall. Then it was back to scrambling again to try to find the path back to join the one on which we had left the monastery. Ahead of us a large herd of goats of all shapes, sizes and colours came running and jumping down the terraces and then stopped and turned to watch us seemingly thinking 'why are those humans stumbling along like that?'

To our surprise we came upon the required path more or less by accident. As described by Clive, we saw the views through an opening in the rocks including back to the castle and gaping above us the cave where apparently the monks used to make cheese. We continued along the path until it joined the original path on which we had set out and we found ourselves back in the monastery yard.

We washed our hands over the stone trough and sat down at the trestle table to eat our lunch. To accompany it we bought a couple of warm Fantas from the friendly woman. Beside the cafe was an ancient unplugged chest freezer of the kind we had found littered around the island including one beside the main road from Chorio to Imborios.

'It's nice to have a Fanta rather than water but I wish it could be cold,' said John.

'Ah well, cold drinks are bad for your blood pressure. Remember what Sofos in Armeniou said when we bought warm Fantas from him,' I joked.

The woman saw us looking at the outside of the little chapel and unlocked it for us so we could enter. She pointed to some of the paintings and was obviously explaining them in Greek. We couldn't understand but we nodded appreciatively as it was kind of her to show us the chapel interior. Afterwards we had another brief rest, then said goodbye to her as it was time to begin the walk back to Imborios. As we went out of the monastery entrance and looked back, we watched her husband throwing stones to discourage approaching goats. Well in that region there was certainly no shortage of either stones or goats.

We set off down the road. At least we knew the way and it was mostly downhill. Starting with the section between Imborios and Chorio, the road to the monastery had been built in stages funded by donations from Halkians living in Florida who named it Tarpoon Springs Boulevard. Having been in the States this title conjured up an image totally contrary to the wild, uninhabited and arid landscape this boulevard transversed.

We got back to the apartment as the sun was setting and the restaurants were getting ready for dinner. There were usually only a few tables occupied in the evening as the main business of the day was at lunchtime feeding the day-trippers arriving from Rhodes. It was dark by the time we went out for dinner. The alleys and the flights of steps between the houses were not well lit. On the first night I put my foot on a non-existent step and nose dived down a small flight of four stone steps and landed flat on my front. I just lay there until John stood me up again and luckily, apart from being shocked and totally winded, I was absolutely fine. From then on I took a torch with me as I didn't want a repeat performance.

We really enjoyed our evening meals by the harbour. While we were in Halki the evenings were beautiful and still, unlike in Kefalos where it was often windy. The waterfront promenade was an idyllic setting. On the hillside there were the lights of the houses and the lit up town hall and by the bay the lights of the harbour and on some of the boats moored stern first on the quay.

One night we watched a huge brightly lit ferry from Piraeus come in and go out again. The spirit of travel and feelings of excitement the ship engendered all added to our sense of gentle adventure and well-being. Each night we tried out a different restaurant for our main meal – all were equally delicious. My favourite dish was chicken and potatoes cooked in the oven in lemon sauce and John's was roast lamb done on the spit with onion rice. Afterwards we moved to a busy cafe bar to enjoy the atmosphere while having cappuccinos and crepes sitting on their comfy rattan sofas. Evenings in Halki were definitely something special.

The morning after we arrived back in Kefalos Jan came around for coffee. 'How is the job going?' I said. 'Are you still enjoying it?'

'It's good. I really like it. It's very varied and the customers are often fun. Andreas is very pleased that this summer the business seems to be going extremely well, that is apart from what happened yesterday.'

'Oh and what was that?' I queried.

'Well on Friday this young guy from Liverpool rented a motorbike from us to go to Sunset beach. Near there he skidded on a track and fell off, was badly shaken and actually broke his arm. A car coming up the track behind him found him lying in the dust and took him to Kos hospital, leaving the motorbike by the side of the road. When he got back from hospital he tried to describe to Andreas's dad where the accident took place but Elias wasn't able to find the bike. Yesterday, which was a couple of days later, Elias persuaded him to go in a car with him and direct him to the site. They succeeded in finding the bike but the tyres, lights, mirrors etc had all been taken off, only leaving the frame. This didn't come as any big surprise but nevertheless it was upsetting.'

'Will the insurance cover it?'

'Only in part because the young man chose to rely on his own holiday insurance and didn't take out the one we offer. He should pay the shortfall, but when he gets back home Andreas says that just won't happen and so the bike will have to be written off as a loss.'

As we chatted, it was obvious that Jan was extremely happy working at Budget and that she was spending more and more time with Andreas. However, she still took me by surprise with her announcement that she had plucked up the courage to phone Regi to say that she wanted a separation from him.

'What did he say? Was he shocked?' I asked.

'Yes he was. At first he just wasn't prepared to believe me and was quite flippant about it. He said I must be suffering from too much sun and once the holiday season finished on Kos and everything in Kamari shut down I'd soon want to come home.'

'How did you respond to that?'

'I said that wouldn't happen because I really like living in Kefalos, I've several friends who live here and my plan is to stay for the winter but if I change my mind and return to England I want to keep my independence.'

'I can imagine he was really taken aback as he wouldn't have seen this coming,' I said for the first time feeling rather sorry for Regi.

'No, he certainly didn't but then he is never aware of, or particularly concerned about, how I feel. He said several times that he couldn't believe that I'd give up my comfortable life with him for the loneliness and uncertainty of staying here. I tried to tell him why I found living with him was often anything but comfortable and it felt really good to be in control of my life again but he wouldn't listen. I did agree with him that separation would make the future uncertain for me but said that to me this was actually exciting and opened up possibilities.'

She turned to me for reassurance, 'I felt so taken for granted by Regi who determined everything that we did and how we did it. I so often felt that I was just existing to support him and now I feel alive again.'

'You didn't tell him about Andreas?' I posed the question suspecting that she hadn't.

'No. I think it's too soon for that. Admittedly, as you know, I really care about Andreas and the time I have spent with him has made me even more critically aware of the shortcomings of my relationship with Regi. Even if Andreas should decide he wants to stop seeing me I don't want to return to my old life,' she said forcefully.

'So what happens now?'

'In two weeks' time Regi is returning from Taiwan as he has to get ready for the start of term and so I'm going back to meet him. I think it's only fair to discuss the separation face to face. Also I could do with getting more clothes and some of my other belongings but I wouldn't want to go and take things without him being there. I'm sure he'll argue really hard to get me to stay,' she sighed. 'I won't find it easy to hold out against him but I'm determined,' she stressed, grinning at me and clenching her fist.

16

Up, Down and Around the Kali Strata on Symi

J oy and I were sitting outside Zephina's cafe. We had bumped into each other while shopping and decided we could make time for a cappuccino. John and I were planning to go to Symi for our final island exploration and, as Joy particularly liked Symi, she was telling me all about it.

'The name Symi is rather special as the island took its name from the nymph Syme who was Poseidon's wife,' explained Joy.

'I guess that like the other Dodecanese islands seafaring was all important to Symi so it's a good choice of name,' I responded.

'Yes seafaring and trading were its lifeblood and the source of its wealth. You'll see it has lots of beautifully decorated mansions which were built by rich sponge merchants and other traders.'

'When we visited Kalymnos and Halki we found

sponges had been really important to the economy of those islands. I guess like the sponge fishing there, the two World Wars followed by the effects of pollution and marine disease killed the sponge trade on Symi.'

'Yes, only about three thousand people live on Symi now but in its heyday the population reached nearly thirty thousand. In the post-war years, as on other islands, Symians left to escape poverty abandoning their houses. Many of these were ruined owing to bomb damage during World War 11. Others were gutted of anything that could be sold in order to raise money so that their owners could emigrate.'

'Lots of the people on Kos have relatives in Canada, America or Australia and younger members of their families visit them quite regularly,' I commented.

'Yes, my husband's grandparents live in Montreal and he has been over there to stay with them numerous times, especially when he was in his early twenties. He told me he seriously considered staying and working there but his parents live in Kefalos and so he set up his business here.'

'Are the mansions on Symi being restored? We've seen this on Patmos and Halki.'

'Yes, foreigners have bought them to do them up as holiday or retirement homes. Also locals, who are making money from tourism, have been able to restore their properties which is really good. Nowadays Symi's architecture is protected and restorations and new builds have to be in keeping with the neo-classical style. You might be able to stay in an apartment in one of them like you did in Halki,' Joy concluded.

On the ferry on our way to Symi we went very close to the Turkish coast and passed where a Turkish flag was flying from the clifftop. As we discovered, Symi lies between two Turkish peninsulas, one only ten kilometres away. Given its location it was unsurprising that Symi became part of the Ottoman empire in 1522 and remained under Ottoman rule until, like the other Dodecanese islands, it was occupied by the Italians in 1912.

The ferry chugged into Symi bay, an oblong shaped east-facing inlet on the island's north shore. We passed the clock tower on the peninsula and entered the port of Gialos. We saw the colourful building by the stone clock, where in May 1945 the Germans signed the Dodecanese islands over to the British.

The island's main town, also called Symi, is comprised of Gialos and the old town of Horio. All around Gialos there are houses, and joined to it on the left hand side as you enter the port, the old town of Horio stretches up the slopes, along the top and behind the mountain. The scene is extremely colourful and impressive. The multi-coloured pastel square and rectangular houses with their tall windows, triangular pediments and red tile roofs are all in similar harmonious neo-classical style. It was reminiscent of Halki but the scene before us was on a much larger scale.

When we disembarked from the ferry we took advantage of a nearby souvenir shop and, as usual, went in to buy a map. I also bought a small guidebook, which in addition to photos of tourist beaches had some interesting geographical and historical information in it.

Pleased with our purchases, we headed for the five hundred steps of the Kali Strata to climb up into Horio. As my newly acquired information source told me, the Kali Strata was built in the 19th century by the rich merchants to provide a convenient link between Horio and the new mercantile area of Gialos. It replaced an old donkey path which climbed up the hillside at the back of the harbour and led to the castle and the oldest part of Horio. As we climbed, we passed shops and cafes and attractive houses in alleyways off the steps. We ventured along a couple of these in the hope of discovering rooms to let but were unsuccessful and so continued to climb to the top of Horio.

'Oh look out,' I said. We hastily jumped to one side as

five mules with empty panniers came down the steps at a gallop and clattered past. During our stay we saw several mule trains. They were usually either taking heavy loads of building materials around Horio or waiting patiently outside houses that were being refurbished for their panniers to be filled with demolished stones and bricks. Perhaps these mules had finished for the day and were gratefully heading home, as they seemed in a hurry and there was no sign of their muleteer.

When we reached the top of the steps we paused to put down our bags and have a rest. The steps were wide and well kept but there were uneven parts and they were slippery in places, particularly where there had been spillages, and so you needed to observe where you were placing your feet. Later, as we kept encountering tourists with legs or arms in plaster casts, we attributed their injuries to mishaps on the steps.

'We haven't made any progress in finding accommodation,' I said as we stood enjoying the wonderful view over the harbour.

'No we haven't. We've only seen one sign for rooms to rent in that partially restored house and it didn't look very promising,' John agreed. 'Let's have a look at the map and see where else we might try.'

Looking at our map we decided that we would carry on to Pedi, which was a couple of kilometres down hill. This turned out to be a good decision as we found accommodation there and we really liked being based in Pedi. It was situated on an almost entirely enclosed bay and its colourful neo-classical buildings were in sharp relief against the brown rocky hillside.

We enquired about rooms in a taverna situated in the middle of the bay and the waiter whom we asked directed us to another taverna at the end of the bay. The owner there said that above his taverna were two studios and he would phone Katerina who owned them to see if one was available. Fortunately one was free and, as she lived nearby, she soon arrived to show us around. The entrance to the studio was through a wrought iron gate in a wall at the back of the taverna and up some stone steps. We were delighted with the studio when we saw inside. It was spacious and had a great view over Pedi bay from the balcony. The balcony was large and equipped with sunbeds, chairs and a table with a sun umbrella. There was even another little balcony outside the kitchen which had a washing line.

We decided that we would have dinner in the taverna below the studio, and so for lunch we thought we'd go back to the one where we first enquired about somewhere to stay.

We told the waiter to whom we had spoken earlier that we were now comfortably settled in a studio. We ordered pork souflaki and, while I suspected that the 'garbage salad' was 'cabbage salad', I decided not to risk it and instead shared a portion of chips with John.

We got chatting to an English couple who sat down at the table next to us. They had also just arrived in Symi for the first time. We thought it was quite a coincidence that, when we told them we had come from Kefalos, they told us that they often stayed in Kefalos because they really liked it and had actually been visiting there in May.

After lunch we relaxed on our balcony reading until having digested his lunch John decided he fancied a swim to cool off. I joined him initially doing more floating in the warm shallows than swimming. Then, while he snorkelled around the rocks, I pulled on my shorts and went for a wander along the beach.

Two young men were painting a small fishing boat propped within a frame of stanchions and struts. One was on a ladder painting the side of the cabin red, while the other was putting a thick black substance on the underside of the hull. As I approached, a small gust of wind blew off the white cap I liked to use as a sun hat and deposited it at the feet of the latter. Grinning he picked it up and handed it to me. 'You'll be glad it didn't blow onto the boat,' he said.

'True,' I replied. 'You are making it look very smart. Is this boat yours?' I asked.

'No, it belongs to my uncle. He owns the boatyard.' He pointed further along the top of the beach where there was a large shed with several boats outside. 'I'm at university in Athens and I usually come and help him in the summer. This year Yiannis has come with me.' He looked up at the man on the ladder who waved his paintbrush at us.

'At lunchtime the waiter told us that shipbuilding had once been extremely important to Symi's economy,' I commented.

'Yes that's right, but there is only a small amount of boat building and repairs done in Pedi nowadays, mainly at my uncle's and the other yard a bit further up. Probably because of my uncle, I find the history of shipbuilding on Symi really interesting. It goes right back to ancient times when the forefathers of the islanders built the Argo for Jason and sent three triremes to the siege of Troy. Then again, when Symi was part of the Ottoman empire, it really flourished as fast boats were built to supply the Sultan's fleet.'

'Back then the boats would all have been wooden and so did they have to bring trees from Turkey or islands like

Nisyros because that's got lots of trees?'

'No, no. It's quite hard to believe that Symi used to be a thickly forested island. It's because of its shipbuilding tradition that it's now predominantly barren and rocky.'

'Well thank you I wouldn't have realised that but I think I'd better let you finish off the hull. Yiannis has finished the cabin,' I observed, as he had descended the ladder and folded it up.

After our leisurely afternoon, we were in the mood to see a little more of our surroundings and so we decided to have an early evening stroll through Pedi and along the coast path to Agios Nikolaos. It was a good path reinforced in parts with concrete and it took us about 30 minutes to arrive at the little beach. Any tourists, who might have been enjoying it, had left and the taverna was shutting up. A small motor boat came speeding in, collected one of the waitresses and speeded out again.

We wandered over to the chapel of Agios Nikolaos, which was open and so we went inside. We were used to island chapels having a few plastic flowers as decoration – unsurprising as real ones were hard to come by and would soon wilt in the heat. However, this little chapel was full of them in many sizes and colours and representing a range of floral varieties.

'Do you think it's a local festival time?' suggested John.

'Maybe or perhaps, whoever looks after the chapel is heavily into plastic flowers,' I suggested.

Back outside we found a comfortable spot on a flat rock and sat in the late afternoon sun enjoying the peace and tranquility. We watched the barren landscape on the other side of the channel turn bronze in the setting sun and on our way back we watched the sun finally disappear behind the houses of Horio.

Katerina had let us know about the Symi bus, which contrary to our expectations based on other island experiences, turned out to be a large coach with automatic doors at the front and back and air conditioning. When we got aboard we felt as if we were about to go off on a day's tour rather than just around the Kali Strata. The bus conveniently turned around outside our studio and left on the half hour for Horio and Gialos. The small square window in the bathroom, at eye level when sitting on the toilet, proved most useful for looking down the street and seeing the bus approach.

The next day we caught the 8.30am, an unusually early start for us but we planned to have a full day exploring. Our intention was to walk to Nimporios on the coast three kilometres to the north west and then continue further west to go to the beach at Toli. We found the street for the start of our walk behind a small bridge in Gialos and were soon going uphill out of town.

We stopped at the Elikoni cemetery, where a priest in Greek Orthodox robes, accompanied by a small group of locals, appeared to be blessing an existing grave. He vigorously swung an incense burner back and forth over the grave and the scent from it, when it reached us, was so strong we happily continued on our way feeling quite intoxicated.

Leaving the cemetery behind us, we walked along the path between dry stone walls and looked over olive groves, almond trees and citrous orchards down to the sea. When we got to the church of Agios Georgios we sat in the courtyard under the shade of an ancient and very gnarled olive tree. The trunk was patched with white painted cement presumably to stop it from cracking apart. From there we had a lovely panoramic view of the port of Nimporios and the bay.

After we had fully appreciated the view and John had taken a couple of panoramic photo shots we set off down the hillside on an old stone path. The path took us past a chapel and around the bay to a narrow beach bordered by trees. There, when we clambered among the rocks, we could see in the crystal clear water shoals of little fish weaving in and out and sea anemones fastened to the rocks. We enjoyed pottering among the rocks looking at the marine life and were surprised how quickly the time went. We could easily have stayed longer but with lots more exploring to be done we retraced our steps climbing up the hill until we came to the red dots marking the path to Toli.

This area above Nimporios, labelled Lykotena on the map, is known for its ancient wine presses. As our guidebook informed us, wine production dating back to Byzantine times was important and accounts for the 130 or so ancient wine presses found across Symi. The white wine was sold to the nearby islands and the Turkish coast, until in the 18th century increasing pirate activity made its export no longer viable. I wasn't sure what the wine presses looked like but given there was supposed to be one on our route, there seemed a good chance that we could come across it.

'Now we have got to where the path is descending through this orchard and the info on the map says we have got to look for a monolith with a groove, a circle and a straight line carved into it,' said John consulting the map.

'What's the significance of the monolith?' I asked.

'Apparently these monoliths were primitive ancient

winepresses and, as the Byzantines continued the tradition of cultivating vines and making wine in the same places, the monolith tells us we are near a Byzantine wine press.'

We looked around but couldn't see any large stones with carvings or anything that might be a wine press.

'Perhaps we need to walk a bit further on,' John suggested. We continued along the path which ran alongside a dry stone wall. About 40 metres further on, John who was in the lead gave a triumphant shout.

'Found it. This has to be a winepress but I don't know what happened to the monolith.' I joined him and we looked at the Byzantine wine press which consisted of a floor of large flat rock with a wall built of large stone slabs all around it and the remains of a roof.

Consulting the guidebook, 'This must be a later Byzantine wine press,' I said authoritatively. 'It says here that only later ones had high walls and a roof to keep dust out and the sun off.'

Pleased that we had been successful in finding it, we continued along the path until we came out on the road by the chapel of Agios Dimitrios. While the chapels are clearly of considerable religious importance to many of the Dodecanese islanders, we always found them to be of great value to walkers as indisputable landmarks and for the provision of shade where trees were non-existent. From the chapel we took a dirt road, and at the point where it joined the main road, we could already see the secluded Toli bay below us.

'I'm definitely ready for some lunch,' I declared, when we arrived at the beach.

'I agree. I think we have earned it,' replied John.

We entered the very attractive looking taverna. It was painted white with blue wooden shutters and blue pots full of herbs. We selected a table on the terrace overlooking the beach under the shade of the vine covered roof trellis. The narrow pebble beach at Toli had a row of sunbeds ranged along it which just fitted in between the water's edge and the few trees that bordered it. Behind the beach the rocky cliffs rose steeply.

There were a number of boats moored in the bay and while we ate our omelettes and salad several motor boats entered the bay and tied up on the two little quays, collecting or bringing visitors, and in one case delivering supplies to the restaurant. It was very pleasant sitting there but by mid afternoon we acknowledged we must be on our way back as it would take us a while to get back to Gialos.

The next day we decided that we should visit a monastery and the castle above Horio, as on our visits to each Dodecanese island we had become accustomed to visiting at least one monastery and a castle. The largest and most well known monastery on Symi is the Panormitis monastery built in honour of the Archangel Michael. This is situated in a bay at the southern tip of the island. While too far for us to walk to it, we could have caught a bus or an excursion boat from Gialos. It is an extremely popular tourist destination but, according to our guidebook, the building is less interesting than you might expect because it was thoroughly pillaged during World War 11. Consequently we decided instead to visit the second largest monastery Mihail Roukouniotis.

This monastery, built in the 15th century by the Knights of Saint John and which once housed 80 monks, is located inland on the west of the island about five kilometres from Gialos. We caught the bus to Gialos and walked up the road to the cemetery as we did on our excursion to Nimporios. From there, as directed on our map, we found a footpath that went up the hill, through three gates and then followed a pipeline to the road. We walked up the road past Agios Fanourios until the road turned into an old stone track which led us to the monastery. Next to the monastery and not marked on our map, nor mentioned in our guidebook, we were somewhat taken aback to find an extensive army base with large sheds covered in soil to provide camouflage and the usual 'no photo' signs all around the area.

The monastery was impressive. It was built in a square and resembled a fortress. With its high white painted walls contrasting with its red tile roof, it looked attractive and well cared for. We tried the old wooden door, which was the only way through the outer wall, and were really disappointed to find that it was locked. However, fortunately a small boy heard us trying to undo it and let us into the yard. Having done so, he immediately disappeared back inside the building, leaving us with the monastery yard to ourselves.

We took our time absorbing the atmosphere and looking around the two chapels. We first went into the old one reputedly built in the 5th century AD with financial aid from the Byzantine emperor Theodosius 11. There we thought about all the pilgrims who had come there through the ages while, as they would have done, we stared at the paintings now too faded to guess what they once depicted. Then we entered the much more recent chapel where there were Byzantine frescos in gold and bright colours and many historical relics, although without any accompanying information we didn't understand their significance.

When we left the chapels we let ourselves back out of

the door. Outside the monastery gate was a huge cypress tree shaped like an umbrella and encircled by a low wall. The sun was high in the sky and we knew the walk back was going to be hot and so we delayed setting off by sitting down on the wall enjoying the tree's wonderfully cool shade. While we sat there an attractive young woman with long brown hair and a floral dress came out of the monastery and approached us.

'Did you enjoy seeing the chapels?' she asked.

'Yes, we did thank you,' said John.

'I thought the old chapel had a wonderful mystical atmosphere,' I added.

'You were lucky my son heard you and let you in, as the monastery is only open to the public in the afternoon.'

'Oh I'm sorry, we didn't realise that. We are grateful to him,' I said. We walked here from Gialos and so we would have been really disappointed if we couldn't have seen inside.'

'Do you live in the monastery?' asked John.

'No, we live in Gialos but we often come here to see my parents. They look after the monastery now there are no longer any monks here. Like you are doing, my son and I often sit under this tree. He likes me to tell him one of the many legends associated with it.'

'It's certainly a magnificent tree and I imagine it must be very old,' John said.

'Reputedly it's a thousand years old.'

Wishing to hear more about it I asked her, 'Could you tell us one of its legends?'

'Of course. Well, as one of my favourite stories goes, the child of a Symian nobleman was accidentally killed by a maid. Very frightened by what she had done, she buried the body and planted a cypress tree over it to disguise the fact the earth had been disturbed. The nobleman thought his child had been kidnapped and constantly searched for him. One day a musician playing under the tree heard a child's voice and the body was discovered. The nobleman then planted another cypress tree as a memorial to the child alongside the original one and in time the two merged. If you look closely,' she instructed us, 'You can identify what is regarded as a seam between the two cypresses.' She watched while we examined the tree bark very closely and managed to find a dark line in the bark.

'Is this the seam?' I asked tracing my finger along the line.

'If you believe the story then you will convince yourself you have found the seam,' she said smiling broadly.

We returned to Gialos by the same route as we had

come, pleased that the walk had enabled us not only to see the Mihail Roukouniotis monastery but also to experience something of the interior of the island. Back in Gialos at the bottom of the Kali Strata we discovered The Fishing Boat a traditional fish restaurant. It looked the part being painted blue and ochre and having pots of shells, stones and driftwood stood around. Nets hung across the roof struts with vines growing through them, along the walls and up the stairs. Paintings of the harbour and fishing boats adorned the walls. We ordered calamari, whitebait and garlic bread.

There were several Greek customers sitting at a table opposite us. When the waiter brought them platters of large fish decorated with slices of orange, tomato and herbs, John thought it looked really good and wondered what it was. When the waiter brought our meal John asked him what the fish was that they were eating and was told that it was gelos. He really fancied trying it, and so we vowed to return in the evening and have some for dinner. We did and the gelos was delicious.

After lunch we were ready to do some climbing. Part way up the Kali Strata we found a signed path to the castle. Getting to the castle on the highest point above Horio was tiring. Our timing wasn't great as we were doing it at the hottest time of day. However, the view was fantastic and made the hot climb worthwhile. On one side we looked over Gialos and out to sea and in the other direction inland over a small valley.

Over the main entrance was the emblem of the Knights of Saint John, now very familiar to us. Like the other castles on the islands that we had visited, this castle was repaired and extended by the Knights of Saint John in and around a Byzantine castle which in turn was constructed on the site of an ancient acropolis. We could see some large rectangular stones which apparently formed part of the acropolis walls. At the top of the castle area was the chapel of Kyra Panagia which was built over an ancient temple to the goddess Athena. We also learnt from the guidebook that there had been a large Byzantine church to the south of the castle, which the Germans used as an ammunition store during World War 11. Sadly when they retreated, they blew it up.

We returned to Horio on a path that took us to the top of the Kali Strata and had an enjoyable hour just wandering through Horio's maze of narrow alleys and steps. Many of the houses had been beautifully restored and we admired their decorative pediments, ornamental doorways and impressive carved wooden doors. Others were still in ruins

437

and several were in the process of being repaired. We encountered the mules again that were vital to the restoration process. Some men passed us leading mules carrying bags of cement. Outside a tall dilapidated vine covered building, a solitary mule waited patiently in the doorway ready to receive his burden of rubble and transport it downhill.

We wandered until we felt we had gained a full impression of the old town. John enjoyed taking his time to get various pics of aspects of ruined and restored buildings in order to select a couple to send to his photo club back home as entries in its competition required photographs of buildings. Having finally exhausted the possibilities, we returned to the top of the Kali Strata and took a path down to Pedi. This passed the old electricity power station which was an amazing rusty primitive looking monstrosity. It was definitely worthy of a photograph and to our amusement subsequently got him first prize in the competition.

'Here it comes,' I shouted from the bathroom on our last day. John picked up his camera case and his rucksack with our bottles of water and I quickly tucked the map into its front pocket and we went out for the 9.30am bus. It was the same driver as on our previous trips, as he told us that he drove the route from Gialos to Pedi and back from 7am to

11pm every day with only a break at 3pm for him to have lunch.

He was a tall, thin, darkly tanned man with classic Greek features, who drove with a cigarette in one hand and a mobile phone in the other whilst chatting to any local passengers who chose to stand alongside him. Doubtless he could have driven the route blindfolded he knew it so well. He judged brilliantly the width of the large coach when weaving it through traffic or squeezing it through seemingly too narrow gaps between buildings and vans. The road along the harbour was incredibly narrow and on the way in, if the coach met a car, it had to go right to the water's edge. When this happened and you looked out of the coach window, it appeared as if you were travelling in the water and I couldn't help feeling fearful that this might soon become the reality.

Today we didn't need to go as far as the harbour. The driver, who was accustomed to stopping the bus wherever passengers wanted to get off, dropped us on the top of the ridge by the windmills, several of which had been converted into stylish accommodation. Up until the first World War agriculture on Symi had flourished. The windmills on the ridge between Gialos and the Pedi valley were used to grind not only locally grown wheat but also wheat brought from Turkey by caique.

We were planning to walk to Agia Marina on the tip of the peninsula stretching out from Symi town. After we had walked past the last mill we came upon the extraordinary pontikokastro – a round building of carved large stones which was covered in earth in the shape of a dome.

'What an extraordinary building, what is it?' asked John.

'No one really knows,' I replied having found the reference to it in the guidebook. 'Some believe that it is a cenotaph to honour Nireas, an ancient king of Symi, while others think it's possibly a monument to an important historical event.'

'Then they don't know who built it. You'd think they might have excavated it to learn more.'

'Probably they don't want to disturb it,' I responded. 'Also such excavations need a lot of financing and as we have seen there are so many ancient sites on the islands.'

'This one is rather unusual though and certainly large.'

'Yes, it says here that it's 18 metres in diameter.'

'Well it's built where it can be seen from everywhere around and so there's a wonderful view of Symi town and over to Turkey from the top of it.' Having climbed up we stood surveying the scene and John took out his camera to take another panorama.

'I've certainly had plenty of practice taking panoramic shots on these island trips,' he said.

When we set off again we went in the direction indicated by blue and red dots. The views along the walk were spectacular. We watched the various ferries heading for Symi including the big tourist boat from Rhodes, which sounded its loud horn to alert stall holders in the port that it was approaching. We could also see the previous day's walk to Nimporios and the houses and chapel of Panagia Hypakoi on the island of Nymos off the northern tip of Symi.

The dots then directed us uphill over the peninsula to the other side. We were in a totally barren rocky wilderness with no vegetation apart from dried up sage and oregano. There were the remains of stone walls and animal pens and at one point in the empty landscape we came across a small deserted house. We thought that indeed the climate on the islands must be getting hotter and drier as the one-time farmers on Patmos had claimed. In the current conditions it seemed it would be impossible to grow anything and any livestock wouldn't be able to find food. Symi has little natural fresh water. It used to have a weekly water delivery by ship and now is served by a desalination plant.

As the morning wore on, the sun got hotter and clambering through the stones and rocks more tiring.

'Ouch!' I gasped as a sharp rock cut into the side of my shoe. 'I don't think I'll be taking these walking shoes I bought in Kalymnos back to England. They're practically shredded with all these rocky paths we've been on.'

'Yes, mine have about had it too,' said John surveying his feet.

We knew we were heading in the right direction but we were no longer on a path and we didn't see any more red and blue markers. When we got our first glimpse of the secluded bay of Agia Marina, it was like stumbling upon an oasis. On the beach, where there were the anticipated sunbeds and umbrellas, we could see not only tamarind trees but also palm trees, and even a lawn greeted our astonished eyes. This we learned later over lunch was achieved through a grey water recycling plant.

The little islet opposite the beach with its landing stage, chapel and a couple of houses looked very pretty in the shimmering green and azure sea. As we enthusiastically approached this enticing spectacle, we realised that the oasis was surrounded by a high wire fence presumably to keep out goats rather than worn out and thirsty walkers. However, fortunately before despair set in, John spotted red and blue dots painted on some rocks and following these we were guided to a gate which allayed our fears that we might be shut out.

On the beach there was a restaurant and circular bar from which we purchased drinks and sat relaxing under a tree. John was keen to go for a swim in the inviting looking crystal clear waters, where as at Nimborios we could see shoals of tiny fish. He swam out of the area, marked off by buoys to keep boats away from swimmers, over to Agia Marina islet and climbed out on the jetty. He found the chapel locked but I reckoned they didn't want too many soggy visitors dripping all over it. Meanwhile I sat in the shade under a tree watching an expensive looking motor boat drop anchor and a couple wade ashore. As they walked past me I realised that, like several of the sunbathers on the nearby sunbeds, they were French. The water taxi from Pidi also turned up a couple of times bringing customers to the restaurant which opened at 1pm.

When John returned and had dried off, we too went to the restaurant for lunch. With its stone walls, open square windows looking out on the water's edge and canvas roof it was cool and appealing. We really appreciated Symi's nice beach tavernas. We had expensive Symi shrimps, which were tiny fried shrimps with their heads removed so you could eat all of them, followed by seafood pasta and lettuce and tomato salad. After which we succumbed to creme brûlée and cappuccinos.

Over our coffee we got chatting to an elderly French couple who substantiated our impression that this particular beach was popular with the French. The couple lived in Nice and came to Symi most years with friends of theirs who sailed to Gialos in their private seagoing yacht. They had taken a water taxi from Gialos to Agia Marina and were fairly amazed, when they looked back over the way that we had come, that we had walked.

After our leisurely lunch absorbing the somewhat Monte Carlo atmosphere, we took the coastal path back to Pedi making our trip a circular one. It took about an hour and a half for us to get back to our studio. The route was marked by blue and red dots and a black water supply pipe that ran alongside the path for part of the way. We stopped several times to look over the inlet to Agios Nikolaos where we had walked on our first evening. We were in no hurry to get back to Pedi because unfortunately we wouldn't be able to do any more exploring on Symi, as the next morning we were getting the ferry back to Kos town.

17

A Festival Finale

Late that evening Jan texted me to say that after a week in Brighton she had just arrived back in Kos airport. Her meeting with Regi had gone more or less as expected and she had achieved a separation but, while she felt relieved, she was also feeling really stressed and unsettled. It would help to talk about it so could we meet up at her apartment asap.

After breakfast the following day I headed off to Jan's apartment. When I arrived, she made us a coffee and we took it out on the back balcony where we could sit in the shade. The minute we sat down she began to recount what had happened with Regi.

'As you know I really wanted a separation from Regi. Being here without him I've felt so unfettered and free to be myself and do what I want. Still I was unprepared for how I felt when I saw him. I just felt so sad and emotional that our marriage, which I had once been so thrilled about, had disintegrated. I thought about how the love and admiration I'd once felt for him had been worn away just leaving dislike and resentment,' she said tearfully.

'You are taking a big step to change your life so I think it's only natural you are upset and wonder how you came to this,' I said feeling inadequate as to what to say.

'Perhaps I should have tried harder to get him to understand what was happening to us but then somehow I don't think I really realised myself until it was probably too late.'

'Maybe you could have done something to save your relationship,' I said, 'but, when you both were staying with us, Regi didn't seem like he was particularly aware or concerned about how you were feeling. Quite possibly he wouldn't have taken any notice if you had tried to get him to see things from your perspective or accepted your reality.'

'Yes, that probably is the case. He would most likely have rejected anything that could be regarded as criticism of him.'

'In your text you said Regi had agreed to a separation. Before you went you were afraid that he would put pressure on you to change your mind, did he?' I said moving the conversation on from what might have been to the present.

'Yes, but not quite in the way I anticipated. I thought he would try and pressurise me by reminding me of the good times we've had, tell me that he loved me, plead with me not to give up on everything we'd done and built together. He didn't at all. Instead he questioned whether I could manage on my own, asked how I thought I would cope without him to care for and organise me, stressed that he was sure I would soon regret any separation. He was really patronising. It made me angry and I shouted at him that I was certainly subjected to plenty of organisation but it was of more benefit to him than me and recently I hadn't experienced much care. I pointed out that the way he ended our holiday together, which he'd promised me for ages, was the last straw.'

'How did he react to that?'

'I think he was really taken aback by my anger because he's got so used to me just putting up with any criticisms. He became a bit more conciliatory after that and even apologised for abandoning our holiday but he still tried to persuade me that I'd soon realise any separation was a mistake.'

'But did he agree to it eventually,' I said, 'though I mean if he acknowledged that you were determined to leave he wouldn't have a choice really would he?'

'We seemed to go over and over the same ground and I began to worry that I wasn't going to get anywhere. Then in the end he suggested a six-month separation because he admitted that he would be in Taiwan for most of the next six months.' He said, 'If I wanted to spend the winter in Kefalos even though he thought it a ridiculous idea he would go along with it. I was just so relieved we had reached an agreement.'

'Presumably that meant he could see you would need more clothes and other things.'

'Yes he realised I would need more than I'd taken on holiday and so getting my things wasn't a problem. We agreed that I could pack another case to take back with me and a small trunk to send out to Kos.'

'And you didn't mention Andreas?'

'No. I did feel guilty not doing so because my feelings for Andreas have strengthened my decision to push for a separation but telling Regi really would have complicated matters. I don't know whether or how my relationship with Andreas will work out. If it does continue to develop then I'll tell Regi, that's only fair, but not yet.'

As I drove home reflecting on what Jan had told me, I thought about how she wouldn't be in the situation she was in if she and Regi hadn't come to stay with us. However, while this probably accelerated the breakdown in their marriage, it seemed obvious that it was going to happen sooner or later. Also by coming to Kefalos she had met Andreas. I believed from seeing them together and from what Jan told me that their relationship would continue to grow stronger. Even if it didn't, it had to be regarded positively because it served to show Jan that she could take charge of her life, set it in a different direction and find someone who made her feel valued. At the end of the month John and I were returning home and so I would no longer be able to observe first hand how Jan used her new independence. Still, our time together in Kefalos had reestablished our close friendship and so I knew she would keep me posted.

As we contemplated bidding goodbye to our friends, John and I found the prospect much more upsetting than we anticipated. In all our positive plans for what we were going to do in our Dodecanese summer, we hadn't really given much thought to the negative aspects of how we would feel when it became time for us to leave. We sought to comfort ourselves with the knowledge that we would keep in contact with our friends through phone conversations and social media and after all we intended to return next summer. However, as before it would only be for a couple of weeks' holiday, we wouldn't be part of the community as we were now. Also I was sad to leave our little house, as we had been so happy and comfortable there, and I would miss the garden that I'd enjoyed making and taken a pride in. I hoped whoever moved in after us would also enjoy it and look after it.

Knowing we were extremely sad to leave Kefalos our friends argued, 'Well why not stay longer or even move here?' We pointed out to them that we needed to go back to England to look after our house and garden there, as the Australian academics, who had rented it, were about to go back to Perth. In addition, equally important for our career prospects and finances, we needed to get back to work.

The Education Department at the university had secured a large grant to research the different attitudes, education experiences and life chances of the millennials and the post-millennials and so we had extremely interesting research awaiting us on which to work. Also, on the plus side, we were both very aware that there was much to look forward to in returning home. John was keen to resume his role as competition secretary in the camera club to which he belonged, playing tennis again and going to rugby matches, whereas I planned to rejoin the local art society and the drama society. Also, we had both missed being able to go to the cinema and theatre and social dances – all of which we did regularly when at home.

The season at Meltemi was drawing to a close and this was the final week for the remaining bookings that the various companies had with Meltemi. Often in early autumn the wind would flutter from the usual off shore to on shore and sometimes nearly die altogether. However, this October it was blowing strongly and, as business was quiet, everyone at Meltemi including John was taking the opportunity to fit in as much windsurfing as possible before the weather changed.

They could be seen streaking across the bay with Seb and Alain performing extraordinary tricks. John's windsurfing prowess had greatly improved over the summer but he could only marvel at their textbook manoeuvres. Then it would be time to thoroughly clean the boards, stack the masts, mend the sails and assess the state of the harnesses and wetsuits etc. Alain was about to return to Athens, Otto was booked to fly home in a week's time and Seb was going on holiday to try out windsurfing in the Caribbean.

This week was also my last opportunity to help out at the Art Centre. The beginners' course in multi-media painting was the final one that Joan was going to put on this year. She thought that she would probably do a few day workshops for locals over the winter, as she had done the previous year and found that they had been well attended and much appreciated. However, basically Kos Creative Escapes was closing down at the end of the week. I would miss the experience of working there as it had been fun and I'd learnt a number of tips from the various tutors.

This final course was run by Sandra, who had delivered several courses at the Art Centre since it opened. I first met her earlier in the summer, when she was running an intermediate course on fantasy painting. She was extrovert in personality and in appearance being tall and striking looking with short bright red and green spiky hair and gold eyeshadow. However, she was also extremely patient and supportive which made her a popular tutor.

Yesterday she had demonstrated how to produce a picture of the harbour using a combination of watercolour paint, collage and ink. This morning course participants were going to take some photos and do some sketches to get ideas for their own coastal scene. Then this afternoon they were to practise the techniques that she had shown them and make a start on their own multimedia picture using everything that they had learned. This week Terry was busy helping a Greek friend to repair his extension and, as today Joan was meeting their accountant in Kos town, I was going to stand in for her.

I joined the group in the studio where they were waiting for Sandra. Several of them were clustered around the easel admiring Sandra's large brightly coloured demonstration painting of Kefalos harbour. The rocks were depicted in painted-over newsprint, the fishing boats were brightly coloured triangles cut and torn from magazines, thin strips of silver paper provided sparkles in the sea and the beach was torn tissue and actual sand, while lines in ink and paint defined key items.

'I think it's brilliant,' a young women said, 'I can't imagine I'll ever produce anything like that but I'm looking forward to having a go.'

'I love it but I find the idea of trying to do something similar awfully daunting,' said her companion somewhat nervously.

'Don't worry she'll guide us through it,' said an older woman whom I recognised from Sandra's fantasy course and so she was speaking from experience.

'I certainly will,' said Sandra as she came up behind us. 'Don't worry, just enjoy it. It will be fun and you will be amazed by what you can do, believe me.'

The group set off enthusiastically with their

sketchbooks plus iPads and phones to take pictures while I drove down to the harbour with an elderly man who was still recovering from his hip operation. Once at the harbour Sandra gathered the group around her.

'Now remember from yesterday what you are looking for are shapes. Regular shapes, irregular shapes. Look at all the squares and rectangles in the buildings along the road, the squares and triangles of the boats and the interesting assorted shapes of the harbour walls and rocks. Try to do a number of quick simple sketches just identifying the main shapes. Your photographs will capture the details and colours of the scene.'

The group spread out and started sketching with most members choosing to go along the harbour promontory to where they could look back and so incorporate the shops and restaurants along the road as well as the boats. However, when a large tour boat arrived from Kos town they soon found themselves surrounded by interested visitors. Some group members, clearly enjoying their celebrity status, explained what they were up to and answered the visitors' queries, while others hastily found themselves an alternative location.

At lunchtime, back at the Art Centre I was busy ensuring everyone had ample quiche and salad followed by the apricots and ice cream Joan had prepared for them. After I had cleared up, I went into the studio to see how things were going. Everyone had used rollers or wet into wet watercolour techniques to paint the sky and the sea and cover their white paper. The almost total silence suggested maximum concentration as they engaged in much tearing and cutting of paper.

'Now be bold,' instructed Sandra. 'Take your first shape and stick it down and build up your painting from there. Use your sketches from this morning for ideas of shapes and their positioning. Look out as you go for opportunities to bring out recognisable objects from your semi abstract chaos.'

As they continued, the group seemed to form naturally into two camps – those who kept moving their shapes around trying to get a satisfactory composition out of the relationship between them before reaching for the glue and those who embarked with gusto on a sticking frenzy.

'I see a few of you are laying out your paper shapes like a jigsaw,' observed Sandra. 'Of course you can do this but too much such planning can make the picture really dull. Be intuitive, be creative and get sticking,' she urged laughingly.

A couple of the shape movers joined the stickers but as one man commented to his neighbour, 'I always like to spend time planning my painting rather than just let it evolve. Although I'm new to multimedia I still think I'll do better if I plan what I'm going to do before I start.'

'Oh no! I've lost my picture!' exclaimed one of the shape movers as her paper pieces rose upwards, drifted around in the air and rearranged themselves on the floor. A tall woman in voluminous clothing had wafted out of the room and unintentionally slammed the door, thus creating a considerable picture changing draught.

'I've certainly achieved abstract chaos,' said one of the enthusiastic stickers but she went on somewhat disconsolately, 'but I can't identify anything remotely recognisable.'

'Let's have a look,' said Sandra. 'Well I can. Look,' she pointed. 'I think that tall thin piece of newsprint could become a lighthouse and those patches of texture would make great fishing nets.'

'Umm, yes, perhaps they could,' the sticker agreed somewhat doubtfully but sounding more cheerful.

'Do you really need all that silver paper or can I have some of it?' a man engaged in paper sticking crossly addressed another sitting in front of a large and ever growing pile of shapes in all different kinds of paper.

'Well I suppose so,' said the paper collector sounding

aggrieved, 'but I don't know yet what I'm going to need.'

'You have made lots of interesting shapes in a wide range of papers,' said Sandra going over to him. 'Let's have a look at your sketches from this morning to see how you might begin to use them.' The collector got out his sketchbook. 'Why you have lots of ideas here,' she said. 'Decide which sketch you like best and use the shapes in that as a guide, just to get started.'

'Oh look I've found a recipe for fish soup in this magazine,' the elderly man, whom I'd driven to the harbour and back, said delightedly, 'Can I incorporate that?'

'Definitely, good idea,' said Sandra. 'Use part of it to paste on the front of one of your buildings to suggest a cafe or on one of the boats. It's fun to use images or print that are related to the scene you're depicting.'

Everyone worked very hard on their coastal scenes through to tea at four o'clock. After tea Sandra reviewed their efforts giving them praise, encouragement and constructive advice for how to continue tomorrow. As she had promised at the beginning of the day, the group were indeed enjoying the process and most of the paintings were developing in an interesting way. I too was definitely enthused and decided that I would start collecting a variety of papers to have a go at doing my own multi-media scene.

The only interruption to the efforts of the afternoon occurred when the tall woman caught her glue pot in her sleeve and tossed it into the air spreading glue all down her front and over her flowery sneakers. She swore loudly and rushed out to wash herself down and rescue her shoes. As she charged past, everyone held onto their paintings and glue pots to avoid further disasters. Sandra went after her to help her with glue removal and provided solvent to rescue her shoes.

When I got back home, almost before I got through the door, John wanted to know if he had got to me with the latest news on the arsonist before anyone else. I assured him he had because I had come straight back from the Art Centre and whatever the news was it hadn't reached us.

'Well,' he said taking a deep breath. 'The developments on that front are really interesting. Just as we had finished packing up for the day Lampros called in because he wanted to tell us what had happened the previous night. Following the fire at Konstantinos's water park, Lampros had decided to sleep at his kitesurfing hut but he kept quiet about his intention. As you know, Kohilari beach is totally deserted after about 6pm when the last holidaymakers have left and so he was really worried that his business was particularly vulnerable.'

'Understandably,' I said. 'He worked so hard all last winter building that much larger hut and there is a lot of very expensive equipment stored in it.'

'Anyway,' continued John, 'Each night around 11 o'clock he has been taking his two dogs and going back to his hut to sleep. Last night about two in the morning he was woken by the dogs getting up and sniffing around one side of the hut. He indicated to them to stay still and quiet and waited listening for any sounds that might suggest whether someone was outside.'

'That would have been really scary,' I commented, imagining Lampros waiting in the dark wondering what was going to happen next.

'For a bit he couldn't hear anything and then he heard a faint swishing and scraping noise. He shot out of the shed and confronted a guy outside, who ran off as soon as Lampros appeared dropping a petrol can as he ran. One of the dogs caught up with him and ripped a chunk out of his jacket just as he jumped in his car which was parked close to the beach.'

'Did Lampros see who it was?'

'No, because the guy was wearing a balaclava but Lampros got the numberplate of the car.'

'Did he give chase?'

'No, it would have taken him too long to get his motorbike out of the shelter behind the shed. He telephoned the police straightaway and gave them the car number and they said that they would track down the car which could have been the arsonist's or a hire car.'

'Has Lampros heard anything from them today?'

'Yes, they found the car in a car park in Kos town and they think that it's likely he has taken a ferry to one of the islands. Lampros says the police are confident that they will catch him.'

'Well that's good. Will Lampros carry on sleeping in his hut until they do?'

'Yes. He's sure the guy won't try again and doubts that he has an accomplice but he's not going to risk it.'

'All the beach businesses will be grateful to Lampros and really relieved if this means the arsonist is caught.'

'Yes, everyone at Meltemi was certainly pleased to hear his news.'

On the Friday morning of our penultimate week in Kefalos, while as usual John and I were eating breakfast on the patio, we watched towers of precariously stacked plastic chairs and plastic tables being placed on the open space at the entrance to the harbour.

'What do you think they're for?' I questioned John.

'I don't know but clearly something out of the ordinary is going to happen. It's possible they are going to hold the fish festival. Seb told me a while ago that it was cancelled last year but is planned to go ahead sometime soon this year.'

That afternoon our sense of expectation was further heightened when a large lorry arrived and three battered stalls were offloaded beside the chairs. As we discovered from Spiros, who called in that evening anxious that we shouldn't miss out, on Saturday the annual fish festival was indeed going to take place.

'It's a great event,' he said. 'You mustn't miss it.'

'So what happens Spiros?' asked John.

'Well in the afternoon fish will be caught in a huge net in the traditional way. Then in the evening the catch will be celebrated with a fish supper for everyone. The fish will have been caught, marinated and battered earlier in readiness for the supper. I'll be directing the cooking and I guarantee the fish will be delicious.'

'We know the fish festival was cancelled last October but does it normally happen every year?' I asked.

'Yes it always has but I think this might be the last one. It's a real shame but the problem is it's a very wasteful way of catching fish. Vast quantities of fry will be caught alongside fully grown fish and this is unacceptable nowadays when fish stocks are diminishing anyway because of climate change and pollution.'

'If it is the last one then we definitely don't want to miss it and so we are grateful to you Spiros for ensuring we knew about it,' I thanked him.

'After the fish supper there will be music and dancing. You will enjoy yourselves, everyone will be there. You will find it an excellent festival finale or indeed a very fishy ending to your stay in Kefalos,' he said chuckling.

Throughout Saturday morning we watched the continuing preparations from the vantage point of our patio. With a speed and precision not normally witnessed, a platform for the band was erected, the chairs were arranged in semi-circles in front of it and floodlights were focused upon it. A small van selling candyfloss and popcorn turned up and announcing itself with a jingle parked alongside the platform. This immediately induced much shouting and arm waving until the driver agreed to relocate his van on the edge of the road.

About three o'clock we watched a crowd start to gather from all directions. Burly men in jeans discussing purposefully, elderly ladies in black arm in arm proceeding quietly, families with excited children several of whom burst into tears when hurried past the van's attractions, young couples holding hands and curious holidaymakers, cameras and mobile phones to the ready.

'Time we went,' said John and grabbing his camera we hastened out of the back of the house and down the track to join the throng. As we arrived at the harbour, an announcement in Greek was made from the platform. Obviously this must have specified that the nets for catching the fish were about to be cast. Everyone surged onto the beach and down to the water's edge colliding with the remaining few sunbeds and umbrellas still occupied by seemingly disinterested tourists.

We watched fascinated as a small boat very slowly traced out a huge horseshoe shape in the sea dropping a gigantic net marked by orange buoys as it manoeuvred. On the beach the burly men busied themselves straightening into two parallel lines, a couple of metres apart, the thick ropes attached to each end of the net. When all was in place to their satisfaction, they picked up the ropes in readiness.

On the signal from the two men in the boat, pulling in the net began. Hand over hand, rope digging into their shoulders the burly men hauled, sweated and strained and hauled some more. The young men egged on by their girlfriends filled in the spaces between them laughing as they also tugged away. A few women not seeing why this should be a male only activity elbowed their way in putting their backs into the task with gusto. A few holidaymakers also briefly did some tugging but mainly to pose for the benefit of friends and family members with cameras.

Small children smiling and chuckling tried to catch hold of the rope above their heads and join in, risking being strangled or trodden on by the men as they staggered backwards, grunting loudly, feet slithering in the shingle. For a full half hour the hauling and tugging went on, halting every so often when first one side and then the other pulled ahead thus upsetting the symmetry of the net.

'It's clearly extremely hard work,' I commented looking at the sweating and straining fishermen. 'In the past I wonder how often fish used to be caught in this way or on this scale.'

'We'll have to ask Theo,' said John. 'I'm getting some great pictures of the action.' He walked along the beach to photograph the scene from different angles.

As the net gradually got closer to the beach some boys wearing goggles ran into the sea and swam above it diving down and gesticulating to those on the shore that, as anticipated, the net was full of fish. As the horseshoe got smaller their calls grew more excited and within it we could now see swirling spirals of fish-filled water with fish jumping in the air as if to try and escape their fate.

Eventually with shouts of triumph the net was hauled completely onto the shore to reveal a terrific heaving silvery grey mass of fish of all sizes. The well-prepared locals immediately pounced on the catch. Men filled crates and carried them off above their heads. Women filled blue supermarket plastic bags and saucepans and hurried off home. The children giggled and shrieked as they picked up handfuls of wriggling fish and felt them slipping through their fingers. The catch was huge and so there was more than enough for everyone.

'We need a container,' I said, 'so we too can have some fish dinners.'

'Definitely, right,' replied John. 'I'll go and get one,' and he ran back up the cliff path returning with the washing up bowl. We joined the last of the locals and helped ourselves to several potential fish dinners for our final nights in Kefalos.

As the locals moved away some of the holidaymakers having managed to procure a bag or container from somewhere also tentatively helped themselves.

'This is truly amazing,' said one as he filled his frying pan with fish. 'I look forward to tucking into these seasoned with plenty of Greek herbs.'

An hour or so later, having stowed their fish back home or in car boots or the back of trucks, everyone reassembled to sit expectantly on the chairs in front of the harbour. When we returned, Joan and Terry and Betty and Mike were already sitting at a table and beckoned to us to join them.

'Smells very good,' said Terry as a delicious aroma of fried fish soon emanated from the stalls.

A few moments after we had sat down, Lampros and his girlfriend Nicola arrived. On spotting John, Lampros left the group he was with to bag a table for them and came over to us.

'I thought that you'd like to know that the police have caught the arsonist,' said Lampros addressing John.

'Really. Great. Oh that's really good news,' responded John. 'Where was he when the police caught up with him?'

'At the airport on Leros where he was waiting for a plane to Athens. Apparently he was hoping to get a plane from there back to England. You'll be amazed when I tell you who it is. You would never guess.'

'Well you said he wanted to get to England so is he English?' questioned John sounding surprised.

'Anyone we know?' I followed up.

'Oh yes, you most certainly do.' He paused. 'The arsonist is Andy.'

'What! Andy who works at Kyrios's?' John sounded incredulous. 'Really! What on earth was his motivation?'

'I've no idea,' said Lampros shaking his head, 'but it seems likely to be due to the fact that his father was a fireman. The police reckon there has to be some psychological connection.'

'That's interesting,' remarked Terry, 'because I do remember reading an article not that long ago about firemen becoming arsonists often in order that they can then become heroes putting out the fires they themselves started. Also it said that, if they have a dysfunctional relationship with their children, this can make the children become arsonists as a way to get back at their parents.'

'Well that is the most extraordinary news and sad too,' said Betty. 'I wonder what Kyrios will do as he is really dependent on Andy. It's a good thing that it's the end of the season.'

'I mean Andy had just bought that shop in Kefalos old town and was going to turn it into a bar,' commented Mike.

'Yes he told us all about the plans he had for it and he seemed really excited at the prospect,' added John.

'What about his girlfriend Tanya. What will she do? She

must be very upset,' Joan commented.

'Do you think she had any inkling that it was him?' Betty speculated.

'I doubt it,' said Lampros. 'I don't think anyone had any idea it was him. It's a real shame because he was very popular.'

'Yeh, I really liked him. When we went to Kyrios's restaurant he was always friendly and joking. It really is a shock,' said Terry.

'It is,' said Lampros, 'but I must say it's a great relief to me and others whose businesses are on on the beach. I'm very pleased that I won't have to sleep in my hut anymore and so is Nicola.' He grinned as he turned to go back to join her and his friends.

'I can hardly believe it,' John reflected.

I agreed. 'Like Lampros said, he was really popular. He knew everyone and everyone knew him. He was certainly a draw for tourists to go to Kyrios's and I'm sure his bar would have done well.'

'He has lived here for at least the last four years,' said Mike, 'and so while the police think they know the underlying cause of the arson attacks I wonder what triggered his actions this summer.'

'Well I guess we will never know. I don't suppose we

will see him again,' Terry speculated.

'If he is convicted and I expect he will be, will he be sentenced to prison in Greece or sent back to England?' wondered John.

As we concluded discussing this astonishing news, there was an announcement that supper was ready to be served. Chairs began to be pushed back as their occupants got up to form a queue in front of the stalls. Tin foil dishes of fish, onions, tomatoes and black and green olives rapidly appeared on the stalls and disappeared as those queuing helped themselves. Several women, including Angela, handed out hunks of brown bread and beakers of red wine to accompany the fish.

'Come on,' said Terry. 'Let's go and get our supper.'

We ate our meal carefully leaving the heads, fins and bones, unlike the elderly Greeks in front of us who downed the complete fish. As these fish were at least ten times bigger than whitebait, for me this wasn't an option. While we were eating, the musicians began warming up and as the last dishes were handed out they started in earnest playing traditional Greek folk music.

The violinist was particularly good putting his own interpretations to the music with his fingers dancing over the strings. However, the female singer, who joined them after a few instrumental numbers, seemed particularly bad, screeching above the music and setting the amplifier into feedback mode. Feet began tapping and an elderly couple stood up and quickly established their position to lead the line dancing. The man, his arms outstretched, dipping and diving to the music, nimbly dictated the steps. He was soon joined by other locals demonstrating their skills.

'I'm going to join them,' said Betty getting up. 'I went to a few lessons in Kos last winter but I don't often get a chance to have a go.'

'I've tried and I'm hopeless,' said Joan to me. 'I need more than a few lessons.'

'Angela is pretty good at it,' I commented as she was dancing confidently alongside her partner.

As more people got up and the line extended, those in the front rows of chairs started shuffling everyone backwards as they sought to create more space for dancing and remove their ankles from the danger zone. The line bent around into a double loop in front of the stage and then began to encircle the chairs and tables. Younger locals joined the line followed by a few holidaymakers stumbling over their own feet. The music grew louder and more frantic causing the dancers to struggle ever more valiantly to keep some sense of togetherness.

Up one end a very large man in a pony tail was enjoying his own individual unencumbered dance. After five lengthy numbers in succession, the line dancers gradually dropped out to collapse back into their plastic chairs. The violinist gesticulated to the large man, whom he obviously knew, to join them on the stage despite the protestations of the wailing singer. The extrovert seemed to need very little encouragement to be heaved onto the makeshift stage where the microphone was then removed from the indignant singer's hands and given to him.

The music started up again and it was immediately apparent that the large man's similarity to Demis Roussos certainly wasn't limited to his appearance. Demis had a moustache and long hair, struggled with his weight and was known for his flamboyant kaftans. In the mid seventies my mum loved Demis's high tenor voice and had several of his albums. Goodbye my Love Goodbye is the song that I particularly remember her playing. The crowd nodded and clapped appreciatively at the replacement of the screeching and wailing by the rich melodious vocals of the interloper, who the violinist later introduced as Stamatis.

When the band and their star performer took a short break, I went to speak to Jan and Andreas who had arrived part way through the entertainment probably because they would have had to wait for some of their hire cars to be returned.

'The band are really good,' said Jan, 'especially the singer.'

'Yes they are but they started initially with a female singer who was pretty awful and then the violinist brought Stamatis on. I don't know where the woman went, replacing her like that was rather unfair but she didn't sing, she just screeched.'

'Did you see the fish being caught in the afternoon?' asked Andreas.

'Yes it was amazing, hard work though pulling in the nets.'

'Dad and I have both helped pull the net in in the past and it certainly is hard work. It's not really environmentally acceptable nowadays though and so we realise it probably won't happen again.'

'Yes Spiros told us for that reason we should make sure we saw the catch.'

'Oh I won't be a minute but I've just seen Joy,' Jan interjected apologetically. 'I want to ask her to fix up some accommodation for us for a weekend in a couple of weeks time, as Andreas is going to take me to Nisyros to see the volcano.'

'Jan really enjoyed her trip to Patmos with you,' I told Andreas.

'I look forward to taking her to Nisyros,' he replied. 'As she will have told you, we get on so well together. In fact I'm hoping to get her to move in with me soon but I want her to tell her husband about us because I know she hasn't done so yet.'

I was saved from having to react to this as at that moment the band started up again with a loud rock-n-roll number and so I was able to respond by putting my hands over my ears, mouth 'excuse me' to him and return to John and the others. However, I thought it extremely likely that Andreas would get what he hoped for.

It was a most enjoyable evening and we were able during the course of it to socialise and say goodbye to the various acquaintances that we had made. It was the kind of evening that you really don't want to end. However, end it did very abruptly at just after 11.30pm, when suddenly the harbour was plunged into darkness and the music petered out to sighs of dismay, swearing and laughter as Kefalos was subjected to one of its frequent power cuts.

As our eyes adjusted, the bright moonlight lit up the harbour replacing the floodlights. For a while everyone continued chatting and the band remained in position but clearly the electricity wasn't coming back on and it was getting late. The crowd slowly drifted away melting into the shadows. John and I walked down the road past Sophia's shop and began climbing up the hill with the moonlight brilliantly illuminating the track and the hillside.

'The night sky here is fantastic,' I said. 'I'm sure the moon is never this bright at home. Look at how it's glistening on the sea. You can see every detail of Stephanos's olive trees and look at the stars, the sky is full of them.'

'We did a bit of astronomy at school but I can't remember much of it,' recalled John, 'but I think that really bright star must be Sirius the dog star and that group of stars is Orion.'

'I'll miss the night sky when we leave Kefalos. I'll miss an awful lot when we leave Kefalos but we have had a truly wonderful summer.'

'Yes, it's been fantastic, even better than anticipated. Tonight made for a really good send off,' said John.

'Yes indeed it did, like Spiros said, it was a very memorable festival finale.'

Printed in Great Britain
by Amazon

21740041R00273